T0304944

Fifty Minutes

Fifty Minutes

Carla Jenkins

First published in Great Britain in 2024 by Trapeze,
an imprint of The Orion Publishing Group Ltd
Carmelite House, 50 Victoria Embankment
London EC4Y 0DZ

An Hachette UK Company

1 3 5 7 9 10 8 6 4 2

A CIP catalogue record for this book is
available from the British Library.

ISBN (Hardback) 978 1 3987 1584 4
ISBN (eBook) 978 1 3987 1586 8
ISBN (Audio) 978 1 3987 1587 5

Typeset by Input Data Services Ltd, Bridgwater, Somerset

Printed in Great Britain by Clays Ltd, Elcograf S.p.A.

MIX
Paper | Supporting
responsible forestry
FSC® C104740

www.orionbooks.co.uk

For Tony. This book wouldn't have been written without you.

'Education is an admirable thing, but it is well to remember from time to time that nothing worth knowing can be taught.'

Oscar Wilde

Chapter One

I chose Richard Goode because his practice is a twenty-minute walk away from where I live, or a few minutes by bus then one stop on the tube.

When he answers the door, he fills the frame. He's tall and wide and doesn't look at all like the photos on his website, those black and white pictures of his stern middle-aged face, one shot of him showing perfect teeth and another of his face in profile, his chin lifted. The photos didn't reveal the size of him.

'You're early. Would you like to sit in the waiting room?' His voice is deep but there's a warm tone to it. I look at my phone. It's four minutes to six.

'I'll come back.'

As I walk down the red and blue mosaic-tiled path, I feel self-conscious about my tight jeans, and I wish he'd close the door. It clicks shut as I reach the gate. I take a pouch of tobacco from my bag, sit on the low brick wall and roll a thin cigarette. I smoke under the bright light of the streetlamp until six o'clock exactly. Then I knock again.

I'm yet to learn about the 'boundaries' that are so strict in psychotherapy: start on time; don't run over; don't try to rearrange the appointment. Or what I should get from a psychotherapist in return: consistency, predictability and security. In other words, the same place, the same hour and a calm environment.

The second time he answers the door, he doesn't say anything, just turns and walks down the hallway. He has dark brown curly hair and a section of it falls over his shirt collar. Everything else about him is neat and clean, no lint or creases on his clothes.

He opens the door on the left and I follow him into the room. People bang on about the beauty of sunrises and sunsets, but I've never seen anything that's affected me like the sight of a wall of books. Nobody I know has such a collection, and I've only seen this many before in a library or bookshop. Two of the walls are lined from floor to ceiling with shelves, muted hues of thick and thin spines. Expensive-looking brown leather armchairs face each other, and there's the therapist's couch with a green checked blanket folded at the end. Beautiful pictures hang on the walls. One is made of lots of beige and brown ovals with dots inside. Another is of dark blue arcs and light green dashes. There's only one picture that has people in it: a watercolour, smaller than A4. It's a girl sitting on her father's lap. The girl's face is partly hidden by the father's arm, and the father is stroking the girl's hair. There's a faint smell of leather. I stand and absorb it all. I don't have to think about my breathing. Sometimes the only way to get a deep enough breath is to make myself yawn, but I don't need to do that now.

'You may hang your coat here.'

He gestures to a couple of hooks by the door. I'm not sure where to sit, and I don't want to get it wrong. I keep my coat on and sit on the chair which has a box of tissues on the table next to it. I put my rucksack by my feet. He sits on the chair opposite, crosses his legs, leans back and clasps his hands together, resting them on his thigh. I like what he's wearing; it seems like the type of thing a psychotherapist should wear – corduroy trousers in a mid-brown. His trouser leg has ridden up to reveal yellow and grey diamond socks. I wonder if he's got lots of pairs in different colours. I look up to see he's observing me and I'm embarrassed he caught me staring at his ankle.

It's so still in this room, and the air is nice and cool. I should say something.

'All right?'

His chin moves down and up again slightly; not quite a nod, more an acknowledgement I've spoken, filled the space a little with those two words. He leans forward slightly.

'Dani, before we begin, I need to tell you that this is a safe space. Everything you tell me will be treated as confidential unless I feel you are at risk of harm to yourself, and then I would have a duty to report it.'

'Fair enough.' I nod. I just want to start.

'Psychotherapy is about exploring your feelings and under-standing them. If you have the courage to be honest, curious and vulnerable during the sessions, you will maximise your progress, but it will take time. And sometimes it can be painful, and diffi-cult feelings will arise, but I am here to guide and support you.'

He speaks so slowly. I try to pace my speech like his but my words come out in a rush, as usual.

'It's what I need.'

I wait for him to carry on speaking, but he doesn't. Looking at the bookshelves, I tilt my head so I can read the titles on the spines: *Clinical Notes on Disorders of Childhood*; *Psychotherapy: An Erotic Relationship – Transference and Counter Transference Passions*; *Class and Psychoanalysis: Landscapes of Inequality*. I tilt my head to the other side to even things up and do a couple of shoulder rolls.

'Oh.' I take four twenties from my bag, stand and walk over to him. 'Eighty pounds for today, yeah?' I hold the money towards him, but he doesn't take it. 'I thought I'd pay you now in case you're worried I won't – after the session, I mean.'

He doesn't say anything. He doesn't take the money. I feel stupid holding my arm out, it's like being left hanging on a high five. I briefly consider letting the notes flutter to the floor, but I put them on the table next to his chair and sit down.

'Why would I think that?' he says.

'What?'

'That you wouldn't pay?'

'Because I could. I could get away without paying. If I decide not to come back.'

I sit up straighter. I've never been in a room like this. I feel a better person just for being in it.

'You've got a lot of books.'

He doesn't answer.

'You like reading.'

The books all seem to be about psychotherapy or philosophy. A light green spine with *French Grammar in Context* stands out.

'Do you speak French?'

Nothing.

I change the inflection.

'Do you speak French?'

He frowns.

'*Vouz parlez français?*'

He stifles a laugh.

We sit in silence until it's broken by a low rumbling coming from the direction of his stomach. I wonder what he had for lunch. Probably something like a quinoa salad or sea bass with lightly steamed vegetables. Whatever it was, it wasn't enough and he's still hungry, or he ate too close to six and he's mid-digestion. There's no other sound in the room except a clock ticking. I tap my fingers on my knees in time to it, then I think it might seem weird and stop. His stomach again. This time it's a low gurgling noise. I wait for him to say something, but he shows no sign of having noticed. I can feel myself blushing. He should eat before, or not eat before, or do whatever he needs to in order not to be making these noises in my space, my time. This is costing me eighty quid an hour – and not even a proper hour, a therapist's hour, which is fifty minutes. I'm paying practically two quid a minute. I've just spent two quid on listening to his gut.

I look at the painting of the girl sitting on her father's lap. I think about how the girl, leaning so far into her father's chest, would be breathing in the smell of his jumper. I wonder if she'd experience his jumper as soft or scratchy against her cheek, if she could feel his heart beating. I raise my eyebrows and smile at my therapist but he doesn't smile back. Fuck him. His stomach again. The sound fills the room but again, Richard's expression doesn't change and he doesn't say anything.

'My dad would've got up and left the room at your stomach making noises like that.'

Richard finally moves – his nose, like he's caught a strange smell in the air and he's not sure what it is.

'We weren't allowed to make any noise when we were eating. Dad would go mental. Once, we were having lunch at my nan and grandad's and my mum burped with her mouth closed. Dad just got up and walked out. Grandad had to give us a lift home. My dad hated going there anyway. He said sparks came off my nan's fork when she was eating.'

I take my rucksack from my feet and put it on my lap. I find my phone and check the time. It's twelve minutes past six. Richard Goode has hardly said anything, and I want my money's worth from this session.

'What do you think? My dad hating noises like that?'

'Misophonia,' he says eventually.

'What?'

'Misophonia. A strong aversion to particular sounds.'

'Okay.'

Suffers from misophonia sounds so much better than *he goes mental when people eat too loud.* This is the benefit of having a wide vocabulary and being learned, as Richard so obviously is – you can explain stuff better.

I picture sitting at the table with Dad when I was a teenager, smoking and playing cards or Scrabble, and how much fun it was. Then I remember how often he used to say to me, *You weirdo piece of shit.* When I make a mistake, they're the words that come: *You weirdo piece of shit.* The words often play on a loop in my head. I might ask Richard how I can stop this.

'Where did you go just then?'

His voice is gentle. Richard Goode is strong, with his broad chest and wide shoulders. He's wearing a thin green jumper over a shirt, close-fitting enough to see there's not a hint of fat. I reckon he's in his late forties, but he's fit. An attractive man in an attractive room. I scratch the back of my neck.

'What do you mean?' I say.

Richard spirals a finger around slowly. His hands are big.

'There was a lot going on there – in the silence after you spoke.'

'I was thinking about my dad, but I don't want to talk about my dad. I want to talk about the bulimia. I need to get it under control. I had to drop out of uni because of it.'

He does the half-nod again.

'I tried cognitive behavioural therapy. I had eight sessions in a group with two other girls. My GP referred me, and the counsellor, the woman running it, was lovely, and it worked for a while but then I swapped one bad behaviour for another. I think, from reading about it, psychotherapy is more effective at getting to the root of a problem and changing it that way, and that's what I need.'

I tell him about the counsellor and how good she was and that it wasn't her fault the CBT didn't work. With hindsight, eight two-hour sessions were never going to be enough to sort out a problem I'd had for six years. Anyway, I had stopped throwing up so much, but I'd started drinking a lot more and taking drugs. I realise I'm rambling and apologise.

He raises his chin.

'Dani, I offer person-centred psychotherapy, which means it's important we focus on the "here and now" and exploring what's happening between us. What you've already brought to the session reveals to me one area that we need to address, which is your relationship with others—'

'I already said I don't want to talk about my dad. Sorry, sorry, I interrupted you. Go on.'

'What you've already brought to the session indicates to me one area that would be helpful to address, your relationships with others. However — and this is entirely natural, as your accounts of them may be biased — it is most useful to concentrate on the one relationship of which I do have the most precise knowledge, and that is our relationship, and what occurs between you and me in this room.'

'Yeah, okay.' I feel the toes of my left foot curling when he says, 'what occurs between you and me'. I look at his chest and try and match my breathing to the rise and fall.

'Embarking on psychotherapy is brave, Dani. And at times it will be difficult, but ultimately, its success depends on your willingness and ability to engage in that which may be un-comfortable. You need to be able to trust that I am here to help you make the changes necessary to lead a more fulfilling life.'

He's not smiling, but his eyes are soft. I love the way he sits in his chair, so elegant, refined, sophisticated.

'I know it'll be difficult but I don't feel I've got any other options. I'm going to keep going round in circles otherwise.'

Richard takes his hands from the arms of the chair and interlaces his fingers. It feels like forever before he speaks.

'I'm interested in something you just said, Dani, about seeing psychotherapy as a way of getting to the root of a problem. This is true, in part, but psychotherapy can also help you uncover strengths and learn new skills that will help you deal with life's challenges in a more managed and considered way. As I've done with every patient I've seen over the past twenty years, I will prioritise the therapeutic relationship because this is integral to self-development, self-realisation and progress.'

'They're all the things I want. I need to sort out the bulimia, though.'

I can tell he's thinking about what I've said. You can tell when someone's listened. It's not just because he takes so long to answer every time I speak. It's more than that.

'You need to "sort out" your bulimia. Dani, I wonder if you make yourself sick because you don't know how to deal with your emotions in a healthy way?'

'That's it! That is it exactly; it's what I need to work on, why I'm here. I need to sort it out so I can get back to university and finish my degree.'

Keeping eye contact after I've finished speaking feels too intimate. I want to pull a face or stick my tongue out at him, make a noise like a squawking parrot. I focus on his hands. He's not wearing a wedding ring. Not that this means anything – of course he'll be in a relationship. There's no way that someone like him wouldn't be.

'Education, being educated, is important to you,' he says.

'I'll be the first one in my family to do it. I need to learn. I love learning. It's so true, isn't it? What they say about the more

8

you know, the less you know, but that excites me. I'd love a room like this one day, so many books ...' I want to run my fingers along the spines but I stay seated, looking at the wall of floor-to-ceiling books. I glance at Richard. He's turned his head to look at them too, and I like the fact we're doing this together.

'When I go in the charity shops for books and stand there looking, I always start to feel calmer, more peaceful. Do you know what I mean? You must be so calm, being able to look at these all the time. There's no books where I'm living now. Well, I keep some in my bedroom, but it's not really my bedroom. I'm staying with my sister and her fiancé, and his daughter comes to stay every other weekend. She's only four, and my sister's fiancé's old-fashioned, so you can imagine what the bedroom's like ... Lots of pastel colours, dolls, teddy bears.' I check my phone then talk faster when I see there's only ten minutes of the session left. 'I don't want you to think I'm ungrateful or for it to seem like I'm complaining. They're doing me a huge favour letting me live with them, and they're not charging me much rent either. They're helping me get back on track. It's why I can afford to come here. Well, I can't really, I should be paying off some debts, but I think having therapy is more important right now.'

Fifty minutes of Richard Goode's professional service costs as much as I earn in a day. Eight hours of pot wash for fifty minutes with him, but my work is unskilled, minimum wage, anyone could do it. He's a professional, educated and well qualified. His rate is high, but I spend more than eighty quid on bingeing some weeks.

'I'm curious as to why you were concerned I might perceive you as "complaining" about your sister and fiancé,' he says.

'Because that would be out of order. I was completely on my arse and they let me move in with them. They're trying to help me.'

9

'And this means that you can't have any negative feelings about them?'

'Of course. If someone's been nice to you, you don't slag them off.'

I wait for him to respond. Perhaps I haven't explained it well enough.

'I had a complete breakdown. I was completely fucked. I started crying and couldn't stop. I never knew the human body was capable of that, you know? So much water came out of my eyes. I was lying on my back in bed and my ears were wet for two days. My sister came and picked me up from university and then I sat on her sofa for another two days, crying. It was the bulimia. I'd had enough. I was so exhausted by it. I was making myself sick every single day, two, three, four times a day. I'd even get the shakes if I hadn't been sick for a few hours – it was like a proper addiction, you know? I wanted to stop so much but I kept failing. My sister said I could live with them while I sorted myself out. She said I needed the support.'

Richard doesn't speak.

'It was kind of them,' I say. I want him to acknowledge it. He doesn't. I feel like he could have commented more on what I've said in this session, asked me more questions, given me more advice, but it's only the first one. Perhaps he'll say more next time. 'Where's the ticking coming from? I can hear a clock but I can't see it. Is that one?' I point to the mantelpiece. It looks like a little travel clock, but it's angled to face him.

'Yes, it's a clock.'

'It's quite loud. If nobody's speaking.'

His eyes go to the clock, and he uncrosses his legs.

'And we'll have to leave it there for today,' he says. And then, in an even softer voice, 'It's time.'

I stand and try to smile.

'Right. Thanks.'

Our eyes don't meet because he's looking towards the window, even though the blind is down. He stands up, walks across the room and opens the door for me. He waits there, with his fingers on the handle. When I get to the door, I pause. I only come up to his shoulder. I want to rest my forehead against his chest.

Chapter Two

In Ealing, in the kitchen of Hall & Walker restaurant, I work in the corner, on pot wash. The Classeq Commercial is a big silver machine and like the fridges, the workbenches, the ovens and the sinks, it's made from stainless steel. Some of us work harder than others at keeping the surfaces clean and smear-free. I stack dirty plates into a large plastic basket and rinse them with the hose. I slide the basket from over the sink to under the stainless-steel hood of the Classeq Commercial and I pull the side handle to bring the hood down. I wait for the whoosh of water and stack the next lot of plates. When the washing cycle's finished, the plates are hot and squeak when I take them out. I slide the next tray of dirty plates over the sink.

Maureen, who does a lot of the cooking, comes over with a baking tray for me and puts it on the draining board. She shakes off her oven gloves and clamps them under her armpit. Her arms rest in a T-rex position.

'You be careful, the tray is hot,' she says. She stands there, looking at me, like she's worried I'll reach out and grab it despite what she's said. She does the same when she brings me knives: 'You be careful, the knife is sharp.' Until I acknowledge I've heard her, she won't leave. I have to stop myself from answering that I know the baking trays are hot because she's wearing thick oven gloves. I know the knives are sharp because knives are sharp. Instead, I thank her each time in a voice that isn't mine.

The working day (excluding lunch and breaks) is divided into four two-hour blocks, and this is what you could be down for: serving tea and coffee, serving hot food, taking payment at the till, food preparation, cooking or pot wash. There's a wipeable staff rota pinned to the wall and Babs, the manager, fills it in every week with the initials of the twelve staff. In the eight weeks I've been here, she's only put me down for pot wash. Babs likes me on it because I'm fast and efficient and nobody can match my speed. If you have to do a job, do it well, else what's the point?

I get two tea breaks and an hour for lunch. The tea breaks are fifteen minutes long, and I spend them outside in the smoking hut. The restaurant's on the third floor of the department store and I take the stairs two at a time, so I've got more time to smoke. The smoking hut is like a large shed with only three sides. Two wooden benches run along the two long sides, and there's a pallet used as a coffee table for the plastic cups of tea and coffee the smokers bring in. There are two metal buckets filled with sand for dog-ends.

When I'm on lunch, I run downstairs for a quick cigarette before I go back up to the staff room. If I'm feeling good, I have a chicken salad and a bottle of sparkling water. I'll eat and drink and chat with other staff. If something's upset me, or I'm feeling restless, I'll choose a seat facing the wall and swallow down the same things, in the same order: cheese and mayonnaise sandwiches on white bread, a scone with loads of raspberry jam, and two packs of cheese and onion crisps. If I'm seriously upset, I'll get Colleen from the staff canteen to make me a steak pie and chips. I drink tea and water while I'm eating because if you don't drink a lot when you're bingeing the food sticks together and is much harder to bring up. I buy a Twix and a Mars Bar and two cans of Diet Coke from the vending machine and put them in my rucksack. I'll eat the Mars Bar while I'm in the staff lift, and the Twix while I walk to the public toilets near the library. I'll lock myself in a cubicle, put my hair back into a ponytail, and drink the Diet Coke. Then I contract my stomach muscles and let it all out.

After the first year, I stopped needing to use my fingers. All I had to do was wrench my stomach in and it would all come up. Now I only need to use my fingers to provoke the gag reflex if I haven't drunk enough. But that doesn't happen much. Six years on, I know what I'm doing.

Three months ago, I was a full-time student at university, studying the American Confessional Poets of the 1950s, a module I chose as part of my degree in English Literature. I loved how these people made poems from their trauma, how they wrote about it with such honesty and depth of feeling. Now I'm a full-time employee at Hall & Walker, and the subject matter of my workmates' lives is no different from the stuff the American Confessional Poets were writing about – mental health issues, abuse and personal failure. While Ginsberg, Lowell and Plath wrote poems about it, my co-workers hint at their struggles, unhappy marriages and disappointments as we sit, side by side, smoking in the hut, united in our black uniforms with green piping and our nicotine addictions. Most often, though, the conversation is mundane. Stuff like,

'I really enjoyed my tea last night.'

'Did you? What did you have?'

But there's rarely a break time we don't end up laughing and there's solidarity among the middle-aged lot. I identify with them and have nothing in common with the girls my age. Yesterday, Leanne and Tulsi were chatting by a workbench covered in crumbs. 'You could wipe the bench down while you're chatting your inane, pointless shit,' I wanted to shout across the kitchen but I've never been one for confrontation. When they moved off, I went and did it myself.

I get on best with Pat. She bustles around the restaurant kitchen as though it's her own. She's a real grafter. She's old enough to be my mum but we hit it off on my first day when she took me down to the smoking hut and gave me two of her cigarettes as I'd run out of Rizlas. I found her easy to talk to. She's the only one I've told about my psychotherapy, apart from my sister. It's not that I'm ashamed, but people don't need to know my business.

Pat and I meet at the back entrance after work. We're going to visit Edie, her mother, in the old people's home. It's the third time I've gone with Pat and I'm grateful for anything that gives me a reason to be out of the flat, where I'll end up watching Jo and Stevie watch *Gogglebox* or some other 'reality' shite.

'I don't know why you want to be hanging around an old people's home. A young girl like you, you ought to be out having fun,' Pat says.

'I am having fun. What's with the flowers?' I nod towards the bunch of pink carnations poking out of her bag.

'It's Mum's birthday.'

'You should have said. I would've got her something.'

Pat pulls off a couple of petals fringed with beige and drops them on the ground.

'That's better,' she says.

I like the way Pat doesn't always respond to everything I say. It reminds me of my dad.

The train arrives. We sit side by side and I think about what I could have got a woman in her late eighties, what she might like. I enjoy buying presents for people, but I feel uncomfortable and indebted when people give presents to me, like I need to give something of the same value back in return.

The nursing home smells like someone's had a shit and sprayed pine air freshener. We go through to the communal lounge where the TV hurts my ears and the heating's on high. Pat kisses Edie and gives her the carnations. Edie smiles at the flowers and strokes them. I watch a resident in a lilac cardigan on the other side of the room rooting around in the back of her mouth with a bent finger. She's getting worked up and keeps looking at the finger before sticking it in the back of her mouth. After a bit, she takes out her dentures and licks them. I tell Pat I'll make tea and wander over to the kitchen. Frank, who was a driver for Margaret Thatcher and took her for weekly meetings with the Queen, or so he says, is leaning against the counter and eating a dark chocolate digestive.

'Dani!' he says. I fold my arms.

'Finished that book yet?' It's how we got talking the week before: I asked him about what he was reading. His book had a picture of a ship with curved white sails on the front cover and I remembered my dad reading one with a similar picture on the front.

Frank puts his hand on my shoulder. I shrug and he takes his hand off.

'Yes, I finished the book,' he says.

'So what are you reading now?'

'Mobile library only visits once a month; I'll have to wait,' he says.

'I'll get you some books if you want. What do you want?'

'You don't need to do that.' He takes a hanky out of his pocket and coughs into it.

'I'm in charity shops all the time anyway. I get all my books from there. What authors do you like? I'll keep an eye out.'

'You're very kind,' he says. He picks up a wide flat tin from the counter and takes off the lid. 'Have a biscuit,' he says.

There are shortbread fingers, chocolate digestives and some kind of cream-filled biscuit.

'Thanks, Frank.' I take one of the cream-filled biscuits and bite into it. The crunch of the buttery biscuit and the smooth cream filling on my tongue makes my mouth fill with saliva. I now want to eat every single biscuit in the tin, and then rush to a fast-food place with a toilet and carry on the binge. I look at the biscuit in my hand and feel hot.

'You all right, love?' says Frank.

'Yeah, fine,' I say. 'It tastes a bit funny.'

What's the point of seeing Richard, paying all that money, if the first day after the session I make myself sick? I shouldn't go so far out of my comfort zone so quickly. I throw the biscuit in the bin when Frank isn't looking.

I take the tea to Pat and Edie and start to take off my jumper until I remember I'm wearing a black bra under a T-shirt so worn it's see-through. I put my jumper back on. Pat's trying to calm Edie, who's complaining about her dinner. There was no gravy, and the potatoes were cold. Pat takes Edie's hand and says she'll talk to Elaine, the manager.

They sit there, just holding hands. I can't stop looking at their hands while I drink the tea that's too hot to get the taste of sugar from my mouth. I remember shaking hands with Dad a couple of times when I was a kid, but that was after he'd gone mental, regretted it and wanted me to accept his apology. Apart from that, I can't think of a time we held hands or touched or hugged when I was little.

Pat and Edie are talking about last night's *Gogglebox*.

'They didn't like it when the copper got shot at the end, did they?' says Pat.

I know the bit she's talking about, because Stevie and Jo had *Gogglebox* on last night too. So now I'm listening to people talking about people watching TV, which is slightly more engaging than watching Stevie and Jo watch people watch TV. But not much.

Chapter Three

It feels good to be back in Richard's office. It feels good to be sitting opposite Richard. He's wearing navy corduroy trousers and a cream jumper over a light blue shirt and again, socks with the diamond pattern. He looks immaculate. If I got close enough, I think he'd smell of handmade soap, something fresh and citrusy. I'm scruffy as usual, no makeup or jewellery. I don't see the point of putting on makeup – I can't see my face, so why put it on for other people? I get changed after work in the toilet cubicle, pull on jeans, jumper and Nike trainers and I always wear black to look thinner. All I do with my hair is brush it. It only goes up when I'm being sick, so it doesn't get in the way. Otherwise I like to wear my hair down, in case my ears are dirty inside.

Richard's chest rises and falls and I try to sync my breathing with his. It makes me feel calmer. He breathes much more slowly than I breathe.

'I've been looking forward to this session,' I say.

'Are you warm enough, Dani?' he asks.

I turn my head back from the books to him.

'Why do you ask?'

'You're shaking a little.'

'I do feel the cold and it's freezing out there. I suppose it should be, in January.' I tilt the side of my face towards him and run my hand down my cheek and jaw. 'That's why I've got this.' I like to point it out before people notice, the thin film of soft hair, my body trying to insulate itself. 'It's okay. I don't mind. I'd rather be hairy than fat.'

'Would you like to use the blanket?' He gestures to the folded one at the end of the couch.

'No. I'd feel like an old granny sitting here with a blanket over my lap.'

He doesn't say anything. I take a piece of paper from my bag. I've made a list of things I want to talk to him about, one, so I don't forget anything and two, to avoid the silences we had in the first session.

'I read on your website you trained first in "body psychotherapy" – it sounds interesting.' I fold the list back in half and push it down the side of the chair.

I've been reading and rereading his website. Richard Goode initially trained as a 'humanistic psychotherapist with a focus on the body' before studying psychotherapy for a further eight years and then gaining a master's in Counselling and Psychotherapy from the 'World-famous Matrix Clinic'. In the seventeen years since, he's run a private practice, worked as an NHS adviser and lectured at the College of North West London. There's a 'publications' tab on his website and details of four pieces he's written, which have gone in academic journals and magazines. He's an intellectual and he's highly qualified. I've always liked clever people. A friend told me I was a 'sapiosexual' but I disagreed because it suggests I'm fussy. I binge on men the way I binge on food, drink and drugs. I go for bulk, quantity. I want to fill myself up. When I'm on Pornhub, I always end up watching the triple penetration videos. I can't get away from the desire to be stuffed, full up.

'I was wondering how "body psychotherapy" is different from normal psychotherapy,' I say. I could have looked it up but I thought it would be better if he explained it.

Richard gives one of his half-nods. 'You'd like to know more about me.'

'No, not really. I think I know as much as I need to.'

'And what is it you know about me, Dani?'

'You've had an excellent education, done loads of training.'

He tries not to smile. I like people's faces when they're trying not to smile – the trembling of the lips, the creasing around the eyes.

'An excellent education, years of training. You would like to have those opportunities.'

'Well, I had the opportunity, didn't I? But I messed it up. I loved university, the library was brilliant, and the lecturers – I loved it, but this time I want to go back and be able to focus.'

'What stopped you from focusing before?'

'It was too hard. It's like I've always got this urge to do bad stuff.'

'"Bad stuff?"'

'The bulimia, or if I managed to get that under control for a while, I'd end up taking drugs or drinking until I passed out. Bad stuff.'

'You mentioned this in the first session,' he says. 'Addiction transfer. What drugs were you taking?'

'Ecstasy, mainly, and I was smoking a lot of weed. I never touched anything skanky like acid or crack. Nothing like that.'

I'd heard about people getting a bad trip and it scared the shit out of me. And the people who took acid seemed grubby, unpredictable.

'There was a correlation between an increase in the "bad stuff" and attending university?' Richard says.

'Probably. I've been bulimic since I was fourteen and drinking since then, but I only started taking drugs when I got to university. I was seeing this guy who used to deal.'

Richard closes his eyes and I stare at his face, his chest, his legs, his arms, back to his face. I can't look at his crotch because his legs are crossed. The silence before he speaks stretches on and on, but I know he's thinking about what I've said.

He opens his eyes. 'What you want is also what you resist, Dani,' he says. 'You desire an education, yet you sabotage it.'

I scan the bookshelves and then turn back to him. His cream jumper is clean and made of quality material. It could be brand new.

'My dad used to sleep in his clothes. He had two jumpers, one black and one white.'

The ticking of the clock is loud. There's no other sound in the room.

'You miss your father.'

The rug in this room is large, with swirly patterns in ochre, red and orange. I try and work out the sequence of how the patterns link but they blur. I wait until I've pulled myself together before I speak again.

'Have you heard of Diogenes? He's my favourite Greek philosopher – well, the only one I know really. Diogenes didn't believe we should have material possessions. He rejected all forms of luxury and my dad was the same. I think it's a good way to be. Two jumpers is probably enough.'

'You miss your father, Dani.'

'If you get attached to stuff, you only get upset when you lose it. Or if it breaks.'

'I think you want to bring your father into this room.'

'He wasn't even that nice. That's why I haven't cried, why I don't need to. I'm not really bothered.'

21

'When did your father die, Dani?'

'I don't know. Ages ago.'

'Ages ago.'

'Twelve weeks, thirteen or fourteen. Something like that.'

I look at the picture of the small girl sitting on her father's lap.

'How would it feel to be sad for your father, here, with me?' he says.

I lower my head and take the neckline of my jumper up over my face. It gets too warm, and I haven't got enough air, so I bring it down.

'There are tissues on the table next to you.'

I take one, scrunch it and blot the water from the corners of my eyes before it falls.

'If I get upset, I might not be able to stop, and then I'd go mad.'

'Your grief is so huge it feels if you let it free, it might overwhelm you.'

Yes, my grief would fuck me over if I let it. I'd rip out my hair, stamp on my own hands and smash my face into a wall. I look at Richard's books.

'I'm not coming here about my dad. It's the bulimia. I'm so desperate to stop it. I'm upset now because it's relief that I'm dealing with it. I haven't made myself sick at all since I started coming to see you, although I've felt like it. I was stupid, I took a biscuit and it made me want to start a binge. But I didn't. I know this is only the second session, but it makes me feel better having this in place.'

'You haven't made yourself sick since you started coming here because you feel supported.'

'Yeah, I mean, I've got Jo and Stevie who are helping, and Pat at work is brilliant, but I want her to see me as nice.' I unscrunch the tissue. It's got a big hole in the middle. I consider holding it up to my face, putting the hole in front of my eye and looking at Richard through it. 'I need this therapy so I can work out why I'm this way so that I can change.'

'You want Pat to see you as "nice". What does nice mean to you?'

'Not hurting anyone. Being clean, not throwing up.' I pause. 'I've made a new friend at Hall & Walker called Del. He works in the warehouse downstairs. I went to his house last night, and we stayed up all night smoking weed and drinking. I know that's still not good, you know, the weed, but it's better than being sick.'

We also spent the night having sex, but it wouldn't feel right to talk about sex in here. Anyway, sex isn't a problem because I love it. After a few cans of Stella and the second joint, it was obvious Del and I would kiss and take each other's clothes off. Lying on my back, I was getting dizzy in the Artex swirls when he said, 'Do you want me to make love to you, or fuck you?' I whispered, 'Fuck me.' Making love is for people who are good and kind and decent. Missionary position, to begin. I wrapped my legs around him and enjoyed the paleness of my skin against the black of his.

'Dani?'

I wonder if Richard could tell what I was thinking about and I blush.

'Your "new friend" Del. Why do you like him?'

The acne scars on Del's face add to his sexiness. His muscles are defined through hard physical work rather than the gym. He smells of baby oil and beneath that sweetness, fresh earth.

'He's chilled out. He thinks I'm funny. We're on the same wavelength.'

The same wavelength means he's also happy to spend the night smoking and drinking, then drink more on the bus to work the next day. I feel good from all the cuddles and proud of another day of not making myself sick. I don't know what Del's motivations are, what he's trying to avoid. Perhaps he's just having fun.

'I had to tell Stevie I was staying at Leanne's, though. It's easier that way, although I feel bad for the lie. Stevie wouldn't be happy if he knew I was staying around some bloke's house who's not even my boyfriend. He's old-fashioned that way. He's even got this calendar on the kitchen wall and he writes stuff on it, like when the football's on or work functions.' I shake my head. 'Who does that?'

Richard's waiting for me to carry on, but there's not a lot more I can say when he's not giving me much back. I look at his feet and wonder how much his shoes cost. They're suede. People who buy shoes you can't wear when it's raining have money. I remember my list and unfold it.

'How long do people usually come to you?'

'How long do patients come for therapy?'

'Yeah.'

Richard clasps his hands together on his lap.

'It depends. Some come for years. Psychotherapy is a type of therapy that is long-term, and it benefits the patients most when they attend for a long period of time.'

'How long will I need to come for?'

'We can say two years, to begin with, at this point.'

Two years is a good minimum. I like the thought of coming here every week for two years. I'll have to manage my money better to afford it, but you can't put a price on mental health.

'This room is brilliant. I'd love to have a room like this, books from floor to ceiling, nice pictures on the walls . . .'

'You have warm feelings towards this room.'

'I'm in love with it.'

I pull my hair across my face so he can't see me. I try not to think about my face burning because that will make it burn more. How pathetic did that sound? In love with a room. I play with my hands and squeeze the tip of each finger. I've bitten my nails down too low and I close my hands into fists to hide them. I remember when Dad cut my toenails, my foot resting on his knee. He cut them too short, and it felt like my toes had been peeled. He gave me a two-pound coin, and I spent it on a Cadbury Fruit and Nut because that was his favourite. He shared it with me when we watched a wildlife documentary together that night. He loved wildlife documentaries, especially if a predator was chasing its prey. He'd sit forward in his seat and shout at the TV. I liked how excited he got just before the leopard or whatever it was finally caught and brought down what it was chasing.

When I look up, Richard is still looking at me.

'I've read your website; I read you've helped loads of people over the years,' I say.

'Psychotherapy is a helping profession, but I like to think of it as a transformative profession. Effective psychotherapy can help the patient transform their life.'

'That's why I'm coming to see you.'

It's so expensive but worth it. It has to be. Nothing else has worked: two types of antidepressants, cognitive behavioural therapy, self-help books. Psychotherapy is my last chance.

Richard looks sideways at the clock. I know what's coming. He gives this little smile like he's sorry for what he's about to say.

'And it's time. We'll have to leave it there for today.' I like the way he makes his voice extra gentle when he says it, like he's as sad as me that time is up.

'I can't believe it's time already. It's gone so fast. I've not even gone through everything on my list.' I shake it at him, but he doesn't look at it.

He walks to the door. Opens it and keeps his hand on the handle. This time I don't risk looking at him when I say thanks, in case he's not looking at me.

I walk home even though it's freezing because being cold speeds up the metabolism. Stonebridge Park, where the flat is, is not park-like and the blocks of flats are just that, blocks. No architectural design quirks or flair. Basic and brutal. Columns and rows of windows that are exactly the same shape and size, uniform as Lego. There are triangles of grass to the side of some of the blocks, studded with shit because people take their dogs there but don't pick it up after. There's the odd tree here and there and I feel sorry for them. I'd like them to live in a nice field or a more natural environment, somewhere with more earth where they could stretch their roots and not get their leaves coated with a film of grey shite from all the pollution. I stop off at the garage opposite the flat because I'm running out of Rizlas and to get a bottle of white wine for Jo and Stevie.

Jo and Stevie's flat's on the sixth floor. I take the stairs because the lift is usually broken and when it is working, it stinks of piss and weed. We've all got metal-bar doors as well as our standard doors. It's prison-like, but as Stevie says, it's what it's like inside the flat that matters, and they've made their flat look nice. When they started renting it a couple of years ago, Stevie painted and put up wallpaper. Jo ordered deep grey curtains and electric blue cushions online from a website that encourages you to pay monthly instead of all at once so you buy more.

I let myself in and walk into the living room. Stevie and Jo are in their usual positions. The chair Stevie sits on has its back to me, and his bare shoulders show over the top. His hairy legs are stretched out, feet resting on the grey velvet pouffe. It makes me start every time; for a moment, I think he's naked, but he's

26

wearing loose boxer shorts. He leaves them on top of the wash basket rather than inside it after his nightly bath. It drives Jo mad. 'I'd never go to bed with a dirty ring,' is something Stevie says so often it's like his catchphrase. Jo, in her shiny satin pyjamas which have little hearts on, is lying on the sofa.

'I got you a bottle of wine,' I say, holding it up. 'I'll put it in the fridge.'

When I come back, Jo pulls her legs up so there's a space for me at the end, then when I sit, she puts her feet on my lap.

'Good time at Leanne's last night?' Stevie doesn't take his eyes from the TV.

'Yeah, it was good, but she snores, so I didn't sleep too well.' This is pre-emptive in case he looks at me and notices the dark bags under my eyes. Jo's too wrapped up in herself to notice. Twenty years old and I've got to lie about where I spent the night. Stevie's taken it on himself to be my father, adviser and moral guardian, but a part of me likes it. He walks into the kitchen, scratching at a hairy bit on his lower back and letting out a loud belch. He makes the belch waver towards the end like a singer experimenting with a high note. Jo says *fucking pig* under her breath. There's the noise of the 'treat drawer' opening, and he comes back holding a pack of Haribo and a green tube of Pringles. He shuffles a wedge into his hand and offers the tube to Jo. She shakes her head. It's the third time recently she's refused Stevie's offerings from the 'treat drawer'. She's growing her nails and keeps looking at them as if the more she does that, the faster they'll grow. I reckon there could be someone else on the scene.

'No point in asking you, is there, Dani?' Stevie says.

'Nah, you're fine, thanks. Does anyone want a drink?'

They don't answer, which means no. I go to the kitchen, take a can of Diet Coke from the fridge. I sit down and open it.

'Your teeth,' says Jo.

'I'm only having two cans a week now.'

I shouldn't have told her I've got tooth decay caused by all the stomach acid. Now she says I should only be drinking milk or water.

'What have you eaten today?' Jo pushes her foot into the side of my thigh.

'The usual. Chicken salad, fruit, yoghurt.'

She nods, not taking her eyes from *Made in Chelsea*. Her question is token but pointless as my answer is the same even when I've binged. I've told them before I have 'safe foods', which don't make me feel guilty when I eat: dry bread, fruit, vegetables, chicken cooked in water and low-fat yoghurt. I don't count the calories for alcohol. I tell myself it's balanced out because it speeds up the metabolism.

Sometimes I watch Stevie eat – sidelong glances, though, or he'd tell me I needed 'a check-up from the neck up', another one of his catchphrases. It's fascinating how he can crunch away, crumbs falling into his chest hair, not giving a shit, putting away mouthfuls of fat, protein and carbohydrate and sit with it, not even hiding the evidence of his gluttony under clothes. I'd like to be like that. Not give a shit. Be able to eat without thinking and not be overwhelmed with guilt at every mouthful.

Chapter Four

It's morning break, and Pat and I are sitting side by side in the smoking hut.

'Look how fat I'm getting, Pat.' I pinch my stomach. 'I've put on three pounds. I feel like a right fat cow. It's disgusting.'

'I was thinking about how chubby you looked. I almost mistook you for Babs yesterday.' Pat stubs out her cigarette, then lights another.

'She must weigh at least sixteen stone. I'm half that and I still feel obese some days.' I say. 'It's the therapy. It's been making me feel more relaxed. I'm eating more.' I've been having coleslaw on my lunchtime chicken salad, and when a couple of people have brought in birthday cakes recently, I've had a slice. I've only made myself sick twice since I've started seeing Richard, but if the weight gain carries on, I'll want to start throwing up again. It's a rock and a hard place.

'There's nothing of you. If you think you're fat, what am I?' Pat says.

'You look great.'

Pat's a little overweight but in a comforting way. I imagine if you leaned against her while you were watching a film, it would feel warm, safe. Even though cooking smells and cigarette smoke cling to her clothes, there's something under that which is clean and soft. Perhaps it's the fabric conditioner she uses.

'How long do you think you'll see him for?' Pat says.

'Who? My therapist? As long as it takes, I suppose. He said two years. What? Why did you pull that face?'

'The more messed up they tell you you are, the longer they can take your money.'

'But I am messed up.'

'We all are, darling.' Pat leans forward and picks something up from the ground. 'Strange things, aren't they? Not sure I'm a fan.'

I take it from her and turn it in my hand. 'A spork. A spoon and a fork in one. I can see the logic. I think they're pushing them again to cut down on waste.'

'Horrible word,' she says.

'Spork,' we both say a couple of times.

'I was on a dating website once,' I say, 'and a couple of people had written they were after a spooning partner, but one guy had written, *I like spooning but I prefer forking.*'

'Did you contact him?' Pat says.

'Yeah. You know I love wordplay.'

'How did it go?'

'His first point of conversation was that some girls on the site were so easy he could go through them like a knife through warm butter, or it could have been a warm knife through butter. It put me off, anyway, the arrogance of him.'

'Sounds like he'd want to talk about cutlery all the time, too,' says Pat.

'Yeah, can you imagine? How long do you think you could talk about cutlery without it getting boring?'

'It depends,' says Pat. 'Just the kind of cutlery you'd find in the average kitchen drawer, or are you including your big utensil pieces?'

'Like tongs and spatulas?'

'Yeah,' she says.

'No, they don't count. Funny word though, isn't it? Spatula.'

'Sounds like a posh girl's name. Spa-choo-la! Hurry up, you're going to be late for polo!' Pat's good at putting on a posh voice.

'Spa-choo-la, supper is ready, come immediately,' I say. 'They say supper instead of dinner, don't they?'

'Who?' she says.

'Posh people.'

Pat laughs.

'Have you heard the latest about Babs?' I say.

'About the ripped trousers, on the arse?'

'No, that's old. Someone saw her leaving the toilet without washing her hands.'

'Dirty bugger.'

'It's not very hygienic, is it? Even if you're not working in a kitchen. When I was at university, my boyfriend, Christy, used to dry his hands on the curtains after he'd been to the toilet.'

'Well, he's a dirty bugger too, then.'

I don't like talking about Christy. I don't know why I said it.

'She was in a mood this morning,' Pat says.

'Babs?'

'Yeah. Leanne and Tulsi both called in sick again. They take the piss, those girls.'

'Leanne's probably hooked up with someone. Did she tell you about her latest date?'

'Possibly. I tend to switch off when that girl starts speaking.'

'The guy had said he was five foot ten but when they met up, Leanne was taller than him, and she's only five three.'

'Funny what people think they'll get away with,' says Pat.

We smoke in silence until the back door slams and Reena from accounts walks across the concrete towards us. I like the way she walks along one line instead of two, like a model. She's very pretty but looks permanently surprised because of the way she draws on her eyebrows. Some people, behind her back, have started referring to her as 'Boo'.

'Hiya,' Reena says, but she's not looking at either of us when she says it. She puts a cigarette in her mouth, stands in front of Pat and holds her hand out for a lighter.

'How's it going, Reena?' I say.

'Fine,' she says and sits next to Pat.

'Hey, Reena – show Pat your impression of that new bloke in accounts.' I wait for her to start, but she doesn't. Perhaps she didn't hear me. I lean forward to look around Pat to try to catch Reena's eye. She's looking straight ahead. 'Reena?' I say.

She's ignoring me and I don't know why. Reena and I get on. Pat starts talking about this morning's staff meeting, but I've gone cold and I'm only half listening.

When I did the CBT course, the counsellor told us about the danger of mind-reading, not to assume you know what someone's thinking. Perhaps Reena's worried about something. I talk over Pat.

'Reena? You okay? What's up?'

Her nose twitches, and with that one little move, her profile changes and she looks ugly.

'Reena?' I say.

Pat stops talking and looks at me.

'If you think about how you spend your evenings, Dani, you might work it out,' Reena says.

I turn to face the other way because my mouth's gone funny, and I need to wait for it to go back to normal. *You weirdo piece of shit.* We sit and smoke in silence until Reena gets up and drops her cigarette into the bucket.

'See you later, Pat.' She walks away. Her hips move from side to side as she does her walk along one line.

'She's not happy with you, is she?' Pat says.

The cigarette Reena dropped is burning into another dog-end.

'That fucking stinks. I wish people would stub their cigarettes out properly. It's not hard.' I pick up a plastic cup half full of cold tea and pour it into the bucket. 'Think about how I spend my evenings? What's that meant to mean?' I try to roll another cigarette but the tobacco keeps falling out of the paper.

'Perhaps she's having a bad day,' Pat says.

I think I'll call Dad then remember I can't. This is the kind of thing I'd have called him about, crying or ranting down the phone. He'd have put it in perspective for me. He had this way of summarising a person even when he knew very little about them. He just got it. I imagine how the conversation would've gone.

'Dad, there's this girl at work, Reena, who works in accounts, and we've always got on, but then she suddenly blanked me and when I asked her why she said something about how I spend my evenings. I've got no idea what I've done to upset her or what she's going on about.'

'Works in accounts?' Dad would've said. 'That's because she's got no social skills so she has to deal with numbers, not people. Don't worry about it. Sounds like a piece of shit.'

And I would have felt better. When I see Richard tomorrow, I'll talk to him about how when something like this happens, I get so stressed I have to binge and throw up. A girl on the CBT course said she kept her emotions in the fridge and down the toilet. We all knew what she meant.

I realise Pat's talking to me.

'Dani, she's a funny one. Don't stress, I can see it in your face.'

'I don't know what I've done to upset her.'

While I'm walking upstairs to the restaurant kitchen, I decide it's too long to wait until tomorrow to talk to Richard. I ask Colleen to make me steak pie and chips for when I'm on lunch. She nods in approval.

'Anything for you, me darlin', you need feeding up.'

I'm late back onto pot wash. Babs comes over to me, looks at her watch.

'Sorry,' I say.

Babs should wear a bigger watch, the one she has is tiny – or perhaps it's a normal size but looks tiny on her forearm, which is the size of a leg of ham. I try to work out why Reena's upset with me. Every time I catch sight of someone in the kitchen, I think 'cunt', 'slag' or 'wanker'. I count down the minutes to lunchtime. *You weirdo piece of shit.* Maureen comes up behind me humming a stupid little tune.

'Dani?'

I pretend I haven't heard her and stack the plates.

'Dani,' she repeats, 'you be careful, this tray is hot.'

I see her out of the corner of my eye with her enormous oven gloves on. I want to tell her to go fuck herself.

'Thanks, Maureen,' I say so she'll leave, but she doesn't. She stands in front of the machine.

'Are you all right, Dani?'

'Yeah, I'm fine.'

'You look sad.'

'Honestly, Maureen. I'm good. Aren't you cooking sausages? They'll burn, won't they?'

'They'll be okay for a minute,' she says.

The machine cycle ends and the red light goes off.

'I need to get there,' I say. 'You're in the way.'

She reaches out. I think she's going to pat me on the arm, so I move.

★

At lunch break, I get two cups of tea from the machine. Colleen brings through my pie and chips. The plate's so loaded her thin wrist shakes, and a couple of chips fall onto the table when she puts it down. I take the food and sit at a corner table facing the wall. There's a grease-stained copy of the *Mirror* with yesterday's date. I read. After I've eaten all of the pie and half of the chips, I get up for more tea. Chips are especially hard to bring up if you don't drink enough while eating them. The chair next to me is being pulled out from underneath the table. I ignore it, but when a big hand reaches across the table and slides my newspaper away, I turn. Del. He leans back on the chair, stretches out his long legs and gives me a sexy look. The last thing I feel right now, my stomach hard with pie and chips and four cups of tea, is sexy, and I stand. His forehead creases.

'Want anything from the vending machine?' I say.

He asks for a Twirl and leans forward to reach inside his back pocket. I tell him not to worry.

'You hungry today?' he nods at my empty plate and then at the chocolate in my hands. I got my usual Twix and Mars Bar and two Twirls for him.

'Yeah. I didn't eat yesterday, too busy – you know what Saturdays are like in here.'

'You've got a little . . .' He strokes his lower lip, where it meets the skin.

'Thanks.' I rub it. 'Gone now?'

He nods, and I get another heavy-lidded sexy look.

'You wanna come over tonight?' he says.

We'll drink and smoke weed. I won't think about food, I won't think about Reena. I'll get lots of cuddles even if Del's cock is inside me.

'I'd better message my brother-in-law. I have to tell him if I'm staying out.'

35

I message Stevie I'm staying at Leanne's again. I don't like lying but . . . Del looks good when he eats, beautiful lips. I take my tobacco from my bag and make a roll-up.

'Been inside?' Del says.

'It's how my dad made them. I copied him when I started smoking. Do you want to meet out front after work?' He nods and I stand up. 'I'll see you later. I've got to pop into town.'

'I'll take a walk with you.' He stands.

'I'm meeting my sister. She wants to talk to me in private.'

The bulimia makes me into a liar, another reason I want to stop. You have to lie all the time, make excuses for why you're starving and need to eat so much, why you need another shower, why you can't go out. Del waits as I get two cans of Diet Coke from the machine. I wish he'd go.

'See you later then.' He pinches my waist. I jerk away because I don't want him touching my bloated stomach. I hear somebody choking. Reena's holding one hand to her chest and one hand on her mate's shoulder. She's laughing, not choking and she and her friend are looking at me and then back at each other. Reena's eyebrows are almost at her hairline they've gone up so high. Fuck them both.

On the way to the public toilet block near the library, I put my hood up so people can't see so much of my face. I drink one of the cans and eat the chocolate. There's a queue for the toilets which means I'll be late back to work. I get a message from Stevie asking me for Leanne's address and I say I'll send it later. It's a good cleaner who does this place. The floor tiles are cracked and old but they never look dirty.

When I finally get inside the cubicle, I pull my hair into a rough ponytail, push the flush, lift the toilet seat, contract my stomach muscles and lean close over the bowl. I angle the sick so it slides down the inside of the bowl which means less chance of splashback. I down the next can of Diet Coke in one, push the flush again and contract my stomach. Wait for the cistern to refill. There's a film of fat floating on the water, so I chuck some paper on top. I light a couple of matches and quickly blow them out. When I asked Stevie why he kept matches in the bathroom at home, he said it was good manners to strike a couple after having a shit because it got rid of the smell, so now I always ask for a couple of boxes of Swan Vestas when I buy my tobacco.

When I come out of the cubicle, I keep my face down to avoid eye contact with the woman who's going in after me because I'm ashamed at the idea that she'll know what I've been doing. She coughs before she closes the door. I know why – it will be the lingering smell of the vomit filling the small space.

There are two trolleys full of dirty crockery and cutlery waiting when I get back to pot wash. When I've nearly cleared them, Babs comes over.

'Is everything okay with you today, Dani?'

'All fine.' I take a step away from her in case she can smell sick. I always smoke then spray body spray all over me and chew strong mint gum after, but I'm still paranoid.

'You were five minutes late back from morning break and twenty minutes late back from lunchtime.' She puts a pudgy finger on the face of her little gold watch.

'I'm so sorry. I'll work late today to make up for the time.'

'It's not as simple as that. I need you back on time after your breaks. We ran out of forks because you were late back.'

Fuck your forks, I think. I put my hand on my stomach. 'I am sorry. It's that time of the month, you know.'

I've not had a period for years, but they're a useful excuse for a time like this.

'You're a good worker, Dani, but you need to keep an eye on

the time. You can't be late back again.' Babs's lips disappear as she taps her watch.

'It won't happen again, sorry.'

I need to keep on the right side of Babs. It's only washing-up but it took me a month to get this job and I can't afford to lose it and then wait a month to get another one.

I feel dirty all afternoon and I can't stop thinking about what I could have done to upset Reena. I keep thinking about her face as she put her hand on her mate's shoulder and laughed at me.

Me and Del get off the bus a stop early to go to Spar. I buy Jack Daniel's, vodka, a bottle of Coke for him and a bottle of Diet Coke for me. It'll make me go overdrawn but I get paid in a few days. My card gets declined so I put the vodka back and my card goes through. I must have reached my overdraft limit already.

While I'm in the shower, Del's mate drops over some cocaine. We listen to rap; we snort lines off his bedside table; we drink all of the JD; we have sex; we watch shit on Netflix. My phone dies and I look in my bag for my charger but I've forgotten it. At four in the morning, I ask Del if he's set an alarm for work and he says yes.

I wake with a stone-dry mouth and a raging thirst. I know it's later than seven because there's too much light coming through the sides of the blinds. I shake Del but he says he's got the day off. I think about using Del's phone to call an Uber but remember I haven't got any money in my account to pay him back. I lie back and close my eyes. I'll call Babs and tell her I'm coming in but I'm running late. I pick up Del's phone. It's got five messages from a girl with a thick pout and fake eyelashes. Babs's line is engaged. I don't shower because I don't want to be any later than I already am.

I chain-smoke at the bus stop and wish I had some juice, a smoothie, water, anything. I have to keep thinking of cold orange juice with ice so my mouth waters and I make enough spit to swallow.

Babs's office, to the side of the kitchen, is tiny and there are no windows. Papers are strewn across her desk, and there are three framed photos of the same orange and white cat, sleeping, stretching and looking out of a window. I put my hands in a prayer position while I apologise. She looks up from her screen.

'Two and a half hours late, Dani.'

'My alarm didn't go off. I'm so sorry, Babs. My phone died.'

'How could you let this happen after the conversation yesterday?' She shakes her head.

'I am truly sorry. You know I've never been late to work before. I was so stressed yesterday so I found it hard to get to sleep which is why I overslept. You can take it off my pay if you want, that's fine. And I'll work Sunday if you want me to.'

'I'll have to give you a verbal warning for this, Dani, which means next time, and I hope there's not a next time, it'll be a written warning.'

'There won't be a next time. I promise I won't be late again. Could you please not give me the verbal warning?'

'You've not given me any choice.'

'Is there any way I can avoid getting it?'

'No.'

'I'm sorry. I'll get to work.' I turn to leave but she holds her hand up.

'I've had someone calling for you all morning. Well, twice.' She looks at the back of her hand and reads, 'Steve, Stevie. He's called twice.'

My stomach twists.

'Can I give him a quick call now? My phone's got no battery.'

39

'Jesus,' she says.

'I'll only be a minute. It's my brother-in-law; he's overprotect-ive. He'll probably keep calling if I don't call him. He's relentless. He thinks I'm twelve, for some reason.'

'You've got two minutes,' she says and leans to the side so I can use her computer to look up his work number. She smells musty, like her clothes have taken a long time to dry. I breathe through my mouth.

'Stevie speaking,' he says when he answers.

'Stevie, it's me,' I say.

'Where are you?'

'Work.'

He doesn't answer and I think maybe he didn't hear.

'I'm at work,' I say.

'Where were you last night?'

'Leanne's.'

'You were supposed to text me her address.'

'I was going to but my phone died.'

'Why didn't you get to work on time?'

I look at Babs, who's not even pretending not to listen and rubbing her thumb across the inside of her fingers. Her skin is dry with lots of little white lines.

'I overslept because my alarm didn't go off because my phone died,' I say.

'Why didn't Leanne wake you up?'

'She overslept as well.'

'Cut the bullshit, Dani. We'll talk when you get home. Don't be late.'

He hangs up.

'I didn't know you and Leanne socialised outside of work,' says Babs. 'And she managed to get in on time.'

I work even faster than usual, so when Babs walks past, she'll see I'm trying to make up for being late. I only take five minutes for lunch and don't take my afternoon tea break, although I'm desperate for a roll-up. I get some Nicorette gum from Tulsi to keep me going.

I feel good for not having eaten all day and my stomach feels flat but that's down to dehydration. My piss is the colour of ear wax. I should drink some water but I like feeling slim again after all the weight I've put on recently. I like it when my work uniform waistband feels loose and my shirt extra roomy. I like putting my hands on my hip bones and rubbing them through the fabric, feeling the shape of them under my skin.

When I get home, Stevie and Jo are sitting in their usual places. Stevie must have turned the TV off when he heard me open and close the front door; they'd never be sitting in here with the TV off. It'd mean they had to speak to each other, which they don't, or not when I'm home anyway.

I smile at them, and when they don't smile back, it makes me laugh, but it's because I'm nervous. Stevie makes me feel like such a kid. He clears his throat.

'Dani, sit down; we want to talk to you.'

I wish they were at least dressed. Stevie's in his boxers again, Jo in a vest and pyjama shorts. It's harder to look sorry when you're being told off by people who are practically naked.

'Actually, I need the toilet,' Stevie says. 'Wait there.'

I wait until I hear the bathroom door close.

'He's not gone for one of his forty-five-minute shits, has he?' I say to Jo.

'You're good,' she says, thumb smoothing over her phone. 'He's already had that one today.'

'Good.'

'It's better that he takes his time. He gets piles otherwise. Then he won't stop going on about it.'

'You're losing weight,' I say to her.

'Stop trying to get on my good side.'

'You are. How much already? Half a stone?'

She smiles but I don't know if it's because of what I said or what's on her phone.

Stevie comes back in and sits down. 'Dani, we let you move in with us to help you sort yourself out. If you're going to stay out all night, then miss work, that's not sorting yourself out. That's disrespecting us.'

'I'm so sorry. My phone died, and I didn't have my charger.'

'Where were you last night?'

'I said.'

'Leanne's? You were at Leanne's house, were you?'

I nod. He's got no way of knowing.

'From now on, when you're at work, you stay here. You don't stay out and fuck up work the next day. And you're not staying at Leanne's again until you give me her address.'

'It's a case of respect,' says Jo, not looking up from her phone. 'We're trying to help you, but you need to help yourself.'

Stevie thinks this is how to help me, and I can't criticise him for it. Part of the problem is that he has such a strong work ethic. He gets wound up by people missing time off work or taking sick days, even when they're ill. 'It's the reason this country is such a mess,' he says. He goes to work no matter what.

'I won't do it again,' I say. 'I'm sorry. I do appreciate you letting me stay here, helping me to sort myself out. I'm sorry.'

'If you do it again,' Stevie says, 'you're out.'

Chapter Five

It's Monday and my sixth session with Richard. Once a week isn't enough. I need more.

'I'd like to come here twice a week, please. Would that be possible? How long have I been coming now?' I know he won't answer, so I carry on. 'About six weeks, I think. I'm not making myself sick anywhere near as much as I did, but I want to stop completely.'

I look at his legs. The trouser leg of the crossed-over leg has ridden up. Today his socks have navy and green triangles. I went and looked in the men's sock section when I was on break at work and found out that the name for the triangle pattern is argyle. I wanted to buy a pink and purple pair for him; I've not seen him wear that colour combination before. I took them up to the till but when the assistant came over, I said I'd changed my mind. I'd look mental giving him socks. Pathetic. Who'd buy their therapist socks?

The room smells good. There is the tang of furniture polish in the air and I wonder if he has a cleaner or if he does it himself. I imagine him polishing the armchairs, long strokes against the leather. Perhaps he has the radio on while he's doing it, some kind of intellectual discussion programme. I smile at him.

'I feel these sessions are making such a difference,' I say, 'but once a week doesn't feel enough. I was wondering if it would be possible to come twice a week?' I'll ask Babs for more shifts and see where I can save money in other places – stop taking Ubers, no more drinking in pubs. I'm already saving money from not bingeing as much. Jo and Stevie not charging me much rent helps too.

Richard brings his hands together and rests his chin on the tips of his fingers. I love the way he moves, what he does with his hands. There's something so humble about it.

'There is a waiting list, Dani. I would have to let you know when a second session becomes available.'

'I'm not surprised you're in demand. I look forward to this session all week. I feel like it's keeping me together, but I had a little lapse last week and Stevie and Jo are pissed off with me because I overslept and got into work late. If I come here more, it would help me to stay on track. Please.'

'Why do you come here, Dani?'

'I told you in the first session. I want to stop the bulimia, get back to university, get my degree.'

'Stop the bulimia, get back to university, get your degree. How will being here help you to achieve those desires?'

'I'll be able to sort myself out. That's what it's all about, isn't it, psychotherapy? You'll be able to help me get what I want. Cure me. No, cure is wrong. You'll be able to help me work through all my issues so I can get on with my life.'

'Dani, my role is to facilitate self-awareness and personal growth in my patients and I have an excellent track record in this, but my success is also dependent upon my patients' ability to engage and trust in my methods. You do need to take some responsibility in this process.'

'I do want to engage. I wouldn't be coming otherwise.'

'How could you increase your engagement?'

'I've just asked to come twice a week, but you said no.'

'How could you increase your engagement while you're in this room with me?'

'I don't know.' I thought I was fully engaged. I don't know what he's after. 'Should I talk about my past more?'

'Feeling one needs to talk about one's past or childhood is a common misconception of psychotherapy. Another misconception is one's relationship with one's mother should be examined.' He pauses and looks at me. I've never mentioned my mum. 'But it is often helpful to deal with more recent material. My work is influenced by the person-centred model of therapy, which is more focused on the here and now.'

'I do, don't I? Speak about the here and now?'

'You're certainly good at telling me what you've been doing on a day-to-day basis, but I feel it's surface level. You stop yourself from going deeper. This is what will help you, to explore your underlying feelings with me, to explore our relationship. Exploring our relationship will help you to explore the other relationships in your life. I know this is a challenge, Dani, but it works. My methods have evolved through years of experience in treating patients successfully. And considerable academic study.' He smiles. 'This is why I have a waiting list.'

I push the back of my trainer down against the chair so I can slip it off and bring my foot up under me. 'You want me to talk about how I feel about the way we're working together?'

'That could be a part of it, but what would also help you is to explore the dynamic between you and me, and the feelings they may echo of other primary relationships in your life.'

'Okay. I'll try.'

'It is important,' he says softly, 'for you to be able to trust me, Dani. If you cannot trust me, you will not be able to confide in me, and the therapy will not be a success. I don't want you to waste your time or your money.'

I take the glass of water from the table beside my chair and take a sip.

'Yeah. That makes sense.'

'It may seem anomalous to ask you so early on, but it's to discover whether there is anything that may inhibit our working relationship. If there is, I would rather refer you to a colleague with whom you may feel more comfortable.'

'No. I don't think I want to see anyone else. I'm used to coming here now.'

'The therapeutic alliance is integral to a positive outcome. This is what I want for you, Dani: a positive outcome with you returning to university and able to focus and succeed in all areas of your life.'

'So do I,' I say. I think about saying, 'We both want the same thing,' but I don't because it sounds corny in my head, which means saying it aloud would sound even worse.

'Authenticity is key. You must feel able to be authentic in this space, Dani.'

I look at his books and think about what he said about referring me to a colleague. Perhaps he doesn't want to see me any more so he's trying to palm me off on someone else. He might think I'm too mental, but it's his job to deal with mental people, so it can't be that – unless there's a hierarchy of mental and he prefers people who are mental in a more interesting way. Maybe he just doesn't like me.

'Do you think I should see someone else? Instead of coming here?' I hold my breath. If he says yes, I'll get up and walk out.

He clears his throat and I hear him take a breath.

'I want your therapy to be a success, Dani. I feel that we have the potential to work well together, but it's important to check in occasionally to hear your thoughts about how the therapy's going and if there is anything holding you back.'

'I'm happy here. That's why I asked for more sessions. It's such a nice room and I love all these books. It feels like we're in a library, or a bookshop or the book section of a charity shop – my favourite places. Anyway, what you were saying about being authentic reminds me of Diogenes. He believed in authenticity. He advocated complete truthfulness at all times. I try and follow his values. He said a lot of things that make sense.'

'Complete truthfulness at all times,' says Richard.

I take a long breath in.

'I'll try to say how I feel but I don't want to get upset in here.'

'Let's stay with that a moment. What would being upset in here, with me, mean?'

'I don't know. I spend so much time trying not to drop my guard.'

'Being upset, here with me, dropping your guard, would mean you're vulnerable. You can be vulnerable in here with me, Dani.'

Vulnerable. I hate the word and everything it connotes. The same first three letters as vulva. Tender, exposed, sensitive. A kick in the cunt. That's what I think of when I hear the word.

I let my hair fall in front of my face. 'It's not something I find easy. Perhaps in a few weeks. I'm not sure I can right now.'

'Those who find it hard to be vulnerable are those who have been harmed in the past. To be vulnerable means putting yourself in a position that could potentially harm you, but trusting your vulnerability will not be abused. You can cry in here. You can release those pent-up emotions. You are safe.'

Each time he says the word, I cringe.

'I can't.'

'You can't?'

'I can't cry. It won't come.'

'You're like an overstuffed tyre, Dani.' He holds his hands like he's holding a beach ball, then brings them closer together. 'We

47

need to undo the valve and let the air out, little by little.'

'It's going to feel very contrived now if I cry, like I have to because of what you just said.' I take my other trainer off and bring my other foot under me. 'Does it look like I've had my legs amputated at the knee when I sit like this?' I pat my thighs and raise my eyebrows at him, but Richard doesn't think it's funny. Stevie did. He took a photo, although why he'd want a picture of me looking like an amputee, I don't know. I tap my fingers on the arms of the chair.

'Relax, Dani. Can you be still for a moment?'

I stop tapping my fingers but then make a clicking noise between my tongue and teeth. 'If I can't come twice a week, perhaps you could give me homework or something.'

'I'm not going to give you homework.'

I love how he's so direct, says things outright.

'I often notice you seem drawn to the picture. What is it about the picture that draws you to it?'

He's caught me looking at it again. The small girl sitting on her father's lap.

'It's a good—' The word 'picture' sticks in my throat. I pull the neckline of my jumper up over my face and hold my breath.

'Dani.' His voice is gentle. 'Dani, can you let me see you?'

It would be easier to keep pulling my jumper up and let him see my tits than my face.

'The picture makes you feel sad, Dani.'

My nose runs. I grope around on the table next to me, and the water glass hits the floor with a thud. *You weirdo piece of shit.* Perhaps Richard will come and pick the glass up. I'd love him to get up and come over, feel his body close and the warmth of it, be able to smell him, but there's no noise or movement from his side of the room. I find the box of tissues and pull one out. I shift in my chair, so he can't see my face full on, and wipe my nose. I get my breath under control and I put the glass back on the table.

'I was so upset at work yesterday. Reena, in accounts, blanked me, so I binged and made myself sick. Then I went to Del's so I wouldn't be tempted to binge again but I overslept and I was late for work. I need to find other ways of coping when I'm upset or angry.'

'What is it about the picture that affects you so much? Is it the relationship between the young girl and her father?'

'I don't want to talk about it at the moment.'

'The relationship between the young girl and her father, a young girl who wants to be loved and to be held by her father.'

I shake my head because if I tried to answer that, the words would stick in my neck like chewing gum and if they did come out, I might lose it completely.

'Dani, I am giving you permission to be sad in here. Your father's death was very recent. I am giving you permission.'

I'm not ready for it. I think about what I'll have for dinner. Salad or vegetables.

'You're all right at the minute, thanks.'

'I want you to open up for me, Dani. Can you open up for me?'

I know he means to be honest, but when he said, 'open up for me, Dani,' I thought of opening my legs. I'd like to be flat on my back on the floor now, not talking and have him fucking me so hard I get carpet burn. No more talking.

He glances at the clock.

'And it's time?' It's better if I say it. I feel rejected when he tells me the session's over even though he uses his soft voice.

'No, the session is not over yet. We have two more minutes.'

Two minutes isn't enough time to start a conversation. In a similar situation, you'd leave an appointment if it was so close to the end. I tried to a couple of sessions ago but he said, 'Sit down, Dani,' so I sat down. Richard's tone of voice and the authority with which he said those three words made it non-negotiable. It's about observing the boundaries – *consistency* and *security*. There's something sexy about being told what to do by someone who's in control. Stevie tells me what to do a lot, but obviously that's not sexy and doesn't count because he's family.

Chapter Six

Saturday's the busiest day of the week in the restaurant and I always work it, but Babs has been off sick, and whoever's done the rota has given me the day off. I don't know what to do with it. I like Saturdays in the restaurant because they're so busy. I like trying to stay on top of the trolleys coming in at twice the usual rate. I like how tired I feel when the restaurant closes because when I'm exhausted, I don't feel so angry. That's why bulimia has always worked for me: after a few hours bingeing and vomiting, you're spent, drained. It's hard to be angry when you're a crust of yourself.

I get up at six as if I'm going to work and I stand at the sink and sip water from Stevie's Ipswich Town tankard while I'm waiting for the kettle to boil. As I'm dropping the tea bag into the bin, Jo walks in.

'Ah, make me a cup, will you please?'

It's the first roll-up of the day that's my favourite. I was seconds from unlocking the kitchen door, taking my tea on the balcony and lighting up. Now I'll have to wait while I make Jo's tea. She takes her cigarettes and lighter from the fruit bowl, unlocks the kitchen door and steps out onto the balcony. She's using a cheap disposable lighter and it's run out of gas. I pass her Dad's Zippo. He gave it to me while he was in hospital. It was the only time he stopped smoking. Jo got his gold signet ring but she'd have preferred the lighter. I wait while she tightens the belt of her dressing gown then pass her the mug. She pulls a face.

'Cows on strike, are they?'

I open the fridge and pretend to add milk. I pass her the mug and sit next to her.

'Why are you up so early?'

She sniffs. 'There's a gym class I want to go to at seven.'

I hold my hand out for my lighter. I love the warm weight of it and the smell of lighter fluid reminds me of Dad. Jo makes loose fists and examines her nails. When she began the affair with Stevie, she behaved the same, eating little and going to gym classes. Once Stevie left Michelle, his pregnant wife, for Jo, she put the weight back on and then some. I want to ask if she's met someone, but I don't dare – and anyway, she'd deny it.

'How's the therapy going? What's his name again?' she says.

I take a long drag on my roll-up and take my time breathing the smoke out. I feel my body relax with the nicotine hit.

'Richard Goode. Yeah, fine.'

I hear him saying the words, *You can be vulnerable in here with me, Dani*, and I picture him sitting in his chair with his legs crossed and I feel warm because he's warm: his voice, his eyes, even the colour of his clothes. I want to be held by him, to curl up in his lap. There'd be no need for a blanket; his warmth would seep through to me. He'd stroke my back, and I'd hold on to a bit of his jumper and rub it between my fingers. What's he doing now at a little after six on a Saturday morning? Perhaps he's still asleep, perhaps naked. There could be a naked wife next to him. Perhaps they're making love in a king-size bed with white covers and art on the walls. Bedside tables with slim volumes of poetry with pages turned at the corner. Lines of poems they'd read to each other and then discuss. He could be going down on her right at this moment while she's drowsily coming to. I pull out a few strands of hair from the back of my head to make me stop the thought.

'Ah, look at that, fucking shaving cut.' Jo moves her fingers to show me a scab on her knee she's been picking. She blots the blood with her dressing gown.

A car alarm cuts through the stillness. One of the cars parked in front of our tower block has its alarm lights flashing and a bloke running from the direction of it. Jo leans forward and we watch him through the pigeon netting, legging it down the road before he's picked up by someone in a car.

'Going well, then? The therapy?' She folds her dressing gown back over her knee.

'Yeah, it's going well. He's . . .'

You can be vulnerable in here with me, Dani.

'What?'

'He's good at listening, which considering how much I'm paying, he should be.'

'And how's work?' Jo rarely asks questions like this.

'Yeah, work's fine. I think I might get to do something other than pot wash soon.'

She and Stevie think it's funny I wash up all day at work and then come home and wash up. When I get back, they've often eaten but not cleared up afterwards. I'll scrape the plates into the bin and turn the taps on, and Jo will shout, 'Leave it, Dan. Stevie'll do it later,' but I want to do it because then they'll know I'm grateful for letting me stay with them.

I turn to look at her profile. She has the same nose as Dad – the Greek idea of perfection. 'I am sorry about what happened the other day. About being late for work and all that.'

She takes a deep drag on her cigarette and exhales the smoke before speaking. 'Stevie was more pissed off than me – you know what he's like. He was fuming when he couldn't get hold of you. Oh yeah, he said to ask you why you haven't paid the rent for this month yet. You were supposed to transfer it yesterday.'

'Shit, sorry, I forgot. I'll do it in a minute.' I didn't pay because I haven't got the full amount. 'I've been thinking, though, if I fill my time with good stuff, it'll keep me more focused. You know I've been going to the old people's home with Pat to see her mum? I might start going there more to fill my evenings, you know?'

'Whatever you need to do. If hanging out with old people is going to stop you chucking your guts up, then go for it.' She wrinkles her nose. 'Why don't you do drama or sports or something that might be more fun, give you a chance to meet people more your own age?'

I start rolling another cigarette.

'I did try an am dram class about a year ago. It was awful, and they were all old anyway – or midlife crisis age. Do you know what the teacher made us do?'

'You're going red so it'll be good.'

'I'm embarrassed to tell you. The memory is almost as painful as the event.'

'You've got to now,' she says.

'The teacher divided the class in two, half at one end of the room, half at the other, and then we had to take it in turns to run across the room, in a goofy way, until you got to the people at the other end and say, "I'm a silly fairy. Wah!"'

'Fuck that,' says Jo.

'Yeah. I only did it once then I went to reception and asked for my money back. But I think going with Pat is a good idea. We get on well and I need to keep busy while the therapy starts to work and then I'll be fine. I'll be able to focus when I get back to uni.'

'Mmm,' Jo says. She and Stevie both think university is a waste of time. They both work in the office of a haulage company. 'I've never met a good graduate,' Stevie says, but I don't take it personally. I like how he's so firm in what he believes; I'm always impressed by anyone who has so much confidence that they can say what they want and not care what other people will think of them.

'How's work going?' Jo told me a few days ago it was pissing her off.

'Yeah, the job's all fine.' She pauses and squints at the tower blocks over the road. Then she gets up and pulls at the handle of the kitchen door, even though it's already shut.

'You're working tomorrow, aren't you?' she says.

'Yeah.'

'Are you going to the gym after?'

'I'd planned to.'

The restaurant closes at four on Sunday, and I go to the gym to kill some time. I try not to invade their space too much.

'Could you go somewhere after?'

I laugh. I can't help it. 'How long do you want me to stay out for?'

She chews the inside of her cheek. 'You can come back at about nine. That'd be okay.'

Stevie's leaving today for a stag weekend in Manchester and not coming back until Monday. Jo clearly has plans. I'll take a book and sit in a pub or go to Del's. I could ask Jo what she's doing, but if she wanted me to know, she'd say.

Jo chucks her cigarette into the plant pot overflowing with rainwater and fat dog-ends. I throw my dog-end in after. It's the one area of the flat Stevie refuses to clean because he hates smoking. She takes her cigarettes from her dressing-gown pocket. I give her the Zippo. I take out another Rizla and spread a line of tobacco in the crease of it.

'Dad used to get me to roll his cigarette when he was driving, and he'd get so angry when I didn't do it right. One day, I hadn't separated the tobacco well enough, and there must have been a lump of tobacco stopping him from inhaling. He was going mental!' I give her a sidelong look. Sometimes she'll ignore it if I try and talk about Dad, but she's up for it this morning.

'It was about the only thing he couldn't do with one hand – drive and make a roll-up. It didn't matter otherwise, did it? His dodgy hand.' Jo makes a claw with her own, then admires her nails before lowering her arm.

'He got round it, didn't he? Most people didn't even notice. Do you want to go through his stuff soon?'

We boxed up some of the things we wanted to keep after he died. Norfolk County Council wanted Dad's house back, so we had to go in sooner than we wanted. We hardly spoke on the drive down, just chain-smoked. If they hadn't rushed us into it, maybe we would have put it off forever. Neither of us wanted to get out of the car when we pulled up outside his house. I hated walking in and knowing he wasn't going to be there. I put the radio on because Dad had the radio on low, twenty-four hours a day, but Jo turned it off. I sat in Dad's chair, and Jo told me to get off it. I found all the birthday cards and Christmas cards I'd ever sent him, in pristine condition, in a clear plastic tub. I cringed at some of the stuff I'd written, trying to be funny. I'd written one birthday card in green felt tip and I thought I should have made more effort and found a biro. His house smelled the same: cold sawdust and Amber Leaf tobacco. The marble chopping board in the kitchen still had the serrated bread knife on it. There was a dishcloth hanging over the tap in the sink. I took it off and it stayed the same shape. Dad could've walked in and carried on with his life. It didn't seem right that the house and what was in it had stayed exactly the same.

We didn't take much: five boxes full of the wooden sculptures he'd carved, and a black washbag he used to keep his driving licence, passport, nail scissors and glasses in. There were also three letters from Boris Johnson's secretary in the washbag, replying to letters Dad had sent. I'm not sure what about as the responses were vague, along the lines of 'thank you for your letter, it has been passed on to the Education Secretary' kind of thing. I packed all the poetry books I'd given Dad, the ones I'd bought for the module on the American Confessional Poets. I'd memorised some parts of the poems I'd really loved so I was happy to give Dad the books. I also wanted him to be impressed by the notes I'd made in the margins.

I opened the volume by Philip Larkin I'd bought him. When I gave him *High Windows*, I put a bookmark at the page, 'This Be The Verse'.

They fuck you up, your mum and dad.

The bookmark is no longer there and I wonder if he read it. I forgot to ask him. It was only a joke, putting the bookmark there.

I took the anglepoise lamp that sat on the table in the living room. Dad used to read by that lamp. The whole room would be pitch black, with the lamp angled at his book.

Mum said we couldn't store the boxes in her spare room, but after we'd both shouted at her, she gave in.

'I don't want to go through them. Not yet,' Jo says.

'She keeps leaving messages.' I do an impression of Mum's voice: 'Dani! When are you and Jo coming to sort out these bloody boxes?'

'Ignore her,' Jo says. 'She does my head in.'

'She's got a new boyfriend, I think. Apart from the messages about the boxes, she's gone very quiet recently.'

'Always the way, isn't it? When someone new is on the scene.'

'I can't believe Dad kept the clay house you made at primary school. It was shit,' I say. 'It was so wonky.'

Jo's eyes fill, and she blinks a few times. I decide to do what Richard does and see if not saying anything makes her talk more.

'I miss his voice,' she says.

I think of Dad's voice, his big loud laugh.

'Haven't you got any saved messages from him on your voice-mail?' I say.

She pulls a face.

'No, I always delete messages after I've listened to them,' she says. 'Go and make me another cup of tea, will you?'

'Isn't it your turn?'

'The last cup was so nice.'

I go and make it because I'm enjoying the chat and don't want it to break. If she goes in, she won't come back out.

I hold the mug so she can take the handle even though the heat is hard on my palm. I light my roll-up and when she puts a cigarette in her mouth, pass her my lighter.

'Have you?' she says.

'What?'

'Still got messages from Dad on your voicemail?'

I take a piece of tobacco from my lip and wipe it on my knee.

'Yeah, loads. I always saved them because they made me laugh. He sings on a couple of them.'

Jo leans forward to stub her cigarette out. She's not even smoked it all the way down. I don't want her to go yet.

'You can listen to them if you want,' I say.

She stands up and tightens her dressing-gown cord. 'I don't know. It seems a bit morbid.'

'You can if you want.'

'I might.'

My feet are freezing and I wriggle my toes to try to get some circulation going.

'What about you?' she says with her hand on the door handle to go back in.

'What about me?'

'What do you miss about him?'

'Advice. Calling him.' It's easier to say the words out of the logical order, trick my brain into not realising what's going on so it doesn't get me too upset.

I also feel sad I won't hug Dad again, but we didn't hug when he was alive. I should have gone for it, leaned into him, a brief contact, my forehead against his chest or something. For a second. I didn't because I was scared he'd push me away. I turn away from Jo, rub my eyes with my sleeve and think of how the back of my head felt when my hair was caught up in Dad's fist as he twisted the back of my leather jacket.

'God, I miss that too – calling him for advice,' she says and I can hear the tears in her voice.

I should try and comfort Jo, but we're not like that. She brings an arm up to her eyes and coughs.

'You got my lighter?' I say.

She gives it to me, and I put it in my pocket. I stand up and pat her twice on the upper arm.

'Fuck off,' she says and moves her arm away.

It was still a nice chat. We don't usually show each other signs of weakness.

Chapter Seven

It's the first time Richard has smiled when he answers the door. He looks like he's just shaved and I'm sure if I ran a finger down his skin, it would feel as soft as velvet. His jumper is a rich, warm shade of burgundy.

As I follow Richard into the room, I want to jump on him, crash my body into his back and put my arms around his middle, hold him as tight as I can and breathe him in and stay like that.

'It feels like ages since I was last here, but it's only been a week,' I say as he sits down. Then I notice. 'The picture's gone.' I point to the space on the wall.

'Please, sit down, Dani.' He sits in his chair, crosses his legs.

I look round the room to see if anything else has changed but it's all the same.

'Why have you moved it? The picture of the girl and her dad?'

Richard leans forward slightly in his chair.

'The painting is important to you.'

'No. I noticed it's not there and I wondered why.' I sit down and play with my hair, twist it around my finger then pull a couple of strands out. I straighten them out on my lap. I can feel him watching me. The room doesn't feel right without the picture, any more than it would if the books had disappeared from the shelves.

'What does the picture mean to you, Dani?'

I sit up straighter and make myself yawn. I'll think about it after the session and why he's taken it away. I don't know why it's pissed me off so much.

'Can I use your loo, please?' If I don't get some space now, I'll cry. I was in such a good mood when I came in.

'Down the passageway, first on the right.'

I pull the light on, unwind some tissue and blow my nose. I look at my face in the mirror and notice how dark the bags under my eyes are. When I turn to chuck the loo roll in the toilet, I see a nugget of shit floating in the water. I flush the chain and it disappears before bouncing back up. If I leave it, Richard will think it was me. Perhaps it's his, but no, it must be from his previous client – this is the clients' toilet. I flush again but this time the shit doesn't even disappear under the U-bend. I'm taking too long; Richard will think I'm having a dump. There's no option but to pick the shit up and break it into pieces. This time when I flush, it all disappears. I use a lot of the lime, basil and mandarin handwash. It smells gorgeous and I imagine it's expensive.

I sit back in my chair and check my hands. 'I think Jo's having an affair. I can see why she might want the excitement, Stevie's not exactly dynamic, but I think it's wrong for her to have another man in the flat.'

Richard looks at the space on the wall again, where the picture was. If he says anything else about it, I'll ask him to stop. I'm paying a lot for these sessions. I should choose what I want to talk about.

'Well? Don't you think it's wrong?' I say.

He doesn't speak for a while. Then he says, 'Why would it be wrong for Jo to have another man in the flat?'

'It's obvious, isn't it? It's disrespectful to Stevie.'

Richard sits elegantly in his chair, leaning back and legs

crossed. Black and brown argyle socks today.

'It's disrespectful, on top of everything else, isn't it?' I feel out of order, talking about Jo, but this is a safe space, confidential. It's not like she'll find out. 'I began to suspect a few weeks ago when she started losing weight. It's what she always does at the beginning of a new relationship, but when I knew for sure is when she told me not to come home after work straight away on Sunday, when she had the house to herself. I mean, it's a good thing she and Stevie haven't got children together, I think then she'd be completely out of order, but—'

Richard uncrosses his legs. 'You stopped mid-sentence there. What were you going to say?'

I shake my head. 'It doesn't matter.'

'I heard the word catch in your throat. It triggered a strong emotion in you.'

'No. I forgot what I was going to say.'

'Then tell me, how does it feel in your body, Dani? How does it feel in your body when you think about somebody cheating on their partner, their children?'

'I don't know how to describe it.'

'Try.'

'It feels like my stomach is being twisted by someone wearing gloves made of sandpaper. Is that good enough?'

There's warmth in his eyes. I now think of brown as the warmest colour. I look for things at home, in the street, at work, the same shade of brown as his eyes, then I stare at them and build the rest of his face around them. I pull my cardigan over my face so he can't see me and take a few breaths. I drag the cardigan across my face to dry it.

'I don't think people should have affairs when they have children. It's selfish. If I have children, I'd never have an affair. I'd never put them through it.'

'Why would the children be aware of the affair?'

'Because people get found out in the end, or they leave for the new person. But the kids don't have a choice. They have to live with the mistakes the parents make and all the hurt that comes after it. When my dad had the affair, Mum divorced him and it marked the start of all the shit that followed. Dad then going to prison, and all that.'

'Are you angry with your father for his affair?'

'No. If my mum wasn't so devoid of any warmth or emotion, he probably wouldn't have had one.'

'You think your father had the affair because of the way your mother was? You blame her for his affair?'

'I don't know.'

'Perhaps it feels easier to be angry at her, than at him.'

'I have more reason to be angry at her than him.'

'But he was the one who had the affair?'

'Yes, but . . .'

I don't want to go into it, yet.

'Have you got children?' I say.

Richard takes a long time to answer.

'You are curious about me.'

'No, not curious. I don't know anything about you, do I? If you're married, or if you've got children.'

'What would it mean to you if I were married?'

'It's none of my business whether you're married, single, divorced.' I look at his left hand, the naked ring finger, but that doesn't mean he's not married. I bet he's an amazing husband. Thoughtful, intelligent, intuitive. Imagine coming home to someone like him. It would feel safe. I'd get home from work and he'd come to the hallway to greet me and we'd kiss and put our arms around each other. I'd have one hand on his back and one in his hair. He'd pull me into him by my hips, and he'd whisper something to me that would make me laugh. I bring both hands to my face. When my cheeks feel cooler beneath my fingers, I lower my hands and play with them on my lap.

'You said you were going to let me know if I can come twice a week. Has another time become available?'

He tilts his head and raises a finger. I realise I'm holding my breath.

'Dani, I have many patients—'

'Why do you call them patients? It's not a hospital.'

'Why do you object to the term?'

'I'm not ill; "patient" makes you think of sickness.'

I close my eyes.

'Patient, from the Latin *patiens* – one who suffers or endures,' he says.

'I suppose it doesn't matter; patient, client, customer, it's just a word. What's your favourite word? Have you got a favourite word?' I smile at him but he doesn't smile back.

'Dani.' He waits until I look at him before he continues.

'How does it feel when you think of me seeing other patients?'

I don't give a shit about the men he sees; that's fine. It's the women. I hate to think of him talking to them how he talks to me, with the gentle voice and gentle eyes.

'It doesn't feel good when I think of you seeing other women.'

'Go on.'

'Shit.' I drum both hands on the armrests then stretch my arms above my head. My back clicks and cracks and I'm embarrassed at the noise. 'I don't like to think of you enjoying yourself with them.'

'I think you want to be special to me.'

'It's pathetic. I feel pathetic for feeling it.'

'What you're feeling, Dani, is not uncommon. Many of my patients want to feel they're special to me.'

I wonder what he'd do if I walked over to him, right now. Sat on his lap and put my arms around his neck.

'Do you think of your clients outside of the sessions?' I ask.

'I'm thinking about my patients all the time. I hold each one of you in my mind, Dani.'

'I like the colour of your jumper.'

'I'd like to go back to something you said earlier, your thoughts about me enjoying myself more with other patients. Why might you think that? Why might you think I enjoy seeing other patients more than I enjoy you?'

'I just do.'

'"I just do" is not an answer.'

'They're better than me.'

'Better? Can one person be "better" than another?'

'Of course they can.'

'What would make one person "better" than another?'

'More interesting, better educated, less fucked up. Loads of stuff.'

'It feels, Dani, you're more comfortable focusing on your faults than on your positive qualities. I think you have a deeply ingrained sense of inferiority.'

He's right. I'm filled with a self-loathing so fierce that I understand why some people take sharp objects to their skin. I've thought about it but I wouldn't want anyone to see the cuts and scars. Ripping my insides up from vomiting doesn't leave visible marks.

'I don't—' My voice disappears. I realise I've never spoken the words aloud. 'I don't like myself, very much.' I start crying before I reach the end of the sentence.

'I can feel that.' His voice is soft.

The box of tissues is empty so I press my sleeve against my eyes.

'And then it feels self-indulgent to be so self-loathing, and then that's another thing to beat myself up for.'

I wish he'd get up, take my hand and lead me back to his chair. Let me curl up on his lap and stroke my back. No need to speak. I should ask him about body psychotherapy. Perhaps it involves touching the client, but I'd have to keep my eyes closed if he was touching me.

'Dani, I think you have a lot of integrity.'

I think about all the lies I tell to cover up the bulimia, the sleeping around and the drugs. 'Sometimes, I shoplift.' I sniff a couple of times. I don't want to use my sleeve for my nose in front of Richard.

He laughs. 'I tell you that you have integrity and your response is to tell me you shoplift?'

'I can't have integrity then, can I?'

'You steal from shops without paying?'

'That's what shoplifting is, isn't it?'

'What do you take?'

'Small stuff, cheap, and only from supermarkets, never from a small shop, that wouldn't be fair. Things I can fit in my hand, so basically chewing gum, it's all that fits, really. I've got little hands. You've got big hands – you'd be able to take much bigger stuff. If you wanted to, which you probably never would, or have before.'

'I think you want me to think poorly of you, but I can't, Dani. You are an intelligent and vibrant young woman.'

Intelligent and vibrant. Weirdo piece of shit.

He glances towards the clock and raises his eyebrows.

'And it's time,' he says. Richard opens the door and waits there with his fingers resting on the handle. I pause when I get near him. I look at his chest and listen to the clock. Four ticks. We just stand there together. I shouldn't have looked up because when our eyes meet, he speaks.

'Goodbye, Dani,' he says and I close my eyes because now he's said that, I have to leave. If I look at him now to say thanks and he doesn't look at me, it'll end the session on a sad note. But I risk it because I've got his voice saying *intelligent and vibrant* on repeat in my head.

'Thanks for today.'

'Goodnight, Dani,' he says.

He must be feeling this between us; there's no way he can't be. If he put his hand between my legs, for one second; held me there; even through my jeans, I'd come.

Chapter Eight

I take my apron from its hook and am putting it on when Babs comes over. She opens her mouth, then closes it, squeezes her nostrils together as she stops a sneeze. She rubs her fingers down the side of her thigh and leaves a thin shiny streak. I cross the apron strings at my back and bring them around to make a bow. I'm proud of my small waist.

'Dani, can you come to my office? We need to have a chat now you've reached the end of your probationary period.'

'Shall I clear the trolley first?'

'No. Come with me now.'

We walk across the kitchen together and I'm sure it will be fine. I'm sure she's not going to let me go. I work hard and everyone comments on it. Best pot-wash girl in west London, they call me. But it's not like it's a specialised job and I'm not indispensable. And there was the time I overslept at Del's and got the verbal warning. There's been another couple of times that I've been late back from lunch and break but thought I'd got away with it. Maybe Babs knew but didn't say anything at the time – she might have been saving it for now.

She sits behind her desk and gestures to the other chair.

'Sit down, Dani.'

'Is everything okay?' I say. I look at her photo of the cat looking out of the window.

'What do you think?' she says.

'Yes. I think everything's good.'

'We're pleased with you, Dani. You're a hard worker — apart from the lateness, of which I'm pleased there's not been any more incidents.' She takes a deep breath, and there's something artificial about her smile. 'You've passed your three-month probationary period, and we'd like to offer you a full-time permanent contract.'

I get a rush of relief that she's not sacking me, and then a rush of shame. I'm now a permanent pot-wash person.

She raises her eyebrows and smiles again. There's a flash of something yellow between her two front teeth. It's the colour of sweetcorn but who eats sweetcorn before nine in the morning?

'Thanks, Babs.'

'You don't seem too happy about it.'

'No, I am. It's good.'

'I could do with another ten of you, Dani!'

Or she could manage the other staff to make sure they were doing their jobs properly.

'You know, Hall & Walker is a great place to build a career. I reckon we could have you trained up on the tills and ordering stock in no time. When you've got that, there's always development programmes in customer services if you're interested. Leanne's just started. Is it something you'd be interested in?' she says.

'It sounds good,' I say. 'I'd definitely like to do anything that will make me go up to the next pay band. Did you manage to look into giving me some more shifts?'

'I've put a couple more on the rota,' she says. 'And I'll look into getting you trained up on the till soon so your hourly rate will increase.'

A phone buzzes, and she moves papers across her desk. When she finds her phone and sees who's calling, two lines shoot up her forehead.

'I'll go back now, shall I?'

'Hang on a minute, Dani.' She answers the phone and listens. 'He isn't . . . not again . . . Christ's sake . . . all right . . .'

Her top teeth suck in her lower lip like her mouth is trying to eat it.

'Yep, I'll call and get it logged.'

Babs puts her elbows on the desk and her head in her hands.

'Is everything okay?' I say.

She drags her palms down the sides of her face.

'My ex being a nuisance.'

I think about what Richard would say.

'That sounds like a difficult situation, Babs.'

She nods while scrolling through her phone. 'He's hanging around my bloody house again, in the back garden. That was my neighbour.'

I keep quiet so she'll carry on speaking. I'm using this technique of Richard's a lot, and it works nine times out of ten.

'He's a bloody arsehole . . . I'll get your new contract ready for you, Dani, don't you worry.'

I point at the door and raise my eyebrows.

'Right. You get back then,' Babs says.

She moves a pile of papers across the desk, and there's crumbs and a green stain underneath.

I pop to the staff toilets before going back to the kitchen. When I come out of the cubicle, Reena's there, leaning towards the mirror and using her little finger to stroke on lip balm from a small blue tin. Our eyes meet in the mirror and I look away first. I wash my hands and think of twenty things I could say to her to try and make it better between us. I look at her reflection in the mirror again.

'Reena, I—'

But she yawns without covering her mouth and walks out.

In the smoking hut at lunchtime, Pat congratulates me. 'So you're a permanent staff member now then?' She lights a cigarette.

'Yeah. I'm not sure if I should've said about only wanting it until October.'

'When you go back to university?'

'Yeah, but it's still seven months away, and it's not even a guaranteed thing. It's not messing them about, is it?'

'You look after yourself, girl.'

'Yeah, I'm trying to, so I don't have to work at Hall & Walker all my life— Shit, I'm so sorry, Pat, there's nothing wrong with it . . .'

Pat's worked at Hall & Walker for more than twenty years.

'I know what you meant,' says Pat. 'No offence taken, love. It wasn't my first choice of job when I was your age either.'

I apologise again, and she tells me to shut up.

'Babs said about these management opportunities. I suppose I could stay and work my way up the chain,' I say.

'Is that what you want, Dani?'

'It's a secure career.'

'I don't think it's you,' she says.

'No. You know, Pat, I want the university experience – to read and study and write essays. I want to go to the uni bar after a lecture and discuss it with other students. I couldn't do it before because my head wasn't in the right place.'

'You want another go at doing it properly,' says Pat.

'Yeah. I want that graduation certificate in my fingers that shows I'm worth something and that I've achieved something.'

'Dani, you're worth something now.'

'Thanks,' I say as that's the quickest way to stop her from

adding more compliments. There's no point telling her that the degree certificate will cancel out some of the times I've been called a 'weirdo piece of shit'.

'You got any plans for the weekend?' Pat says.

'Working both days here, then I've got Richard on Monday.'

'How's that going?'

I lean forward so I can chuck my dog-end into the metal bucket. 'It's hard at times but I'm getting used to the way it works.' I realise that sounded too negative. 'Actually, he's brilliant, Pat. I feel so much more together since I started seeing him.'

'He's brilliant, hey?'

'He gets me to speak about difficult stuff. You know how hard it is to talk about stuff you've always kept to yourself because you're ashamed or whatever. Sometimes he gets me saying stuff I didn't even know I felt. It's hard to explain. When I speak, sometimes he's quiet for ages after, and that's when I say stuff I didn't even know was in my head. I kind of blurt it out. He gets me.' I feel my voice catch. 'Why are you looking like that?'

'Dani, if you feel it's working for you, that's good, but don't get too dependent on him. My sister-in-law was having counselling once and got to the point where she couldn't do anything without her counsellor's approval. I don't want you to go down that route.'

'No, I won't. I just find it useful to have someone I can tell everything to who won't judge me.' I can't be explaining it right, else she'd be more enthusiastic. I try again. 'Even when I talk about feelings, like jealousy, he says it's understandable. It's weird to have those kinds of feelings accepted. I could tell him everything bad about me, all my bad thoughts and bad stuff I've done and he wouldn't think any less of me.' I picture Richard, the way his face doesn't change even when I've told him something that puts me in a bad light. 'I think, Pat, that's what's good about therapy. You can spill your guts out and not worry about what they think of you because you're paying them.'

As I'm saying it, I know I'm talking shit. I do care about what Richard Goode thinks of me. His opinion is the most important.

'We've all got our skeletons, Dani. You're nothing unusual there, love.'

'But I think if I tell people what I'm like, they won't want to know me.'

'I'm sure that's not true. Why would you think that?'

'I don't know. It's probably from when I was quite young, like primary-school age, and when I was kicking off, my mum would say, "I'm going to tell people what you're *really* like." And that scared the shit out of me because I was well behaved at school and at friends' houses and what she was threatening was, if people knew what I was *really* like, they wouldn't want to know me.'

'What were you kicking off about?'

'Not seeing my dad, mainly. I was furious about it. Anyway – this is too heavy for a weekday lunchtime.'

A couple of guys from the warehouse walking over catch the end of the conversation. 'Heavy?' says Marco.

'We were speaking about the staff canteen,' says Pat. 'About our favourite meals. I like the chicken curry because it's hot and heavy and fills me up.'

'Do you like being full up, Pat?' Marco winks at her.

'I love it,' says Pat. 'But I prefer blonds, Marco.'

This is what I like about Pat: she can hold her own.

When I get home from work, Stevie is on his laptop in the kitchen and so I know it's because he left work early so he could pick up Ellie. There's a court order in place for contact and Stevie has her every other weekend, but Michelle has recently started asking him to have Ellie at other times if she has to work, which he always jumps at.

Ellie's sprawled out over the living-room floor, surrounded by ripped-out pages from a sketchbook and every felt tip and colouring pencil she owns. I lie down on the floor next to her, take a pen and paper and start to draw. I've stopped saying hello because she kept blanking me. Stevie never pulled her up on it because he found it funny. Now I wait for Ellie to speak first. She stops what she's doing to watch me draw.

'What's that?' She puts a pink-ink-stained finger on the page and taps it.

'It's obvious,' I say.

'No it's not.'

'It is. Look. Here's the mouth, here's the nose, and here are all the brains spilling out of the goblin's skull and being eaten by seagulls.'

She screws up her nose but lies closer to me so our sides are touching.

'The seagulls are gobbling up the goblin,' she says after a while.

'Very good, Ellie,' I say.

She smells of coconut shampoo. Stevie calls her 'Princess'. I'd like to ask him why he can't get more with the times, call her 'Pilot', 'Doctor', 'MD' – something more aspirational, but he'll get annoyed.

'Dani,' she says.

'Yep?'

'Do you want to play Barbies?'

'No.'

'Why not?'

'It's boring.'

'What do you want to play then?' she says.

'Where's that slime kit?'

'Daddy put it in the bin.'

'Why?'

'He said it was too messy.'

'What about baking then?

'With our hands?'

'Yeah.'

Ellie puts her pen down and I can see she's thinking about it. She's been brought up never to get dirty. She freaks if she gets paint on her hands, doesn't want to stick her hands in a mixing bowl, cried when she sat on some dried bird shit when I took her over to the park recently.

'Okay, baking,' she says, but she doesn't sound keen.

I pull a chair up to the counter for her and take a unicorn cake kit from the cupboard. Stevie won't have bags of flour in the kitchen as he says they make too much mess when they spill.

'Look, we're baking, Daddy,' Ellie says. He watches us for a moment.

'Dan, I still haven't had the rent,' he says.

'Yeah, I'm so sorry. I've got some of it, but I was going to wait until I had it all before transferring it.' I take the box of eggs from the fridge.

'Why haven't you got it all?'

'The therapy's costing a lot, but I've got some extra shifts at work. I'm sorry.'

'Do you owe your therapist money?' he says.

'Of course not.'

'So you manage to pay him on time?'

'So far.'

'How far down the list of priorities are we?'

I open one of the cake-mix packets and give it to Ellie to shake into the bowl.

'I'll pay you as soon as I can.'

'You need to pay your rent first, Dan. If you can't manage your finances, make your therapist wait, not us. Another important life lesson for you is always prioritise your rent. If you don't have somewhere to live, that's when you've really got problems, so prioritise your rent above all else.' He walks out and I clench my hands so I don't give him the finger behind his back.

'Crack this egg in there, Ellie,' I pass her the egg.

'Naughty, Dan,' she says. 'You need to give my daddy the rent.'

Chapter Nine

I'm early for my session with Richard. I sit on his neighbour's wall and roll a cigarette. There's banging behind me, and an old woman at the window pulls her net curtain to the side and makes sweeping gestures with her hand. I walk further down the street. This is a good road. The houses are large, detached, worth millions. Most of the front gardens have been paved over but have earthenware pots with little trees or shrubs in them.

I'm down to the last of my tobacco, and it's more like dust. Tiny pieces of it keep hitting the back of my throat and making me cough. I think about my posture as I stand and smoke, in case Richard's watching me out of the window. I imagine there's a line going through my spine being pulled out of the top of my head. I put my shoulders back and suck my stomach in. It's uncomfortable.

Ten minutes to six. Seven minutes to six, five minutes to six. I keep looking at my phone. I'm halfway through typing a message to Jo when Richard's front door opens a little. It stays like that for ages, then it opens wider, and a woman with a blonde bob steps out, turns to face Richard who is standing behind her. He laughs and puts his hand on her arm, above the elbow, and keeps it there. I feel hot and wish he'd take his hand off. He's never touched me, not once. We've never stood in the hallway chatting. I always assumed all his clients start 'on the hour' like me, so they should finish at ten to, a fifty-minute hour. She's had extra time and is practically running into my session, and he's touching her. I look away, to the other end of the street, look at the dark grey sky, the pavement. When I look back, he's still got his hand on her arm, and he's rubbing it up and down. She's looking up at him and smiling. I bet she's got a cute dimple on the side of her face I can't see. How can he be ready for me when she's only just left? One in, one out, as quick as that. He should have some space in between, some thinking time. Now he'll still be thinking of her, and that's bang out of order because it's my session time and I'm paying shitloads for it, and it should only be about him and me.

She's slim, wearing a brown leather jacket and long boots. Slim hips and shiny blonde hair. Not as thin as me but a much better figure and bigger tits. She points a key fob at her car, a black Audi parked opposite. I look at my trainers and notice a small hole on the side. The woman takes a parking permit from the dashboard and does one of those slow runs, when a walk would be quicker, across the road and hands it to Richard. He watches her walk back down the path and shuts the door when she reaches the gate.

When her car's turned at the end of the road, I knock. It's two minutes past six, and I know it's my responsibility to be on time, but I didn't want to come so quickly after her when he'd be more likely to notice the contrast. Glossy, scruffy, sophisticated, rough, charming, awkward.

He doesn't come. I knock again. Five past six. I can't knock a third time. I take my phone and am about to call him when he opens the door.

'Daaani.' He draws out the first syllable of my name like he's singing it. He's doing it because he's happy after spending time with her. I can see it in him. She's bright and entertaining. She's got difficulties, but they're problems that she's working through in an intelligent and endearing fashion. She and Richard are developing a meaningful relationship grounded in mutual respect and admiration. After sessions with her, he feels content and like he's done excellent work. He'll leave a lasting impact on her, which makes the rest of her life better, and she'll remember him with warmth and affection, strong and sensitive Richard Goode who helped her lead a better life.

The room stinks of her perfume. I shrug off my coat and drop it on the floor in front of the hooks. The picture of the girl sitting on her father's lap is back in its usual place on the wall. I'm too agitated to sit. I touch the spines of some books, then I walk over to his desk. There are always the same three things: a closed laptop, a notebook and a pen. Today there's a book on the edge of the desk: *The Cultural Context of Sexual Pleasure and Problems*. He sits in his chair, watching me. I turn the book over so it's face down on the desk and pretend to read the back of it, but a line jumps out at me: *this edited book contributes to our efforts to help individuals and couples increase their sexual satisfaction*, and I blush. I wonder if that's why the woman comes to him, if they've been speaking about 'sexual satisfaction'. I'm fine fucking someone but talking about sex? Even fucking a stranger is more comfortable than speaking about sex.

I want Richard to tell me to sit down or ask what I'm doing but he doesn't.

I sit down in my chair, kick off my trainers and bring my legs up under me. I feel like I'm sitting in the shadow of her smell. I drum my fingers on the arms of the chair. Five minutes pass, then ten. I look everywhere but him. I think about how he prefers seeing her to me, probably because of all the weight I've put on lately. Then I think how stupid I'm being, how pathetic it is to pay eighty quid to sit in silence. I should be using this time to make me better. He looks amused. I want to shout at him, *you weirdo piece of shit*, but I need to feel what's behind the words. Richard always tells me to feel what's behind the words.

'I'm feeling annoyed today,' I say.

'Can you tell me more about that, Dani?'

'I want to shout at you. I want to call you a "weirdo piece of shit", but I worry about how you'd react if I did, about what you'd do.'

He nods. 'A weirdo piece of shit.'

'Yeah. Or a cunt. It's always the first thing that comes into my head when I'm angry.'

I want him to ask me why I'm so upset. I'd say 'her' and he'd know what I meant, then he'd tell me she's boring, and he only sees her for the money. Richard leans forward in his chair so his elbow rests on his crossed-over knee and his chin is in his hand.

'Dani. Can you tell me what is happening between us at this moment?'

'That's your job, isn't it? To interpret what goes on in here?'

'I want you to tell me how the room feels to you at this moment.'

'It stinks of that woman. I saw her, the one here before me.'

'How does it make you feel, Dani? That I have other patients?'

'It's your job.'

'Yes, it is. But I want to know, how does the room feel to you? Right now?'

I don't speak.

'Do you feel safe to express yourself in this room, with me?' he says.

'I don't know. I'm trying.'

He sits back and uncrosses his legs.

'I wonder if you're feeling jealous, Dani. I think you would like to have me all to yourself.'

'Didn't we go over this a few sessions ago?'

He closes his eyes, and I have a good look at him. His flies are half undone.

'It's probably her I'm jealous of. She's got money, takes care of herself. She must have some issues, or she wouldn't be coming here, but on the surface, she looks good: designer clothes, nice Audi.'

'Compare and despair,' he says.

'I'm not comparing myself to her. Can you come up with something better than the words you'd find on a meme?'

'You would like me all to yourself, Dani.'

'You just said that.'

'Would it be possible for you to say it?'

'In my family, we never even said hello and goodbye.'

'You referred to her as "a woman".'

'Who? The woman? Yes, I referred to the woman as a woman. You were rubbing her arm.'

'Do you feel you are a woman, Dani?'

I feel like a frightened little girl most of the time. I'd like to be bundled up and rocked, like the girl in the picture, until I feel like an adult.

'No.' The word comes out in a laugh. 'I don't feel like a woman at all.'

He closes his eyes and I quickly look at his crotch again. I want him to do his flies up.

'I wonder if you keep so thin to avoid being womanly,' he says.

I'm flattered he's referred to me as 'so thin', but then I think about what he's said.

'I'm not sure a person's size relates to if they're a woman or not.'

'Breasts, hips, laying down fat, being fertile. Fertility can only occur when a woman is a certain weight. Fertility embodies what it is to be a woman.'

He's studied at top institutions, has a master's. I disagree, but he's the educated one.

'I think a woman can be a woman whatever her size, but I accept different people will have different ideas about what it is to be a woman,' I say.

I hate myself for not saying what I believe. Stevie would get into a full-blown argument protecting what he believes in. When I'm passive like this, too scared to say what I truly want to because I'm worried about how the other person might respond, it's another layer on the stack of reasons to feel shit about myself.

We don't speak. When I look at Richard, it looks like he's working at something stuck in a back tooth and I wonder what it is, what he's been eating.

'I've not made myself sick for a long time,' I say.

'You're becoming more self-aware, Dani.'

'I still get urges to do it but not as much as before.'

'You're controlling the bulimia, rather than the bulimia controlling you.'

'Yeah.'

I want him to praise me more, tell me I'm doing well. I want him to like me more than the woman who came before me. I want him to recognise how well I'm doing and that it's because of him.

'I was thinking, recently, of something else that may help you, Dani. I would like to invite you to write down your feelings, perhaps in a journal-style format. It can be an effective way to propel emotional growth and I feel it would give you more fluency in our sessions if you'd already thought about some areas you believe would be beneficial to speak about.'

'You think writing would help me?'

His forehead creases slightly and he takes a sip of water.

'Do you think it would help you?'

I don't like the way he turns my questions back towards me.

'If you think it would help me, I'll try it. So, like homework?'

'No, Dani. It isn't "homework". I don't give my patients homework. It's an invitation to take some ownership of your feelings in between sessions. Writing can provide direct access to the subconscious and you may find it empowering.'

I'm pleased the tension in the room is easing. I think of an article I read a few days ago.

'Why do you think I'm like this? Do you think I'm bipolar?'

'I think a diagnosis like that would be unhelpful.'

'Why?'

'When such a diagnosis is made, it lessens the potential to relate to the other as a person. They become a set of expectations according to the diagnosis. It limits the vision.'

I recognised all the symptoms in the article. I get manic highs and depressive lows. There hasn't been a manic high lately, but it's because I've been working at getting better, and Richard is keeping me anchored. If I keep coming to the sessions and telling him I've been sick, he won't think he's helping me much. Besides, I've not even wanted to do it recently.

'I don't think you understand what I'm trying to say to you,' I say. 'I don't think I'm explaining it very well.'

'What I'm hearing is you think having a diagnosis means it would be easier to find a "cure"?'

'No, that's not it.'

'Perhaps you could help me find some of my blind spots.'

'What?'

'If I'm not hearing you correctly. You could help me to understand why I haven't understood you.'

83

'You want me to tell you where you're going wrong?'

'It could be helpful for us both.'

'Okay. That will be eighty pounds an hour. Not an hour, fifty minutes.' My voice comes out louder than I wanted. It always does when I'm making a joke. Then I feel ignorant.

He presses his lips together.

'Sorry, it was a joke.' I shake my head and look at the floor. Stupid. I pay for his expertise. I should treat him accordingly. 'Maybe I'm a highly sensitive person then, not bipolar.'

He does a half-nod. I know he doesn't want to talk about that any more. I try and be as engaging as the woman who came before me. Lighter.

'Are you enjoying your book?' I say.

'My book?'

'There's not usually a book on your desk.'

'You're so attentive to change in this room, Dani.'

I bet the woman before me addresses him by his name. I can't. I remember something else I wanted to ask him.

'Would it be possible to have the full hour instead of fifty minutes? It feels like we just get going, then we have to stop.'

'My sessions are fifty minutes.'

'The woman you saw before me had nearly an hour.'

'In certain circumstances, the sessions can run over.'

I think about all the times he's spoken about the importance of boundaries. We sit in silence.

'I've been reflecting on something you said in our last session, Dani, that your parents' divorce marked the start of a traumatic time for you.'

'Yep.' Because of what happened before the session, and in the first part of it, I'm pleased Richard's brought this up. It gives me somewhere to put the anger. 'When they divorced, she started having loads of boyfriends over.' I try and keep my face neutral because I know how ugly I look when I'm angry. 'Some of them would come in the middle of the night, some for weekends. It's because they were married. There was never a proper boyfriend, it was a series of men who were all disgusting in their own horrible grubby way. I hated them – all of them.'

'You hated them.'

'I hated them for being scummy, but most of all, I hated them for not being my dad. They were in the house because he wasn't.'

'And how old were you when your mother had these men in the house?'

'Ten.'

'Ten,' Richard says softly.

'You'll make me upset if you speak in that tone of voice.'

'A little girl. Ten.'

I don't know how long I cry for.

'Dani, I want to thank you for your courage today.'

'Is it time?'

'I'm afraid so. We've gone slightly over.'

'Okay. Thanks.' I speak to his chest. I can't look at him.

He stands at the door, and as I'm walking past him, he says, 'Remember, Dani, that I am on your side.'

I can hear Stevie and Jo arguing as I walk down the corridor towards the front door. I consider leaving, going to the pub and coming back later, but I'm too tired. I let myself in and shout that I'm home. Stevie comes out of the living room. His face is red and he's in jeans and a T-shirt. He must be going out, or he'd be in his boxers. Jo's flicking through the TV channels.

The front door bangs while I'm putting shorts and a T-shirt on. Stevie's gone without saying goodbye. In the kitchen, I take a potato from the cupboard and push the roots off with my thumb. I stab it a few times and put it in the microwave. I slice a tomato and some cucumber. I feel weak after the session with Richard but I also feel like something has shifted. I get the fleeting thought I could binge and throw up now as Stevie's gone out, but I don't want to. I cut the potato open and add salt and vinegar. Nourishing. I want nourishing things for once. There's an avocado on the side but I'm not ready to go that far – too many calories, even if they are nutritious ones.

I think of the vitamins and the good it's doing me while I eat. But as I start to feel full, I get the urge to add butter and cheese to the potato, put a microwave meal in, run over to the garage for biscuits and cake and crisps and chocolate and ice cream. I've tipped. There's a point when I'm eating, even if I planned to keep it down, where it suddenly feels like I've eaten too much and I need to turn it into a binge and bring it all back up.

I could scream with the craving, but Jo is in the next room and she'd freak. I stare at my plate – the potato skin, the cucumber. I want to do it. I don't want to do it. I want to do it. I can't do it. I have to stop doing it. I lean down to the plate and whisper, 'Fuck you.'

I pick the plate up and take it over to the sink. I squirt washing-up liquid over it and scrape it into the bin.

'What's the matter with you?' Jo says, walking into the kitchen. 'You look like you're about to cry.'

'No, I'm fine. Just a bit tired.'

I'm going to write about my feelings like Richard suggested. I breathe through the feelings of fullness and try to describe why feeling full is so uncomfortable. When I feel full, I feel fat, but I should rationalise and not feel so guilty because everyone needs to eat. I need to focus on nourishment. Richard said that before he eats, he thinks, 'Is this nourishing?' What was the expression he used earlier? Holding his clients in mind. And when I was leaving today, he said that he's on my side. *I am on your side, Dani,*

I write at the top of several pages of the notebook, so that each time I start a new page, I'm reminded that Richard is with me.

I write for over an hour. The fullness has gone down a little.

I stand at the end of the sofa, wait for Jo to shift her legs up so I can sit down. When she puts her feet back on my lap, I see she's had a pedicure.

'You all right?' I say.

'Stevie's being a dick.'

'That's a shame.'

She changes channels.

'I like the colour.' I squeeze her foot, and she kicks out with it, so I let go.

'Thanks.' She cranes her neck for a second to look at her flexed toes.

On TV, a couple are in deep discussion, sitting up in bed, side by side. He's bare-chested; she's wearing some silky negligee thing. What must it be like to be part of a couple like that? I think of Richard and his wife, if he has one, side by side in bed, talking, intellectual and respectful conversation. I think about what's led up to the evening before they got to bed. She gets in from her creative and well-paid job. He's run her a bath and put little scented tea-light candles around the side. He comes into the bathroom with two glasses of good red wine in big wine glasses, sits on the side of the bath and passes me one. He asks about my day, and I ask him what the psychoanalytic perspective might be of the poem I'm currently studying. He thinks about it before he answers, and I close my eyes and the water feels smooth because of the sensual bath oil he's put in. The radio is playing classical music and Richard says something about the composer of the piece. I refer to a similar composer and link the two together in an insightful and relevant way. Richard tells me to relax, he'll make supper. He bought swordfish from the local fishmonger's and will steam some asparagus. He says he's bought a rather decadent dark chocolate torte from the local patisserie for pudding, or whatever the word is posh people use for dessert.

Jo's phone rings. She reaches for it too fast, and it thuds on the floor. She grabs it up and leaves the room, slamming the door behind her. She doesn't come back for ages, and when she does, her face is flushed. She takes her usual position on the sofa and then stretches like she's had good sex.

'Who was that?'

'Hayley from work.'

'Yeah, right.'

She laughs and kicks me.

'Where's Stevie gone then?'

'Pavan's birthday, they've gone out for dinner. That's why he had the hump; he wanted me to go.'

'Why didn't you?'

'Couldn't be arsed.'

She changes the channel, watches an angry woman banging on a door, then changes the channel again.

'He does so much for you, Jo. I know he can be a prick but his world has you at the centre. How can you not like that?'

'You know what it is about Stevie? He needs to be needed.'

'It would have been nice going out for dinner, wouldn't it?'

'Pavan and his girlfriend are boring.'

Stevie needs to be needed, but Jo needs to be indulged. I can't say it though. I'm her little sister and until recently, I could barely function. She won't take advice from me.

'Do you think Stevie'll still be annoyed when he gets back?' I say.

'Be quiet,' she says. 'I'm trying to watch this,' and changes the channel.

Chapter Ten

Reena's on her own in the smoking hut, sitting at the end of the bench. I sit at the other end, roll a cigarette and stare into the middle distance while I smoke. I tried a mindfulness video on YouTube once but realised I do it all the time anyway when I'm smoking. Those minutes enjoying the hand-to-mouth action, the sucking in, the taste in my mouth, the hit at the back of my throat, the filling of the lungs, the keeping it in a few seconds. The slow exhale. Perhaps that's why more people are doing mindfulness stuff now – they miss that quiet time they used to have when they smoked.

Reena and I sip our tea, smoke and ignore each other. The inside of my chest starts to burn like I've got indigestion.

'Reena?' She doesn't make any sign she's heard; just puts her tea down, takes out her phone and starts scrolling.

'Reena, I was thinking about what you said, about how I spend my evenings, and the only thing I think it could be is Del. I seriously had no idea you liked him. If I had, I wouldn't have gone near him. I'm not like that. I'm truly sorry.'

'It took you a while to work that one out.'

'I had no idea, that's why.'

'Seriously? He never said anything about me?'

'Nothing at all.'

'Tosser.' She shakes her head.

'I'm sorry, Reena. If I'd known—'

'Okay,' she says.

At Roden Court, Pat goes to speak to her mum and I go to make the tea. Elaine, the manager, is in the kitchen wiping down the work surfaces and we make small talk about the shitty weather we've been having lately. She complains they're short-staffed but luckily have just had a 'lovely young man' start called Elijah, with 'lovely green eyes'.

'Speak of the devil,' she says as Elijah comes into the kitchen.

Elaine doesn't introduce us. A resident warbles from the lounge and Elaine throws the dishcloth in the sink and goes to assist.

'Who do you belong to?' Elijah says.

'I don't have any relatives here. I come with my friend, Pat; she's Edie's daughter. I talk to Frank sometimes.'

'Margaret Thatcher's ex-bodyguard?'

'He told me he was her driver.'

'He mixes it up. Sometimes it's her chef.'

'Is it dementia?'

'No, he's having a laugh. He's a Labour supporter.'

I squeeze a tea bag against the side of the mug. Pat likes her tea strong.

'Sorry, what's your name?' he says.

'Dani.'

He doesn't say anything.

'Well, that killed the conversation, didn't it?' I say.

He laughs.

'How are you finding the job?' I say.

'Hard and low-paid, but apart from that, it's all right.'

'I admire people who do this work. I like chatting to the

people here but I'd struggle to do the caring part. That makes me sound awful but it's true. So well done you – and that sounds patronising. Sorry.'

Elijah laughs again. 'I'm on break now. Come and join me for a cigarette if you want.'

'How do you know I smoke?'

He nods towards my right hand and I close my fingers into a fist, embarrassed. He noticed the nicotine stains on my fingers.

'Being a good observer helps in this kind of work,' he says.

We go outside and sit on a wooden bench by the flowerbeds, which contain only a couple of scrubby little plants. Elijah takes his tobacco from his rucksack and while it's open, I see a couple of books inside.

'What are you reading?'

'This is between you and me, okay?' He's got excellent teeth, white and straight, like Richard's. I always notice teeth as mine are all yellow and shit at the back. I'll get them sorted when I have the money. Elijah pulls two paperbacks out and puts them on the bench between us.

'Early Greek philosophy for when I'm on the tube and want to look intelligent, a Jack Reacher for when nobody is around.'

There's a mug ring on the Jack Reacher and I run my finger around it and look at him with eyebrows raised.

'Charity shop. Wasn't me, I promise.'

'I buy all my books from the charity shop. Except if I know it's got sex in it, then I buy the book new. I'm worried I might find a pubic hair in it otherwise. Is Diogenes in your book of Greek philosophers?'

'From pubes to Diogenes.' Elijah puts the books down and rolls a cigarette. 'Diogenes. No, I've never heard of him.'

'He was rude and sometimes lived in a big wine casket.'

'Doesn't ring any bells. What did he believe in?'

'His thing was authenticity. He wanted to cut through people's pretences, so he spoke the truth. And he pissed on people. And shit in the theatre and tossed off in public.'

'I didn't know any of that. I'm still on Socrates.'

'I like some of the stuff Diogenes said. When he was jerking off in public, he said, "If only I could cure my hunger by rubbing my stomach."' I put a hand on my stomach. 'It would be good, wouldn't it? If hunger could be satiated so easily.'

'Do you know many Greek philosophers?'

'Not personally. Only Diogenes. My dad used to talk about him. When the king came to see him – Diogenes, not my dad – he asked Diogenes if there was anything he could do for him. Diogenes told him to move out of the way as he was blocking the light.'

'Say what you mean and mean what you say. Are you so honest with people?'

'I only say what I'm honestly thinking about five per cent of the time, and even then, I shit myself and worry I've caused offence. It keeps me up for ages, stops me sleeping.'

'Is this the five per cent?'

'It's the five per cent. But I am trying to increase it, get it up to ten or fifteen. Pat told me the other day that the bigger the difference between what you're feeling and how you're acting, the worse your mental health will be. So I'm working on it.'

Elijah starts laughing and gestures to the window. 'Look at Frank.' I watch Frank pulling faces behind another resident's back. He's pulling the sides of his mouth apart with his fingers like a six-year-old and sticking his tongue out. Elaine's laughing at him and shaking her head.

'Sorry, was I boring you?' I say.

'Yeah, the pants off.'

I love people who take the piss. One of the first friends I

made at uni was a girl who called me a stupid fucker the first time we spoke. I knew we'd get on.

'Frank's doing well, considering.' Elijah takes a pull on his roll-up. I like the way he smokes, licks his top lip before exhaling.

'What?'

'I thought you'd know. He's quite poorly.'

'Nobody's ever said.'

'Lung cancer.'

'I didn't know. How old is he?'

'Late seventies. And it's just spread to his liver.'

'Shit. Is he having treatment?'

'Refused it. Said he'd rather enjoy the time he has left.'

'I can understand that. Does he get many visitors?'

'Not that I'm aware of. He's got a son, but Elaine said he doesn't visit.'

Elijah has his sleeves rolled up and his forearms are a beautiful shape. His skin is so pale I can see the veins clearly in his arms and there's something sexy about it, being able to see underneath him.

'How do you deal with it? You must get close to them, then they die.'

'It's part of the job.'

I'm not sure I want to spend so much time with Frank now. I stub my cigarette out. I'll give it some more thought later. I hope his son visits him soon.

'Going back to Diogenes,' I say, 'I think he had the right idea. He wanted a simple life. He wanted to show you could be happy without a lot of material possessions, do you know what I mean?'

'I do,' says Elijah. 'The best things in life are free.'

'A cliché but true.'

'What do you do? Are you working? Studying?'

'I'm on a year out from uni, trying to keep busy. I've got a job in Hall & Walker washing up in the restaurant, but I was thinking about coming here more, talking to the residents who might like the company. At the moment I only really chat to Pat's mum Edie, and Frank. I thought I could come at a different time and visit someone else.'

Elijah smiles. 'Sweet,' he says.

'I'm so self-indulgent I thought it could be good to try and give something back to others, so I stop thinking about myself so much.'

'Why don't you see if you can get paid work here?'

'No, I couldn't wipe their arses or anything – but I'm happy to come in and chat to them.'

Elijah grinds his cigarette into the concrete with the toe of his boot and stands up. 'Right, good to meet you, Dani.'

'Shit – have I offended you?'

'Not at all.' He looks at me. His eyes. They are the most beautiful eyes I've ever seen. 'Some people are squeamish about stuff like that. No big deal.'

I watch him go back into the building and imagine what it would be like to have a boyfriend like Elijah, roughly my own age and intelligent, nothing wrong with him. He has a job trying to help others but isn't square with it. Clean. I wouldn't be good enough for him. Too worn and weathered like an old shoe on the side of the motorway. I like him. There's an energy and optimism about him. He's not jaded.

Chapter Eleven

Richard's room is stuffy today and the first thing I see is a small box under the couch. It's a little wooden box, and I recognise the carved swirls on it. It's usually on the shelf on the left-hand wall, in front of *Psychoanalytic Explorations* and *The Intimate Hour.*

'That box usually goes there.' I point to the shelf. Richard's hair looks damp, flat on his head and he looks like he's been holding his breath. 'Have you just had a shower?' He's not wearing argyles. 'You're wearing different socks today – well, I'm sure you wear different socks every day, but in all the time I've been coming here, you've always worn argyle socks. Are they sports socks?'

'What have you brought to the session today, Dani?'

I can't think about that when things aren't right in here. The box, his hair, his white socks.

'Do you want me to put the box back in its place?' He ignores me. 'It's close in here. Would you mind opening a window, please?'

'Perhaps you could remove your jumper if you're too warm,' he says.

I've only got a vest on underneath. If I take my jumper off, he'll see the silver stretch marks streaking my inner upper arms. The room doesn't feel right. He doesn't feel right. I think about what could be wrong with him, why he's annoyed.

'Did you get my email? I'm sorry I haven't paid you for last month yet. I will, of course, when I next get paid. I got behind with the rent and Stevie was getting pissed off so I had to pay him and I didn't have enough to pay you as well. I'm sorry.'

Richard strokes his temple with his finger. Usually, I love it when he does that but he's made me tense like him.

'Dani, I've been meaning to discuss my fees with you. I can see this is an issue at the moment. I do have a low-cost session that has become available, and I would like to offer it to you. It's at seven on Monday, my last session of the day, an hour later than you currently have, so you would need to come at seven instead of six. Would that be possible?'

I like the idea of being the last client of the day, coming at seven instead of six. Seven o'clock has got a different feel: unwinding, relaxing, shaking the day off. What do people do in the evening? Eat, relax, go to bed.

'Seven is fine. I can do that; it's not a problem.'

'And just pay me half of your outstanding fee for last month. The low-cost sessions are forty pounds.'

'Are you sure? I don't mind paying the full amount for last month.'

'You're making good progress, Dani, and I don't want cost to be a barrier or create more stress for you. Most therapists offer some low-cost sessions to make therapy more accessible for a wider range of people.'

'Okay. Thanks. A hundred and sixty then.'

'I'd have to check. Numbers aren't my strong point. I'm slightly numerically dyslexic.'

'You mean you're shit at maths?' My voice. Too loud again. Ignorant. He doesn't smile. He's been so generous, and I insulted him. I apologise. I'll buy him a present with some of the money he's let me off. We sit for a while, and I look around the room.

'Do you move stuff around to see if I'll notice? You did the picture, and today you've moved the box. Is it a technique or something?'

'Do you think you spend time looking at the books and art because it's easier than looking at me?'

'No, I just love books. I like seeing so many in one place. You should have seen the library at my uni; it was fantastic. I know a lot of stuff is online nowadays, but nothing competes with a library. You need to be able to hold the book in your hands, stroke the cover, smell it. It's one of my favourite smells, you know? When you flick through the pages of a book, that warm papery smell that wafts up. I'm surprised it doesn't come up on those top ten lists that get compiled. It's always boring smells like bacon or freshly cut grass. Or paint. Stuff like that.'

'Dani, I feel you look at the books to avoid looking at me, particularly if we're exploring something painful to you.'

'No, I don't think so.'

'I wonder if it feels too intimate for you when we look into each other's eyes.'

'It's fine.' I look at him and smile.

'What are you feeling in your body at this moment?'

'I don't know.'

'You must be feeling something. How would you describe it?'

'I'm not feeling anything, to be honest. Same as usual.'

'You broke eye contact with me. Before you broke eye contact, I want to know what you were feeling inside your body. Perhaps there was a heaviness, or a tightness, or a tingling or fizzing. What was it?'

I'm not the kind of girl who says words like 'tingly' and 'fizzy'. People use words that suit them. I wouldn't say 'tingly' or 'fizzy' any more than I'd say 'fab' or 'yay' or 'meh'. I hate people who say 'fab' and 'yay', especially when they draw the word out.

'Dani?'

'Yes?'

'What are you thinking about? Right at this very moment?'

'Hamsters.'

'Did you say hamsters?'

'Yes.'

'Why hamsters?'

'You said about tingling and fizzing and it made me think of other words I don't like, and I thought of 'yay' and 'fab' and 'meh' and then 'bedding', because when people speak about bedding it makes me think of hamsters. You know that shredded paper they have for bedding?'

'I see. Are there any other words that evoke such strong reactions?'

'Maureen at work is always saying she needs to eat some food. That bothers me. What else is she going to eat? And it also winds me up when people say they were thinking in their heads.'

'Where else are they going to think?' Richard says.

'Yeah. I've been thinking in my knuckles.'

The room softens.

'You were looking at me then,' he says. 'It's easier for you, isn't it? When we're speaking about the everyday, and avoiding difficult subjects.'

'Yes.'

'Why is eye contact so hard, Dani?'

I take a deep breath and try not to look away from Richard when I speak.

'My dad could never make eye contact when he spoke to me. Perhaps for a second or two but never for any length of time. And his pupils were tiny. He had light blue eyes and tiny pupils. They were like dots. And when I saw him again, when I'd not seen him for a few years, he looked like he'd suffered so much.

It was in his mouth, his eyes. His face at rest was sad. Even when he was laughing his eyes stayed sad.'

'You feel loss at the fact your father didn't look at you.'

'No. It's the way he was. I was used to it. He spoke to my shoulder or the top of my head. If we made eye contact by accident, he'd look away.'

'Dani, a child needs to feel their parent is present, so they know they are worth thinking about. This is how a child builds confidence. A parent making eye contact with their child is fundamental to the relationship.'

So they know they are worth thinking about.

'A child needs to be shown by one or both parents that they are special and loved and a pleasure to be around,' he says. 'This is subtly done through cues like eye contact and tone of voice. When this doesn't occur, it can lead to feelings of worthlessness in the child that they then carry through to adulthood.'

He's right. I do feel worthless, but if I tell him that now I'll cry.

'In lots of ways, it was a great relationship with my dad. Even though he struggled with eye contact. He'd have done anything for me.'

'How do you know?'

'Just because my dad struggled in some ways, it doesn't obliterate all that was good about him. He had this huge sense of fun and he was always pushing me to learn, get a good education, go to university, do what he hadn't done. But I'll tell you about a relationship that's bothering me right now. Remember I told you about Reena? Blanking me in the smoking shed? Well, I found out why. She likes Del, and I think they had something going on, but I didn't know, else—'

'Dani changes the subject when Richard speaks of things that can be painful,' Richard says.

'So I felt good when I worked out why Reena was angry because it meant it wasn't me. Well, it was in a way, but I didn't know she liked him and they had something.'

'You had done nothing wrong.'

'No.'

I listen to the clock.

'I'd like to talk about what came up in the last session,' he says. 'About after your father left.'

'I don't want to. Not today.' I rub my hands against my face and then rub them together. I clap a couple of times and stretch my arms out in front of me. 'Ask me about something else.'

Richard runs a tongue over his teeth. His mouth is closed and it makes a little ripple across his top lip.

'I can hear your reluctance.'

'I'm not in the mood.'

We sit in silence for a while.

'I've been writing a lot at home. And in my lunch break at work. You're right: it's helping me a lot. Sometimes I don't even realise what I'm feeling until I see it written down.'

'What have you been writing about?'

'I wrote about the Del and Reena situation. I end up giving myself advice, telling myself not to feel bad. It helps. Thanks for suggesting it. I find that I often end up writing down the advice my dad would've given me.'

'The advice your dad would have given you, if he was still here,' Richard says gently.

I nod because I don't trust my voice.

We sit in silence and I look at the books. Eventually, Richard speaks.

'You've mentioned your workmate Del a few times. I'm curious about what the sex is like with Del.'

I feel my shoulders rising and I shake my head. 'I've never said that he and I—'

He sighs and closes his eyes.

'What?' I say.

'Dani, you come to therapy to examine your inner life and the motivations behind your behaviour.'

'I come here because I want to sort out the bulimia. I don't think sex has got anything to do with it.' I do this fake laugh to soften what I've said, so it doesn't seem too abrupt.

He presses his lips together. I don't want him to be angry with me. I try not to speak. I feel too uncomfortable.

'Yeah, it's fine.' I try not to squirm.

'Could you give a little more detail?'

'Not much to say about it. Normal.'

'What is normal sex for you?'

He's probably asking to make sure I'm not into S&M or some kinky shit.

'Normal positions, normal.'

'Normal positions, normal sex,' he says slowly and I clench my feet so I can try and keep my face neutral, but I can feel one eyelid beating and the eye becoming smaller.

'Yeah. Normal.'

It wouldn't feel right to say words like reverse cowgirl or doggy style in this room. I wonder if there are more middle-class names for those positions. I might look it up.

'Dani, I'm going to pin you down here. I am not going to let you evade this question. I want you to tell me about what normal sex is for you.'

I run my forefinger across the skin between my nose and mouth.

'Missionary position,' I say. That sounds sophisticated. Almost biblical.

'Missionary position,' he says. 'The man on top.'

I wonder why he so often states the obvious.

'Yes,' I say.

'Contraception?'

'Sorry?'

'Are you using contraception?'

'No.'

I bring my hands to my face because I should use contraception, a nice girl would use contraception, but I never have because I don't care enough about myself. *Weirdo piece of shit.* I get now why he asks me questions that make me feel uncomfortable. It's because of what they reveal about the way I feel about myself. He's clever.

'Dani.' He says my name so softly. 'Dani, can you look at me?'

He's so kind. He's still talking to me in a kind voice, despite what I've just said. I move my hands so they only cover my eyes and so my words won't be muffled.

'How long will I see you for?'

'We spoke about this, remember? Some people have psychotherapy for years.'

'I think I need to come for a long time. I think I'll need it for years.'

Then I realise if I do sort myself out, it will mean I'm finished here. The thought of not coming here any more, of not seeing Richard any more, is unbearable. I need to keep seeing him. I don't know how I'd manage without him.

Chapter Twelve

Now Richard has changed our session time to 7 p.m., I could leave work at 6 p.m. like everyone else, but I'm not going to tell Babs I don't need the early finish on Monday any more. I'll use the extra time to go home and get changed. It'll be nice to shower before seeing Richard instead of walking into his office stinking of chip fat. It'll be nice to get changed in my bedroom instead of the toilet cubicle at work.

As I'm pulling clothes out of the tumble drier, looking for my silky black top, I see Jo's been buying new underwear, shiny and blue. It looks so cheap it must have been expensive. I feel sorry for Stevie. I go to their bedroom and spray Jo's perfume on my neck, wrists, and all over the front of my top. I put on some of her mascara.

It's raining heavily so I order an Uber to Richard's because I don't want the mascara to run. The driver gets out and opens the back door for me.

'I'd prefer to sit in the front,' I tell him. I'd never sit in the Uber like a royal being driven around by a chauffeur.

'King's Road?' he says and I nod.

'Wet today.' He increases the speed of his windscreen wipers.

'That's why I thought I'd book you; usually, I'd walk such a short distance.' I don't want him to think I'm lazy. His ID badge is stuck to the dash. In the photo, he's smiling in a way that makes him look a bit simple.

'How's your day going so far, Naz?'

He laughs. 'Busy. Good weather for Uber drivers.'

We pull up at some lights. They change to green, but the car in front doesn't move. Naz beeps the horn.

'Come on, sleepy face,' he says.

'It's sleepy head.'

He doesn't respond. I shouldn't have corrected him. I like his version better anyway; it makes more sense.

I take my phone and check my face in it. I put lip gloss on.

We reach King's Road. Naz stops outside Richard's and points to the door.

'Mr Richard. Miss Becca.'

'You know him?'

He nods.

'Miss Becca, nice lady, she makes wedding cakes, birthday cakes – big, beautiful cakes.'

I can feel my heart beating in my neck.

'Is that his wife? Are they married?' It could be his daughter.

Naz shrugs. 'His woman.'

'Where do you take him? Do they go out together?'

'Theatre, West End, other houses . . .'

'Does anyone else live there?'

He shrugs again. I can't sit here with the engine running, pumping the driver for information. I pull the visor down and check my face in the mirror.

'Can I have your number?' I say.

Richard opens the door and I follow him to his room. I stand with my back to him, take my coat off and then check the pockets before hanging it on one of the hooks. I want him to have a minute to admire my hair, my small waist. I sit down and fold my arms.

'I got an Uber here today. The driver told me some things about you and your wife.'

Richard clears his throat but doesn't say anything.

'Don't you want to know what he said? About you? And your wife?'

I keep looking at Richard in the silence that follows but his face stays expressionless.

'In the last session, you seemed to become rather upset when we spoke about contraception. Can you tell me more about how you were feeling at that time?'

'Let me try to remember.'

I can remember, but I'm stalling for time. What else is there to say about getting upset?

'In the last session, you became upset when telling me you did not use contraception with Des. Can you tell me more about the feelings you had? The feelings that were behind the words?'

'Del. His name's Del, not Des.' I speak to the floor in front of my feet. 'The contraception thing made me realise it's all connected with my feelings of being worthless. If I felt better in myself, I'd use it. That's why I got upset.'

'You feel worthless.'

'My dad spent a lot of time telling me I was a weirdo piece of shit. It's hard to shake that off. I know I shouldn't be so sensitive. It's just something he said when he got angry. He was a great dad in so many other ways, but he had a temper.'

'Your father's words hurt you.'

'That's why I'm determined to finish my degree. I need it to show I'm not worthless, that I've achieved something, do you know what I mean?'

'That you're not a weirdo piece of shit.'

'Yeah. Although I might still be a weirdo piece of shit – but I'll be a weirdo piece of shit with qualifications.'

'You need a piece of paper to make you feel you have achieved? To make you have self-worth?'

'That's why I'm here. I need to get back to uni and get my degree. Unless I sort out the bulimia, I won't be able to do that.'

'Thinking about the lack of contraception, what about pregnancy, Dani? Don't you worry about sexually transmitted diseases?'

'I don't think I can get pregnant; I think the bulimia messed that side of things up.' I move on quickly in case he asks me about periods. 'With the STDs, I don't think about them, to be honest, and I've always got away with it. I convinced myself I had syphilis once, but it turned out I was bored.'

'I'm not sure I understand.'

'I thought I had syphilis, but I was bored.'

'You were so bored you fantasised about having syphilis?'

'I didn't want to have it. When you say fantasy, you make it seem like I wanted it.'

'In psychotherapeutic terms, fantasy is anything imagined. It doesn't have the same meaning in everyday English where it is most often used to describe a sexual desire or something much wanted.'

I like how psychotherapy has its own definitions for things, like a separate world – Richard's world. Every time I learn something new like that, I step further inside it.

'You said you fantasised about having syphilis?' Richard prompts.

'I imagine bad scenarios if I don't have enough to think about. It must have been a boring time in my life. I kept looking at the palm of my hand and imagining it was red.'

'Why would you imagine the palm of your hand was red?'

'Red palms are a symptom of syphilis.'

I'm surprised he didn't know that, but why would he? I doubt he's sat in a sexual health clinic on a sunny afternoon, working his way through all the leaflets and the posters on the walls to alleviate the boredom while waiting to be seen. Me and Christy went after we'd started going out as we both had rashes. Christy went in first. When he came out, his face was pinched and pale. He told me he had HIV. I felt awful for him because he was so distraught. I didn't care about the unprotected sex we'd had since day one: I didn't care about me. Christy came clean after half an hour. He had a strange sense of humour at times, but looking back, the joke was on him. He was expecting me to shit myself but I wasn't bothered. The health-clinic worker told us to use non-biological washing powder because, as we'd discovered, the cheapest biological stuff can cause irritation.

'Nice word, isn't it?' I say. 'Syphilis. There's something soft about it. It's close to Sisyphus. All the gentle "s" and "f" sounds. Do you ever feel like Sisyphus? I—'

Richard cuts me off. 'At the time you fantasised about having syphilis, were you having intercourse with many men?'

'Loads.'

'Loads. Were they fleeting encounters?'

'Yeah, you could call them fleeting encounters.'

So fleeting I didn't even lie down for some of them. The ticking clock is suddenly loud in the room and I'm aware of Richard's breathing. I start to count the books on the top shelf. Before I'm halfway across, he speaks.

'Euphoria. You would have experienced a euphoria at having sex with many men. There is a euphoria attached to reckless sex; it makes one feel alive.'

I want to tell him he's wrong, that most of the time, it's for the hugs. I'd love to hug Richard. Have his arms wrap around me, nuzzle my face into his warm chest, sit, not moving, stay like that for hours with his arms around me. Breathe him in.

'Are you with me, Dani?'

'Sorry?'

'I sense you aren't entirely with me today.'

'I was thinking about what the Uber driver said.'

I wonder how old his wife is, how attractive, and if she's clever. Naz said the cakes she makes are beautiful. I wonder how talented she is and if she makes a lot of money.

'Dani. The email you sent last night . . .'

I cover my face with my hands. 'I'm not sure I can talk about it. It's embarrassing.'

'Why did you send the email?'

'I don't talk about things I should. There's stuff you should know. If we work through it, it will help. When you got me talking about why I don't use contraception because of my low self-esteem, it made me realise I need to talk about the difficult stuff. Things happened when I was with Christy I should talk about. I thought it'd be easier to write about it first.'

'It took courage to send the email.'

'I'm trying hard. There's no point coming here unless I'm going to do it properly.'

'The more you engage, the more helpful psychotherapy is. The more I can help you. Be authentic, Dani. Be your true self.'

I know I'm paying to be here, but he cares. I can feel it.

'Diogenes believed in authenticity. He thought everyone was a bullshitter and was so desperate to find an honest man he'd walk around in broad daylight with a lighted lantern. I often think of him. He's like my guide. He had good ideas and principles.'

'Tell me more about Christy.'

'Diogenes another time then. I thought Christy was so attractive. He was so funny; he could sing, write poetry . . .'

'He sounds like a creative man. His creativity attracted you.'

'It did, but it was his looks first. He was good-looking. He even used to get work from this lookalike agency as Gerard Piqué.'

'I'm sorry. Piqué?'

'Yeah, the footballer. Plays for Barcelona, good-looking.'

Richard shakes his head.

'He used to go out with Shakira. The singer? Hips don't lie? Everyone knows that one.'

He still looks blank.

'I was just trying to make the point that Christy was good-looking. You'd probably recognise the song if you heard it.'

There are a few beats of silence.

'I've got the song in my head now,' I say. 'That's annoying. There's a spider, look.' I point to the ceiling. 'It's crawling towards the light. Do you believe spiders can feel sad?' Richard doesn't look at the ceiling. He sighs.

I shift in my seat so I'm facing the bookshelves and not him. I start counting the books on the top shelf again.

'Dani, saying things that may make you feel uncomfortable is a fundamental part of the therapeutic process. It's good that you're beginning to share difficult experiences with me through email, but it is also important that you're able to speak about them too.'

'I'm not sure I can. That's why I emailed you.'

We sit in silence. I imagine Richard getting up and getting a book off the shelf. He beckons me over with a tilt of the head to read something on the page. When I stand next to him, I'm aware of his body heat and how clean he smells, then he puts the book back on the shelf and puts his arms around me, and we kiss. We move over to the couch and lie down and I come although all we're doing is kissing.

'In your email, Dani, you described some sexual behaviour with Christy I would describe as dysfunctional.'

I pull a couple of hairs out from the nape of my neck. I take one of the hairs and start wrapping it around the knuckle of my index finger.

'Yep, he used to hold me down.' I pretend I'm someone else when I say it, an actor.

'And then?'

'You read it in the email. I put the details in the email.'

'You need to be able to talk about it.'

It's the stuff I wrote in the email. He knows it already.

I pull more hair from the nape of my neck, placing it on my thigh so I can take it with me when I go and not leave it behind for Richard to be disgusted over, shedding hair over his lovely chair and rug like a moulting dog.

'Christy used to hold me down and call me names. You know what I said in the email. It felt like he was punching me with it.'

At the time, it didn't bother me. Being with Christy was so exciting at first. It'd been my birthday a couple of weeks after we'd met and he did me a treasure hunt in the garden. He hid a bottle of vodka, a gram of coke and a silver vibrator in the shape of a massive bullet and gave me clues in the form of handwritten poems to find them. My mate Bethany's birthday was the same day and her boyfriend gave her a green tartan blanket from Primark and a box of Ferrero Rocher.

'Where did you go just then, Dani?'

'You've put the box back.' I point to it on the shelf. The box is back in the same place, in front of *The Intimate Hour*. I suppose *The Intimate Fifty Minutes* wouldn't have the same ring.

'Stay with what we're exploring, Dani. In the email, you wrote it felt like he was "punching" you with it. You felt like he was "punching you" with his erect penis?'

I nod.

'And I'm curious as to why you felt this was acceptable.'

'Low self-esteem, I suppose.'

I look at the picture of the girl and the man on the wall.

'I'm wondering if there is a sense you believe this is what you deserve,' Richard says.

'It connects with low self-esteem, doesn't it? Letting people treat you badly.' My chest has gone tight and I'm getting a head-ache. I need to change the subject. 'I'm going to Del's after this,' I say.

Richard's eyes narrow and I know it's because I should stay with what we're talking about. 'I'll think about what you said. I haven't thought about that before, about why I put up with shit from people.'

'I wonder if there is a part of you that feels like you need to be punished,' he says.

'You're probably right. Don't you want to know what my Uber driver said?'

Richard looks at me for a while before speaking. 'I think you like withholding the information. I think it makes you feel powerful.'

'Now you've made me feel bad, and I come here to try and make myself feel better.'

'Dani, my goal with you, as with all of my patients, is to fa-cilitate personal growth and basic character change. Today I feel you are somewhat distant, and this is creating a barrier in our relationship.'

I feel cheap. Like I'm wasting the session. I reset myself by reading a few book titles, then I look at Richard's chest. I wonder if it's hairy or smooth. I wouldn't care either way.

'I was a downer for most of the time I was with Christy. I mean, it was only six months we were together, and the first few weeks were brilliant, but looking back, I think he was a bully.'

'Go on.'

'He'd wake me up in the night and call me names. He'd shake me to wake me up and call me a fucking bitch and a dirty slag. I hadn't even done anything. It was the middle of the night and he was drunk and he wanted someone to have a go at. That's what he used to call me all the time when we were having sex too. I'd forgotten. "A dirty slag." I thought I'd be able to stop him drinking.'

Richard opens his mouth to say something, but I carry on speaking.

'But it was understandable, why he drank. When he was seventeen, his younger brother was killed in a hit and run, then within the year, his mum killed herself, took an overdose, so that's a lot to cope with when you're only seventeen. She and Christy had had an argument and when Christy got home the next day, she was slumped in her armchair, packets of Prozac, paracetamol and an empty bottle of Bacardi at her feet and "Everybody Hurts" playing on repeat in the background. That's why he drank. He felt like his mum's death was his fault. And that's tragic, isn't it? To carry that weight? There were such good things about him, though. He was sensitive, he wrote poetry, he could walk in a room, tell a couple of jokes and everyone would be laughing. He just needed someone who understood him and could care for him and make him better. That's what I was trying to do, but I couldn't do it.'

'Dani, I'm interested in what you were thinking, what you were feeling during the sex. When you felt like you were being punched with his penis, while he was calling you a dirty little slag, what were you feeling?'

'Dirty slag.'

'I'm sorry?'

'You said, "dirty little slag".'

'Okay. What were you feeling?'

'I felt like a piece of meat. Not even a good piece of meat, like a steak or a decent piece of chicken, but something shitty and processed. It's like I gave over my body because I felt so connected to him. I wanted to make him better. It was like, take what you want of me. Will that make you better?'

'Was there any part of you that felt it was wrong? That you shouldn't be treated in that way, that making love should be warm and caring and loving?'

When Richard says, 'warm and caring and loving', it makes me feel sick.

'It's just the way he was. He'd had a terrible life. It's understandable the way he acted. I read somewhere there's not a person alive you couldn't love if you'd heard their life story. And people sometimes say things like, isn't it terrible or shocking that this person has had so many bad things happen in their life, but it's not shocking, because once bad stuff happens, it triggers other bad stuff, like a chain of events, so I'd say it's more logical than shocking that bad stuff then keeps happening to a person. Unless you try hard to drag yourself out of it. That's why I've got to get back to university. I have to get educated. I need to have those options that a degree will give me.'

'Can you feel sad about the way Christy treated you?'

'What would be the point? How's that going to change anything? Forward not backwards. My dad said anything shit that happened was character-building.'

'You chose to bring your father into the conversation. We were speaking about a violent man, and you chose to bring your father into the conversation.'

'Because I agree with what he said – shit that happens *is* character-building. Anyway, Dad and Christy hated each other.'

'People often seek to replicate the relationship they witnessed between their parents. Was your father a violent man?'

'He was a good dad.'

My words hang in the air.

'Did you ever witness your father being violent?'

I want to tell Richard to fuck off, but I nod then I cover my face with my hands. I don't know how much time passes.

'Could you try to tell me about it, Dani?'

I look at the floor and let my hair fall over my face.

'When I was about six or seven I saw him holding my mum up against the living-room wall by her throat. And there were a couple of times when he went for me when I was a teenager. He didn't hit me, but he used the fact that he was much bigger and stronger to intimidate me. But I don't think these are the reasons I feel shit about myself. They weren't even that bad. Nobody ended up in hospital. There was no blood, no broken bones.'

'Dani, victims will often seek to minimise their trauma, especially when it is at the hands of someone they love.'

'I keep telling you, he was brilliant in many other ways. But he had a temper he struggled to control. It feels like you want me to slag him off, and it doesn't feel that helpful. I read this thing about when you feel angry with someone, it's like drinking rat poison and hoping that they die.'

'I think it could be helpful to you to accept that you were growing up in a climate where you would have felt fear, and at risk, and perhaps explore the impact that this has had. I want you to talk about what the Dani at five, six, seven, eight would have been feeling.'

'Yeah, okay.'

'Dani, until you're able to, I'm concerned that you will go on with your self-harming behaviours.'

'Okay. I'll think about it,' I say. He looks at the clock and I know what's coming.

'And it's time.'

We say it at the same time, and I stand.

I'm wired from divulging so much. I do a full-body stretch before I get my coat from the hook. I take out the present.

'I'll do this quickly as I know my session time is over and you're strict on time and all that. I wanted to get you something for letting me off the money.' I hold it out to him and he takes it. I thought he'd talk about boundaries or something. 'You can open it later.'

I walk out. I don't want to see Richard's face when he opens it in case he doesn't like it. It's a gold-plated Zippo lighter with RG engraved in italics on the front. I doubt he smokes, but a lighter is always useful to own for lighting candles and stuff. I wanted to get him something small and classy.

I wait at the bus stop for the bus to Del's and smoke. I hold Dad's Zippo lighter and think how me and Richard are linked now through our lighters. I hope every time he uses it, he thinks of light and warmth and connects it with me. I know that's cringy but I don't care.

There's only a couple of people on the top deck of the bus. They've both got earphones in so I'm not bothered they'll over-hear. I sit at the front and call Pat.

'You're just out of your session, aren't you?' she says.

'Yeah. I'm on the way to Del's now.'

'All okay?'

'It was a good session. We talked a lot, about loads of different things.'

'Your voice sounds a bit funny, Dani.'

'It's, well—'

I check the people behind me haven't taken their earphones

out. 'I think I need more time to process some of the stuff he says. Do you know what I mean?'

'Like what?'

'He said . . . ah, I'm embarrassed to say this. He says there's a part of me that wants to be punished.'

'Right,' Pat says. I hear the click of a lighter and a heavy inhale. 'Thinking about it now, it makes me feel shit.'

'These people need to be careful about what they're doing. They can open cans of worms they can't get back in.'

'I don't see how else I can sort myself out. I need to get rid of this anger. And therapy's meant to be hard, isn't it? Because you're dredging up all this stuff you normally try and keep down.'

'Your anger isn't the problem, love; it's how you deal with it. We all get angry.'

'Yeah, but I feel angry too much. It is helping – the therapy, I mean. He's got a lot of experience. He's very clever.'

'You seem better within yourself recently, but remember he's only a person, love, he's not some god.'

'I want someone I can put on a pedestal. I keep trying with different people but they all fall off.'

'You're after a hero.'

'Yeah, I—'

I stop because I can hear her husband John in the background calling her.

'You got to back yourself, Dani, put yourself on a pedestal. We'll speak tomorrow. You be good.' She always says be good at the end of a call. Be good. I'm trying to be.

Chapter Thirteen

Del, lying on his side, is propped up on one elbow. He's twirling strands of my hair around his finger. We're both stoned, and everything moves in slow motion.

'Ginger,' he says.

'Mmmm.'

'You're my first ginger.'

'Bullshit,' I'd say if I could speak.

I keep my eyes closed, too stoned to move my head. The hash Del gets is strong, and he puts loads in when he skins up. I'm knocked out after a few puffs. Del's fingers move from my hair to my collarbone, and he strokes it. He pushes his fingers into the hollow.

'You could keep something in there,' he says.

His hand moves to where my tit should be. There's hardly anything there when I'm upright; lying on my back, even less. I put my hand on his thigh. I need to wait a few minutes before I can move again. I stroke his thigh with one finger. He groans and moves on top of me. I think of Richard. I imagine there's more foreplay than a finger in the collarbone, a hand on a tit, a stroke of a thigh. I picture Richard's strong hands stroking his wife's body; I bet he goes down on her for ages. Del tries to push it in. He's close, but I can't even lift my hips to help. He guides it in with his hand. 'Jesus,' he says. He always comments on how wet I am. He must have had some shit sex.

After Del's come, I move slightly so he can put a T-shirt on top of the wet patch. He pulls up a blue carrier bag from the side of the bed and passes me a bottle of Ribena; he buys me the low-sugar version because he knows I prefer it. When we're both sitting propped up against the pillows sipping our Ribena, and have lit our cigarettes, I turn to him.

'Del, I can't come here any more. I'm trying to sort myself out. Coming here, there's too much temptation.' Stevie's at a work conference and away for the night, else I wouldn't be here now. I came to say goodbye.

'You ditchin' me?' He says it aggressively, but it's an act. It's only ever been casual between us.

'It's been great, and I like coming here, but I need to sort my shit out, get back to uni.'

'Thought there was loads of drugs at uni?'

'Yeah, there is, but when I go back, I want to be able to focus, so I need to get my shit together now.'

I lean over to pull my rucksack up from the side of the bed. I unzip it all the way around, take out a wrapped present, and put it on the duvet in front of Del.

'You always pay for the gear, and I wanted to say thanks.' He's never accepted my offers of money and I feel I owe him. Now Richard's dropped the session fee, I'm okay-ish for money. Del unwraps the present, a pair of Nikes.

'You didn't have to do that, baby.'

'I wanted to. Make sure you wear them, hey?'

'Why wouldn't I?' He brings one of the trainers to his face and smells it, breathing in deeply.

'Sometimes people are funny about new stuff. When me and my sister went to my dad's house after he'd died, we found a brand new pair of trainers Jo had given him years before. If anything was new, he wouldn't use it. Everything was from car boot sales or charity shops. The trainers he wore when he went to hospital were falling apart.'

'You giving me your old man's trainers?'

'Course not. They're new. He had smaller feet than you, anyway.'

'What are you going to study at uni?'

'English Lit. Same as I was studying before.'

'I hated English when I was at school.'

'You must have had a dodgy teacher. There's a few of them about.'

'What can you do with English Lit?' he says.

'Yeah, it is a weird one. It doesn't qualify you for any specific job. But I've always thought I'd like to teach. It's a long way off, though. The first thing is to get the degree – that's going to be enough of a mission.'

'You gonna be a teacher?'

'Yeah, that's the ultimate dream. Not kids, though. I wouldn't be able to handle teaching in a secondary school. I remember how bad I was at school and I'd hate to teach kids like me. I want to teach adults to read. When my dad went to prison, he learned to read and write properly. It let him access stuff: Shakespeare, poetry, Greek philosophers. He couldn't do that before when his reading wasn't so good.'

'Did it help him get a job?'

'No, but he got so much out of reading. I want to do that for other people. Reading is a basic human right.'

'Would you want to teach in a men's or women's prison?'

'I don't know. I generally get on better with men. I feel drawn to teaching in a men's prison. Maybe because I saw what a positive effect it had on my dad.' A lump starts to expand in my throat. 'Let's watch a film.'

We smoke another joint with the new trainers on the bed between us and watch *The Shawshank Redemption*. I can't believe Del's never seen it before. Del opens a bumper bag of pink and white marshmallows and I can tell he's enjoying the film because sometimes he holds a marshmallow in front of his mouth, with his mouth open, and forgets to put it in.

Stevie's sitting with the remote control in one hand and a mint Cornetto in the other.

'No Jo?' I pick up a sparkly pink cardigan from the back of the sofa, fold it, and then place two little pink and white socks on top of the cardigan. I sit on the sofa, at the end, as if Jo were still in her usual position.

'Gym.' He takes the top of the whole Cornetto in his mouth and bites. On the floor around him are Haribo packets and cans of Coke with twisted crisp packets sticking out of them. We stare at the TV.

'She's going to the pub after, with Hayley.'

'Nice.'

Jo hasn't told me outright she's seeing someone, so I can act like Stevie – aware of the possibility but not sure.

'She's been going to the gym a lot lately,' says Stevie.

'Probably trying to get skinny for summer. You had a good day?'

'A lot of running about after Ellie. I reckon she opened every single packet in the treat drawer, then she emptied all the packets out. Made a total mess.' He smiles. Whatever Ellie does, even if it's naughty, he'll find it funny. 'At least it tired her out – she fell asleep on the sofa, bless her.' He drinks some Coke.

'Well, I'll leave you to it.' I get up and as I'm walking out, Stevie says something I don't catch.

'Sorry?'

'You're doing well, Dan. Work, gym and all that. It's good.'

'Yeah, all right.' I hover in the doorway, looking at his shoulders and the back of his head. I could go back in and make conversation, try and cheer him up. He laughs at something on the TV and lets out a long, bubbly fart. He'll be all right.

I sit at the kitchen table and open my collected poems of Robert Lowell, one of the American Confessional Poets I was studying at university. He was mentally and emotionally fragile, and in and out of hospitals for years for bipolar disorder. Despite that, he wrote all this poetry and won loads of awards. Perhaps the poetry wouldn't have existed if it hadn't been for his mental health struggles. I admire and respect the way that people can make art from their trauma. Writing about my feelings is helping me, but it couldn't be considered art. I read 'Waking in the Blue', one of the poems we studied, and try to work out my scribbled notes around the sides. I remember being so immersed in writing that assignment that I didn't realise it had got dark and when I went to stand up, I couldn't because my legs had gone numb.

I hear the TV go off and Stevie's chair creak as he gets up. Thank god he's gone to bed so I can now go and sleep on the sofa. I realise I haven't got anything to sleep in and I couldn't be any quieter when I slide the drawer open, but Ellie sits up in bed.

'What are you doing?' she says. Her face is flushed from sleep.

'Go back to sleep, Ellie. It's late.'

'You woke me up.'

'I'm sorry about that but go back to sleep, please. I need to get some pyjamas.'

'I'm telling Daddy.' She pushes the duvet back.

'Ellie, your dad has gone to bed. I'll read you a story, come on, back to bed.' She's standing in the middle of the bed with her fists clenched.

I close the door and take a step towards her and she tips her head back and screams. Within seconds, the door is flung open and Stevie's there in his boxers.

'What's going on?' He reaches towards Ellie and she clambers into his arms.

'Dani hit me,' she says.

I laugh. 'Come on, Ellie. You mustn't tell lies. That's naughty.'

'You hit me,' she says.

'I was trying to get some clothes out of the drawer,' I say to Stevie. 'I was being quiet but she woke up.'

'Dani was making lots of noise,' Ellie says.

'Dani, you should be more organised,' Stevie says. 'Remember to take what you need out of the bedroom before Ellie goes to sleep.'

'Sorry.'

'Do you want to watch some TV with Daddy, Princess?' he says.

Now I'll have to wait even longer before I can go to bed.

'Ellie, do you want to say sorry for telling lies?' I say and she turns her head so Stevie can't see and sticks her tongue out at me.

'Can I have an ice cream, Daddy?' she says.

'Stevie, I didn't hit her.' I want him to make her apologise.

'She probably had a bad dream and got confused,' he says, and then to Ellie, pushing her fringe away from her eyes, 'What ice cream do you want, Princess?'

At half past midnight, Stevie comes into the kitchen to get a pint of water. He tells me to tell Jo to keep the noise down when she gets in. I get the spare duvet from the hall cupboard and lie on the sofa, put the TV on, turn the volume right down and the subtitles on and watch a documentary about obese people. This woman has what looks like a Chinese set meal for four piled on one plate and as she's bringing forkfuls of noodles to her mouth, she's saying, 'It makes me feel good while I'm eating it but afterwards, I'll feel bad.'

'Throw it up, love,' I whisper. 'You'll feel so much better.' And then I remind myself it doesn't make you feel better.

I hear Jo's key in the front door, turn the TV off and pretend to be asleep but she taps my shoulder then starts shaking me so much I can't keep pretending to be asleep.

'Coming out for a fag?' There's wine on her breath.

'Jo, I was asleep.'

'Sleep when you're dead. Come on.'

'Stevie said don't wake him when you get in. You need to be quiet.'

'Ah, leave it out. Come on. Now.'

If I don't, she'll get louder. I wrap the duvet around me and we go on the balcony and light up. Jo can't stop smiling.

'It's freezing out here.' I pull the duvet up so it's around my shoulders and bring my feet up so they're not on the floor. 'Ellie was a little shit earlier. She told Stevie I hit her.'

Jo laughs. 'I probably shouldn't tell you this but I found your toothbrush on her bedroom floor this morning.'

'I thought it tasted funny when I cleaned my teeth.'

'She can be a little shit. It's Stevie's fault. And Michelle's. She spoils her, too.'

'How's Hayley?' I say.

'What?'

'You went out with Hayley this evening.'

'Oh yeah.' She laughs.

'Jo, don't do this to Stevie; you're out of order.'

'He had an affair when he was married.'

'With you.'

'His choice. I'm not going to feel guilty about it.'

He does, I think. That's why he indulges Ellie so much.

'Why do you stick up for him so much all the time, anyway?' she says.

'I like him. I know even when he's being all strict with me, it's his way of trying to help. He's not perfect, but he tries to do the right thing and Jo, he really cares about you. I don't think you always see it.'

Jo shrugs. 'I had such a good night,' she says.

'Where did you go?'

'A bar in east London.'

I can see she wants to tell me.

'With?' I say.

'One of the drivers from work.'

'Shit. Do he and Stevie know each other?'

'Yeah, but they're not mates. Stevie thinks he's a prick, and Doug can't stand Stevie either.'

'Jo, what are you doing? You're going to fuck things up with Stevie.'

'I want to have some fun. He's so fit. And he was in the same prison as Dad at the same time. How funny is that?'

'Hilarious.'

'He doesn't remember Dad, but Dad might have known him.'

'What are you going to do when Stevie finds out?'

'He won't. I don't care. We're done. I'm just waiting for the right time to tell him.'

'Be careful. This might end badly.'

'All right, who the fuck are you, Captain Sensible?'

Chapter Fourteen

I meet Pat after work as we've planned to go to the old people's home. We sit side by side on the tube.

'Babs's ex-husband was put in prison yesterday,' says Pat. 'No wonder she's been all over the place.'

'Really? What for?'

'Stalking and harassment, she said. Been going on a while, apparently.'

'Stalking? Shit.'

'Hopefully she'll be happier now.'

The bloke sitting opposite us has his legs wide open and I can see the outline of his cock through his beige trousers. I wonder if Pat's noticed.

'My mum was happier when my dad was put inside,' I say.

'I reckon a lot of women are.'

'You don't hear of it being the other way round a lot, do you?' I say.

'Women harassing men?'

'I'm sure it happens, you just don't hear about it. They haven't got kids, have they – Babs and her husband?'

'No, she couldn't have them. Don't mention this to anyone at work, Dani.'

'No, no, I won't.'

I look at Pat and think Babs must confide in her as much as I do. There's something about Pat; she's so easy to talk to.

'I missed my dad when he went to prison. And it was so quick. One day he was there, and the next, gone.'

'Got to be harder on the kids,' Pat says. 'No say over any of it.'

'I was gutted.'

'Poor old thing.'

'Nobody spoke about it. Even Jo and I didn't speak about it.'

'How old were you?'

'About ten. He got out when I was fifteen. Then my mum said she was going to make sure he went back to prison and I'd never see him again.'

The tube pulls into a station and the doors open. The bloke with the beige trousers gets off and a few people get on. When we pull away again, I speak.

'I've been emailing uni. I should be able to go back in October, pick up where I left off.'

'That's what you wanted, isn't it?'

'I need to make sure I can handle it this time.'

'You will, love. You put some of that energy you put into pot wash into your uni work, and you'll do great.'

'All this work I've been doing with Richard has put me in a much better position. I'll be fine when I go back. I'll be able to handle it this time.'

Frank's in his usual chair, head bowed and reading. I watch him for a while. His eyebrows move up and down and occasionally the left side of his mouth droops. I think about what Elijah told me; how ill Frank is. While my first reaction was to back off, I then thought that wouldn't be fair, especially if his son doesn't visit. I decided to still speak to him, but not as much or for so long. There's no point getting too attached. I poke the back of the book. He looks up, irritated until he realises it's me.

He reaches for my hand, and his skin feels like cold paper. I shake it away. It's the skin-on-skin contact that bothers me.

'Want a coffee?' I say.

He tries to reply but his words come out as a croak and he coughs. 'Why not?' he eventually manages.

I look away as he tries to get up from his chair. He takes ages. I offered him help once, but he shook his head and looked pissed off. That's the good thing about my dad dying young. He'll never reach the age where every movement is painful. When I visited him in hospital a couple of days before he died, he said, 'Fifty-five – not too bad, is it?' And I wanted to shout at him that making it to fifty-five was nothing to be proud of; perhaps a hundred years ago but not nowadays. He was propped up on the hard hospital pillows with his hands resting on the covers. I wanted to rest my hand on his, the tobacco stains between his index and middle finger as bright as orange felt tip. But I couldn't, because in my family we didn't make noises when we ate, and we didn't touch each other either.

In the kitchen, I watch Frank struggle with the lid on the coffee jar for a few seconds before holding my hand out. I open it and pass it back.

'I loosened it for you,' he says.

'Not managed to get to the gym lately?'

'We did some chair yoga this morning.'

'I love yoga. When he was in prison, my dad got into it. He even had his picture on the front page of the prison magazine, doing a shoulder stand. When he came out, he kept telling me how brilliant it was and that I should do it.'

Frank passes me my coffee, and we go and sit down. Sometimes we don't speak much, but the quiet is comforting.

'What was he in prison for?'

'My dad? Fighting.'

'Did he win?'

'Frank!'

'Who was he fighting with?'

'I don't want to talk about it.'

'Must have been tough, your father being away,' Frank says.

'Yeah, but shit happens, doesn't it? He got eight years, but he was out in five.'

'And how about you?'

'What?'

'Like father like daughter? Are you a fighter?'

'No, physical violence disgusts me. Always has. I'd never fight.'

'It's for animals,' says Frank.

Elijah comes to get me when he's on break and we sit on the bench outside and smoke.

'Good chat with Frank?' Elijah says.

'It's always a good chat with Frank. He reminds me of my dad. Less mental but he likes the same kinds of books and he's quite direct in the way he speaks.'

'I see Frank reading most days.'

'My dad got into reading when he was in prison,' I say. 'He learned a lot. Before he went in, he wrote in capital letters; when he came out, he could write properly. He went to English lessons, and he told me this story about how the teacher gave them all some worksheets. He said the pair who completed the activity first could have the lunch his wife had made, and he put two huge sandwiches, roast chicken, on his desk. My dad and the bloke he was working with won the competition, and then, even better, the bloke he was working with was a vegetarian, so Dad got to have both sandwiches. He said they were the best sandwiches he'd ever had.'

'That's a good story,' Elijah says.

I wonder if that's all it was, a story.

'What does your dad do now?'

'Nothing.' I can't continue because it feels like a lorry has parked on my chest. 'He died a few months ago.'

Elijah briefly touches my arm.

'It's good your dad learned while he was in there.'

'He learned a lot.'

'When you see any documentaries about prison, it seems so bleak,' Elijah says. He checks his phone and stands up. 'I've got to get back.'

Elijah walks away but I stay on the bench. *A good story*, Elijah said. I wonder now if Dad made up these stories. If prison wasn't as good as he made out. Elijah's right, prison is bleak, but then Dad had this capacity to get huge enjoyment from the tiniest of things, the colour of a cup of tea, a lion chasing a gazelle on a wildlife documentary, a good joke – he'd throw his head back and slap his thigh and laugh and suddenly that's all there was.

While I'm smoking another roll-up, Jo messages me to say that Stevie is doing her head in and she'll pick me up from Roden Court in an hour so we can go for a drink. I go back in and sit and chat with Mary. Elaine told me she never gets visitors and she'd be glad of the company. Mary isn't as entertaining as Frank but she tells me about growing up in the East End and about her beloved Aunt Eve. I say things to her like Richard says to me, so that she knows she's been heard.

Chapter Fifteen

It's pissing it down and I get wet in the few seconds it takes to run to Jo's car. We drive to a pub a couple of minutes away. Jo has Heart radio on loud and I take this to mean she doesn't want to talk until we get to the pub. I start picking up empty cigarette packets and empty water bottles from the footwell and put them in a carrier bag. In the car park, Jo reverses into a space. She turns the engine off and shifts so she's facing me. The rain's so heavy everything through the windscreen is blurry.

'What's up, then?' I say.

'I fancied having a drink with my little sister.'

'I thought it was because Stevie was doing your head in.'

'Yeah, that as well,' she laughs.

'Nice.' Jo's been more light-hearted lately, lifted by her illicit affair and the pumping endorphins.

'Well, I wanted to ask you a favour, actually,' she says.

'What?' I get a heavy feeling in my stomach.

'I want to spend the night with Doug and I need you to cover for me.'

'How am I supposed to do that?'

'I'll tell Stevie me and you are going away for the night. I'll drop you off somewhere, then pick you up again the next morning.'

'Where will you say we're going?'

'Back to see some old school friends in Norfolk.'

'Right.'

'I'll give you some money to stay in a Premier Inn or go and stay at one of your mates. If Stevie calls, don't answer. Even better, keep your phone off. I'll tell him where we're going has bad reception.'

'When's this supposed to be happening?'

'Not sure exactly. I wanted to do it next weekend but Stevie wants to go out for his birthday when we've got Ellie. Make sure you're available for that, yeah? Saturday night.'

'Why don't you finish with him so you don't have to sneak around?'

'There's always an overlap with one relationship ending and another one beginning. I can't finish with Stevie so close to his birthday. I'll wait until after.'

'That's going to be a fun evening.'

'He's booked a table at Louis and Luna's.'

'Ellie's favourite,' I say.

'I'm seeing it as a goodbye dinner.'

'It's his birthday, Jo. It's not nice to be looking at it like that when he doesn't know.' She shrugs. 'Will you move out?' It's a selfish question. I want to know for me, not her. If she moves out, I'll have to look for somewhere else.

'I'm hoping he will. You might need to pay more rent.'

How will I afford that? I'm already overdrawn at the end of each month. Stopping my therapy would save money, but I can't stop seeing Richard. I'll look into taking a loan.

'Is it serious with this new one then?'

'Not sure. I prefer being with Doug to being with Stevie.'

'Because of the novelty.'

'No, he's got more about him.' She looks at her nails. 'I

remember once, Dad told me not to have kids with Stevie.'

'Did he? Why did he say that?'

'Because evolution would start going backwards and we'd all end up as apes.'

I clear my throat to cover a laugh.

'Dad told me that I'd only know a man was truly in love with me if he killed himself,' I say.

'Yeah. I don't think Dad gave the best relationship advice.'

'What do you think he'd have made of Doug, then?'

'No idea – but he's definitely something special.'

'It's because it's early days and you're both on your best behaviour. In a year's time, you'll be sitting with him in your PJs watching TV and bored again.'

'No, he's not like Stevie. He's the exact opposite. He hasn't even got a TV at his flat. He goes out all the time.'

'Where?'

'Out and about.' She turns the engine on so she can open the window slightly and lights a cigarette. 'He's got a court case coming up soon.'

'Yeah?' I take my tobacco out from my bag and make a roll-up.

'He was at a traffic light and this guy behind was beeping him to go even though the light was red.'

I nod like Richard would at this point.

'You don't do that,' says Jo. 'So Doug jumped out of his car, took a baseball bat from the boot and started bashing the bloke's car. He didn't break any windows or anything, just dented the bonnet and doors a bit. The guy was crying his eyes out.'

'Jo, seriously, this impresses you?'

She flicks ash out of the window. Her eyes are bright. 'You shouldn't beep at someone to go through a red light.'

'You're looking for excitement. Why don't you do a skydive

or something? Is bungee jumping still a thing?'

She adjusts the rearview mirror and strokes her neck.

'Completely lost my double chin. Have you noticed? I put on so much weight when I got with Stevie.'

'You can't blame him for that. You're the one holding the spoon.'

She smiles. 'When me and Stevie first started going out, we were eating ice cream in bed and I dropped some here.' She raises a hand to her breastbone. 'I said, "Stevie, sort this out for me," and do you know what he did?'

'I'm not sure I want to.'

'He leaned over me, scraped the ice cream off with his spoon, and ate it. It says all you need to know about him. It wouldn't have been like that with Doug.'

'Yeah, yeah,' I cut her short. We don't talk about sex.

'You're looking good at the moment,' she says.

'Thanks. The therapy's helping.'

'What do you talk about?'

'Lots of things.'

'Like what?'

'Last session it was about Mum's boyfriends.' I can't see Jo's face as she's looking out of her side window. 'Who did you hate the most?'

She takes a long inhale on her cigarette and exhales slowly.

'Mike,' she says. 'Definitely Mike.'

The rain sounds harder on the windscreen. The smell of the air freshener hanging from the mirror, a pink and a purple jelly bean, competes with the cigarette smoke. I think of Mike's yellow-tinted glasses.

'Anyway, probably the weekend after next then,' she says.

'Weekend after next?'

'Going to Norfolk.'

'Right.'

I try to get Mike's face out of my head.

'Tell me some news, then,' Jo says.

'It's all going quite well, actually. I don't want to jinx myself but I feel like I'm getting my shit together.'

'That's great. Are you chatting to anyone at the moment?'

'Not interested, to be honest. I don't want to end up with another Christy.'

'Christy.' She wrinkles her nose. 'Do you ever hear from him?'

'Nothing. When we broke up, he told me I was a one-hundred-and-eighty-day one-night stand.'

'What's that supposed to mean?'

'We were together six months. He was going for the jugular.'

'Dad hated him, didn't he?'

'I thought they'd get on because Christy was so funny, but obviously not.'

'That time he asked Christy to leave the house . . .'

'Stevie was good, trying to keep the peace.'

'Christy was off his face, wasn't he?' she says.

'Yep. Even more than normal.'

The rain stops.

She opens the car door. 'Are we going in for a drink or what?' she says.

Chapter Sixteen

'How are you and I in this space today?' says Richard.

'I can't speak for you, but I'm okay. I had a good chat with Elijah on Thursday. He works at Roden Court.'

'Roden Court?'

'The old people's home, Roden Court – where Pat's mum Edie lives, and Frank.'

'Oh yes.'

'He's a nice guy. I like him.'

'What position does he hold there?'

'He's just a carer, I suppose. I'm not sure of his official job title.'

'A junior position.'

'He's passionate about his work. He's nice to talk to. I was talking to him about my dad.'

I notice a smear on the mirror above the fireplace and take a tissue from the box on the table next to me. Richard doesn't say anything as I rub the smear until it disappears, then throw the tissue in the bin. There's a blue cheese-and-onion crisp packet in the bin, but it can't be Richard's. I doubt he eats crisps. If he wants a savoury snack, he probably has a slice of brie on a wholewheat cracker or pretzels dipped in a dip with a name that's hard to pronounce.

'I don't think you've ever told me your father's name,' Richard says.

'Haven't I?'

'No.'

'Or perhaps I have, but you just don't remember. Like you didn't remember what Roden Court was.' Even with Richard cutting his fee by half, the sessions are still expensive and I think he should remember what I talk about.

'Your father's name?' he says.

I don't answer and then I worry he'll say what he did before, that I like withholding information because it makes me feel powerful.

'Danny,' I say. 'My dad's name was Danny.'

'You were named after him?'

'Yeah.'

'How do you feel about that?'

'Good. I like the name.'

'One might say it's a narcissistic trait, naming one's child after oneself.'

'Or traditional,' I say. 'My dad wasn't a narcissist. Not at all.'

'That triggered something in you, didn't it, Dani? You look annoyed.'

'Is that why you said it? Are you trying to annoy me? Sometimes I think you are, to see how I'll react.'

'It might be useful to explore why you're feeling angry about what I've said.'

'I don't like hearing people say things about him that aren't true. My dad wasn't a narcissist. He beat someone up, but he was punished for that. He served his time.' But then he died four years after he got out and I feel cheated that he was taken away twice. I look at the picture of the girl and the man and bite the inside of my cheek so hard it stings.

'You've told me before that he was in prison for fighting but not given me any more detail. It could be helpful to explore further.'

'I will, just not yet.'

'How long was your father in prison for?'

'Five years.'

'Did you visit him there?'

'There was nobody who'd take us. It was far away.'

'Did you write to him?'

'No. But he wrote to us. Jo found letters from him on top of Mum's wardrobe. Then he stopped writing, or perhaps Mum found a better hiding place.'

I've still got the letters he sent. I keep them in a clear plastic document wallet with my university essays. Dad would like that.

'I imagine you had a great sense of loss during that time of not seeing him.'

Yes. There was a great gaping wound that made me feel hollow. I ate to try to fill it. It didn't work. I take some tissues.

The room is still. Richard doesn't speak. He doesn't try to deny my feelings, minimise them or make me feel better. He sits with me.

I look in the direction of the picture but I can't see it properly because my eyes are full of water.

'He's gone for good this time, hasn't he?' I say.

Richard closes his eyes and gives the tiniest of nods.

I don't know how much time passes. I keep taking tissues from the box until there are none left then I go to the client bathroom to get more tissue. I splash water on my face and dry my face on my T-shirt because I don't want to use the hand towel.

'You said to think about the impact the atmosphere at home would have had on me when I was a child. Before he went,' I say when I sit back down.

137

'Yes.'

'It was bad, but there were fun times too, because Dad was so dynamic and so much fun and he laughed and joked all the time. He'd take me and Jo to the forest and he'd pretend there were witches or trolls chasing us and we'd run until we couldn't breathe or we fell over. He'd take us to the beach in the evening and pay us to go in the sea. He had to offer money because it was so cold. He'd get us to jump off the shed roof and catch us.'

'Happy memories,' says Richard.

'We had an open fire in the living room and he'd build it up until it roared and read me and Jo stories. He'd put music on, get up on the table and dance. Mum never joined in, so when Dad left, it was all just shit. She was out working more than full time and we never saw her. She'd come home late, eat the dinner we'd left her in the microwave and go to bed. So yes, the times when he was laying into Mum or exploding about things were stressful, but he was so good in other ways. And those were the things I missed. I felt weaker without a dad. When he went, I felt like there was nobody there to protect me.'

'You didn't feel your mother could protect you?'

'God no.'

'Tell me more about your father,' Richard says.

'When he was in prison, he got into English and yoga, he learned good things. That's why I went for English at uni. After Dad came out, he used to speak about Shakespeare a lot. *Richard III* was his favourite. And poetry. He wrote a lot of poetry. Sometimes he'd send it anonymously to the woman in the post office. He pushed me to go to university. It was so important to him I went. He knew Jo wasn't interested but he stood a chance with me going. When I started there, he wanted to hear all about it – the lectures, the tutors, the other students. He loved it.'

'Was he able to hold on to this goodness? These things that were nourishing that he learned in prison?'

'He still mixed with people who were dodgy but not as bad as before he went in. He didn't want to go back. He carried on reading.'

'He liked to read.'

I look at Richard's books and nod.

'When he got out, he was put in a house with two men. They were both called Martin, so Dad called them Six Foot Two and Six Foot Five.'

I can see by Richard's face that he doesn't get it. For an educated man, he can be slow.

'Their heights. Six Foot Two got a girlfriend who couldn't read and write. Dad wanted me to teach her, but I said no, so he got the woman who lived over the road to teach her.'

'He valued education.'

'Yeah, he did.'

'What will becoming educated mean to you, Dani?'

'People won't be able to look down on me.'

'Why would they?'

'If I haven't been to university, there's nothing to prove I'm worth something.'

'Why do you feel you need to be educated to prove you're worth something? You are important, Dani, educated or not.'

'It's okay for you. You've studied, you've learned, you've achieved. Would you still feel as confident without your qualifications?'

'I would still have self-worth.'

'Until I get that certificate stating I've got a degree, I won't feel I'm worth anything. The certificate will be the beginning of all things good.'

'I can hear how important it is to you.'

'Good.'

We sit for a while. I feel a bit worn out from all the talking but I'm pleased I've shared so much about my dad with Richard.

'Diogenes said something I love,' I say. 'When he saw a girl learning to read, he said, "I see a sword being sharpened." Isn't that great? It's power, isn't it? When you're educated, you have more power.'

'That's true,' he says. 'Dani, at the start of the session, you were speaking about Elijah. I wonder if there is anything else that draws you to him, apart from that you find him easy to talk to.'

I think about it.

'He's good-looking, I think I told you before, but it's in an unconventional way, and he doesn't realise how attractive he is. He's got good principles. But, carrying on with what I was saying before, I think it's linked with when I feel a bit depressed, this feeling I'm not worth anything, and I can't see a way around it, apart from getting a degree, getting a good job and being able to help others.'

'Do you remember a time when you felt good about yourself, Dani?'

'Not really. The doctor put me on Prozac when I was fifteen but I stopped taking it because it made me aggressive. I came home from school one day and thought someone was in the house, so I got the biggest kitchen knife we had and went around kicking all the doors open. That wasn't me. I didn't like the fact I'd done that, so I stopped taking it. Then I got depressed. People talk about depression being like a black dog, but it's a bit of white ceiling.' I stop to let Richard speak because he's raised his hand like a traffic warden and is shaking his head. 'What?'

'Slow down, Dani. You speak so quickly.'

'Sorry.' I make an effort to speak more slowly. 'All I want to do when I'm feeling low is lie on my back and look at the ceiling. A single patch of white ceiling. I'm feeling okay now, so that's why I can talk about it clearly. If I was in it at the moment, depressed, I'd find it harder to talk about.' There's something else I want to tell him. He could pass it on to another client, and it could help. 'The best thing I ever learned about how to deal with depression is to take it hour by hour. Focus on getting through the next hour, or if that's too much, getting through ten minutes.'

Richard leans forward.

'What makes you feel good about yourself now?'

'I'm trying to get my self-esteem from other places, not from men finding me attractive. That's how I used to feel good about myself. I think I need to work at developing my self-esteem in other ways.'

'Feeling attractive to men, feeling that male gaze is something that makes you feel good.'

'Yes, but it's a cheap fix that quickly goes. I made a list once of all the men I'd slept with. I wrote down their names and where they were from. I can't remember all the names but I remember the places: Essex, Italy, Nigeria, Spain, Northern Ireland, Bulgaria, Colombia, Jamaica, Liverpool, Hartlepool, London. I wish I'd visited all those places – well, I'm not bothered about Hartlepool – but I wish I'd visited those places rather than sleeping with people from them. Do you know what I mean?'

'Do you think you have a "type"?'

'No. But I suppose if I had to say, it would be tall, dark hair, well educated, clever, someone who likes reading.'

I turn from looking at the bookshelf to Richard and cover my face when I realise what I've said.

'How are you and I in this space today?' Richard says again.

'It's okay, same as usual. I feel better about telling you stuff I haven't before, about the Prozac, and about feeling shit about myself. I suppose there's an element of having to work through all this stuff to get better. I'm talking a lot today, aren't I? It feels productive.'

'I think you're doing well, Dani.'

'I'm grateful for your help. It's making a difference. I feel better in general, like I'm finally getting my shit together, you know? On the right track.'

'Anything else?' he says. 'About the space between us?'

I scrunch down into the chair and make my hands into fists. 'Can we go back to the depression?'

'I think you are scared of being vulnerable, in here, with me. Paradoxically, it's being vulnerable that will make you stronger. We have discussed this.'

'I know. I am trying. I've told you things I've never told anyone before.'

He smooths his hands together. He makes circles on the palm of one hand with his thumb.

'That's good, but I need to hear you speak about your feelings towards me.'

'They're good feelings,' I say and then make a weird whistling noise like I'm trying to call a dog back.

'You have good feelings towards me, Dani,' he smiles.

My heart is beating out of its chest. My mouth has gone dry. As if I could sit here and talk about how I've fantasised about lying on his swirly rug with him fucking me hard. I've written about it. I got so turned on when I was describing it that I had to go and have a shower. I stood under the warm water and rubbed a bottle of Dove shower gel against myself until I came. My face is hot and it's made worse by the thought that Richard can read what's in my head.

'How are you feeling, Dani? Right now?' says Richard.

I can't tell him I'm thinking about what it would be like to lie on the couch. Would I need to take my shoes off? Would I cover myself with the folded blanket at the end of the couch, or would Richard put it over me? I imagine coming in one day and telling him I'm ready to try it. Lie there with my eyes closed, warm under the blanket. It does feel easier and I tell him things I've never told anyone. I imagine Richard listening to me and responding in his gentle voice. Then I imagine him getting up from his chair, kneeling down by the couch and sliding a strong hand under the blanket. We don't speak. There's no need to speak.

'We talk a lot in some sessions,' I say eventually. 'I need a little more time to think about what we've talked about, to be honest.'

'I know sometimes it's hard for you to engage with what we're discussing, and how difficult feelings must arise, but I admire your strength, and you are doing well.'

'I've never thought of myself as being strong.' I try to think of a time when I could say I've been brave or held it together. None come to mind.

Richard looks at the clock on the mantelpiece.

'And it's time,' he says. 'I'm afraid we have to leave it there for today, Dani.'

I hold a hand up. 'Just one more thing, quickly. Did you like what I gave you?'

He pauses.

'The lighter?' I say.

'The lighter was a thoughtful gift, Dani. And with my initials engraved too. Yes, I like it. Thank you.' He stands.

As I get up, my foot catches in the strap of my rucksack. I fall forward and land on my hands and knees. I try and get up as fast as I can. My face is burning. Graceless, clumsy, no finesse. Richard comes over.

'Are you okay?' he reaches a hand towards me. I take it, and he

143

pulls me up. I've never stood so close to him. It's the first time we've touched and his hand is firm around mine. He brings my hand up in the thin space between us and for a moment, I think he's going to kiss it, but he lets my hand go and opens the door.

'I look forward to seeing you next week, Dani.'

I call Del as I'm walking down the road and ask if I can come over. I fidget the whole time on the bus. I keep looking at my right hand because Richard held it, and wondering what he was thinking as he held it. I hope that Richard didn't notice my bitten-down nails. I practically run from the bus stop to Del's house. His mum lets me in, and I go straight to Del's bedroom. He's lying on top of his duvet, watching TV and smoking a joint. I love the shape of his arms, the sleek bulges. I love his long legs, I love the hint of a six-pack.

'Thought you weren't coming any more?'

I take my coat and T-shirt off and drop them on the floor.

'I won't do any drugs.'

He watches as I take my jeans off. It's fine being here, even though I said I wasn't going to any more, because I'm getting it together.

'You missed me?' he puts his joint in the ashtray, lies back on the bed and opens his arms wide.

'Yeah.'

He's already hard. I lie next to him and he's inside me within seconds. I close my eyes and wrap my legs around his neck and pull him into me so he can get in deeper. I get him on his back, so I can grind down on him. I think of Richard holding my hand and the way he looked at me just before I thought he was going to kiss it. Del keeps slipping out because I'm so wet.

Chapter Seventeen

Stevie drives us to Louis and Luna's. I sit in the back with Ellie and we play I-spy. The atmosphere is good. Stevie and Ellie are happy to be going to the restaurant. He likes the big portions and she likes the kids' play area, which has lots of soft foam cushions in primary colours. We're taken to our table. We read the menus and the waiter takes our order.

I give Stevie an expensive T-shirt that I got from the men's department. I used my staff discount card and got twenty-five per cent off. He holds it up at arm's length and smiles at it. Jo gives Stevie tickets for the next Ipswich match and says she doesn't mind if he wants to take Pavan rather than her and make a day of it.

Jo and Stevie take Ellie to the play area and hold hands while they walk across the restaurant. She's making an effort as it's his birthday but it seems duplicitous. Because it is.

I stand the menu up in front of me and think about Dad's last birthday. He unwrapped the first birthday present, held it, then rotated his wrist to look at it from another angle. It was a Swiss army knife, inexpensive because I was a student and didn't have much money. 'That's shit,' he said, placing it to one side. He picked up the next present and opened it. A lavender-scented candle: I thought the smell might help him

relax. Again, a rotation of the wrist as he looked at it from another angle, another 'shit' as it joined the Swiss army knife. Third
present. I held my breath. He rolled a thin cigarette, lit it and
balanced it on the edge of the ashtray. He tore at the paper,
saw a hint of what was inside and coughed to hide a smile. It
was a brown and white plastic cow, about the size of a toaster.
He'd seen it in the window of the Sue Ryder charity shop as
we were walking past the week before and, pointing, said, 'You
can get me that, for my birthday, if you like.' He moved the
cow around in his hands, smoothed its flanks with his thumbs,
and stood it up on the table in front of him. He took a drag
from his roll-up, exhaled the smoke through his nostrils and said,
'Good.'

Jo and Stevie come back. Ellie's pink in the face. Stevie has
his arm around Jo's waist and tells me they're popping out so Jo
can have a cigarette.

Ellie takes a yellow crayon from the plastic cup and starts to
colour in the dinosaur on her large paper place mat.

'Can you help me, Dan?'

I take a blue crayon and start to colour the sky.

'No.' She snatches the blue crayon out of my hand and shoves
in an orange one. 'Do the slide first.'

We colour for a couple of minutes. Ellie slips off her chair and
comes to sit on my lap.

'Don't you want to sit on your chair so we have more space?'
She ignores me. I watch her scrawling over the shapes. She
makes no effort to stay in the lines.

Stevie and Jo come back and the starters arrive. Jo and I didn't
want any. Ellie stays on my lap and eats her ovals of green-
specked garlic bread. I watch Stevie digging into his mussels.

'Aren't you checking for beards?' I say.

'What are you on about now, Dan?'

'Beards on the mussels. You should check in case they've not taken them all off.'

'Beards?'

'Have a look at where the lips of the mussel meet. If there's a tangle of these thin brown thread things, pull it off. You don't want to eat the beard.'

'I don't want to eat any of it now, Dan.' He pushes the bowl away from him and throws his serviette over the top of it.

But isn't it better to know about the beards than eat them? 'I'm sorry, I didn't realise you'd react like that.'

'Dani, why did you have to tell him about the beards?' Jo says.

'I thought I was being helpful. Isn't it better that he knows, instead of eating them for years and years and then finding out?'

'He probably would never have found out,' says Jo. 'And what you don't know can't hurt you.'

I shake my head at her. She's well out of order.

The waiter takes away the starters and brings the mains.

Stevie ordered a massive combo platter, Jo a chicken salad, dressing on the side, Ellie fish fingers. I ordered soup, the least calorific dish on the menu. Stevie stares at his plate a moment, then calls the waiter back and tells him they've forgotten to add the breaded prawns.

I start to ask Stevie if he knows about the shit-line in prawns but decide against it. I'm about to tell Ellie to go back to her chair when she reaches out and grabs at my soup bowl. She has dimples instead of knuckles, and these fold over and clasp the rim of the bowl.

'Ellie, don't do that please.' I could unpeel her fingers from the bowl, but I want her to listen to me and do what I'm telling her to for once. 'Let go, Ellie,' I say in a stern voice. The bowl moves slowly, closer to us. 'Stop it now, Ellie.' I'm not backing down on this one. 'Enough,' I shout. Stevie turns from his conversation with Jo; his face creases as he sees what's happening and he reaches across to take Ellie's hand away, but he's not quick enough, and the soup bowl jerks to the edge of the table and pours onto Ellie and me. There's a second of silence, and then as I lift her to put her down, she screams, and Stevie jumps up so fast his chair falls back behind him. I take a serviette from the table and brush at the soup running down Ellie's sparkly tights. Stevie grabs hold of Ellie, who's still screaming, lifts her with one arm around the back of her legs and runs towards the restaurant kitchen. Jo says, 'Christ,' and leans forward.

'You all right, Dan?'

'Yeah, it wasn't that hot,' I say, although my thighs are burning. I take a serviette and wipe it off my jeans. There's not much. Most of it went on Ellie. Jo heads after Stevie and Ellie. The people next to us are staring and not even trying to hide it. I want to shout at them, tell them their dinner conversation must be really fucking boring if they can be so easily distracted.

I lock myself in a toilet cubicle and rest my head against the door on a poster about bowel cancer. I gently bang my head a few times then I wipe my jeans with tissue. It disintegrates on my thighs. I don't want to leave this cubicle. I don't want to walk back to our table with the untouched meals, and the people looking. I flush the chain, unlock the door and come out. I wash my hands and look in the mirror and hate my face.

At the table, there are splashes of soup on the floor around my chair. I stop a waiter going past me and insist he gets me a cloth. I'm on my hands and knees cleaning up the soup when Jo's shoes appear in front of me.

'Leave it, Dan. The waiter'll sort it out.'

I sit back on my heels.

'How's Ellie?'

'Stevie wants to take her to hospital. I think he's overreacting but—'

'Shit. Is it that bad?'

'Well, her legs are red; I think he wants to be on the safe side . . .'

Stevie comes over, still holding Ellie, who's sobbing into his neck.

'What the fuck were you playing at, Dan?'

'What?'

'You pulled her back when she was holding the soup.'

'I was trying to make her let go.'

'Where was your brain? What is going on in there?'

He jabs a finger twice at his temple.

'Come on, Stevie,' Jo says. 'Don't blame Dan. It wasn't her fault.'

'I'm taking Ellie to hospital. Are you coming or not?' He walks away before Jo can answer.

Jo takes her bag from the floor near her seat. 'Can you pay, please? I'll sort you out later or you can take it off the rent.'

'Yeah,' I say, although I know there's not enough in my account.

'Dani, that wasn't your fault,' Jo says again before she walks away.

I sit at the table with the cooling jumbo platter, chicken salad, fish fingers and the soup-stained tablecloth. I drink my wine, then Jo's wine. I drink Stevie's wine and finish the bottle. The waiter asks me if he should clear the plates and I say yes and ask him for a double vodka and Diet Coke. When the waiter brings it, he puts the bill on the table although I haven't asked for it. I finish my drink and I know I can't sit here any longer. I call Pat and she transfers money while I'm on the phone. She cuts me short and says she knows I will when I say I'll pay her back as soon as I can.

At The Green Man across the road, I order a double vodka and Diet Coke and sit outside and smoke. I message Stevie that I'm sorry. A drunk guy with hair only above his ears, who smells like he's shit himself, comes and sits next to me.

The drunk guy asks where I'm from and when I say Essex, he tells me I'm lying because with hair and eyes like mine, I must be Scottish. He's from Scotland, and he prefers Scottish people to English people. The drunk guy says honesty is important and that's why he likes people who are from Scotland because they don't tell lies.

I tell the drunk guy I have to meet a friend and leave. I go to another pub around the corner.

I order two double vodkas with Diet Coke. I go outside and over to a couple of blokes sitting at a table that has a spare chair.

'Mind if I sit here?'

'Go for it,' the one with the baseball cap says. We introduce ourselves. The one with the baseball cap is Al, the one without the baseball cap, Eduardo.

'You having a good night?' Al says.

'Yeah, great.' I roll a cigarette.

'Waiting for a friend?' Al says, nodding at my two drinks.

'No, it saves going back to the bar.'

I take Dad's Zippo and try to light my cigarette, but it's run out of gas. Eduardo leans forward and lights my roll-up for me, then picks up telling a story that it sounds like he was halfway through before I interrupted. I try to follow, but I can't concentrate. I try to catch Al's eye but he's too busy listening to Eduardo. I stretch my arms above my head, and when I bring my arms down, I put my hand on Eduardo's thigh. He looks at me briefly but carries on talking to Al. I slide my hand further up his thigh and rub it.

'You all right, love?' He smiles but doesn't take my hand away.

'I'm good, you?'

He finishes his pint.

'What are you drinking?' he says.

Eduardo goes to the bar, and I look at Al.

'You're incredibly good-looking,' I say. I stretch my leg out and run my shin up his lower leg. He returns the pressure.

'So are you.'

Al's wearing sunglasses so I can't see his eyes but he has a sexy jawline and I like the way he was so attentive to Eduardo, listening to him and enthusiastic about the story, laughing and smiling in places.

I half stand over the table, lean forward and knock my forehead on his cap before I find his mouth. Eduardo comes back with the drinks and says, 'Hey! You moving in on my woman?' He sits next to me, and I put my hand back on his thigh and start rubbing again. Ash from my roll-up drops onto his jeans, and I like how he brushes it off without saying anything. Eduardo puts his arm around my waist and squeezes. I pull his hand up higher so his hand covers my tit. He mouths something at Al. I rub Eduardo's hard-on through his jeans, then I put my hand on the back of his neck and pull his face towards mine. We kiss.

'Let's go somewhere else,' I say.

'Al, back in a minute,' Eduardo says.

'We can't leave Al here on his own,' I say. Al stubs out his cigarette and stands up.

I know Eduardo has somewhere in mind as he's walking with a purpose. I stumble over a kerb, and he and Al are protective, grabbing at my elbows and making sure I don't fall. We get to Mecca Bingo, and Eduardo leads us round the back, where it stinks of piss and bins.

Me and Eduardo put our arms around each other at the same time and kiss, then I stop and pull Al so he's behind me and push my arse into his crotch while I'm kissing Eduardo. I want them both at the same time. I want to be full up. I want to feel of service.

When they asked Diogenes what they should do with his body after his death, he said he wanted it thrown outside the city gates for the dogs to feed on. I understood why he said that. Letting others, even dogs, benefit from your body. Feeling of use.

I undo Eduardo's belt and unzip his flies. He's not wearing boxers so his cock springs out and feels like warm velvet in my hand. I push my jeans down and Eduardo pulls at my knickers until they rip. It's clumsy for a moment while Eduardo lifts me. Al tries to help him. I wrap my legs around Eduardo's waist, and he lowers me down onto him. I want Al too, but the angles aren't right. I get down and put my hands against the wall. The floor slides back and forward beneath me so I close my eyes. I don't know which one is fucking me but he's doing it so hard my arms give and the side of my face grazes the bricks.

'Smile,' one of them says, and I realise he's filming. I tip my head forward so my hair falls over my face.

The one fucking me grunts and pulls out. Then I like it more because the other one's a lot bigger and it fills me up better.

They don't say goodbye. As they walk away, they're laughing. One of the legs of my jeans is damp when I put them back on. I roll a cigarette and take out Dad's Zippo but I can't get a flame.

I walk down the high street until I get to Kam's Kebabs and ask a man queuing if I can have a light. I smoke my roll-up until it burns my fingers, then I go in. I order a quarter-pounder burger and chips, a large lamb doner kebab and a bottle of Diet Coke. The lights are too bright in the shop and the canned drinks behind the glass too colourful. I go back outside and call Naz to come and pick me up. I don't want to go back to the flat, but I've got nowhere else to go and work tomorrow.

I've finished the doner by the time Naz arrives. When I get in the car, I eat the burger. I hold a chip in front of Naz's face. He shakes his head and pushes my hand away.

'Good night?' he says but he's not looking at me. He keeps his eyes on the road. Naz could pull over somewhere and fuck me. He wouldn't even need to take my knickers off because they're somewhere behind the bingo hall. I wouldn't care. I am a dead Diogenes carcass letting people benefit from me. Naz could lean over, recline my seat, climb on top, unzip his jeans and pound away. I'd turn my head to the side and breathe through my nose so he didn't get my burger and onion breath.

'Been to the pub?' Naz says.

'Yeah. I've been to the pub. How are you, Naz? You been busy tonight?'

'Payday next weekend, this is a quiet weekend.' He stares in front.

I eat like a dog. The burger slips out of the bun when I pick it up and the sauce goes all over my hands and fingers when I try to put it back in. Sauce runs down my chin and drips on my chest. I wipe it away with the back of my hand. The tray shifts and a few chips fall on the floor. I see Naz look at the floor in front of me and shake his head.

'You got a problem, Naz?'

'You're making a mess.'

'For fuck's sake, I'll sort it out in a minute, okay? When I get home.'

Naz pulls up in front of the flats. A crowd of blokes are hanging around the entrance, drinking from cans and smoking. I bend forward to pick up the chips, but Naz tells me to leave it. He nods towards the men.

'You know them?'

There's nobody I recognise.

'Yeah, it's fine.' I give Naz a tenner and tell him to keep the change. I slam the car door harder than I mean to.

'All right, lads?' I say as I get close.

They're lit up in Naz's headlights and I wonder why he's not driven off yet. Probably still picking up chips.

One of the men says something, they all laugh, and one of them barks. I push through the heavy doors and when the lift comes, I don't hold my breath, although the smell is worse than ever. I let myself into the flat and bend down to take my shoes off. My stomach is bloated hard with the burger and chips and kebab, all the vodka and Diet Coke. I belch and it tastes of garlic sauce and doner meat. I want to make myself sick, but Stevie would hear.

When I'm on the toilet, I see the medicine cabinet is slightly open, and I catch sight of familiar-looking packaging. Laxatives – the same brand I used to take every day. It's a box of thirty and there's only a couple missing. I pop ten through the foil and hold my head under the tap to wash them down. As I'm bending over the sink, my jeans feel even tighter around my stomach. I take another ten and put the box back. I'll buy some more tomorrow and replace them before anybody notices.

Stevie's sitting on the sofa with Ellie leaning into him, asleep. She's got a bright white bandage on her arm.

'I'm so sorry, Stevie.' I can't look at him.

'It's done now.'

'How is she?'

'You're drunk. We'll talk in the morning. Have Ellie's bed. I'm going to sleep here with her. She wants to be with her dad.'

Chapter Eighteen

The bed is wet. I've pissed the bed. I shouldn't even be in the bed – it's Ellie's weekend so I should be on the sofa. I push the covers back, and then the smell hits. I am a disgusting piece of shit. I have shit Ellie's bed.

The diarrhoea has gone up my back and down my legs and my T-shirt is stuck to my skin. I sit up and realise if I move off the bed, it will drip over the carpet. *You weirdo piece of shit.* I take a pillowcase off a pillow, try to mop some of it up. The smell makes me gag. I take off my T-shirt and put my dressing gown on, wrapping the cord tight around my waist. When I take the sheet off the bed, there's a deep yellow stain on the mattress. I spread a towel over it, pick up all the filthy sheets and creep to the washing machine. I add seven capsules and turn it on to a ninety-degree wash. I shower, and wash my dressing gown by hand. I shampoo my hair twice, as fast as I can. I'm terrified someone will walk in the bedroom while I'm in here and see the stain and I'll hear a shout of disgust. When I get out of the shower, I put my dressing gown over the chair on the balcony to dry. I make half a cup of instant coffee and fill a bowl with water and washing-up liquid. I pour the coffee over the stain and scrub at the mattress. I pray nobody will come in and catch me. The stain spreads but weakens in colour. Better. It's better than it was, but still bad. I open the window and hope as the mattress dries, the stain will fade. When I'm dressed for work, I look round the living-room door. Stevie and Ellie are sleeping on the sofa. I leave a note in the kitchen saying so sorry for spilling coffee over the bed. I want them to see it before they see the bed. I could text, but Stevie will see the note against the kettle quicker.

I go straight to pot wash when I get to work, and every time someone comes near me, I move away from them in case they can smell shit. I showered on the hottest setting and used a whole bottle of shower gel but I don't know how long I was lying in the shit and I feel like it's seeped through my pores.

'You all right, love?' Pat says.

I hold up my palm and shake my head. I can feel my mouth going.

'You know where I am.' She puts her hand on my shoulder.

'Give me some space,' I say.

I have a banging headache, and I'm so thirsty, but I won't let myself stop and have a drink.

'Careful, Dani, this tray is hot. Why are you crying? Are you all right?' Maureen says.

'Just a headache.' I touch my head. 'Hangover.'

'Well, you've only got yourself to blame.'

'You're right,' I say as I know the quickest way to get rid of her is to agree.

On my lunch break, I stand around the corner from the smoking shed so I have some privacy and call Jo to ask how Ellie is.

'She's okay. Stevie got her into the kitchen and under the cold water tap so quickly it wasn't as bad as it could have been. The kitchen staff were brilliant too. You know what Ellie's like; she can make a right fuss.'

'She's all right then?'

Jo exhales. I picture the smoke coming from her mouth and fading into the air.

'She's fine.'

'What about her arm? I saw she had a bandage.'

'Stevie put it on to distract her while the nurse was looking at her legs. What time are you back?'

'Usual time. I'm not going to the gym. I didn't have time to pack my stuff after spilling the coffee.' I remember I need to replace the laxatives. 'But I might be a bit later as I need to go to the shops.'

There's a couple of beats of silence.

'Right,' she says.

'Do you need anything from the shops?' I say.

'Nah, I'll ask Stevie; hang on.' She shouts to him. 'Nah, you're fine,' she says. I hear a door shut. 'I'm going out tonight, but Stevie's got the hump about it. He thinks I should stay in because of Ellie.'

'I thought you said she was okay?'

'She's fine. He's using it as an excuse to get me to stay in.'

'Okay.'

'Anyway, it was just to give you a heads-up.'

'Shall I make dinner?' I know this is what she's angling for. Stevie always cooks, but he'll be wanting to give Ellie his undivided attention.

'Yeah, that would be good. Not soup, though.'

I feel sorry for Stevie for getting involved with this family. His girlfriend shagging a lorry driver from work and her younger sister shitting his daughter's bed. He should have stayed with Michelle.

After work, I buy macaroni, cheddar and a jar of deluxe cheese sauce. I pick up the biggest, most expensive Easter egg I can find for Ellie and two smaller eggs: one for Stevie, one for Frank that I'll take next time I go to visit him at the old people's home.

When I get back to the flat, I go straight to the bathroom to replace the laxatives but the box isn't in the cabinet. I'm sure I put it back last night, but I must have chucked it. It wouldn't be the first time I've wiped something I've done while pissed. I take out the couple that were missing from the original box and put the new box in the cabinet.

I stand in the doorway to the living room. Stevie and Ellie are pretty much in the same positions they were in last night – she's nestled in the crook of his arm, and they're watching *Trolls* again with the subtitles on as Stevie thinks it helps Ellie learn to read. Ellie's sucking her thumb.

'Are you okay, Ellie?'

She ignores me.

'She's all right. We've been having a chill-out day,' says Stevie but he stays watching the TV and doesn't look at me when he says it.

While I'm unpacking the shopping, Stevie comes into the kitchen.

'I'm so sorry about what happened last night. I wanted her not to ignore me for once,' I say.

'I accept I might have overreacted – but you should have stopped her when she had her hand on the bowl.'

'I wanted her to listen.'

'You shouldn't have left it to chance.'

'I know that now. I'm sorry.' I open the fridge door to put the cheese in and so I can speak without Stevie seeing my face.

'And then I spilt my coffee over the bed this morning. I'm so sorry – I'm messing up left, right and centre at the minute.'

'Dan, you took a load of laxatives and shit the bed.'

'No.'

'You did.'

'Stevie. Please. No. That's not what happened.'

'My mate shit the bed on a rugby tour,' he says. 'Stop thinking you're something special.'

I pick up a tube of tomato puree and dig the sharp corner into my head, just above my ear where it won't leave a mark.

'I was so drunk; I didn't know what I was doing. I'll buy a new mattress, and I replaced your things in the bathroom.'

'Forget about the mattress. I was going to get a new one anyway – and get your head out of the fridge; the food will be getting warm.'

'I'll pay you for it.' I close the fridge door and look at a piece of onion skin on the floor by the bin.

'You can't keep up with the rent, Dan. How are you going to afford a mattress?'

'I don't know. I can borrow the money off someone.'

'You need to stop that. It's part of sorting yourself out – money management.'

I pick up the onion skin and put it in the bin. I still can't look at him.

'We said you can stay with us because we want to help you. I don't have any experience of eating disorders, Dan. I eat like a pig, you know that. I don't know how to help you. I do what I think's right but it doesn't seem to be working.'

'I am so sorry, and I'm so grateful to you and Jo for letting me stay here. The therapist I'm seeing is excellent, and it's helping a lot. I just need to focus on not slipping backwards when something bad happens. Things had been going so much better up to Saturday night. I'm changing, I really am changing, Stevie. Please, I don't want to move out.'

'I'm not asking you to move out.'

'I slipped, but I'm not going to slip again. Things were getting better.'

'But you took a load of laxatives because you were upset about what happened in the restaurant?' Stevie takes the biscuit tin from the cupboard and looks inside it.

'Basically. I felt so bad.'

'You're lucky she wasn't seriously hurt.' He takes out a custard cream and eats it.

'I know.'

'I can see you're trying to sort yourself out, Dan – the job, the gym, the therapy, the old people's home stuff. All of that.'

'Yeah.'

'What happened with Ellie was bad, but on the whole, you're doing all right.'

I blink a few times to get rid of the water and tear off a piece of kitchen roll to wipe my nose.

Stevie takes another biscuit.

'You were grey when you first moved in. Jo says you're getting your sparkle back.'

'I get filled with this self-loathing, and I don't know what to do with it.'

Ellie calls for him from the living room. Stevie looks like he's about to say something but then he pauses. I think he's going to hug me, but Ellie shouts for him again. He puts a flat palm between my shoulder blades as he walks out.

On Easter Monday, I go for a four-hour walk. I didn't plan on it being that long but I had a lot to think about. When I get back to the flat, Jo is alone watching TV. Stevie's gone to take Ellie back to her mum's. Jo moves her feet up so I can sit down.

'I'm going to bed, Jo.'

'It's five o'clock,' she says.

'I know. I've got a headache.'

'Shall I wake you up for dinner?'

'No thanks. I ate when I was out.'

I don't deserve to eat. I don't want to eat.

At work the next day, I have to take an early break because I'm shaking so much. My whole body is vibrating and my head feels like it could detach and float up to the ceiling, bob against the strip lights like a helium balloon. It's because I haven't eaten for so long. I don't want to pass out because I don't want the attention, so I get a ready-made cheese sandwich from the vending machine, eat half and throw the other half in the bin. Pat comes over when I'm back on pot wash.

'We still on for today?' I say.

'I spent all day with Mum yesterday,' Pat says. 'So I'll leave it today. You can still go, if you want to? They all love seeing you, but don't feel pressure.'

'Okay,' I say. I'd like to be able to tell Pat that I want her to come too. That I feel like shit and being around her makes me feel better but I don't know how to ask for it.

'How was Stevie's birthday dinner?' she asks.

'Not good.' I scrub at a baking tray with a scourer, trying to get the burned bits off.

'What happened?'

'I can't talk about it. I don't think it could have been any worse. Thanks so much for lending the money, though. I'll pay you back as soon as I'm paid, okay?'

'Are you struggling for money, Dani?'

'It's fine. As long as I keep getting extra shifts from Babs, I'm okay. And Richard cut my session fee by half, so that makes things a lot easier.' I put the baking tray on the draining rack and start on an industrial-sized saucepan.

'He cut it by half?'

'Yeah, he gave me a low-cost session so it's only forty quid a week now.'

'Okay,' Pat says. 'I didn't realise it cost so much in the first place. Eighty pounds an hour is a lot of money.'

'Fifty minutes,' I say. 'A therapist's hour is fifty minutes.'

'Okay,' she says.

'I didn't see him yesterday because he doesn't work bank holidays.'

'Do you still have to pay? Or are you seeing him another day to make up for it?'

'No, to both.' My throat clogs like a plughole full of hair. 'He didn't offer me another session. He probably couldn't. He's got a waiting list. I think that shows how good he is. He wouldn't have a waiting list, otherwise.'

'What are you doing after work tomorrow? Do you fancy going for a drink?' Pat says.

'Yeah,' I say.

It's another six days before my next appointment with Richard. Six long days. I leave pot wash and go to the toilet. I don't even know what I'm going to say but I need to hear his voice. I lock myself in the end cubicle. Richard answers on the third ring. His voice is warm and although all he says is 'Hello,' I wonder if he knows it's me, if he's stored my number on his phone.

'Hello?' he says again. Soft, gentle voice.

I press mute so he can't hear me breathing.

'Is anyone there?' he says. 'Hello?'

I take the phone off mute. I want to say, 'I need you.' I open my mouth but the words don't come out. I kill the call and go back to pot wash.

Frank's in his usual place with a newspaper on his lap. His hands are resting on top of it, and his eyes are closed. There's a rattling noise each time he exhales. Elaine, the manager, comes up to me. She's carrying several mugs and has a tea towel draped over one shoulder.

'He's not been too good lately.' She nods towards Frank.

Although he's asleep, it feels disrespectful to be talking about him while we're so close. I lead her away.

'What's wrong with him?'

'Off his food, getting up later and later.'

'He looks worse than usual,' I say.

'That's because he is,' she says. 'Shame, he's such a lovely man.'

I sit next to Frank and take out one of the books I've brought him. I open it, but I don't read. I think about how just before Dad died, I didn't know what to do with the information then either. Emphysema, lung cancer and acute paranoia, the doctor said. How do you respond to a list like that? Dad was convinced that the doctor was trying to kill him and that they were using him for an experiment. Dad was so adamant I started to believe it too. Then Dad made me practise this thing where he took my hand and pressed his thumb into my palm three times. 'If I do that, it means put a pillow over my face.' Then he made me do to the palm of his hand what he'd done to mine to show I understood, but I messed it up and he got annoyed.

After a while, Frank lets out a loud snore and opens his eyes. He looks around like he's seeing the place for the first time.

'Coffee?' I say.

He nods and leans forward to get up. I tell him to wait while I make it. When I get back, he's more with it.

'You been at work today?' he says.

'Yep – and all over the Easter weekend, which is fine, I'm not bothered about Easter. It's for kids really, isn't it? All the chocolate and Easter egg hunts.'

'Christians like it too, I believe,' Frank says.

163

'You feeling okay?'

'I'm fine, Dani. Don't you worry about me. How are you?'

I wonder how Frank would react if I told him about the soup accident, the sex with two blokes behind the bingo hall, waking up drenched in diarrhoea in Ellie's bed.

'I'm fine. Just working a lot lately.'

'Working all day, then you come here and visit me,' he says.

'Well, I wanted to bring you these.' I take the books out of the bag. The Easter egg seems like a stupid idea now and I leave it in the bag.

Frank takes the books and puts them on his lap on top of the newspaper.

'You should be hanging around with kids your own age,' he says.

'I've always hung about with older people.'

'Old head, young shoulders.'

'I feel about sixty,' I say.

'I'd love to be sixty,' he says. We watch a woman with a head like a dandelion moving across the room on her Zimmer frame. 'You're young, Dani. Be careful with youth, for it flies from us. That's a line from a poem I liked, but I can't remember the poet's name or the name of the poem.'

'I think my youth flew from me a long time ago. When I was a teenager, someone told me what old eyes I had.' I feel old in some ways but like a child in others. I wish I could lose that child part and be a woman who knew what she was doing. 'Do you remember any other lines from the poem? I'll try and find it for you.'

'Just the one about being careful with youth because it flies from us. I think it was an Italian poet. Lorenzo something, I think was his name. I used to write poems for my wife, leave them around the house.'

'That's romantic. What did your wife do?'

'She was a nurse, not a great one. She wasn't keen on blood.'

'And you? What was your job? Were you really a driver for Margaret Thatcher?'

He smiles. 'I wouldn't be here if I was. I'd have driven into a brick wall.'

'That's a bit violent, Frank.'

'I did a few things and worked a few different jobs, but carpentry was my main trade. I wish I'd done something else, though – where I could have worked abroad, somewhere hot.' He takes a handkerchief from his pocket and coughs into it. 'You always regret what you haven't done, not what you have.'

'That's why I want to go to university. If I don't, that's what I'll regret. And my dad really wanted me to go, although he'd never been himself. It's like I'm still following his orders even though he's dead.'

'Daddy's girl,' Frank says.

'I want him to be proud of me, even though he's not here any more. Is that stupid?'

Frank's coughing again. I'm not sure he heard what I said.

I go to the kitchen to get him some water, and when I come back, he looks pale. He needs to rest.

Chapter Nineteen

I breathe in the smell of the room, such a good smell. Books and furniture polish. It's only been two weeks but it feels like months since I was last here. I sit down and smile at Richard.

'How are you, Dani?'

'Pleased to be back.'

His brow creases as he studies my face. 'Have you been poorly? You look pale.'

'I'm fine.'

I look around the room to make sure nothing has changed.

'How did you feel about not having the session with me last week?'

'Lots of people don't work bank holidays. Just the way it is.'

I picture him and his wife exchanging Easter eggs from Waitrose and roasting chicken for an extended family gathering. A beautifully set table with polished cutlery, glasses of chilled white wine and warm, affectionate conversation. I tried to shag two blokes at the same time and slept in my shit.

'What did you do, at the time you would have been here, with me?'

'I can't remember. I worked. No, the restaurant was closed. I went for a walk, I think. And I went to see Frank — no, that was Tuesday. Or was it Monday? It doesn't matter, does it, which day? I always find it strange when people start trying to remember the precise day something happened when they're telling you a story and you're like, it really doesn't matter, just get the fuck on with the story – whether it was Wednesday or Thursday is irrelevant. Anyway, me and Frank talked about people's ages. It made me think about how I always hang out with older people.'

'You always hang out with older people. And why do you think this is, Dani?'

'I feel I have more in common with them.'

Richard waits.

'My first kiss was with a paedophile,' I say.

'Your first kiss was with a paedophile?'

'That's what I said. You repeat things back to me a lot, don't you?'

'A paedophile. How old were you, Dani?'

'Thirteen. He was twenty.'

'Can you tell me more?'

'Perhaps he wasn't really a paedo. I said I was sixteen.'

'And where did this happen? This first kiss?'

'Someone's house. I can't remember much about it. I was pissed out of my head. I remember being very grateful someone wanted to kiss me because I was so fat. All the other girls in my year had been getting off with boys for a long time. Sad, isn't it? Gratitude for a paedo with a leaning towards little fat girls. You know what? I didn't look sixteen. It would have been obvious to him I was much younger.'

'You like older men. There is something that draws you to older men.' Richard picks up his glass and takes a sip of water. 'I thought we could speak about your mother in this session.'

'Nah, you're all right.'

'I think we need to speak about your mother, Dani. You've been resisting it for a while.'

'Didn't you say once it was a common misconception of psychotherapy? People speaking about their mothers? You'll be asking me about my dreams next.'

'I may have said that, but what you've brought to the sessions makes me believe it is important.'

I shift in my seat and breathe out. I can feel a headache coming on; my temples are being squeezed.

'She's not maternal. Will that do?'

He leans back in his chair. I wrap my arms across my body and squeeze myself. For as long as we're speaking about other things, I can avoid telling him about what happened at the weekend. If we get a silence, it might burst out.

'I never give her a Mother's Day card. I can't bring myself to do it. Every year, I look at the cards in the supermarket and I'm angry that I can't buy one.'

'Why can't you?'

'They all say slushy, caring things.'

'Why does that make you angry?'

'Because I want one that says, "Happy Mother's Day" and nothing else. But there's never one like that. They all say things about love and hugs and being the best mum.'

'Go on.'

'And I don't want one like that.'

'Why not?'

'Because I can't stand her.'

'You can't stand your mother?'

'Yeah.'

'What causes the hatred, Dani? Where does it come from?'

'I wouldn't say it's hatred. That's too strong. I mean, if I was out with her, and she had a heart attack, I'd look for a defibrillator.'

'What does it mean to not be able to "stand someone"?'

'I find it difficult to be around her, and I disagree with basically everything she says or does. I don't feel so strongly all the time. If things are going okay, it's more like ambivalence. But when things are bad, I can't stand her.'

'When you speak about her, you become agitated. You're moving around a lot.'

'It's because I feel uncomfortable. I can feel myself getting angry.'

'It's coming out in your body.'

I try to keep still but then I get the urge to scream. I start fidgeting again.

'What causes the anger? Where is it coming from?' Richard speaks even more slowly than usual.

'Probably from when my dad first moved out and she was having boyfriends over.'

'To your home?'

'Yeah. They were morons. She didn't go out with them for dinner or anything normal. They couldn't, because most of them were married and she'd have been ashamed to be seen out with the ones that weren't. They were thick. Ignorant. And she was always threatening me and Jo not to talk about "her business". Always worried what people would think of her.'

'She wanted you to collude in something that made you feel uncomfortable.'

'Yeah. It wasn't as bad for Jo; she was out a lot, anyway, staying over friends' houses. Dad wouldn't have let Jo do that so much if he was still at home, but when he moved out, it all changed. Mum didn't give a shit.'

'And how old were you at this time?'

'Ten. I mentioned it before. Jo was sixteen. Our house was small; I'd get woken up.'

I close my eyes and wait a moment.

'Her headboard. Banging against the wall. I wouldn't be able to go back to sleep. I'd wrap my head in a towel but it still wouldn't block the noise out.'

'You felt unsafe.'

'It's hard to speak about. I could write it down if you want.'

'You need to be able to speak about it, Dani.' His voice is gentle.

I take my phone out and read the news headlines. Richard watches me. I don't look up from my phone when I start talking.

'There was one guy, Mike, with tinted glasses, who gave me the creeps, even more than the others. I told my dad. That's why he went to prison. He beat the shit out of him. I mean, it wasn't that bad, Mike didn't go to hospital or anything.'

Richard waits a moment before he speaks.

'What did you tell your father about Mike? Your father "beat the shit out of" Mike because you told him he gave you the creeps? I want to understand, Dani.'

'I told Dad about Mike always leaving the door open when he went to the toilet. That was it. There might not even have been anything in it – there was a dodgy lock on the bathroom door and it could have been innocent. I don't remember all the details. But that's why my dad went to prison. It was my fault. I carry a lot of guilt for that.'

I look at the picture of the young girl sitting on her father's lap. When Richard says my name, I turn to face him.

'Dani, your father's imprisonment was not your fault. Can you say that?'

I shake my head.

I take tissues from the box and bow my head. Each time a tissue gets too wet, I put it up my sleeve and take another.

'Thank you, Dani, for sharing that with me,' Richard says in his gentle voice.

'I've never told anyone all this before. Or about how difficult it is with my mum. Only Jo.'

'There's something else, isn't there, Dani? That you're holding back. Another reason for the hatred towards your mother.'

'How do you know?'

'I can feel it.'

I speak to his shoes. 'She doesn't love me. She never did. But it doesn't matter because I don't want it now. It's too late.'

'She never made you feel loved,' Richard says gently.

'I feel pathetic for saying it. It makes me cringe.'

'It is a basic human need, Dani, to be loved. Nobody should ever feel ashamed about wanting to be loved. We all want, and need, to be loved. And we are hardwired to want a relationship with our mothers.'

I cry for a little longer. I feel something has shifted. Richard's getting all the most filthy, disgusting things about me today. Why stop?

'I did some bad things on Friday night. There was an accident with Ellie, which was my fault so I went out and got drunk.'

'Ellie had an accident?' He sounds so concerned it makes me start crying again.

'I don't want to go into detail. Ellie got hurt, and I blamed myself, so I went and got drunk and had a one-night stand.'

I try to think of when I've had sex not drunk. With Christy at university, yes. But he was an alcoholic. He was the drunk one.

'Are you able to tell me more about how you were feeling when you were drinking?' Richard says.

'I wanted to get out of it, to forget.'

'The one-night stand . . .'

'What?'

'You had a one-night stand with a man you met while you were drunk?'

'Two men.'

I make this room dirty, this beautiful room with the books

and the art and the furniture. I contaminate it with the dirt that comes out of my mouth. When I'm educated, it'll be different. Richard pours water into a glass. It sounds like someone taking a piss. I talk to cover it.

'When I drink, I care about myself even less. Last year I got off my face at Notting Hill Carnival and crashed out on the grass outside some flats. When I woke up, this little Jamaican guy was sitting there, looking pissed off and he said, "I've missed *Love Island* because of you." He'd sat there watching me the whole time to make sure nobody did anything to me, but the point is, I wouldn't have cared if they had. Then he offered me a cup of tea and I said no thanks and went off to meet up with my mates. I've always felt bad for not thanking him. I didn't recognise how nice it was, what he'd done, because I wouldn't have cared if anything had happened, but that doesn't take away from what he did.'

'You're diverting from what we were speaking about. Stay with what we were speaking about, Dani. Tell me about the sex you had on Friday night.'

I massage my temples.

'There's not a lot to say. I was drunk.'

'You said you had sex with two men. I want you to tell me more about this. Did you take both men in at once, Dani?' There's a break in his voice when he says my name, like he ran out of breath.

I can't speak. I feel so dirty.

'Do you want to change, Dani?'

'That's why I'm here.'

'Unless you engage with your therapy, you won't make progress. Change and loss are deeply connected. If you want to change, you have to be prepared to lose those parts of yourself that may so far have served you well but ultimately will inhibit your growth.'

Change and loss are deeply connected. I store the sentence away to think about later.

'I just had sex with them.'

'With both men?'

I give Richard a thumbs up.

'You had sex with both men at the same time?'

'It was difficult, outside.' I can feel myself burning up. I'm about to say I don't want to talk about it any more, even though I know I should, when Richard stands up. He comes over to my chair and kneels down in front of me. I've got my legs crossed, and he takes the shoe of the leg that's crossed over in his hand. I stopped wearing trainers to come here when my session time changed to seven. My shoes are dainty, almost. High-heeled with a thin strap. I hope I've not trod on anything and there's no saliva, chewing gum or dog shit on the shoe he's holding. He is holding my shoe. Richard Goode, my psychotherapist, is holding my shoe. His thumb strokes the top of my foot, and then he folds his fingers around the heel.

'How many men have you kicked with these, Dani?'

'What?'

He laughs and leans back, lets go of my shoe.

'Perhaps you think about having sex with me?'

I didn't mishear him. He speaks slowly and pronounces every word carefully.

I shake my head and look at the books but I can't see them properly. My chest throbs. He puts his hands on either side of my thighs and leans forward.

'Can I kiss you?'

His breath is stale.

The clock is loud.

I can't move.

This is a therapeutic technique to see how I'll respond. He's trying something different. He's asked me before if I wanted to role-play.

'Is this part of my therapy?'

He smiles.

'I find you very attractive, Dani.'

'Am I paying you for this session?'

He laughs. It goes high-pitched at the end.

'No, you don't have to pay me for this session.'

I can't speak. My chest is throbbing. I'm trying to breathe through my nose but I'm not getting enough air in so I open my mouth and take a deep breath and hold it in.

'You are so loveable, Dani.'

I exhale slowly.

'What?'

'This is not part of the therapy,' he says. 'I find you very attractive, and I think you feel the same way about me.' He bows his head to kiss the top of my foot and I see a thinning patch of hair on the back of his head. I try to yawn so I can get a deep breath in. I want him to go back in his chair. 'You have been trying to seduce me. You are always so seductive, and now you have succeeded.'

He puts his hand on my knee and cups it, then makes slow circles with his fingers. I can feel my shoulders up by my ears but I can't bring them down. I can't look at him.

'Okay,' he says. Stands up. Sits back in his chair and smiles at me.

Attractive. Seductive. I cover my face with my hands.

'Don't be shy,' he says. 'You don't need to be shy with me, Dani.'

'Don't you think I'm disgusting? After everything I've said to you? All of the horrible things that you know about me?'

'You are not disgusting,' he says in a gentle voice. 'You are beautiful.'

I lean forward and rest my face on my knees. I stay there for a long time.

'What are you thinking?' he says.

I sit up and push the hair from my face.

'Have you done this before, with a client?'

'Once, many years ago. When I was practising body psycho-therapy, it happened.'

'What happened?'

'I was giving her a back massage. She turned over and kissed me.'

'And then you started seeing each other?'

'Yes.'

'How long for? How long did you have a relationship for?'

'Three years.'

That's not a fling.

'When was this?'

'Around fifteen years ago.'

Fifteen years ago; so long ago, it doesn't count. You can't hold something against someone that happened fifteen years ago.

'And nobody since then?'

'No.'

'What about your wife?'

'I'm not married.'

'My Uber driver said you live with Becca.'

'Becca is my partner. She didn't know about it.'

'And now?'

'Now we're in the process of separating.' He rubs a hand over his chin.

'How old are you?'

'In my forties.'

'Have you got children?'

'One.'

'Boy or a girl?'

'A daughter.'

'How old is she?'

'She's eighteen.'

'Is she Becca's?' Stupid question. She'll have grown up with Mummy and Daddy – two attentive and loving and professional parents.

'Yes.'

I wonder if she still sits on his lap. I think of his stale breath and there's a part of me that knows he should not have done what he did. There is a part of me that knows psychotherapists should not make passes at their clients even if, as he said, I seduced him.

'What would you do if I report you?'

The question hangs in the air.

'I'd deny it.'

'You'd deny it?'

He waits a moment before answering.

'Yes. I would deny it.'

'What about my therapy?'

'We can continue with our therapy, or I could refer you to another therapist.'

'How could we continue after . . . ?' I move my finger back and forth between us. I laugh. It would be impossible. I think about the options. Another therapist, another room, another beginning. He's given me three options, but there's only one. When anything momentous happens, I imagine picking the phone up.

'Dad, my therapist made a pass at me.'

'Piece of shit,' he says.

'Dani, I'm afraid we have to leave it there for today,' Richard says.

'It's time? We're still following the session time after what's happened?'

'It's twenty past eight.'

Half an hour extra.

'Can I phone you?'

'Yes, you can call me.'

He gets up and walks to the door. As he walks past me, I punch him – not hard, but he holds his arm where I hit him and makes an expression like he's in pain, like it hurt.

'That's unacceptable, Dani.'

'I was only messing around.' Considering what he just did, his reaction seems over the top.

'Phone me. Let me know how you wish to proceed.'

Proceed. An odd choice of word. Yes, I'd like to proceed, please, Richard. I think I can call you by your name now, after what's happened.

I walk out of his house, buzzing. The cold air makes my headache disappear. I pulled a psychotherapist, and they're difficult to pull. A real professional, on a par with a doctor. I haven't even got a degree. I walk home, feeling weightless.

At home, I can't eat. I don't need food. I take a glass of water to the bedroom and lie on my back on the bed. You won't report him. Who would believe you, Dani? Twenty years old and washing up for a living. Bulimic. Promiscuous. You fuck men behind the bingo hall, *you weirdo piece of shit*. Richard Goode is an experienced and well-respected psychotherapist, a professional who's studied for years. He has a practice so successful he has a long waiting list. He has a beautiful home, a long-term partner, a daughter.

And he wants me.

Despite all the disgusting stuff I've told him, the bulimia and the shagging around, he still finds me attractive. What else was it he said? Loveable. I've never been called that before. I've never felt that before. *Yes, my partner's a psychotherapist. I know a lot about Jung.*

We're having a dinner party. The other guests are doctors, professors and writers with names like Allegra, Rupert and Clement. I can hold my own around them. Richard's cured the bulimia, and I'm still thin. At the dinner party, where we will have five small courses, there is a lot of laughter and intellectual conversation. Richard reaches out to me occasionally and tucks a strand of my hair behind my ear or adjusts my dress's shoulder straps, which fall down when I make expansive hand gestures. He looks at me with adoration and tells anecdotes about me. When the guests have all gone, the last thing on my mind that I would ever do now, is carry on bingeing and then chuck it all up. I'm full with the stimulating conversation, satiated by the success of the evening, and loved by Richard. Richard and I carry delicate espresso cups and saucers through to our beautiful kitchen with marble worktops, and when we've placed them on the surface, because he finds me so irresistible and can't wait until we get upstairs, he pulls me towards him and I can feel his enormous hard-on against me and he leans in to kiss me but his breath is stale.

I take my phone and message him. 'Please could I have a session tomorrow?' I need to speak to him. I need to make sure what happened really happened. It feels surreal. I keep checking my phone, but there's no response. I try calling him but it goes straight to voicemail. What does he do at eleven o'clock on a Monday night? Perhaps he's in bed asleep. He could be on the sofa with Becca, drinking wine and watching a foreign film with subtitles, but I doubt that as they're in the process of separating. Although they're probably separating in a civilised way and will remain friends and could still watch films together.

The last time I check my phone, it's the early hours of the morning, and there's still no message. My alarm wakes me at six as usual. There's a message from Richard. 'Hello Dani, I could see you at 19:00 hours today, R.'

Chapter Twenty

I'm having a smoke with Del outside the back entrance of work to kill time as I don't want to be early for Richard's when Pat comes out of the door.

'Ready when you are, Dani,' she says.

'Ready for what?'

'We're going for a drink, aren't we?'

'Shit. I'm sorry, Pat. I completely forgot. Can we do it another time? Something's come up.'

'Right then. Another time. Can I have a word a moment, Dani?'

We move away from Del.

'Is everything okay with you?' she says.

'Everything's fine, Pat.' I turn away from her and grind my dog-end into the pavement.

'I'm worried about you. You haven't seemed yourself lately.'

'God, you don't need to worry about me. Everything's fine. I'll call you later, okay?'

Pat looks like she's going to say something but doesn't.

'What was that about?' says Del. We watch Pat as she walks away.

'She's lovely but she can be overprotective. I think she forgets I'm twenty.'

'You're looking good,' Del says. I ran out at lunchtime and bought a black denim skirt and silky black top and got changed into them after work. I got seventy-denier hold-ups, the most expensive ones.

'Does it look all right?' It's not the type of clothes I'd usually wear.

'You look hot,' Del says.

I'm fifteen minutes late when I knock at Richard's door. He looks at my legs before he turns and walks down the hall to his room. He doesn't say anything about me being late. I sit on my chair and he sits on his.

'How are you?' he says.

'Good.'

'Well . . .'

'Here we are,' I say.

'Yes.'

'This feels strange, doesn't it?' I smile at him.

'I've been thinking about you,' he says.

'Have you? What have you been thinking?'

'About holding you, kissing you.' He sighs. 'I've not been able to stop. I've found it hard to concentrate today. You've been on my mind.'

I want to tell him I've been thinking about him all the time too, but those kinds of words are hard to say.

'So, Dani,' he says when I don't respond. He looks at my legs and shakes his head. 'You shouldn't keep legs like that hidden.'

Suddenly, despite the two cans of vodka and Diet Coke I had on the bus, I'm shitting it.

'Have you always been a psychotherapist? It must be hard to do the job when you're young. I'm sure most people would prefer to see someone with some life experience.'

He laughs. 'No, I haven't always been a psychotherapist. I used to be a musician. I played lead guitar in a band. We supported some big names. Never quite made the big time, but we came close.' He nods and runs a hand through his hair. 'I'll play for you one time, if you'd like.'

Lead guitar in a band. I bet he had this real stage presence. It's a turn-on. I imagine people in the crowd watching him on stage, wanting him. People always want to bang musicians.

'What kind of band was it? What kind of music?'

'Britpop. We supported some big names: Supergrass, Elastica, Echobelly. Have you heard of any of those?' He raises his eyebrows.

I shake my head even though I have. Stevie listens to Elastica all the time in the car.

'I can't imagine you in a pop band. I wouldn't think it's your kind of music.'

'No, it's not the type of music I listen to nowadays. But I enjoyed it in my twenties.'

I'm not sure what to say. I wish I'd had another couple of cans. The conversation would be easier then.

'Have you still got the guitar you had when you were in the band?' I say.

'Not the one I played onstage. But the one I have now used to be owned by Jonny Greenwood. You know who that is, don't you?'

I shake my head.

'Should I?'

He laughs.

'Can I see the guitar?' I say.

'Give me a moment.' He leaves the room and closes the door behind him.

I look at the top drawer of his desk and think about opening it, but as I stand up, Richard comes back with a guitar.

'Can you play something for me, then?'

He tunes the guitar. Then he plays. I don't recognise the tune, but he's good. I have to look away because I'm turned on and embarrassed in equal measure.

'Did you do many big gigs, festivals, that kind of thing?' I say when he stops and carefully leans the guitar against the wall.

'Glastonbury, a couple of years running.'

'I bet you've got some good stories. People in bands always seem to have crazy lives.'

'We weren't as wild as some, but yes, we had some pretty exciting times, got to tour all over Europe, always straight in the VIP areas in the top clubs. It wouldn't happen now, I'd have to queue like everyone else.' He smiles.

'You play so well,' I say.

'I put the hours in. You have to if you want to be any good.'

I look at the guitar leaning against the wall. I can't think of any more questions to ask about it, or the band.

'Are you from London originally?' I say.

'Cornwall. But I've lived in London for thirty years. You want to know about me, Dani.'

'Yes. I'm interested. You didn't say anything in the session about yourself or your background.'

'The sessions were about you.'

I tap my foot in time to the ticking of the clock. Fifteen ticks, fifteen taps. I wish I'd had another can on the way over.

'You haven't got anything to drink, have you?' I say.

'I could offer you a glass of wine. Would you like that?'

I nod.

He comes back with two large glasses and hands me one.

'Shiraz,' he says.

I drink it quite fast and it goes to my head. He still has a lot

left and I want to ask him if he's going to drink it, but before I
can, he speaks.

'Would you like to sit on the couch?'

'No thanks, would you?'

He laughs and it breaks some of the tension.

'You're exquisite, Dani. There's something about you that is
quite remarkable.'

'Did you like me when I first came here?'

'I thought you were very beautiful but off the wall. But as I've
got to know you, I've seen there's something very special about
you, something irresistible.'

'But you could have anyone.'

'I want you.'

I can't look at him. He takes my hand and leads me to the
couch and sits next to me. We kiss. His breath isn't stale like last
time and I taste the antiseptic tang of mouthwash under the
wine. I open my eyes while we're kissing to see if his eyes are
closed. Thankfully, they are. He moves his hand up my thigh and
when he realises I'm wearing hold-ups his mouth is harder on
mine. He goes to the wall of books. He comes back and puts
a small foil packet on the windowsill next to us. We kiss again
and he goes straight for my tits, makes a short noise in his throat
when he realises I'm not wearing a bra. He pushes me so I'm
lying back on the couch and pulls my jumper up, helping me to
take my arms out of the sleeves. He leaves the jumper bunched
around my neck and sits back, stares.

'I'm so flat-chested,' I say.

'It doesn't matter, as long as they're sensitive.'

He stands and undoes his belt and pushes his trousers down,
kicks them off. He tries to open the condom. I reach up to take
it, but he bats my hand away. He tears it with his teeth, squeezes
it out of the packet and then turns it a couple of times before

putting it on. My legs become triangles on either side of him. He kisses my neck and his breath is hot in my ear. He raises himself up so he's looking at me so I turn my head to the side. 'Look at me, Dani,' he says. I've never made eye contact when I'm having sex with someone, except by accident. It freaks me out. He keeps saying, 'Look at me, Dani,' until I do. Then he says, 'Don't look away,' and goes slow until I come.

Richard pulls out, takes my hand and puts it on the warm latex. He puts his hand around the top of mine, and after a couple of strokes, he comes. I sit up and pull my top and skirt down. Richard lies on his back, panting and smiling, happy as a dog at the beach.

'That was lovely,' he says and pulls me back down towards him so we're lying on the couch together, him behind me and the full length of our bodies touching.

The blanket that sits at the end of the couch has fallen on the floor. I pick it up, refold it and put it back while he's putting on his trousers. He pours some water from the jug into a glass and passes it to me. I look in the mirror above the mantelpiece and talk to his reflection because it's easier than looking at him.

'Am I still coming for therapy? What are we? Still therapist and client?'

'What do you want it to be?'

'I don't know what's going on.'

'Come and sit down. No, no, here with me,' he says as I go to sit on my chair. I sit on his lap and he puts his arms around me.

'Perhaps we should let this evolve,' he says.

'Am I still coming for therapy?'

'You can still come for therapy.'

'I don't see how it can work now with what's happened.'

'We need to take it slowly, Dani. Becca and I are in the process of separating, and it wouldn't be right for her to know I've met someone else so soon.'

'How will we see each other then?'

'You can come here at your regular session time, or we can meet elsewhere. Would I be able to come to your home? You said your sister and her husband work full time.'

'Her fiancé. I suppose you could come over.' I think of Richard in the lift, breathing in the piss and weed, looking at the sticky amber corner as the lift groans and rises. 'But I don't think you'll like it, where I live.'

'I'm not judgemental, Dani.'

He shifts so that we're looking at each other.

'But I'm too old for you. I'm not sure you would want a serious relationship with me because of the age difference.'

I look at the floor. 'I don't care about age. You said you're in your forties; that's not that old.'

'Did I say my forties?'

'You're not?'

'I've just turned fifty-one.'

'You lied then.'

'A little white lie. I feel in my forties.' Richard takes his arms from around me and pushes me off his lap so he can stand. He opens the blinds slightly so he can open the top window. Letting the smell of sex out, I think.

'You tell me what you want to happen, Dani.'

'I've always hung around with older people. I don't have much in common with people my age. My boyfriends have always been older. Are you and Becca still sleeping together?'

'Not for a long time.'

'Weeks? Months? Years?'

'A long time.'

'How long?'

'Many months.'

'Why are you still living together if you're in the process of separating?'

Richard sits down. 'These things take time and we have to consider our daughter – she's just started university, and we wanted her to transition smoothly.'

'Did you say university or primary school?' He looks like he doesn't understand. 'Don't worry. Did she start in October?'

'Yes.'

'What's her name? What's she studying? What uni's she at?'

'That's a lot of questions.'

It's a real novelty now I can ask a question and he'll answer. I imagine Richard's daughter at university, sitting in lectures and looking thoughtful. I picture her stirring a wooden spoon round a saucepan of pulses in her student kitchen, laughing with her housemates. I imagine her in a stripey jumper in the pub with friends. And while she's doing all those things, underneath all that, knowing she has a professional father working from a room like this, and a creative mother, who live together. It would be so easy to succeed and be happy with that kind of security.

'I've been coming here for four months, and I hardly know a thing about you. I'm interested.'

'My daughter's name is Phoebe. She's studying medicine.'

Phoebe. I'm not surprised she has a name like Phoebe or that she's studying medicine. I bet they call her 'Fifi'. I bet she has long limbs and has never had a problem with her weight.

'Medicine, lovely.' I imagine meeting her and what it would feel like if she brought along a boyfriend her age, our age.

'Dani, come here.' He holds his arms out, and I sit on his lap again. I keep some of my weight on my feet.

'Am I too heavy?'

'Not at all.'

We sit like this for a few minutes. My thighs begin to ache.

'You're beautiful,' he murmurs into my ear. 'I can't believe you're interested in me, like this. You could have any man.'

'Yeah, right.'

'You're a genie. There's something magical about you.'

'Don't talk shit.' But I file the words away to think over later.

He pulls me further onto his lap and we kiss. He groans and pulls away.

'Dani, we have to leave it here, I'm afraid.' He shifts in his seat so I stand up.

'What?'

'I have another patient.'

'Oh. Okay. When can I see you again?'

'Come to your session on Monday. We can talk then.'

'Could we go for a coffee or something?'

'I'm not averse to the idea, but best to carry on coming here at first.'

Stevie's eating a pizza from the box. The smell of hot pork and melted cheese fills the room. Jo's painting her nails burgundy. I sit with them and pretend to watch some D-list celebrities in a jungle choking and gagging over parts of animals we don't eat. Stevie holds the pizza box towards me. I look at the little orange pools of grease and my mouth waters. I say no thanks.

I banged my therapist today; you know, the psychotherapist I'm seeing? We fucked on his couch. We looked into each other's eyes while we were doing it. I wonder what they'd say.

I still can't believe he's interested in me, especially with all the stuff I've told him. I imagine saying, 'My partner's a psychotherapist.' I'm attracted to him; he's attractive. His position of power, his authority, they're a big turn-on. If we could have met somewhere else, it would have been better. I still can't believe he likes me like that. I pulled my psychotherapist.

★

One of the best things about kids is they don't hold a grudge. But Ellie's not like most kids. She sticks her bottom lip out as soon as she sees me and carries on playing with her little plastic horse, putting it in a little plastic horsebox, closing the doors, driving it around, then taking it out again.

I watch her for a while, then go and sit on the floor near her. Stevie's in the kitchen, making her macaroni cheese. I break my rule of not initiating a conversation.

'Can I play, Ellie?'

She ignores me.

'Ellie? I'm sorry about the soup.'

She sticks her bottom lip out even further.

I pick up two of her plastic figures and hold them so they face each other. I move the man up and down. 'Do you think Ellie's gone deaf?'

I shake the woman from side to side. 'Why do you say that?'

Ellie keeps her hand on the horsebox but stops pushing it.

'Dani's said two things to her, and she hasn't responded.' I move the man up and down again.

'Perhaps she has gone deaf then.' A shake of the woman.

'What?' I turn the man so his ear is against the woman's mouth.

'You heard. You're as bad as Ellie.'

'How can she be deaf? Look how big her ears are. They're massive, she can't be deaf with ears as big as that.'

'Shut up,' Ellie says. She twists the plastic man from my fingers and bangs me on the head with it.

'Ah, good. You can hear,' I say. 'How are your Scotch eggs?'

'What?'

'Your Scotch eggs. Your legs. Doesn't your dad teach you anything?'

'My legs are better now.' She gives me a big smile and comes to put an arm around my neck. I remember Richard saying how children need eye contact. I push her back so I can look at her and smile.

'Dani?'

'Yes, lovely?'

'You shit the bed.'

I have to wait for Stevie to go to bed before I can sleep because Ellie is here and I'm on the sofa. I want to message Richard but I can't while Stevie is still in the room in case he asks me who I'm texting. I'll have to lie and he'll know I'm lying and it will make a bad atmosphere between us. Stevie goes to bed just after eleven and I message Richard straight away.

Hey, how are you? How's your day going? I don't know whether or not to put a kiss after, or two kisses. I could do the posh thing like he did, that seems to be the way posh people convey intimacy, just my initial. I try it. I add the 'D' after the message but it just makes me think of a shit school grade. I add two kisses then delete them and add a smiley face. Pathetic. I just send the words.

I wait ten minutes and when he doesn't reply, send another message.

I'd love to talk to you now, if you're free?

I keep checking my phone, but nothing.

I want you to tell me something to make me feel secure, I send.

Then I send, *I'm sorry for being insecure. Please don't keep me waiting for a reply.*

It's nearly one now, and he could be asleep, but that's not certain. He could be one of those people who stay up late. If he hasn't replied by one, I'll send one more message then leave it.

God I hate having to text what I want to say. My rational side says you've fallen asleep or your phone has broken. Fine – I can handle that, but the other side is having thoughts I don't want to have. Maybe you're shagging Becca and you're not serious about me after all. You know how I feel about you. If you could just send me a quick text to let me know everything is fine, I'd appreciate it. D x

I try to sleep but the more I try, the more wide awake I feel.

Whatever happens, I hope that you'll always be my friend.

I manage to doze for an hour. It's just gone four and there's no point trying to sleep now. I make tea quietly in the kitchen. One more message. I want him to know.

Mr Goode, I adore you. I don't care if you wake me up, well you won't anyway because I'm awake. You can call if you'd prefer that to texting. I just want to say that I can't believe you're interested in me, like that. And please don't hurt me. I'm not sure I could handle it.

When I'm standing at the bus stop I try calling him and he picks up.

'I'm sorry for all the texts,' I say. 'I'm such an idiot sometimes.'

'You're not an idiot.'

'I panicked. I don't know why.'

'Dani, I absolutely adore every little bit of you that builds into the whole that makes you who you are. Divine. Don't panic,' he says.

'It just feels so unreal. I never thought anything like this would happen.'

'I couldn't resist you. You were so seductive. I could feel how much you wanted me.'

'Can we have longer than fifty minutes on Monday?'

'It's not possible, I'm afraid. But what are you doing today at lunch? Could we meet?'

'I'm in my uniform. It's embarrassing.'

He laughs.

'I don't care about that.'

Chapter Twenty-One

Pat brings over some big serving dishes for me to wash up.

'You seem like you're happy, love.'

'Yeah, it's going all right.'

I hum to fill the space where I'd usually tell her why.

'Do you fancy coming into town with me at lunchtime?' she says. 'I want to get Megan a present to say well done on her promotion. I thought you could help me choose some earrings; you know more about what's fashionable than I do.'

I vaguely remember Pat telling me about her daughter, but I wasn't really listening. 'I would if I could. Sorry, I can't today.' I don't even look at her when I say it.

'No bother, another time then.' She walks away.

Richard and I arranged to meet at the Wetherspoon's on the high street. I spend the morning thinking about whether I'll be brave enough to kiss him when I see him, whether he'll kiss me.

I'm five minutes late arriving, but when I walk in, I can't see him. I wait at the bar to get served. I check my phone in case I've missed a message, but there isn't one. The barman's serving someone further down and I wish he'd hurry up. At the back of the pub, a man sitting with his back to me turns, and I see his profile. Richard. I didn't recognise him from behind because he's wearing a green gilet and a T-shirt the colour of margarine.

Richard raises an arm as he sees me walking towards him. He's got a big smile on his face, a different kind of smile to the ones I saw during the therapy sessions. Less professional. He doesn't look like a psychotherapist. He could be a plumber on his lunch break. I don't have anything against plumbers, but I wouldn't date one in his fifties.

'What do you want to drink?'

'Oh, hello, that's very abrupt!' He stands up and moves towards me but I step back. His clothes have freaked me out. He looks much better in his therapist's gear.

'I'll get the drinks if you tell me.'

'I'll come with you to see what they have.'

'It's fine, just tell me.'

'Why don't you want me to come to the bar with you, Dani?'

'It's easier if I get them – you keep the table.'

He looks around. Only a couple of tables are taken.

'Well, I'd like half a bitter, please.'

'You stay here. I'll be back in a minute.'

'Can I give you some money?'

'No. I'll get these.'

I order a large white wine and a pint of bitter, take them back to the table. I take out my tobacco and roll a cigarette. Richard watches me as if I'm doing something fascinating. The wine goes straight to my head, and after a few sips on an empty stomach, I feel better about being here with him dressed the way he is. Everything's easier when you're pissed. He picks up my pouch of tobacco and reads the writing on it.

'Amber Leaf Hand Rolling Tobacco.' He puts it back on the table and pats it like it's a small animal.

'You don't smoke then?'

'I've tried it before, but it's not for me.'

'Even when you were in the band?'

'Even then,' he says.

'I need to give up.'

'And why is that?'

'It seems stupid to carry on when my dad's side of the family all die of cancer in their fifties.'

'Then yes, Dani. You should give up.'

'I'm going out to smoke this.' I hold up the roll-up. 'Do you want to come?'

He looks at me like I said I'm going for a shit under the table.

'What's the matter?'

'We've just got our drinks,' he says.

'We can take them with us.'

As we're walking out, he puts his hand in the small of my back and it feels like his hand is on fire.

Outside on the street, a grey-faced man in a dirty beige jumper is smoking and every time he inhales, he coughs and brings the back of his hand to his mouth. Richard looks at him for longer than I think is polite.

'You look glamorous when you smoke,' he says.

'Thanks. Why are you wearing that?'

'What?' He looks bemused.

'This yellow thing.' I take a bit of the sleeve between my thumb and finger and pull at it.

'This old T-shirt? I don't want Becca to suspect anything. If I come out wearing old clothes, she won't.'

'I thought you're splitting up?'

'We are, but it would be crass and insensitive if I made it obvious I was already seeing someone.'

I've only got a drop of wine left. Richard hasn't asked if I want another one. He's only had a sip from his pint; it's almost full.

I chuck my roll-up on the ground and stamp on it.

'I'm going to get another drink.'

'Oh right, going back inside, are we?'

He comes with me to the bar.

'Do you want another one? I'll get it. You can wait for me at the table.'

'No, no. Oh, some nuts perhaps?' He puts his hand on my hip before walking away.

It didn't cross my mind to ask him if he wanted to eat. I can't imagine him choosing a burger and beer meal deal, fifty pence more for extra cheese.

I order another glass of wine and peanuts for Richard. I ask the barman if he thinks my lunch is nutritious to make him smile, because I think Richard will be watching. I want him to see a different side to me than what he's seen in his room. Light-hearted.

'I didn't know which ones you like, so I got you dry roasted.' I chuck the nuts on the table, and they slide onto the floor. Richard goes to pick them up, but I stop him, pick them up myself, rub them on my top and hand them to him.

I watch him struggling to open them. I'm halfway through my second glass before he manages and a waft of fart comes from the open packet. He pours some into his hand but doesn't offer any to me. He reaches across the table and strokes my arm. I pull it away.

'Have you got many clients today?'

'Yes, two this afternoon and two this evening. Well, one this evening and afterwards I'm seeing a beautiful young woman.' He reaches across and strokes my nose when he says, 'young woman', and his finger feels warm and greasy from the peanuts. I wonder how long I can leave it before taking the serviette that's wrapped around the cutlery and wipe my nose without it seeming rejecting.

194

'I wanted to ask your advice on one of my patients,' he says.

I try not to smile. I'm flattered.

'Go on, but I've only got twenty minutes before I need to get back, yeah?'

He laughs, but I didn't mean to be funny.

'I have a patient who is in a long-term relationship but she feels disappointed because her partner is not sexually adventurous. She loves her partner and thinks they are compatible in every way apart from sexually.'

I nod and try to look intelligent.

'Has she tried speaking to her partner about it?' I say.

'No, I don't believe she has.'

'I thought you said they were compatible. If everything's so good, why can't she talk to her about it?'

'Oh, I believe she may have broached it, but her partner wasn't forthcoming with reasons and my patient didn't want to push her.'

'Have they been together for long?' I say.

'Around a year.'

'Skinner's rats.'

Richard tilts his head.

'Go on,' he says.

'She needs to praise her girlfriend every time she does the slightest thing that's not so vanilla. Positive reinforcement, isn't it?'

'I hadn't thought of that. You are so insightful.'

I'm warmed by the alcohol, warmed by him.

'Mariella Frostrup used to do this excellent advice column. I always read it. I learned a lot of good shit from that. You know?'

'You're naturally intuitive, Dani. You could be a therapist if you wanted to. You could be anything.'

'Not until I've been to university. I need to get my qualifications.

Nobody would listen to me until then. Are you going to drink that?' He's barely touched his pint.

'Help yourself,' he says.

I take a sip. 'I love drinking. Anything. I can't think of a single drink I don't like.'

'What else would you advise in terms of my patient?'

'They need to talk more. I can't believe you're asking me for advice. You're the one with all the training.'

'You make some very salient observations. I enjoy hearing them.'

'Thanks.'

He brushes a strand of hair from my face and I smell the peanuts on his fingers. 'Have you been with a woman before? I bet you have.' I take his hand and stroke the back of it. There are three big dark brown freckles.

'I'm not against the idea; I've just not met one who does it for me.'

'I thought you'd be more worldly in that regard.' He takes his hand away and leans back.

'I've kissed a couple of girls, but it didn't go much further.'

'And did that happen recently?'

'When I was at university. There was one girl I liked. It was the first time for both of us, with another girl, I mean. It was a real mental connection, and she was an amazing kisser, so gentle, and I was—'

The alarm goes off on my phone.

'I need to get back,' I say. 'Let's sit over there a minute.' I nod towards a more secluded booth. I catch sight of Richard's jeans as he gets up. They look as soft as pyjamas. He does a stiff-legged walk to the booth, and I slide in after him.

'I need to go. I wanted to say goodbye.' I can look him directly in the eye now as I've had two large glasses of wine and most of his bitter on an empty stomach.

I kiss him. His mouth tastes beefy from the peanuts but it's better than how his mouth has tasted before. He pulls back and laughs and says, 'Dani,' because I'm sitting astride him, but I can feel he's excited. I take a scrumpled serviette from the table, take out my chewing gum and wrap it up.

'Did you just take some chewing gum out?' he says.

'Yeah?'

'You've drunk two glasses of wine and almost a pint of bitter with chewing gum in your mouth?'

'Yeah?'

I kiss him again and somebody shouts across the pub, 'Get a room!'

Richard pushes me away. His face is flushed.

'Dani, I can't wait to have you again.' He moves close so he can whisper into my ear. 'And I want to hear the rest of the story about the girl at university and about the other girl. I want you to tell me about it while I'm pulsing inside you.'

'Pulsing?'

'What? Why are you laughing?' Richard moves away from me and pushes me off his lap.

'You said "pulsing". You made yourself sound like a food processor.' It's hard to get the words out and my eyes are watering. I try to take a deep breath. 'Thanks for that. I'll add it to my bank of sex quotes.'

I've never seen Richard blush. 'Do you want to tell me one of them?' he says. 'See if it tops "pulsing"?'

I could refuse, let him sit there feeling like an idiot, but I want to be nice. I could tell him about Dave, who told me he was giving me a 'monster fuck', but I've got a better one.

'My friend went out with a Welsh bloke and every time he was about to come, he said, "I've got spunk at the end of my cock for you."'

Richard fakes a laugh.

'It was funnier when she said it. She's good at doing accents.'

I take my phone out and hold it in front of us.

'Smile,' I say and lean back into him. I take a picture.

'Delete that, please, Dani,' he says.

'Why? I want a picture of us on our first date.'

'Delete it, please. I cannot bear the whole selfie culture.'

'Come on, it's just one photo.'

He takes my phone and deletes the picture.

'Fine. You didn't look too good in it anyway.' I take my phone back and he takes my hand.

'I'm not some Gen Y, Dani, who needs to document every waking moment.'

'Okay, it's no big deal. Neither am I,' I say.

I had to get drunk to get over what he's wearing, but this meeting's gone okay. I still can't believe a psychotherapist, someone with so many qualifications and so much status, would be interested in someone like me and be asking for my advice.

I bump into Pat on the walk back to work. We fall into step and I consider telling her I just met my psychotherapist in the pub, but I don't think she'd approve.

'Did you get the earrings?' I say.

'I did indeed. I had to go to four shops before I found these.' She takes a small silver box out of her bag, takes off the lid and passes it to me. 'What do you reckon? Think she'll like them?'

'Yeah.' I take one off the cotton wool and hold it up. 'They're lovely.' I go to put it back in the box and drop all of it on the pavement.

'Careful, Dani,' she says.

'Okay, calm down, it was an accident.' I crouch down to pick up the earrings and box. I put my hand on the ground to steady myself. I pass it all back to her.

'One of the feathers has fallen off,' says Pat.

'If you'd got better-quality ones, it wouldn't have.'

Pat looks like I slapped her. It's fleeting and then her face returns to normal, but I saw it.

'Sorry, I was only joking.'

'Have you been drinking?'

'I've had a couple of glasses of wine.'

'We're going to be late back,' she says and walks off.

Pat doesn't say anything on the short walk back, doesn't wait for the lift and goes straight for the stairs. She doesn't wait for me. I go to the loo and have a piss so good and long it makes my gums ache.

I get stuck into pot wash. Because I haven't eaten, I feel drunk for longer.

'You look like you're in a good mood, Dani,' Maureen says, bringing some knives over. She tells me to be careful because they're sharp.

'I am in a good mood, Maureen. Are you in a good mood on this lovely sunny Tuesday? Not that we can see it in here as we have no natural light, but we get to enjoy it in our breaks, don't we?'

'I'm looking after my neighbour's cat,' she says. 'He's at his girlfriend's place again.'

'Your neighbour's cat is at his girlfriend's?'

'Dani, are you winding me up or do you honestly not understand?'

'Yes, I was joking. That's kind of you.'

'It's a nice cat. Gives me some company.'

'Are those knives *very* sharp?' I say to her.

'Yes, you be careful,' she says.

'I will. Thank you for warning me, Maureen. I used to get annoyed with you sometimes, but I've worked it out. You're actually a very caring person.'

'If you care about people, then they care about you back,' she says.

I put six tabs of chewing gum in my mouth so I don't smell of wine. I go over to Pat and apologise for the earrings and she says not to worry about it, but she looks over my shoulder when she says it. I could keep saying sorry, but I can see she needs some space.

On my afternoon break, I go to the smoking hut. Reena is there alone.

I sit as far away from her as possible and look the other way, but I can't bear the tension.

'Look, Reena, I didn't know you had a thing about Del. I wish you'd said—'

She sighs. 'I didn't have a thing about him, Dani. We had something going on. He dumped me when you came on the scene.'

'He never said. If I'd known, I wouldn't have gone near him.'

'It was only casual,' she says. 'But he was still out of order. I'm with someone else now, anyway.'

'Are we good then?'

'We're good.' She smiles. 'I've missed our chats, Dani.'

'So have I. We always got on so well. I always looked forward to coming to work when I knew I'd be chatting to you. You make me laugh so much.'

'You make me laugh too,' she says. 'Although much of the time it's unintentional.'

'And we have so much in common,' I say. I use my fingers to count: 'We both love reading, we both have an older sister, we both like an ice cube in our glass of white wine.'

'We both went to Majorca the first time we went abroad,' she says, pulling on my ring finger.

'So much in common,' I smile.

'We go together like Greek yoghurt and honey,' she says.

'We both work for the same company,' I say. 'Am I the yoghurt or the honey?'

'You can be whatever you want to be, Dani.'

'I don't think I've asked you before if you like a shot of almond syrup in your coffee,' I say.

'I can't see any reason why I wouldn't like it,' she says.

I'm deciding what to wear for Richard's. I thought Jo was out, but then I hear the toilet flush and she comes out of the bathroom.

'Cigarette?' she says.

We have our best chats when we're smoking. We take our usual places on the balcony. Jo lights up and exhales heavily.

'Stevie's moved out.'

I turn to look in the kitchen, as though she's joking and I'll see him in his boxers and poking around in the biscuit tin. There's nobody there.

'Where's he gone?'

'He's staying with a mate from work.'

'How long for?'

'I don't know.'

'We won't have to do the whole Norfolk thing now then,' I say.

'Oh yeah.'

'Did he find out about the other bloke?'

'He's not said anything. Can you imagine Stevie keeping quiet if he knew?'

'True.'

Jo looks at her nails. Hot pink with diamante gems. 'We need some space, a bit of time apart. It might only be for a few days.'

'I thought you were going to finish with him?'

'I'm still thinking about it. He's so boring it does my head in. All he wants to do is watch TV.'

'Hasn't he always been like that?'

'Not as bad as this. He doesn't even want to go on holiday this year.'

'Why not?'

'He wants to save for a mortgage deposit. Do you think he knows about Doug?'

'How would I know?'

I think of the time when he told me Jo was at the pub with Hayley, sitting amid a pile of junk-food wrappers, trying to eat away his worries.

'Did you think it's obvious?' she says.

'You've lost loads of weight. That's always a giveaway.'

'A stone and a half now. Can't eat.'

'Stevie's not stupid, Jo.' I want to go and shower and get ready for Richard. I think about telling Jo about him but she's too full of her own stuff. 'Do you want to break up with Stevie or not?'

'I want some fun. I feel like an old woman.'

'So you're keeping Stevie on the back burner for now?'

She shrugs.

'Is he that exciting? The new bloke?'

She nods. 'He's so fucking hot.'

I picture Stevie in his pants in front of the TV eating pizza, the box on his lap, his thighs pinkening under the heat of it.

'I didn't think you went for looks,' I say.

'Doug's not just a driver; he does other stuff on the side, some dealing.'

I can see that excites her. I drop my roll-up in the plant pot.

'What will you do if Stevie finds out?'

'He won't, but even if he does . . . ah bollocks, I don't know.'

I stand up. 'I've got my therapy at seven. We can talk after if you want?'

She nods but she's lost interest as she's got a message and is tapping out a reply. I take a can of Diet Coke from the fridge, tip half of it down the sink and top it up with vodka. I drink some of it while I'm in the shower and finish it while I'm drying my hair. I wear the black denim skirt and hold-ups again but don't put on any underwear. I call Naz to take me to Richard's.

'Nice hair, Naz.'

There are tiny straight hairs on his ear and neck.

He licks a finger and runs it across his eyebrow to make me laugh. We pull onto the main road.

'I like being in the car with you. It reminds me of when I used to go in the car with my dad.'

'Was he a good driver?' Naz says.

'Very good – although one of his hands was bad, he was still a great driver.' I'm chatty from the vodka. 'He fell out of a tree when he was a kid and nobody took him to hospital, so it didn't heal well.'

'Poor dad.'

'It didn't stop him doing stuff. Well, he didn't work any more after he and my mum broke up, but he used to sculpt things out of wood.'

'Revenge on the tree,' says Naz.

'I never thought of it like that. He was good at it. He made faces from the wood and put them on little metal poles.'

Naz smiles and indicates right, waits for a space to pull out.

'Last year, he wanted me to help him make a totem pole. He had this piece of wood that was about two metres long, and he carved all these scary faces down it and we painted it in really bright colours.'

'What did you do with it?'

'Dad attached it to the front of his house. It pissed the neighbours right off.'

Dad was pleased when he was invited to a parish council meeting where the totem pole was on the agenda because of all the complaints. Dad said he tried to look all serious when he was invited to speak, but every time he put his glasses on, one of the lenses fell out.

I'm pleased Richard's wearing his usual expensive shirt and trousers and not the cheap T-shirt and old-man jeans. I much prefer him looking like a psychotherapist – a professional. I stand in the middle of the room, and he comes behind me, moves my hair to the side and kisses my neck. He smells good. His hands are on my hips and he pulls me back into him, whispering he's been thinking about me, about this, from the moment he woke.

'You are so beautiful, Dani.'

I turn to face him and we kiss and I tell him to talk to me more because it turns me on. He strokes my hair and tells me he gets hard every time he thinks of me. We start undressing each other.

'You don't need to,' I say.

'What?'

'Use a condom. I can't get pregnant.'

'There are other reasons to use a condom, Dani.'

'You think you're going to catch something from me?'

'It's sensible.'

Sensible. I'm having sensible sex. I've never had sensible sex before. Drunk sex, stoned sex, reckless sex, rough sex. Sensible sex? A first.

I ride him and lean back, put his fingers there. I'm riding my psychotherapist in his office, on his couch, this educated, sophisticated psychotherapist.

Afterwards, we straighten our clothes. Richard folds tissue around the condom and puts it in the bin. He sits by my side on the couch.

'Dani, I do need to apologise. I have a busy week coming up, and I'm not sure I'll be able to see you until next Monday. I'm sorry. I appreciate it's not what you'll want to hear.'

'Next Monday's ages away.'

'It's only a week, Dani.'

'Can you come out at lunchtime again?'

'I'm afraid it won't be possible.'

I sit on his lap and put my arms around his neck. I put my mouth close to his ear and speak gently. 'But a week is such a long time. Can I come here another time?'

'I suppose it could be possible if I have a cancellation.'

I stop kissing his neck.

'But I might not make it because of work. I could pull a sickie,' I say.

'Sometimes the cancellations are last-minute, so it may not be helpful to you, anyway.'

'Can we talk in the week? Can I call you?'

'Yes, you can call me. Daytimes are best. If I'm seeing a patient, I'll call you back.'

I move so I'm sitting astride him but talk into his neck.

'It's going to feel so long.'

'It will give me a chance to speak to Becca. I want to get things moving along. At the moment, we're in disagreement about who is going to move out.'

I need to show I can be a supportive and understanding partner.

'I understand. Perhaps the following week we could spend longer together one day?'

'That would be lovely.'

'Do I need to leave at ten to?'

'Yes. Becca thinks I'm working.'

It's quarter to – five more minutes. I struggle to think of what to say now we're no longer therapist and client. Sex would be easier, but there's not enough time. I get off him and go to his desk. 'Have you seen any good films lately?' I ask.

'Oh, I don't have the time to watch films. Usually I read, or study.'

'Oh, what are you reading? Or studying?'

'I'm currently writing a paper on the importance of the therapist–patient relationship, how it is fundamental in enabling the client to make progress, and how shorter-term therapy cannot offer this. You see, there's this huge focus on wellbeing at the moment, and some therapists are even incorporating it into their therapeutic practice, but it's nonsense, and this move, this demand for a shorter model of therapy is quite frankly absurd. It's only through a sustained and regular commitment to therapy that the patient is able to make changes and . . .'

I keep taking a breath so I can comment, but he doesn't pause. It's like he's making a speech, and there's no audience participation allowed.

'. . . and without this sustained period of time—'

'Do you think—'

'I haven't finished,' he says. 'All the great psychotherapists advocated long-term therapy in order for the client to immerse themselves in the therapy and commit to . . .'

I'm finding it hard to remain focused without being able to ask the occasional question.

'And it is unjust that some patients are being short-changed in this way, that short-term therapy is being promoted and advocated as the best course when it is absolutely entirely unsuitable for some conditions, such as trauma.'

When he hasn't said anything for a minute, I know he's finished and isn't pausing.

'Right,' I say.

'That's what I'm currently working on. It will be my fifth publication.'

'What is short-term therapy? How short would it need to be to be classed as short-term?' I say.

'Anything under a year could be classed as short-term therapy,' he says.

'My therapy with you was short-term then. I only came for four months.'

He shakes his head like that's got nothing to do with what he's been talking about.

'You, my little darling, seduced me. I could not resist you. I don't believe many men could.'

I can feel myself blushing. I'm not as attractive as he makes out.

'Look at the time, Dani. I'm sorry – you must go.'

Chapter Twenty-Two

The week drags on. I go to work, I go to the gym, I go home to an empty flat as Jo's always out.

She's bought a lot of new clothes and bags which she leaves draped over furniture in the flat. She doesn't earn enough to pay for all these new things so she must be running up her credit cards. When I'm smoking on the balcony, I notice the ends of joints in the fag bucket. I find king-size Rizlas on top of the microwave and put them under the plastic divider in the cutlery drawer. I do it out of respect for Stevie; he's anti-drugs and this is still his home. I message Jo to say where I've put them.

I send Richard texts and long emails saying how I can't believe he's interested in me, that I miss him and can't wait to see him. He doesn't message or email back but when I call him a couple of times he picks up. I love hearing his voice over the phone. He says nice things, that he's looking forward to seeing me, that he misses me, but he needs this week to talk to Becca.

'Stop panicking, Dani,' he says. 'This will happen. Give me some time.'

I don't have any urge to binge and throw up after. I think this is it. The bulimia has been cured. Richard has cured my bulimia.

I ask Pat if she wants to go for lunch one day but she says she's busy. I consider telling her about Richard but I'm worried about how she'll react. I have a feeling she'll tell me it's not right and I don't want to hear that. I want people to be happy for me when I'm ready to tell them.

On Friday, Reena and I have lunch together in a new Turkish café that's recently opened near work. I love the way she eats; she's so dainty. I eat with my knife and fork in the wrong hands. When you don't learn something properly the first time around, it's harder to fix.

'Tell me about your new man,' Reena says.

'He's clever.'

'Another Del, then.'

'No, but come on, look at Del's body, you can't have it all,' I say. 'Richard's a professional, sophisticated. He's a psychotherapist.' I want Reena to be impressed. I want to feel elevated in her opinion, that I'm with a psychotherapist so there must be something in me that he can see. I feel more worthy by association. She takes an olive stone from her mouth, puts it on the side of her plate.

'Doesn't he try and analyse you all the time?'

'No, not at all. We discuss his work, but it's not like I'm in a session with him. Sometimes he asks my opinion on clients he's seeing.' I sit up straighter.

'How did you meet?'

'We just got chatting down the pub. What about you? Who's this new guy?'

'An old school friend – his name's Solomon. We got back in touch through Insta. Such a cliché.'

'Who cares? I don't think it matters where or how you meet.'

'And he's my age for once. I think that's where I've been going wrong. Del was five years younger than me, too much of an age difference. It's not healthy in a relationship.'

'I don't think it's that much of an issue. You see loads of people in the public eye with big age-gap relationships that seem to be working.'

'I think it's disgusting.' She sucks on another olive stone before removing it from her mouth. 'Why would someone want to go out with someone old enough to be their dad? Or their mum? But it's usually the first way round, isn't it? I think some women are after a sugar daddy. It grosses me out.'

'Richard's a lot older than me.' I feel better pre-empting it in case she asks. 'I think there can be advantages, and you can't help who you fall for, can you?'

'How old is he?'

I shake my head. 'I'm not saying.'

'That much older, then?'

'In his forties.'

'Shit, Dani. And how old are you?'

'I've always liked older men.'

She turns her head and appraises me with one eye. 'Get with someone younger, Dani. It's prematurely ageing for the younger partner to be with someone older, and, I don't know, lascivious of the older one, all that feasting on firm young flesh. What's in it for the younger one? Who gets turned on by saggy jowls and beer bellies? Who gets turned on by fleshy necks and liver spots and nasal hair?' She puffs her cheeks out to indicate she's pretended to be sick in her mouth.

'What are liver spots?'

'Age spots. They look like big freckles, or brown stains.'

I think back to when I was stroking Richard's hand in Wetherspoon's.

'That's all so superficial, though. You shouldn't care what somebody looks like,' I say.

'I do. But come on, even disregarding appearance, the age

thing filters through. Do you honestly want to be having conversations about blood in your shit, rheumatism and thinning hair before you're there yourself? Prematurely ageing, Dani. We should enjoy being young.'

'Reena, I'm sure older people have more to talk about than their bodies falling apart and illness. You're simplifying it. What about all the life experience? That's attractive.'

'I prefer younger people. More energy, more dynamism, and they smell better. Seriously, any object over forty years old is gonna smell however much you wash it.'

'A lot of young people only want to go out and get wrecked all the time. I want a relationship that's a little deeper. Do you know what I mean?'

'What's wrong with getting wrecked?'

'I want more.'

'I suppose older guys can be better lovers, more experienced.'

'That's not too much of an issue for me.'

'What do you mean?'

'The whole sex thing between two people. It's overrated.'

'Why do you think that?'

'I once had three orgasms all on my own with no touching involved. Just sitting there, next to the taxi driver when he was taking me home.'

Reena's eyes widen.

'Dani, you've got to tell me more.'

'I'd had such a good night, up at the bar chatting with this lovely Geordie guy, and the music was Northern soul, which I love, and it was the first time I'd tried Corona and lime which was a beautiful taste experience. The whole evening was so good. I got a taxi home and while I was thinking about the evening, all this, like, euphoria started washing over me in waves.

I had to keep leaning forward each time I came and pretend I'd dropped something.'

'Are you shitting me?' she says.

'Straight up,' I say. 'That would be a weird thing to lie about.'

'The power of the female mind,' says Reena.

'Yeah. I don't think you need to be with someone to have good sex.'

'You prefer it on your own?'

'It's different. I wouldn't be with someone just for sex. It comes far down the list of reasons why I like to be in a relationship. There are other things that are much more important.'

'Such as?'

'Conversation, going to interesting places together, sharing things.'

'God, you do need to go out with old men. You sound about sixty.'

I take some hand cream out of my bag and squeeze some onto my palm.

'Aren't you going to eat that?' Reena nods at my salad. I've barely touched it. I'm too high for food. I push the plate towards her.

'So what's your weekend looking like?' I say. 'You're lucky you work in accounts and get every weekend off.'

'I'm going to the new bar that's opened by the bus station tonight. Do you fancy it?'

'With people from work?'

'No, with my football team. Come with us.'

'Okay,' I say.

That evening, Stevie comes into the living room where I'm lying on the sofa and writing in my notebook. I'm dressed and ready to go out with Reena but killing time writing as it's too early to leave. The room's a tip. Stevie looks at the clothes draped over the back of the sofa, shoes all over the floor. He sits on the arm of his chair. He's lost weight and his face looks thinner. I wish I was the type of person who could give him a sisterly hug to make him feel better, but I'm not.

'I'm sorry, Stevie. If I'd known you were coming, I'd have tidied up.'

'I'm not staying. I've come to pick up some more clothes.'

I put the lids on my pens so I don't have to look at him. I don't know what to say.

'How's Jo?' he says.

He sees her every day at work, so much more than I do.

'Yeah, she's fine; I don't see much of her.'

'Where is she now?'

I shrug.

'Is she out with Hayley?'

'She wasn't here when I got home from work, so I don't know.'

'Doesn't she text you to let you know where she's going?'

'No, never.'

I draw blue stars on the side of my notes.

I want to ask him how he is, but I don't want him to think I'm prying. 'Where are you staying? Jo said with a mate?'

'With Ronnie from work. He's got a spare room.'

'What will you do when you have Ellie?'

'I'm taking her away next time I have her, going to get a hotel in Great Yarmouth and take her to all the arcades; they've got this Disney Magic show there.'

'She'll love that.'

'She'll miss Jo not being there with us.'

'She'll love having you to herself.'

'Then hopefully, the next time I'm due to have Ellie, me and

Jo will have sorted stuff out, and it won't be an issue.'

There's a pause. I want to say something nice to him, but I'm not going to bullshit.

'It's not the same without you here, Stevie. I have to do the cleaning.'

He looks at the clothes on the sofa.

'It's not up to my standard, but I wouldn't expect it to be, coming from you.'

It's funny how an insult from a person can be nice because they're telling the truth and it highlights how you can be honest with each other. And sometimes, people have to insult you as a way of being affectionate because they can't do it any other way.

Chapter Twenty-Three

I sit in the smoking hut with a hangover but know that I'll feel fine in a couple of hours. Reena and her football team are big drinkers: pints and shots and cocktails.

I messaged Richard on the way to the bar to show him I wasn't sitting at home on a Friday night, that I do have a good social life and there are people who want my company. After a couple of hours, I sent him some selfies inside the bar, of me and Reena and the football girls laughing, holding up our cocktails. He called me as soon as I'd sent the pictures. I couldn't hear him too well as it was so loud in the bar, so I went outside. Reena kept messaging me while I was on the call, asking me where I was, but Richard wanted to chat and was very animated so I stayed on the call with him and texted Reena I wouldn't be long. Richard wanted more advice on another one of his clients, a guy with depression. I reminded him what I'd said about getting through hour by hour, or if that was too much, ten minutes. I think Richard might be asking me advice to make me feel important, but I'm trying not to second-guess everything or it starts to do my head in.

'There are lots of men behind you in the photo you sent,' Richard said.

'Yeah. I've already been hit on a couple of times.'

'I'm not surprised. You're irresistible, Dani. You could take your pick.'

'There's someone else I like.'

'But these men are so young and handsome. Don't you want to be with someone your own age?'

'No. And I'd never be unfaithful in a relationship. I'm a bit pissed now so I can say it. We're in a relationship, aren't we?'

He laughs but doesn't answer. It annoys me so I end the call. I go back into the bar and chat to one of Reena's mates.

'Love those earrings,' I say. 'Where did you get them?'

'My friend makes them,' she says and I ask her for her friend's details.

I try to make more conversation and she's lovely but I keep thinking back to Richard not answering my question and it's putting me on a downer.

I tell Reena I'm leaving and get the bus instead of the tube so I have reception and can talk to Richard.

'We're in a relationship, aren't we?' I say. My voice doesn't sound how I want it to. Not strong enough. I shouldn't have drunk so much. It's making me too emotional.

'We are,' Richard says. 'Relax, Dani.'

★

This is the fifth time we've seen each other since we stopped being therapist and client. I walk around Richard's room, touching things, stroking them. I pretend I live here, that I've popped in to see him in between his clients, my clever professional partner. I entertain him and he's grateful for the distraction, the light relief I bring in the breaks between the important work he's doing. He watches me move around the room; I know he's enjoying it.

'You move like a dancer,' he says.

I told him once I wanted to do ballet as a child but couldn't because I was so fat. I pick up a small rock from a bookshelf. It

216

has a fossil in it. I pretend to be much more interested in it than I am. I want him to admire how curious I am. I put the rock back.

'I didn't have you down as a fossil hunter,' I say.

'Is it not something you'd like to do together, Dani?' He smiles.

'Are you taking the piss?'

'What's wrong with that idea?'

'Nothing, I suppose. I just couldn't see myself putting it down on my CV as an interest.'

'So what would an ideal day out be for you, if not fossil hunting?'

'I don't think I've ever really had any hobbies as such. I like to swim, but I've not been for a long time.'

'I love to swim too. Perhaps we could go together. What's funny about that?' he says.

'Usually, people go out for drinks, or dinner, in the early stages of a relationship. Not fossil hunting and swimming.'

'Why not? You've always struck me as a rule-breaker, Dani. Why not break from convention?'

'I suppose you're right,' I say. I pick up the carved wooden box from a shelf.

'Dani, put it back, please.'

'Why?' I read playfulness is a quality people value in a partner. Richard comes towards me. I hold the box above my head and smile. Playful.

'Why don't you want me to look at it?'

He reaches for the box so I bring it down quickly and behind my back. He moves forward and there's awkward fumbling as he tries to take it from my hand while I hold on to it more tightly. His shoulder bumps my top lip, and it feels so ungainly I let the box go. It falls to the floor, and flashes of silver spill out. I pick one up. Durex, extra thin, extra sensitive. Richard crouches down and gathers them up.

'Are you fucking other clients?

'Dani!'

'Seriously, are you fucking other clients?'

'No. I am not fucking other clients.' He closes the lid on the box.

'When I came in a few weeks ago, this box was under the couch.' I take the box from him and put it where I saw it.

'Dani, I'm not sleeping with my patients. I don't know how you could say such a thing.'

'Why was the box under the couch that time?'

'I don't know. Are you sure? I don't see why it would have been.'

'Don't try and make me doubt myself. I know what I saw.'

He stands up and puts the box back on the shelf, puts his hands on his hips.

'Let me think. I'm sure there's a logical explanation.'

'The logical explanation is that you're fucking other clients.'

'You're jumping to conclusions. Calm down and stop shouting.'

I walk to his desk and spin his chair around. Stand behind it. I want a barricade between us. I point at him. 'When I came in for my session the time the box was under the couch, your flies were half undone. I specifically remember because I found it unsettling and wanted you to do them up. I'm not stupid.'

'A perfect example,' he says calmly, 'a perfect example of a flawed interpretation which says more about the person interpreting than the one who is being accused. Why did you choose that interpretation, Dani? Could there be others? Could you pause, slow down, think for a moment?'

'I'm not stupid. Don't try and mug me off.'

'If a man's flies are half undone, does it automatically mean he's been having sex? Come on. Don't be so crass.'

'I know what I saw.'

'You're looking for monsters, and when people look for monsters, they find them.'

'What was the reason, then?'

'Why don't you think about how you could be wrong? Could you stop spinning my chair, please?'

'Why don't you tell me why I'm wrong?'

'You're relentless, aren't you? You're not going to give up. You're like a scrappy little terrier shaking a rat between its teeth.' He moves across the room and reaches out to touch my face but I jerk my head back and push his hand down. Richard goes to the mirror and looks at himself before turning to face me.

'Now I remember. If you must know, it was Becca. She came in one night when I was working late.'

'You said you hadn't slept together for months.'

'We haven't. We hadn't, except for that one time. It was only the one time.'

'So you lied to me.'

'I did not lie to you, Dani. It was so insignificant I forgot. It was nothing.'

He sounds sincere. He looks distressed. He's not lying. I know he genuinely does forget stuff sometimes from my therapy sessions. I thought it was a technique to make me work through important issues that needed going over twice, then I realised he really had forgotten.

'You should've told me. It wouldn't even have mattered. I don't want any lies between us.'

'Didn't you tell lots of lies around your bulimia?'

'That's different.' My face is warm.

'I'm sorry. I shouldn't have said that.'

He comes over and pushes the chair out of the way. He holds my upper arms, looks into my eyes.

'I am an honest person. I promise you. I don't tell lies. That's not me. I may be forgetful at times but I'm carrying so much up here.' He taps a finger against a temple. 'I'm seeing thirteen patients a week, Dani. Have you any idea of the emotional and psychological load I carry?' He goes and sits in his chair. Tips his head back and closes his eyes.

Of course he's honest. He's clever and sensitive and honest. That's why I'm so surprised he's into me. And he's right. I've lied loads in the past. If I get annoyed at people lying, it makes me a hypocrite on top of a liar. I should be more tolerant and realise it may not always be intentional. I sit in my chair.

'I still don't understand. Why do you keep a box of condoms in here, your therapy room?'

He doesn't open his eyes when he speaks.

'There was a phase, about a year ago, when Becca and I were going through a difficult time, and so I started sleeping in here. When things were getting back on track, she'd come in, and we'd make love, but we were still sleeping in separate rooms. That's why the condoms were kept here. I forgot all about them until the time Becca came in a few weeks ago. There, you demanded the truth, and you have it.'

'How old is she?'

'Why do you want to know?'

'I thought she was the same age as you but obviously, I'm wrong. Women in their fifties don't have to worry about getting pregnant.'

'She's forty-two. Why does it matter?'

'There's an age difference between you two as well then.'

'Does it matter?'

'She was young when she had Phoebe.'

'Dani, this is not important. We are important.'

'You said it was a phase. So you went through a phase of not getting on, you sleeping down here, but then you moved back into the bedroom?'

Richard opens his eyes and his tone is impatient, louder.

'Yes.'

'So you and Becca are good again?'

'Jesus, no, we're not. We're in the process of breaking up.'

'So why are you sharing a bed?'

'Because we couldn't care less, this time. We're not even trying to get through this. We know it's over.'

'How did you have sex? When she came in here? What position?' I say.

'Why would you want to know?'

'I just do.'

'I can't see why you would want to know,' he says.

'You constantly asked about my sex life.'

'That was part of your therapy.'

'Are you going to tell me?'

'You're not going to stop on at me until I do, are you?'

'No.'

'She came in and kept trying to talk to me. When I wouldn't give her any attention, she got in front of me, unzipped me, and started pleasuring me with her mouth.'

'Where were you? When was she doing that?'

He points to the desk.

'I was sitting there, working. Do you honestly want to know all this?'

'Is that something she did a lot?'

'What?'

'Head, giving you head?' I can't bring myself to say, 'pleasuring you with her mouth'. It's like something Enid Blyton would say if she wrote porn.

'No, never. She'd had a few drinks; she must have been feeling horny.'

'Go and sit on the chair,' I say. My voice sounds odd. I'm not used to giving orders.

He laughs. 'What are you thinking, Dani?'

'Do it.'

He gets up and sits on his desk chair.

'There, like a marionette, I have moved to your will. What would you like me to do next? Dance?' He moves his arms as though they are being yanked upwards by strings.

I walk over and kneel in front of him. I don't look at him but go straight for his flies and unzip them. I get a waft of lemons and washing powder.

'What are you doing, Dani?' he laughs but lifts his hips to make it easier for me to take it out. He undoes the top button of his trousers.

'So she came in like this, did she, and started . . .'

When he's fully hard and has both hands on my head, groaning, I stop and look up at him.

'And then you fucked her?'

'After a while.'

'How?'

'What?'

'How did you fuck her?'

'She leaned over the couch and I took her.'

He takes my head and tries to get me to start again. He pushes me down and keeps me there until I gag. I try to take his hands away and his thumbnail scratches my temple. He holds my head tighter, and I dig my fingers into his forearms. I take a deep breath when I come up and wipe a line of spit from the side of my face against his corduroy knee.

'Show me,' I say.

'What?'

'Show me how you fucked her.'

'You want me to pretend you're Becca?'

'I don't care. Show me how you fucked her.'

He stands up, takes my hand and pulls me up off the floor, over to the couch. He pushes me forward and stands behind me. He tries to unbutton my jeans but he fumbles so I push his fingers away and do it. I rest my hands on the couch and wait, feeling like an idiot while I listen to him unwrapping a condom. When he's inside me, he takes my arms and pulls them back and I feel the crease between my shoulder blades. I wonder, if I made some loud noises, would Becca hear? Would she barge in? I picture her doing a double-take. I want there to be another few seconds before we realise Becca's standing there, watching Richard fucking me. I want her to see that he's more turned on than he's ever been inside her.

Richard comes quickly, and I start pulling my jeans up, but he tells me to lie on the couch. When my jeans are on the floor and his head is between my legs, I think about Becca, how she could be in the next room, one wall away, while Richard's doing this.

I cover myself with the blanket and sit up. Richard's lips are shiny and his forehead is covered in a film of sweat. He rubs his fingers over his mouth and then brings them under his nose and breathes in.

'I love the taste of you, Dani.'

I reach down to get my jeans.

'Yeah, but don't sniff your fingers. It's weird.'

I get dressed and Richard strokes his hair back into place in front of the mirror.

'Don't you ever worry about Becca walking in?'

'She would never do that when she knows I'm seeing a patient.'

'What if she heard something? If she was going out and heard something when she was walking past?'

He turns round from opening the window.

'The room is soundproofed,' he says.

Chapter Twenty-Four

Four more months of Hall & Walker and I'll be back at university. While I'm stacking plates into the plastic tray, I think about last night. I saw Richard at the usual session time and for fifty minutes. The moment I walked in he said, 'Let me take control,' and was more physical than usual, rougher. He wanted me to ride him on the couch, then he suddenly dragged me up his body until I was on his face. I thought again of Becca opening the door and seeing us. When we were dressed, Richard said he was sorry but I had to leave on time as Becca was home, and Phoebe was back for a visit.

'Becca is cooking paella,' Richard said as he did his belt up, and I could see the moment he said it, he regretted it.

'You're going to go and be with your family now? Sit and have dinner whilst you can still taste me?'

'Dani,' he said. 'You're showing a remarkable lack of maturity.'

'You're making me feel used.' I took a book from the shelf: *Couch Fiction, A Graphic Tale of Psychotherapy.* 'Can I borrow this?' I wanted something of his to take home.

He peered over. 'Yes, that will be good for you. It's written in comic-book format.'

'You can fuck off.'

He laughed. It's all good for Richard. A quick fuck with me, then dinner with the family.

'So, Becca is making paella. How lovely. Are you having friends over too or is it an intimate family gathering?'

I pictured the three of them laughing around the table and I burned. 'Make sure you compliment Becca on her cooking, and I'm sure Phoebe will regale you with lots of exciting university tales.'

'You're being very manic. Calm down. I want to be with you. I will be with you. You expect me to up and leave my family within a matter of weeks? Come on. We've talked about this. I need you to find your adult self.'

I grabbed his hand and put it down my jeans so his fingers got me on them and walked out without saying goodbye. I hoped he forgot to wash his hands before he ate. I hoped Becca asked him to pass her the bread, the salt, the pepper.

In the hall, standing by the open front door, were a couple of girls. I could tell straight away which one was Richard's daughter. She had the same hair colour, the same brown eyes and confident curve of the mouth. We made eye contact and I knew she and I wouldn't get on. She wasn't good-looking but held herself as if she were. She looked at me with the arrogance of a person who's grown up thinking they're special because Mummy and Daddy have always indulged them. Fashionable clothes, subtle makeup, an out-there necklace and a lip and nose piercing. I've always thought people who get their faces pierced do it because they need a conversation-starter. Same with tattoos. I'm sure it does have immense significance to you and you've rehearsed a story about why you got it, but I don't want to hear the story as it won't be anywhere near as profound as you think it is. You think you're interesting and rebellious getting your tattoo, when in fact you'd be more original not following the crowd and not having one done at all.

'Enjoy Mummy's paella, and your dad's cock is smaller than average,' I wanted to say to Phoebe.

'Thanks,' I say to the floor as they move aside to let me pass.

On afternoon break, in the smoking hut, Tulsi is whinging about her girlfriend again and I think if people stopped listening to her, indulging her, commiserating, placating, Tulsi would have to speak to Lily instead. When Tulsi ramps it up even further and starts crying pretend tears, I've had enough.

'Tulsi, if you're not happy, end it.'

It probably came out more aggressive than I wanted it to. I'm still pissed off about last night. The conversation in the hut stops.

Pat looks at me like she wants to ask a question and then shakes her head. I look at a couple of dog-ends on the ground. Pure laziness when we have the bucket ashtrays.

'If you're not happy with a situation, don't keep talking about it; do something,' I say. 'If you're eating an apple, and you find out it's rotten, would you carry on eating it? That's what I was trying to say.' I chuck my dog-end in the bucket and stand up. 'Sorry if it came out wrong.'

I go back up to pot wash but I'm only there a couple of minutes and haven't even stacked the first tray before Babs calls me into her office. The room is still a shit tip and smells like old milk. I breathe through my mouth.

'Close the door,' she says.

'Everything okay?' I say.

'I'll get straight to the point, Dani. Did you tell Maureen to fuck off this morning?'

'What?'

'After you got back from tea break.'

'Tell Maureen to fuck off?'

'She wasn't going to say anything, but she looked upset and I asked her what was up.'

'I didn't mean for her to hear.'

'You did say it then?'

'Do you want me to apologise?'

'Do you think you should?'

'I will. I didn't want her to hear. I was wound up about something and she got me at the wrong time. I think she was telling me off about something. But that doesn't excuse it, I know.'

Babs shakes her head. 'I'm going to have to give you a written warning for this, Dani.'

'Seriously?'

'You can't treat your workmates like that.'

'Please don't, Babs. Can't it be a verbal warning? If you give me a written warning the next thing's the sack, isn't it? I don't want to lose this job. I can't lose this job. I need the money.'

'You won't lose the job if you toe the line. It's simple. Don't be late and be respectful to your colleagues.' She bites the side of her thumbnail. 'Is everything okay, Dani? You've seemed distracted lately.'

'Everything is fine.'

'Another thing. It's been brought to my notice that you've been leaving the kitchen when it's not time for your break. What's going on?'

I've been going off to call or message Richard, but I've not been gone that long. I'm pissed off someone's grassed on me. I work harder than everyone in that kitchen except Pat.

'Probably the toilet. I've got a problem when it's that time of the month, you know.'

'Have you been to the doctors?'

'I'm going to book an appointment.'

'Make sure you do.'

'I'm sorry, anyway.'

'Go on,' she says. 'Go and apologise to Maureen, and don't do it again. If you do, that will be it.'

After work, I go to the gym. I'm managing to maintain my weight despite not throwing up. I can't be bothered to eat and am smoking a lot more. When I'm finished in the gym, I meet Jo in a bar in Ealing. Nowadays she wants to be out all the time, wearing her new clothes and going to new places. She's enjoy-ing the attention she's getting because she's thinner and holding herself with more confidence, but the attention she's getting is more to do with the loved-up glow. People can sense it and it's appealing; they respond to it. I go to the bar for vodka and Diet Cokes and take them back to our table.

'We went to Doug's brother's house for a party on Friday night, and you know who was there?' Jo can't wait to tell me.

'No idea,' I say and down half of my drink. She names some reality stars who have made their names and become famous by displaying ignorance about simple facts or doing makeup blogs on social media. She's star-struck and basking in the glory of having puffed on the same joint as one of them, got makeup tips from another.

'This type of thing would never happen on a night out with Stevie.'

'Not his crowd, is it?' Stevie watched all the reality crap on TV with Jo but he wouldn't be in awe of them.

'Stevie just wanted to eat out. Or watch Ipswich. Doug gets out and about more. He knows people.'

'Stevie's not moving back anytime soon then?'

'No,' she says. 'He's staying at Ronnie's and I'm having some fun.'

'Aren't you worried he'll find out?'

'Why would he? You're the only one who knows.'

She's getting off on the secrecy of it all. My relationship with Richard is also secret, but whilst Jo's enjoying that aspect of it, to me, it feels dirty.

Chapter Twenty-Five

Richard's coming over to the flat today, and he's bringing lunch. I picture him carefully choosing ingredients in Waitrose without looking at the prices. I can't settle, and keep going to the balcony to see if I can see him. He's coming at twelve. I've been cleaning, and then pacing since six this morning. I paint my nails luminous orange then smudge them while I'm plumping up the sofa cushions. I walk around the flat, trying to see it from his perspective and imagine what he'll think. There are no bookshelves. There are no pictures on the walls except two large canvas pictures of Stevie and Jo. They went to a professional photographer and both had their hair cut before.

While I'm in the toilet again, the intercom buzzer goes. He's ten minutes early. I consider making him wait till bang on twelve but it wouldn't be nice to leave him hanging around the communal entrance. I pick up the handset and say hello like I don't know who it will be.

'Hello, Dani.'

'Hi.'

I love how he sounds on the phone. I wonder if we'll have sex before or after lunch.

'Could you possibly buzz me in?'

I open the door to the flat, then think it looks too keen to be standing there as he walks down the corridor. I shut it again and go to the kitchen. I realise I haven't cleaned inside the microwave and unplug it. If he wants to use it I'll say it's broken. I hope he doesn't want to use it. Microwaved food isn't romantic.

Richard knocks, and I take my time getting there.

'I meant to tell you the lifts aren't working,' I say.

'Yes, I gathered. Rather a long way up.'

'At least we're not on the eighth floor.'

'Can I come in, please?'

I stand back to let him step through. He's carrying a large shoulder bag and an Asda carrier bag. I've forgotten what to do.

'Are we just going to stand here?' He smiles.

'This way.' I walk through to the living room.

'That's quite a TV.'

'Stevie's into his sports. Likes to watch them on a big screen.'

'It's like a cinema in here.'

We both look at the TV mounted on the wall, seventy-five inches of spotless black glass. I look at Richard's reflection on the screen and see him briefly wrinkle his nose.

'I don't watch much TV. I prefer reading,' I say.

'This is a nice colour scheme.' He looks around. 'Nicely decorated, all blues and greys, like a stormy sky, shades like the Van Gogh painting.'

'Yeah, Jo likes stuff to match.' I think it's nice of him to find something positive to say when he probably doesn't like it. It's so different from his therapy room.

'I haven't asked you about the artists you like, Dani.'

'I used to think Neil Buchanan was good.'

'Buchanan? I've not heard of him. A modern artist?' Richard brings a curved finger to his chin.

'Used to present *Art Attack*.'

'Ah. You're joking with me, aren't you?'

'Yes. I was. Ha ha,' I say.

I pick up one of the cushions from the sofa but don't know what to do with it. I throw it back down.

'Do you want a beer?' I say.

'A cup of tea first, I think. Rehydrate a little after all those stairs.'

'You work out though, don't you?'

'I do, but I took the stairs two at a time.'

'Why?'

'To get to you more quickly.'

I don't know whether to tell him to sit down on the sofa or ask him if he wants to come with me. When I'm in his room, I can sit and read all the book titles or look at the art on the walls. In here, there's not a lot to look at when the TV's off. He never takes his phone out so I doubt he'll sit and look at that.

While I'm getting the milk out of the fridge, he comes in.

'Lunch,' he says, holding up the bag.

'Do you always shop in Asda?'

'Sometimes, yes.'

'What about the other times?'

'It varies. Mostly Asda, or Waitrose if we're splashing out.'

'So I'm not worth splashing out on?'

'I didn't shop today. I wanted to, but I didn't have the time, I'm afraid. I brought these things from home. This was the first bag I came across.'

He takes stuff out of the bag and holds it up to show me.

'A very nice tuna,' he says, holding out a tin. 'Some good crackers.' The box is open. 'Olives.' He puts the carton down on the kitchen worktop. 'And some . . .' – he reads the front of the pack – 'blush sun-dried tomato and mozzarella – oh, these are from Hall & Walker, you're in luck!' He shakes out the carrier, flattens it on the worktop and folds it into a small square. He hasn't brought any wine. Lucky I went out and got a bottle earlier; I thought it would be our second. At least he won't want to use the microwave.

'Oh, you use the tea bag in the mug method.'

He comes over and peers into the mug as I'm pouring boiling water in it, like I'm making an unusual recipe with exotic ingredients.

'Don't most people?'

'I always use loose tea and a teapot. You can taste the flavour of the tea.'

'Well, I hope this is okay for you; the flavour is Tetley.'

He laughs.

'Are you okay with normal milk?' I say, holding the carton up at him. 'I'm afraid we don't have any made from soya or nuts or anything like that.'

'Good old cow juice is fine,' he says. 'Cow juice,' he repeats.

'Yes, I heard you the first time. It just wasn't funny.'

'You,' he says and pokes me in the ribs with a pretend angry expression on his face.

I take a bottle of low-calorie beer from the fridge. I'd usually drink it straight from the bottle, but I take a glass from the cupboard.

'Shall we go through and sit down?'

'I'm going to prepare lunch, Dani. I'm a little peckish.'

'Oh, that reminds me of another word I hate.'

'Peckish?'

'Yes.'

'Right, let me add this to the list of words I'm not allowed to say in your presence. Meh, yay, fab, tingly, fizzy and peckish. That right?'

'That's good. But don't forget "bedding".'

'Got you,' he says.

'Are there any words you don't want me to use around you?'

He puts a hand on my shoulder.

'Dani, I'm touched you asked, but I'm generally okay with any words you choose to use. Use any you want.'

'Okay, shall I stay in here and talk to you while you make lunch?'

'Why not. Unless you have anything you need to be getting on with?'

'I'll stay. It's okay.'

He opens the mug cupboard.

'Knife? Plates? Tin opener?'

I hand him a knife, and he stabs at the mozzarella mix, peels back the lid. I put the tin opener and plates on the counter next to him. He opens the tin of tuna and arranges a few crackers on two plates.

'Do you have any mayonnaise? It might be nice to mix the tuna in with some mayo; I forgot to bring any,' he says.

'Becca might've wondered where it had gone,' I say. I get it out of the fridge and put it on the work surface in front of him.

'Oh, a squeezy bottle.'

There is a volley of farts as he squeezes it out. He's putting far too much in; it'll be like tuna-flavoured mayonnaise. He eats a sun-dried tomato and sucks his fingers. I wait for him to go and wash his hands but he doesn't. If I was preparing food for someone, I wouldn't be licking at my fingers while I was doing it.

'Nearly ready,' he says.

'Great. Do you want a glass of wine?'

I've finished my beer and I need another drink.

'Go on, I've nearly finished my tea. What wine is it?'

'White wine,' I say.

'What kind?'

'Waterfall Hills.' I take it from the fridge and unscrew the lid.

'That's not a type of wine,' Richard laughs. 'It's a brand name.'

I look at the bottle again. Pinot Grigio, but I don't want to pronounce it wrong.

I pass the bottle to Richard.

'Waterfall Hills Pinot Grigio,' he says.

'I got it from the garage this morning. They don't have a big selection.'

I'm sure Richard knows a lot about wine. I usually drink vodka or whisky with Diet Coke as it's got fewer calories. He takes a sip of his wine and puts it down on the worktop.

'You look beautiful, by the way,' he says. 'Come here.'

He holds out his arms and I go to him. I close my eyes and I like the feel of his arms around me. He keeps trying to stop the hug but I hold on to him until he laughs, says my name and takes my arms away.

'Are we eating in here?' He nods towards the kitchen table.

'Yes, if that's okay, or on the balcony?'

I spent a long time cleaning it up. I emptied the fag buckets as well. It didn't look too bad after.

'In here is fine,' he says. He bites into a cracker.

'Mind if I put the radio on?' I say. The Heart jingle fills the room. 'Jo likes Heart.' I turn the dial, trying to find another station.

'Oh, wonderful – leave it please.' Richard speaks with his mouth full as I hit a classical music channel. I take a long sip of wine and look at my tuna crackers with the olives on the side. I have one ball of mozzarella and two sun-dried tomatoes. The way he's presented it on the plate is good. Artful. Richard closes his eyes and sways his shoulders to the music. Is this what middle class is? Good tuna on crackers, and classical music?

'Brahms – wonderful. What kind of music do you like, Dani?'

'I haven't listened to much classical music.' I know the names of some composers but if I say one, he might expect me to say more about it. Richard's eaten everything on his plate. He uses the tip of his forefinger to dab at cracker crumbs on his plate and put them in his mouth. His eyes follow my hand as I pick up a cracker and take a bite. He does the same when I eat an olive. I consider holding the next olive up to the ceiling to see if his eyes will still follow.

'I'm sorry. I must have wolfed that; I was terribly hungry. Are you enjoying it?' he says.

'Yes, it's fine.' I push my plate towards him. 'But I had a big breakfast so I'm not that hungry.'

'Are you sure?'

I can't sit and eat while he's watching me like that. I pour us more wine.

'Tell me about when you were in the band,' I say. 'What was your best gig?'

'The first Glastonbury,' he says. 'The atmosphere was unreal.'

'Are you friends with the band, still?'

'We meet up once a year or so, have a bit of a reunion.'

'Do you ever think about re-forming?'

'No, it's in the past – but it was great while it lasted.'

'Is there anything online of you performing? I'd love to see it.'

'There are a few videos on YouTube, I think. The quality isn't great. We're going back a while, Dani.'

'I'm going to look,' I say and grab my phone.

'Hang on a moment,' he says. 'It might be better for you to use a bigger screen.' He goes to his shoulder bag and reaches inside it. 'I thought you might like this.'

'You're lending me a laptop?'

'No. It's for you to keep. I wanted to get you a present. Take it, it's for you.'

'Thanks,' I say.

'I'm afraid it's not new, but I only got it last year. I've restored it to its original settings. For when you return to university. And before that, you can use it for your writing.'

My first laptop. I wash my hands before I open it and turn it on. Throbbing winged hearts flutter across the pink screen. It asks me for a password.

'I don't know what to say. I've always used my phone. Thanks.'

'You deserve nice things, Dani.'

'Don't you need it?'

'I've bought a new one.'

'Thanks. I don't know what to say,' I say again. I reach out and take his hand. 'What's the password?'

'What do you think?'

'I don't know.'

'It has four letters.'

'Shag?'

He leans over and spells out each letter as he types in 'l o v e'.

'It will help with your studies, with writing your essays.'

He sits back on his chair and smiles.

'Thanks.' I want to hide my face.

'Come here, you,' he says.

We kiss, and I lead him to my bedroom. It's good I've not eaten much – my stomach's still flat. He makes little moaning noises when I ride him and gets out of breath. I wonder why when it's me doing all the work. After he's come, I go to the toilet, and when I come back, he's kneeling on the floor, leaning over the side of the bed.

'What are you doing?' I say.

'Just cooling down,' he smiles at me.

He's like a bear with alopecia. There are patches of hair over his back – hairy shoulders like wings.

I pull my dressing gown around me. Seeing him like this feels more intimate than the sex.

'I'm going for a cigarette.'

When I've lit my second roll-up, he comes out on the balcony and touches me on the shoulder.

'Smoking again.' He sits down in the chair beside me.

'Got your breath back, have you?'

'What are your plans for next week, Dani?'

'I'm going for a drink with Elijah and his girlfriend on Thursday. We've both got the day off.'

Richard's dressed but left his shirt untucked. He's not wearing socks, and his big toenails are pale yellow with lines on them.

'Elijah? The carer from the old people's home?'

'Yes.'

'I was going to suggest we meet Thursday evening. I'm going to see a friend in Wales next weekend. I thought we could spend Thursday night together.'

'The whole night?'

'Yes. I'll book a hotel.'

'What about Becca?'

'She doesn't need to know I'm going to Wales a day later.'

I blow smoke out of the side of my mouth so it doesn't hit him in the face.

'Where's the hotel?'

'Central London. I know a nice one, intimate.'

A whole night together. We'll be like a proper couple. I drop my dog-end into the plant pot.

'Coming back in?' I say.

We sit on the sofa. He looks at the two canvases of Jo and Stevie and smiles. In his room, there's lots of stuff to make conversation about. Apart from the TV, the pictures of Jo and Stevie are the only things on the walls in here.

239

'Thanks again for the laptop,' I say.

'That's enough thanking me, Dani. I know you appreciate it.'

I wonder if he gives Becca such good presents. It's not even my birthday. I think about being with him, celebrating our birthdays and Christmas together. Special events where we could be even more thoughtful to each other than usual. Give each other presents that had been carefully considered and wrapped in expensive paper and watch the delight on the other one's face when they opened it.

'Jo and Stevie are exactly as I imagined them.' Richard is staring at one of the canvases on the wall.

I'm not sure what he means by that. I'm not going to ask because I don't want to talk about them. That's what we did in therapy.

'Actually,' he says, 'Stevie looks like a patient I was seeing. He had a stroke recently and he's now unable to elucidate his thoughts verbally, so he's had to stop coming. Terribly sad.'

'Do you know what Diogenes did one time?'

'Now there's a shift in subject.'

'Is that okay?'

'Sure,' he says.

'Diogenes had this ongoing feud with Plato because he thought he was pretentious. Plato described a human as a "featherless biped", so Diogenes plucked a chicken and took it to Plato's academy. He went to one of the classrooms and chucked this chicken up in the air and said, "Behold – Plato's human being."'

'And?'

'So Plato had to add "with broad, flat nails" to his definition.'

'What made you decide to tell me that little anecdote?'

'I don't know.'

'I'm sure you have a reason. It didn't come from nowhere.'

'When you said about your client who had the stroke. You said, "unable to elucidate his thoughts verbally". You could have said, "can't speak".

'You study English. Why not use the beautifully descriptive words we have at our disposal?'

'I do. In essays.'

'You're so endearing.' He leans into me, and we kiss.

'Thanks for the laptop.'

'What are you doing to me, Dani?' He takes my hand and puts it on his erection. 'I've not made love twice in such a short time for years.'

We do it on the sofa.

He says he has to go or he'll be late for his patient and books an Uber. We walk to the front door and when I open it, we can hear lots of banging in the corridor outside. Richard doesn't move.

'Are you going to see me out?'

'I am.'

'I mean, come downstairs with me.'

'I hadn't planned to.'

'What is all that noise?'

'Probably kids fighting. It happens a lot. They chase each other up and down and use the lifts and the stairs. One time this kid was running around with a plank of wood with nails in it.' I smile but Richard's brow creases.

'Come with me, Dani; you're braver than I am.' He says it in a jokey voice but I remember he told me once, "There is much seriousness in jokes".'

'You want me to walk you out?'

I get dressed and we walk down the stairs. At one point, there's a huge bang and a couple of men shout and swear at each other. Richard pulls me in towards him.

'I'll protect you, baby,' he says in an American accent.

'You're so big and strong,' I say.

'I'm shitting myself really,' he says. 'I just wanted you to think I was brave.'

'Are you a lover not a fighter?' I say and he nods.

'Me too,' I say.

In the hall, I open the main door and Richard walks to the Uber, gets into the back. I wait in case he turns and waves as the car drives off, but he doesn't turn around.

As soon as I get back in the flat, I remember he said about the videos of his band on YouTube and look it up on my new laptop. He was gorgeous, even better-looking than he is now. I was right – he has complete stage presence and I love the way he interacts with the other band members and ignores the crowds. I watch it a few times.

There's not much to clean in the kitchen. I thought he'd cook something classy with a scattering of pomegranate seeds or something like that on top. The Asda bag has a receipt in the bottom. Three days ago, he, or Becca, bought an eight-pack of value toilet roll, some long-life semi-skimmed milk, and cheese and onion crisps.

Chapter Twenty-Six

I need to spend time with Pat. She wasn't as friendly with me for a few days after the earring incident, but then it was like she'd completely forgotten about it. Anyway, I've been avoiding her, because I know if we get chatting and it all goes back to normal between us, I'll tell her about Richard, but I'm not ready to hear her opinion. I go and find her at her station, and her face softens when she sees me coming over. We arrange to have lunch in a nearby café.

I take our cups of tea to the table.

'I'm sorry about the earrings.'

She waves a hand at me. 'Forget about it. It's in the past.'

'Aren't you still annoyed?'

'Life's too short, Dani. It's not a big deal. And the ones you replaced them with were nicer. Megan loved them.'

'They're handmade. I got them from one of Reena's mates. I thought you were being funny with me, Pat.'

'No, Dani.'

'How's your mum?'

'She's good. Still complaining about the food.'

'I'm sorry I've not gone with you lately. I've had a lot going on.'

'It was nice of you to come all those times when you did;

there's no obligation for you to come. Elijah was asking after you the other day, said to say hello and tell you that he's started buying his books from a good charity shop near work.'

'I'll message him. I feel bad, though – I set something up with Frank, coming to see him every week. And I was going to start chatting to some of the other residents too – the ones that don't get visitors. I only did that once, with Mary.'

'Frank understands you're busy, and don't worry about Mary. Don't feel guilty about things you've got no need to feel guilty about. You need to focus more on self-compassion, love. You feel it enough for other people. You need to start being a bit more compassionate towards yourself. Would you be as hard on other people as you are on yourself?'

'Never.' I look at the laminated menu but there's nothing on it I want. 'Is Frank all right? I didn't realise how poorly he was until Elijah told me.'

'He's not good at the minute.'

'Shit. I'll go after work today.'

'It's his son that should feel bad, Dani. Not you. He's not visited him for months.'

A woman with a buggy is struggling to push the door open to come in but before I can get up to help, Pat is there, holding the door open.

'You still on track for uni in October?' she says when she sits down again.

'Yeah, it's all going well. I'm going in for a reintegration meeting in a couple of weeks to see the head of department. I might see if Babs will let me carry on working at weekends. I'll still need a job. The student loan only really covers the fees; there's not much left over.'

'I'm sure there's not. How's your therapy? Is it still going okay?'

244

'Yeah.' I slide the menu towards her. 'Did you want a sandwich or anything?'

'No, love. I had my lunch at break.'

I check my phone and put it back on the table. I could tell her now, about Richard. The café's quiet and we've got another forty minutes before we need to get back. But I think I know what Pat would say and I'm not ready to hear it.

'I'm stressed about Jo,' I say. 'I think she's making a big mistake and she can't see it.'

'With the guy she's seeing from work?'

'Yeah.' I feel guilty using Jo to change the subject, but I probably would've talked to Pat about it even if the stuff with Richard wasn't going on. 'If Jo had partied more when she was younger, she wouldn't be acting like a teenager now.'

'She's hardly that old now, is she?'

'Old enough. She's twenty-six. If she'd done all her partying when she was younger, different boyfriends and all that, she'd have got it out of her system. She's been with Stevie since she was twenty. Before that, she was in another long-term relationship. She should be single for a while, play the field, have fun.'

'Have you said any of that to her?'

'She'd kill me.' I smile. 'Who am I to be passing judgement and giving out words of wisdom?'

'You're entitled to an opinion, love.'

'Jo won't want to hear it.'

'Finds it hard to listen to little sister, does she?'

'Exactly. She still tries to pull rank.' I rip bits off a serviette and make a pile of the shreds. The woman Pat held the door open for has put her toddler in a high chair and is feeding her the contents of a little jar with a plastic spoon.

'That reminds me,' says Pat. 'It's Tia's birthday coming up. Megan's asked me to come over and do the party food.'

245

'How old will Tia be? Is it two or three?' I know she's somewhere thereabouts.

'She'll be three,' says Pat. 'And Tyler five on his next birthday.'

'How are they all?'

'Dani. I love them dearly, but I don't want to turn into one of those grandmothers who always talk about cute things the kids have done that should be kept within the family.'

'They're lucky to have you,' I say. 'I can't wait to have kids. I've always thought I'll want my first kid at twenty-seven.'

'You've never told me that before.'

'It's another reason I want to sort myself out. I want the degree and a good job, but I have these really strong maternal feelings. And when I have kids, I'll think about how my mum was with me and Jo and I'll do the opposite. I'd like the chance to experience a good mother–child bond. I need to have my own kids to do that.'

We watch the toddler batting her mum's hand away as she tries to give her another spoonful.

'It's never as easy as you think it will be,' Pat says. 'But I think you'll make a lovely mum.'

'I know I will be. I'm going to do all the things I wish my mum had done with me.'

'Like what?'

'Play board games with them, do their hair, take them to school and pick them up. Sit at the table and have dinner. Go on bike rides, go swimming, ask them questions and be interested in their answers. Loads of things like that. I can't wait. And I'm going to make them lovely lunchboxes for school.'

'Sounds good,' says Pat.

We drink our tea.

'I think my mum might be autistic,' I say.

'There's a lot of adults being diagnosed nowadays.'

'Some of the things she's said to me, or done before. I mean, she gave me a birthday card when I was sixteen and it was still in the cellophane. She said sorry she hadn't had time to write in it. I know these things are little things, but—'

'They hurt,' says Pat.

'Yeah,' I say. 'Anyway, this girl at school, Carly, always used to have cheese and pickle – and her mum grated the cheese and the bread was homemade – and Carly used to chuck them in the bin half the time because she didn't even want them.'

'Always the way,' says Pat.

'So my children are having cheese and pickle on homemade brown bread in their lunches. It's the first thing I'm going to make them. And I'm going to plough so much love into them it will be untrue.'

'Ploughman's the love into them,' says Pat, and I laugh. 'You've got it all planned out, haven't you?' she says.

'It's important to always think of a good future. If you think of it, imagine it, believe in it, then you're some of the way there already.'

247

Chapter Twenty-Seven

If we're on our own, or if I'm drunk, the relationship with Richard can be excellent. I love how he'll respond to my questions from a psychoanalytical angle. I love how he understands people, their behaviour and why they act as they do. He's very clever and he's good at explaining stuff. I love the way he speaks, his gentle voice and the tone of it – deep and warm and unrushed. It's when I imagine what other people are thinking that I get stressed. People might think he's my dad.

He called last night and said he was free tonight as Becca had decided to go to her mother's in Staffordshire or somewhere equally boring-sounding. I asked if he'd spoken to her yet and he said he was getting closer to it. I suggested the theatre as we would have the whole evening, and he was all over it. I bought tickets for a modern dance performance.

We go for dinner first at a small restaurant with cream table-cloths and a short vase with one flower on each table.

'Have what you like, Dani. I'm getting this as you got the theatre tickets,' Richard says.

The waiter comes, and I tell Richard to order first as I'm still deciding. He asks for a sirloin and a bottle of red wine, then checks I'm okay with red.

I order pasta, not something I could have kept down before.

'What did you think when I came for my first session? I can remember you answering the door. I thought you'd be much smaller for some reason. You don't think of psychotherapists being these great, huge people.'

'Six foot two, Dani; I wouldn't say huge.'

'You're well built as well. What did you think of me?'

He sits back in his chair and smiles. 'Thank you. My first impression of you? I thought you were annoying.'

'Annoying?'

'Attractive, but annoying. But as I got to know you . . .'

'That often happens. People don't like me at first.'

'Why do you think that is?'

'I can come across as a bit in-your-face, I suppose. My dad said . . .' I lose my train of thought. 'He wouldn't have liked you. If my dad was alive, I wouldn't be sitting here. He'd have thought this is wrong.'

'Is there a part of you that's projecting your feelings onto your father?'

'Projecting?'

'Yes, that's what I said.'

'I don't know what "projecting" means.' I take the flower out of the vase and smell it. Plastic. 'You studied psychotherapy for years, but you use these terms like I should know them. Why would I? People can't know stuff unless they've been taught.'

The waiter brings the wine and opens it at the table. He asks Richard if he'd like to try it first and Richard says yes. The waiter pours a small amount into the glass and stands back. Richard picks it up, swirls the liquid, takes a deep sniff, pauses and sips. He makes a motion with his lips like a baby sucking on a teat.

'It's fine. You can pour,' Richard says.

I wait until the waiter has gone.

'I could never do that.'

'Do what?'

'Smell and taste the wine with the waiter and the other person watching and waiting. Doesn't it make you want to laugh?'

'Why would it?'

'It all seems very intense,' I say.

'It's important to sample the wine,' he says.

I realise how immature I'm being.

'What's the best thing that's happened to you today?' I say.

'Oh, I don't know, Dani. I read a fascinating article earlier, probably that.'

I was trying to lighten the mood but I think Richard prefers to speak about more serious subjects. We take sips of wine and I think of what to say. Richard is looking at a couple of women laughing at the table next to us.

'What was that you were saying about projection?' I say.

He turns his attention back to me.

'Projection? Projection is a defence mechanism when a person gives characteristics or feelings to another person to displace their own negative feelings. It might be what you feel, Dani, but you don't want to own it, so you attribute it to your father's beliefs.'

'No, it's not projection. My dad would have hated you. He would have thought you were a piece of shit for making a pass at me. I imagined phoning him up when you did, and that's what he would have said. I know it. He thought everyone was a piece of shit – the people who weren't absolutely brilliant. There was no in-between.'

'A man of extremes.'

'Aren't we all?'

'Some of us are more emotionally measured.'

'By measured you mean stable. Someone who thinks before they act?'

'That can be one aspect.'

'Yeah. I don't think my dad did that. I remember him ripping a shed door off its hinges once because it had swung back at him. Ripped it off and threw it on the floor and stamped on it. And he used to have fights with the hoover all the time, if the wire got tangled up. He'd be like, "Cunt, cunt, cunt!"'

'Dani, make your voice a little lower.' Richard looks at the women next to us again.

'Sorry.'

'Uncontained rage. It must have been difficult, being exposed to such anger.' Richard reaches out and squeezes my wrist and I cough to clear a block that's trying to slide across my throat.

'It was a part of him.'

'Did he get angry with you?'

I pour wine into Richard's glass and then into mine. I twist the bottle like the waiter did.

'Sometimes. You know he used to shout I was "a weirdo piece of shit" over and over. But he was always so apologetic afterwards. He'd be like, "Dani, I sincerely, sincerely apologise." And I could tell how bad he felt, and that made me feel sorry for him. There were some other times when he shouldn't have done what he—'

I stop talking because Richard's looking at a plate of food a waitress has put down for the women next to us. I'm not going to tell him personal things while he's staring at someone's dinner.

Richard looks back at me and reaches across the table to take my hand.

'Go on,' he says.

'I remember now. I wanted to ask you how I could make it stop,' I say.

'Make what stop?'

'I used to always think to myself, "you weirdo piece of shit," every time I did something wrong. I was going to ask you how to stop that happening. But it comes less nowadays anyway. Maybe that's why I forgot to ask. And I've been working on self-compassion. I even gave myself a foot massage the other day.'

'You're not a weirdo piece of shit, Dani. You are a beautiful and intelligent young woman.' He leans forward over the table and lowers his voice. 'And I'd like to massage your feet too.'

I wonder if he'd then expect me to do it to him. I think of his big yellow toenails with the lines on them. But isn't this what intimacy is? Giving the person you're with a foot massage? Touching each other in a way that isn't always sexual?

Our food comes. While we're eating, Richard looks at my food a couple of times and I wonder if he's expecting me to offer him some. I think about a time, early in the relationship, when I rang Christy and he pulled over into a layby because he was driving. I wanted to talk to him about the essay I was writing. We used to do that at the beginning before it all turned to shit. We were chatting for over an hour, then he moved the phone and I saw a KFC bag on the passenger seat. He'd let it go cold because he wanted to talk to me.

'I think you have a lot of suppressed rage, Dani.' Richard puts a big piece of steak into his mouth, chews it a couple of times and before he's swallowed, he's got the next forkful lined up and waiting at his chin.

'I wouldn't disagree. You eat quite quickly, don't you?'

It's not just the speed but the noise. I'm not sure I can eat my pasta in these conditions. Richard doesn't swallow his mouthful before answering. He brings his hand in front of his mouth to cover it and talks through the food.

'I'm famished. How's yours?'

'Fine.' I put my fork down.

'Good. This is tasty.'

I hate that word. It makes me think of dogs snuffling around the food bowl to get every last smear of food from the edges. I could tell Richard to add it to the word list but I don't want him to think I'm too controlling.

Richard swishes his little finger over the plate to wipe up smears of sauce.

'Aren't you hungry?' he says, nodding towards my bowl. I've only had a few mouthfuls.

I push it towards him.

'I'm just going to the loo.' I'd never usually leave a person I was in a restaurant with to eat alone, but I know he won't care.

In the toilets, I look in the mirror and wait until I think he'll have finished before I go back. I stop at the bar, order a vodka shot and down it.

'Dani, you weren't . . .' he says as I sit down.

'God no,' I say. 'Please.'

I could tell him that I'd never bother being sick after eating so little, but I don't want to talk about bulimia while we're out for dinner.

When the bill comes, Richard pays with his card and he leaves a twenty-pound note on the table.

At the bar of the theatre, I order two large glasses of wine. Richard goes to the toilet and as he moves across the room, I imagine he's a stranger. What would I think of him, if I didn't know him? He's tall and fit and the type of good-looking that makes people look a bit longer. Dark hair, dark eyes and strong jawline. He moves well, he's graceful and coordinated. I see a woman staring at him, probably thinking the same as me and I feel a hot wave of jealousy. Richard comes back to stand with me at the bar and the woman looks from him to me. I smile at her.

The announcement to take our seats comes over the tannoy and people start moving. I quickly finish my wine. Richard calls over a young barman who's standing down the other end of the bar checking his phone.

'You see this woman here?' Richard says. 'Isn't she absolutely beautiful?' The barman laughs and Richard puts his arm around me. 'I am absolutely mad about her and you can see why, can't you? She's exquisite. Look at her red hair, those blue eyes you can lose yourself in. She's utterly gorgeous, isn't she?'

The barman is blushing now. He doesn't look old enough to be working behind a bar.

'Yes, she is,' he says.

'And what makes her even more special is that she's so intelligent too,' Richard says.

If I wasn't so pissed, I'd be mortified.

'Let's go in,' I say to Richard.

We find our seats. I've booked good ones, and we're right in the middle of the row, facing the stage. The people already sitting pretend to squash themselves into their seats, and we pretend to stretch ourselves taller so we can get past them without touching. We sit down. There's the hum of chatter, and the atmosphere is good, expectant. I can't think of anything to say. The last time I went to the theatre was at high school. I resort to what I'm good at, what will give me something to do and remove the need for speaking. I lean back into Richard and put my hand around the back of his head, pull him down and kiss him. He tries to pull away after our lips have briefly met, but I pull him in again and use my tongue. There's tutting, and I hear the word 'appalling' whispered loudly. I ignore it and sit up, lean over and put a hand behind Richard's head, kiss him hard and make a low moaning noise.

'Appalling.' She's said it again. Louder this time.

I let go of Richard and look at the women behind us.

'What the fuck are you looking at?'

Richard puts his hand on my leg and turns round to face the women.

'I'm so sorry,' he says. 'My friend has had a little too much wine.' He does this fake laugh.

'Why did you do that? You don't need to apologise to her; we weren't doing anything wrong. If she's so dried up she's got a problem with two people kissing, fuck her.'

'Dani, you need to be quiet,' Richard says.

'Why should I?'

'Seriously, Dani. This is embarrassing.'

'You think I'm embarrassing?'

'Not you, this situation. Please, Dani.'

The woman behind me has two big moles on her cheek. She's speaking to the side of her friend's face and unwrapping a sweet. I point at her.

'Could you keep the noise down, please? Your sweet wrappers are very noisy. Rustle rustle rustle, it's so distracting.'

'Sorry, sorry,' Richard says.

'Why are you apologising? You think it's okay for her to call me appalling?' Some people in the seats in front of us are turning to look. The man next to me tells me to, 'Be quiet,' like I'm a five-year-old.

'Dani, please,' says Richard.

'Let's go. This place is full of middle-class wankers. They're giving me dirty looks.'

'Dani, you are projecting massively,' Richard whispers into my ear.

'Projecting, projecting, stop using your fucking therapy terms with me.'

The lights suddenly dim and the chatter stops. A spotlight

appears on the stage, with a dancer in a green leotard twisted around another dancer like a weed around a lamppost.

Richard stands up.

'Where are you going?' I follow him, walking past the row of people, bumping into their knees, treading on someone's foot and kicking over a drink. He keeps walking, out of the theatre into the foyer. 'Where're you going?'

The electric doors part and we're outside. He turns to face me.

'Your behaviour in there was appalling. I can see why that woman used the word. If we hadn't left, they'd have asked us to leave.'

'They were looking down on me.'

'They were, not unreasonably, upset by our kissing. There was no need to react in the way you did.'

'Where are you going?'

'I'll find a bar. I can't go home yet. Becca will wonder what I'm doing back so early.'

'I thought she was at her mum's?'

'Change of plan – her mother came to us.'

'Isn't that awkward?'

'Isn't what awkward?'

'If Becca's mum knows you're breaking up?'

'She hasn't told her.'

He walks fast, and I have to run every few steps to keep up. I try to roll a cigarette, but the tobacco keeps falling from the paper. When it happens for the third time, I give up. We pass bars, but they're busy. We walk for a long time before seeing one with only a couple of people smoking out the front.

I ask for a Diet Coke. It's the first time I've ordered a non-alcoholic drink in a bar. We sit at a table near the toilets. I pick up a beer mat and tap it on the table.

Richard stares at a row of naked bulbs dangling above the bar.

'I'm sorry. I get so angry sometimes,' I say.

'I would never have noticed.'

'You know my dad had misophonia? I think I have it too. I was getting agitated in the restaurant by all the people around me eating so loudly.'

'So why didn't you say something?'

'I didn't want to ruin our evening out.'

Richard closes his eyes. I know he was looking forward to the show, and now we're in some dingy little pub, missing it. Richard turns the stem of his wine glass.

'It seems you have two conflicting desires, Dani. You want an education, but your behaviour, at times, could be described as feral. What do you want to be? Educated or feral?'

I need to show I'm thinking about what he said. I pause before I answer. I learned it from him.

'Can't I be both?'

'Educated and feral? That's not possible. I often see patients who want to change, are determined to change, but do you know what stops them? It's not external forces, but themselves. The behaviours they want to change are so entrenched they form a part of their identity. The patient is often fearful of stopping a behaviour, even when it is destructive, because it forms a part of their identity, and they cannot give that up. Will you make yourself sick, sleep around, take drugs, break the law when you're educated?'

'No, I won't,' I say.

'You will need to accept the change higher education will necessitate, Dani, if you want to be a professional and lead an enriching and worthy life. I imagine the bulimia escalated when you were at university because you struggled to keep in what was good. You were "throwing up" your education. The very thing for which you strive, and you rejected it.'

I watch the barmaid flirting with a guy sitting at the bar. She keeps flicking her hair back and then she licks her lips in such an exaggerated way I have to laugh.

'Sorry,' I say to Richard and try and compose myself. 'I think the bulimia was about having a sense of control over my life. I think when I'm throwing up it's somewhere to put the anger. It has to go somewhere.'

'I'm sure it gave you a sense of control when you were in your teens, but now you do have control of your life. At university, you had control, you could make your own decisions, yet you continued to make yourself sick. I think you resist letting go of these damaging behaviours because without them, you won't know who you are.'

'When I used to think about stopping the bulimia, I didn't know who I'd be without it or what I'd do with all the extra time.'

'Tonight, an opportunity to watch a theatre show which would have been enriching, enjoyable, and you throw it up.'

He takes the beer mat from my fingers.

'I know,' I say. 'I do want these things, but when I get them or get close to them, it doesn't feel right.'

'University, culture, me – a good, intelligent man and a relationship that nourishes and enriches.'

'Perhaps I should stop trying.'

'You want enrichment through education, but there's a part of you rejecting it, and your extreme reactions to people you view as "middle-class"—'

'It's like they can see through me.'

'You have a sense you don't belong?'

'I don't belong anywhere. I don't want the kind of life my dad had. I want to listen to classical music, watch ballet, but—'

'You can like what you want to like, Dani, whatever it is.'

'I can't. Things like ballet and opera and all that. It's fine for the upper and middle classes to do what they want, but it's not the same the other way round. I keep trying to climb out of my old life but I always end up falling back down.'

'We are all in the gutter but some of us are looking at the stars,' he says.

'Are you going to pretend that's something you've made up?' I smile so it doesn't come over as too hard.

'People see what you present them with, Dani. People can't see into your past. You have to be prepared to let go of your damaging behaviours if you want to change.'

Richard takes my hand, and we hold hands under the table. I put my head on his shoulder. He tells me I need to have more confidence in myself and stop feeling inferior to people. He tells me to believe in myself and that I am vivacious and intelligent.

'Do you think more self-compassion would help?' I say.

'That's absolutely right. Compassion for the self is fundamental, Dani.' He carries on speaking and his voice is so soothing I fall asleep.

He wakes me and says it's time to go home. He's already called a cab and it's waiting outside. Richard tells the cab driver my address first, and we sit in the back. His arm is around my shoulders and I keep my face in his chest. I can feel his heart beating.

Chapter Twenty-Eight

On Thursday afternoon, I go to the Rose and Crown to meet Elijah and his girlfriend, Teejay. They introduce me to their friends, Matt and Samuel, who've recently got together and are completely loved-up. While I'm waiting at the bar to buy a round, Richard messages to say he's at the hotel. I message back to say that I'm on the way, but I don't feel like leaving the pub. I'm enjoying the conversation and being around people my own age.

I take the drinks back to the table and the chat is relaxed, good. We speak about where we're from and how it compares with London living. Teejay looks at Elijah even when he's not speaking and laughs hard at his jokes. He does the same to her. Elijah suggests another pub with live music, but then Richard messages again to ask where I am, so I say goodbye to them all and go.

I check the name of the hotel against the details on my phone. The way Richard described it, I was expecting something more special. I tell the receptionist my partner has booked a room. She can't find anything under Goode, so I call him and he says it's booked under my name.

The room is on the third floor, and I take the stairs. I'm not in a rush. Richard is standing half in the doorway of a room down the end of the corridor. He's wearing a T-shirt and light blue boxers, and I feel like a visiting sex worker he's begun to strip off in advance for so he can get more for his money.

'Why didn't you book under your name? I thought it would be a better hotel than this.' I wanted it to sound like I was joking but my voice has come out hard.

'I'm sorry, Dani. What is it you don't like?'

'You made it sound better than this.'

'I like this hotel,' he says, stepping back to let me in the room. 'It's intimate.'

I look around. 'Do you mean small?' There's a shitty print of a flower on the wall, some red cushions on the bed that look flat, and a bottle of wine on the desk, half drunk. I think of Elijah and Teejay and Matt and Samuel in a bar, dancing, drinking, laughing.

'Dani, it's a four-star boutique hotel. Why don't you like it? Okay. It doesn't matter. Would you like a glass of wine?'

'What's going on with Becca?'

'Dani, what is the matter with you? You're being incredibly hostile.'

'Am I?'

'You're over an hour late, you say nothing about it, no apology, and you don't even say hello.'

'I forgot.'

'You forgot to say hello? God, I forget how young you are sometimes, then it comes back to me in one sudden swoop.' He sits down on the bed, but I stay standing by the door.

'Well?' I say.

'Well what?' he says.

'Becca. When are you going to tell her you're moving out?'

'You really are so young, Dani, aren't you? Not just in age but in your emotional intelligence too.'

'My age is a problem now, is it? You knew how old I was when you made the pass. I never pretended. You're the one who lied about his age. You said you were in your forties and that was a lie.'

'What is wrong with you tonight, Dani?' he says in a soft voice.

'You've gone quiet lately about moving out. I want to know what's happening. I don't want to be mugged off. I want to know why you still haven't told Becca.'

'It's the angry Essex girl I'm dealing with today, is it? With her cockney expressions and attitude. Come here and say hello properly.' He holds his arms out but I shake my head.

'I think you're taking the piss. Why haven't you told her about me?'

'As I explained before, that would be inappropriate. We've been together for over twenty-five years. I can't suddenly tell her I'm leaving because I met someone else.'

'Why not? When are you going to tell her?'

'Dani, I need some time, please.'

'What's going on then?'

He sighs.

'Becca doesn't want to move out because of her studio in the garden where she does all her cake design and decoration, and I don't want to move out because it's my practising address; it would be unsettling for my patients.'

'Unsettling for them. I'm unsettled. What about me?'

'Dani, you wanted me, you actively pursued me, and now it feels you are rejecting me.'

'You made the pass.'

'Because you seduced me,' he says. 'Take some ownership of the situation.'

'You told me I had to trust you. And that I should be honest about the way I was feeling. That's what I did.' There are lamps by the side of the bed that Richard has turned on but the light they give out is not soft and pleasant but harsh and unflattering. Richard gets up to refill his glass and I look at a sticking-out vein on the back of his calf. 'I wanted you to be my therapist. You spoke about boundaries. Why didn't you keep them? I've been reading about transference. It's common, lots of people have strong feelings about their therapist, but the therapist is supposed to hold the boundaries.'

Richard hands me a glass of wine and I put it on the table. 'No. It wasn't transference, Dani, because you'd barely been coming for therapy – what was it? A few weeks? There wasn't time for the therapist and patient roles to become firmly entrenched, firmly established. What happened between you and me was simply a strong sexual attraction between two adults. There was a strong sexual attraction, and we, you *and* I, acted upon it.'

'I came for four months, not a few weeks.'

'Can you keep down something good for you, something nourishing? Or will you keep throwing it up?'

'I wanted my therapy. I wanted you as my therapist.'

'You haven't made yourself sick since we've been together. I did good work with you as a therapist, and you're still benefiting from my knowledge, but now, you get it for free.'

'It's not the same.'

Richard shakes his head.

'The anger is still finding a way out, like with what happened at the theatre. I wanted to sort myself out, go straight for once, follow the rules, from start to finish. But now you're something else to add on to a big list of not doing things properly.'

'I did good therapy with you, Dani, in the short time you came.'

'And If I want to carry on getting advice from you, I have to

263

have sex with you. I wanted a therapist. A nice, normal therapist who would help me sort out my problems. You've added to them. I could have been out tonight with people my own age and having fun and I'm with an old man in a shitty hotel room. I wanted my therapy.'

'Dani, I know you're feeling angry, but you cannot keep rejecting what you want. You wanted me, now you are rejecting me. You must recognise this is a pattern. You want it, but when you get it, you don't want it any more.'

'I wanted therapy. I was paying for therapy.'

'You tried to seduce me, and you succeeded. Now you want to reject me.'

'How did I try to seduce you?'

'The way you smiled, the way you flirted in the sessions. It's all seduction, Dani.'

'I read that therapists are supposed to hold the—'

'Wait, wait,' he says and goes into the toilet. I can hear him pissing. I drink some wine from the bottle.

There is truth in what he's saying. I admire something from afar, but the moment I get my hands on it, it becomes contaminated, loses its shine, gets dirty. Once I've become friends with someone, I'm disappointed that their standards are so low they think I'm worth spending time with. I'd think better of someone who didn't want to associate with me.

'What will happen if neither of you wants to move out?' I say when he comes back and sits on the bed.

'I suppose I'll have to go. Becca invested more when we bought the house. She had some inheritance from her grandmother. It's fairer I go. I'm just digging in at the moment.'

'Where will you go?'

'I'll stay in the area so it's less disruptive for my clients. And you can come and see me all the time, Dani. You can move in.'

'What will you get? A house, a flat?'

'I'll buy a house. I must have a garden.'

Even when he breaks up with Becca, he'll have enough money to buy a house with a garden. You've got to be rich to have a house with a garden in London. He fills my glass with wine and puts his hand on my arm.

'We can decorate it together. Think, Dani. Walls lined with our favourite books, elegant furniture, art on the walls. You won't be living in some grotty student house or having to sleep in a four-year-old's bedroom.'

I imagine us having late dinners with expensive wine and the radio on in the background. In the summer we'd sit in the garden with our morning coffees and breathe in the scent of the flowers and listen to the birds. I could wear a silky kimono. I'd have given up smoking so there'd be no dirty ashtray on the table.

'What do you think of the wine?' he says.

'It's all right.'

'I bought it on the way here. It's a young red, that's why the purple is so vibrant.'

'It's nice.' I could learn so much from him, about psychology, literature, people, wine.

'So, our house,' he says. 'I need somewhere big enough to work from home, but there'll be a separate space for you to study.'

'An office each?' I say.

He smiles at me. 'Yes, one each, although of course I'll need the larger space for my practice.'

'I wouldn't need much space, anyway. Just enough for a desk.'

'You will have it.'

He looks into my eyes and I try hard not to look away. He's trying to give me what I want, what he knows is so important to me. And lots of couples have big age gaps in their relationships.

'I'll carry on working at weekends when I'm back at uni. I'm going to ask Babs. I'm sure it'll be fine as weekends are the busiest.'

'No, Dani. Weekends will be for us. I don't want you to feel you have to work. I earn ten times more than you. Forget about it. I want you to have the time you need to devote to your studies, and a peaceful environment to do it in.' He picks up the room service card. 'Let's order another bottle on room service – splash out, as it's our first whole night together. I want to spoil you, Dani.'

When he's on the phone to room service, I tell him to order some vodka shots as well.

'Absolut, not Smirnoff,' I say so he thinks I know something about drinks too.

The drinks arrive, and we do the shots. I pour us more wine and Richard strokes my hair.

'I've seen a desk I'm going to get you. In an antique shop in Fulham. You will have all the time and space you need to study and to succeed.'

I get on all fours and Richard fucks me from behind. The bed creaks and when the headboard bangs against the wall, I get up and move to the floor but he says it hurts his knees so we move back to the bed.

Richard falls asleep and I turn on the TV. I keep it on mute and put the subtitles on so the sound doesn't wake him. He wakes up after I've watched a couple of episodes of a cooking programme.

'Bit of a comedown for you, a little TV like this,' he says.

'What?'

'Your sister's TV.'

'I don't see your point.'

'It's enormous,' he laughs.

'They've got a big TV, so?'

'It was only an observation, Dani. Please don't get angry.'

I go downstairs to smoke, and when I come back, he's drawn the sheet up to his chin like he's in a morgue and someone's peeled back the sheet to identify him. Old face. Old-man lips. He dozes and snorts. I take my jeans off and get into bed, lie on my side on the edge. He moves over and runs his hand along my side. His cock nudges my lower back.

'I'm sleeping.'

'Dani, I booked this room especially for us to be romantic, a couple; stop being punishing. I apologise for my comment about the TV.'

He tries to put it in. He spits in his hand and then his cock slides in with more ease. He moves me so I'm face down on the bed and carries on. I think of a wall lined with bookshelves and studying at my antique desk.

In the morning, I wake up to his face above me. He's shaking me gently. I bury my face in the pillow.

'I have to go, Dani. I have to catch my train.'

'What's the time?'

'Eight o'clock. Check-out isn't until eleven so you can stay in bed a little longer if you wish. I've paid for the room and room service from last night. You don't need to contribute.'

'When am I next seeing you?'

'I'll call you tomorrow to arrange.'

'Why not later today?'

'I'll be with Geoff. It would be rude.'

In the bathroom, there are a couple of pubic hairs over the toilet seat, and the hand towel is on the floor. This is the first time we've left each other without having the next meeting planned. I have the day off work, but I don't want to stay in this hotel room. I go to a café and order two cups of tea and a pint of water. I look up therapy websites on my phone and read about having a relationship with your therapist.

267

Chapter Twenty-Nine

I write Richard an email when I get home.

I know we've only been 'together' for five weeks and I know I overthink things and can be a bit paranoid, but it's so hard for me to trust people. I've been reading more about transference and learned there are different types. I recognise I had positive transference towards you, and I think erotic transference too. It said some clients are so desperate for a god that they project this onto the therapist. That makes sense, doesn't it? If you're sitting with someone week after week and telling them all your deepest secrets and fears and things you're ashamed of, you've got to believe the person is godlike or you wouldn't be trusting them with all your secrets.

It said the therapist needs to be able to handle erotic transference, see it for what it is. Otherwise, if they identify with the client's projections and think they're godlike, they can act abusively. I'm not saying you're an abuser; it's what it said on the website. It said that therapists and clients shouldn't get into a relationship until at least two years after the therapy has ended.

I tried to be completely honest about my feelings as I thought the therapy wouldn't work otherwise. Then I realised the feelings I had for you were mixed in with feelings I had about my dad and that's freaking me out because we've had sex. I used to think about coming home to you, and you'd be sitting in silence reading by the bright light of an anglepoise lamp, and I never even connected it but that's what my dad used to do. And it said online about how the therapist would be able to hold the boundaries if they had strong morals and if they had enough intimacy in their private lives and they didn't need to live 'vicariously' through their patients. I know you and Becca are in the process of breaking up so that might be why you were looking for intimacy. Is that what it was?

It also said all this stuff about how if the therapist and client were genuinely compatible, it could heighten the desire, and the environment could become charged. It was the 'genuine compatibility' that got me because whilst you have so much to offer – your knowledge, your professionalism, attractiveness, all the qualifications, your beautiful home – what do you see in me? A twenty-year-old bulimic university dropout, in debt, living with her sister, never achieved anything, rough background. What makes us compatible? What did you see? What do you see?

I wanted someone to listen, just listen. I've lost that and I want it back. One of the best things about therapy is you don't have to consider the other person's feelings or ask about how they are because you're paying them to do a job and perform a role that lets you be at the centre. Now when I speak about my feelings, I'll have to consider how it impacts your feelings. I can't speak to you about our relationship.

I'm sure I've learned some good stuff with you, and you made me feel a bit more confident, but what's happened between us now seems to be wiping that out in terms of how insecure I feel. I appreciate you reducing the fee but I wonder if it would have been better to pay full price and get what I was coming for.

I always wanted someone who I could look up to and admire and who wouldn't do anything to fall off that pedestal, and it's what I thought I'd found in you. Maybe this is my problem – the fact this is what I needed. I know nobody is perfect but I wanted to imagine that you were.

There's an old song I keep listening to, 'The Dark End of the Street', a soul song from the sixties and the lyrics are really speaking to me . . . hiding in shadows . . . living in darkness to hide our wrong . . . There's something about us that feels sordid and wrong and that's why I need to drink when I see you. I drink to make that thought go away. The age difference is part of it.

Another website says clients are vulnerable and the therapist should not get into a relationship with them. It says therapists should discuss feelings they have about their clients with their supervisor. I don't know if you've ever done that. Have you got a supervisor? Did you speak about me to them?

I also read that therapists don't get sent to prison for having sex with their clients in the same way a GP could, and although all the websites say it shouldn't happen, there's no real consequences for the therapist if they do, apart from being struck off from their professional association – but there's not even a fine, or anything worse than that. So this makes me think that maybe it's not that bad what's happening between us. I keep getting so confused.

I've lost you as my therapist, and that was what I was after all along, a therapist. Not a boyfriend. I didn't want a relationship until I'd sorted myself out, otherwise I'd keep getting ones like Christy who were as messed up as me. I know it's stupid but can you recommend a therapist? I need to speak to someone.

I wanted to be able to look back on this period of my life as a time when you helped me, and it went well, and you didn't do anything dodgy and I would have loved you and been grateful to you forever.

I send the email and get under my duvet. I'm about to fall asleep when my phone rings once. A missed call from Richard. I call him back.

'Did you call me? Are you still in Wales?'

'I'm on the train now, travelling back. Yes, I tried to call. The reception is not so great. I got cut off.'

'You read my email.'

'I did, and Dani, I know these feelings are difficult but try and keep a steady ship.' He pauses. 'I love you, Dani. It's all going to be okay.' His voice isn't the same as usual. His words are joining together. It's the first time he's said he loves me outright. He called me loveable when he made the pass, he set it up as the password when he gave me the laptop. But it's the first time he's said it.

'I'm struggling. You could probably tell from the email.'

'It will all come good. Can we meet tomorrow morning? Go for a walk? I need to see you.'

'Need to see me?'

'You sound like you need my support, Dani.' I hear him take a deep breath. 'I'm concerned for your mental health.'

'Just because I sent that email? There's nothing wrong with me.'

'You're reading things online and comparing our situation, but it's not comparable. What we have is different, Dani. It's like looking up symptoms on Google when you're unwell – it will produce millions of inaccurate results. Stop it. I'm going to take care of you like nobody has ever taken care of you before. Let me do that. Please, Dani. Stop reading rubbish online.'

We agree to meet at the park at seven-thirty the next morning.

It's gone midnight and I'm smoking on the balcony when Jo gets in. She looks fantastic in a shiny black dress with her new haircut, but as she comes closer, I can see a cold sore under the foundation and when she speaks, her voice cracks and breaks.

'You got a cold?'

She sits down and lights a cigarette. 'Yeah. Doug was going to another party but I told him to drop me home. I'm knackered.'

'Go to bed then.'

She holds up a joint. 'I'll smoke this first. It'll help me sleep better.'

'Have you spoken to Stevie lately?'

'I see him at work but we don't chat much. We're meeting next weekend to talk. I'm going to tell him then that it's over.'

'It's going well with Doug, then,' I say and try to keep my face neutral because I don't like the sound of him. I like Stevie. I know even when he's being horrible, it's because he cares.

Jo goes inside, I have another roll-up then go to her bedroom. She's sitting at her dressing table, taking her makeup off.

'Don't you think you've gone from one extreme to the other?' I say.

'Maybe,' she yawns. 'I'm having a good time, though.' She chucks a foundation-caked wipe at the bin and it misses.

'Why do you like Doug so much?'

'He's exciting. We took a boat out today, got stoned and listened to music. Then we went clubbing. Stevie and I never did stuff like that.'

'You could have. On the weekends you didn't have Ellie.'

'He wouldn't have wanted to.'

'Did you ask him?'

'Leave it out, Dan.'

'Has Doug got kids?'

'Yeah, a few, but he doesn't see all of them. There are two baby mothers and one of them is mental. She won't let him see them.'

'That's unlucky.'

'Some women are bitches.'

'What was Doug inside for?'

'GBH. But it was self-defence. He got tucked up.'

'All right,' I say. 'I'm going to bed now.' I can't listen to her keep talking such shit.

I pull the duvet over me and wonder about why Jo is so loved-up with Doug, who seems like a complete prick, rather than Stevie, who has always put her first.

Chapter Thirty

On Sunday morning, Richard is waiting for me when I arrive, sitting on a park bench opposite a red dog-shit bin.

'Morning.' I feel softer because of what he said on the phone last night. He looks like he hasn't slept and the bags under his eyes are fat little pouches.

'Dani.' He stands up. 'Thank you for the email. It had so much emotion in it.'

'Shall we walk?' I throw my hand towards the park. I don't want to sit facing the dog-shit bin and have to mouth-breathe every time someone lifts the lid. We head towards the pond.

'I felt better for writing it all down. I'm trying to work out why I keep feeling so angry towards you, and about us. I think it's because we were getting to the root of it all, about why I feel so shit about myself. The therapy was working. Then you made the pass.'

'I'm sorry you feel this way. I thought it was what you wanted. I can't think of a time when anybody has tried as hard to seduce me as you did. The way you'd smile at me in the sessions, Dani. My god—'

'But we should have talked about why I was doing that. If we'd carried on with the therapy, I could've worked through those issues with you and got better. Now I'm back to square one. No. Worse because I've got all this shit now with you to add to it.'

'Dani, we can still work through some of your feelings.'

'It's not the same. When I was coming to therapy, it felt like I was working towards sorting myself out.'

'We can still do that.'

'I was starting to trust you.'

'You can still trust me.'

'I wanted a therapist to work things through with.'

'You have me, and your writing.'

'It's not the same.'

'Aren't I supporting you?'

'It's all messed up. I still want to work on some issues I was coming to you for. I can't do that with you now.'

'You don't need more therapy. Your bulimia has stopped. You're making your way, Dani.'

'I still don't feel right. I need to get my head around us. It doesn't feel right.'

'So talk to me.'

'I can't talk to you about us.'

'Why would you need to talk about us?'

'I can't make sense of it sometimes. That's why I wrote the email.'

We stop walking and face each other. There's a muscle going in his cheek. A poodle-type dog runs up to us and starts sniffing at Richard's feet. 'Fuck off,' he says, kicking at it. It's the first time I've heard him swear. He puts the tip of his finger just below my neck.

'I can't stop you from going to another therapist, Dani, but you must not mention my name.'

'I won't.'

'The therapeutic community is a small one. I could get into

serious trouble over this. Is that what you want? Would you do that to me?'

'No. I don't want to make any trouble for you. It's not like you'd get put in prison or anything. I read about it, what happens to therapists who have relationships with their clients. And it's nothing. No consequences.'

'Jesus,' he says. 'I could be struck off!'

'You could still carry on working. Anyway, you said you'd deny it.'

He shakes his head.

'Come on, Dani. I think seeing a counsellor is entirely unnecessary. You're in a better place now than you've ever been. I did good therapy with you. Why can't you recognise that?'

'I need to speak to someone. Someone who'll stay my therapist.'

His mouth falls open.

'That is a low blow, Dani. You orchestrated something in a very considered way and now you're throwing it back at me? Yes, I was weak to capitulate, but you wanted this.'

'If I change your name, you could be anyone. You're being paranoid.'

'You have no idea of the impact this could have on my work.'

'I need it. I need to talk to someone.'

'If you must talk to someone, you cannot give my name, and you mustn't say where I practise from either. Dani, this is serious.' He brings a hand to his forehead. 'You shouldn't go. It's utterly unnecessary.'

'Is our relationship always going to have to be a secret?'

'No, it won't. But you're in this mad rush all the time, Dani. I keep telling you, let me tell Becca I'm moving out in my own time. Then when I've moved out, after a reasonable length of time, you can move in and we can begin our lives together.'

'Have you still not told her about us yet?'

He doesn't answer.

'That's a no, then.'

'Oh, give me some space, Dani. You've shocked me to my core with the way you're being.'

We walk around the pond and my mouth keeps moving of its own accord like I've taken a load of Es and can't stop gurning. I put a hand over to cover it.

'The weather's nice today,' I say but he doesn't answer.

'I need to go home,' he says after a few minutes. He gives a short laugh. 'I'm shocked. And sad. I need some time to process all of this.'

'You're going already?'

'I thought we'd be together longer too, Dani, but after everything you've said, the way you're being, I need some time alone.' He puts his hand in his pocket and pulls out the lighter I gave him. 'I don't smoke but I carry this around with me because then I'm reminded of you. I've never done anything like that before. I've never carried around some token or object that makes me think of Becca.'

I look at the lighter in his palm. He puts it back in his pocket and rubs the top of my arm.

'You are important to me, Dani, and I'm sorry that what happened is now not what you want; that you pursued me, actively, but now you've changed your mind. You wanted me, now you don't want me.'

'I'm confused.'

'You'll be more confused if you reject me now and start therapy with someone else. Think about that, Dani. Do you want to start all over again? And is this it for us? Our relationship, in whatever capacity, over? Because if that's what you really want, let's call it now. We never need to see each other again. Ever. You will never see from me or hear from me again.'

I feel a sudden urge to piss and look around to see if there are any toilets about. I can't handle the thought that this could be the last time I'm with him.

'Look, I'm sorry. If it bothers you so much, I won't see someone else.'

'You don't need to. You really don't.' He pulls me into a hug and when I look up at him, there are tears in his eyes. He strokes my hair and I close my eyes.

'Thank you, Dani.'

'I don't want to upset you and I don't want us to stop seeing each other.'

'That's the right decision, Dani. You don't need to see anyone else. You've learned strategies to cope. You have your writing and you'll soon be back at university. Focus on your education. Make that your priority. It's what you always wanted. And now I can help you, support you with that.'

He holds my hand and we start walking again. He stops to take off his jumper and then puts it over his back like a cape, tying the sleeves together at his neck.

'So when do you think you'll tell Becca?'

He clears his throat.

'I'm building up to it.'

'Do you think it will be much longer?'

'Dani, please.' He smiles and it takes the edge off his words. 'It's hard enough as it is without pressure from you. I've been with her for twenty-five years. I'm not going to spring it on her.'

'I'm worried you won't do it.'

'You need to trust me.'

'I'm trying.'

'You find it so hard, don't you? Trusting someone . . .'

A good-looking couple in their twenties is jogging towards

us. I drop Richard's hand and look at the floor to avoid eye contact. I'm still embarrassed to be seen with him unless I've had a couple of drinks. He's never seemed to care about the age difference. When they've passed us, I take his hand again.

'When are we next seeing each other after today? Shall I come at my normal session time this week?'

'I meant to tell you. I'm afraid I've taken on a new patient at that time.'

'So when are we meeting?'

'Becca's going to visit our daughter at her university digs on Friday night, and she's staying over, so you can come over then.'

'Can I stay the night?'

Richard sighs.

'I don't think that would be appropriate, unfortunately. But you can certainly come for the evening.'

I look at the trees around the park's edge.

'I was stressed when I was writing the email. I read all that stuff about transference and it made me feel disgusting.'

Richard stops walking and puts his hands on my shoulders. 'It wasn't transference, Dani. We are two people genuinely attracted to each other. It was clear from the first time we met. The attraction was so strong it was impossible to resist.'

'Loads of the articles I read said that the therapist should always maintain boundaries.'

'Of course that's what they say. I told you, they're writing for the masses, and I agree, it's an important part of psychotherapy that boundaries are maintained, but what was happening between us was an exception. You're an exception. Normal rules don't apply to you – you transcend normal rules. There is something quite remarkable about you, Dani. I do believe you'll go on to achieve great things.'

'Shut up,' I say. I've always found it hard to take compliments and he's being well over the top.

'Anyway, I've been looking at houses and I've found one.'

'You've found a house? Where is it?'

'Not far from where I am now.'

'What's it like?'

'It's a Victorian terrace, three floors, good size garden. It will be perfect for us,' he says. 'Just stop trying to pressurise me all the time and let me work at my own speed. This will happen, Dani. Just have some trust in me.'

Chapter Thirty-One

I don't bake cakes and biscuits. I've always thought adults who bake without a child are tossers. Why not buy the cakes and biscuits and do something more productive with your time? But I'm baking today. I get up early so I can make brownies before work. I'm putting in the hash I got from Del because I want Richard to loosen up a bit and drop his guard. Then I'll be able to find out if he's serious about leaving Becca or if he's just bullshitting me. I put the brownies in a Celebrations tub and mean to put them under my bed but forget.

When I get home after work, Jo and some bloke who must be Doug are lying on the sofa listening to funk-soul music. It must be Doug's taste because I know it's not Jo's. She's been out so much lately I wasn't expecting her home and I'm pleased to see her.

'All right,' I say.

'Yo, yo, yo,' says Jo. She only moves her mouth, the rest of her stays still.

I wait for her to introduce me to Doug, but she doesn't.

In the kitchen, the Celebrations tub is open and about half of the brownies have gone. I go back to the living room.

'How many of those brownies did you eat?' I say.

'A couple,' Jo says.

The smell of weed is strong in the air. They were going to get stoned anyway.

I call Naz to give me a lift to Richard's because I want to arrive fresh and don't want to be taking public transport with a tub of hash brownies. I look at Naz as he drives. I don't know much about him and I wonder if that's why I like him. When a person is mostly a blank canvas, you can make them what you want. I've never seen Naz eat, walk, or speak to anyone apart from me. I know him in one context only, sitting behind the wheel and driving me where I want to go.

'What's in there?' Naz points at the tub on my lap.

'Cakes.'

'Nice.'

'I would give you one, but they're actually not that great.'

'No problem,' he says. 'For Mr Richard?'

'Yeah.'

Naz nods.

'Busy man,' he says.

'What do you mean?'

'Lots of people going there for appointments.'

'Yeah, I think he's quite good, that's why. He's got a waiting list.' I look at Naz's profile. 'Have you ever had therapy?'

He smiles.

'No. When I'm sad, I go for a run, or talk to a friend.'

'That's nice.' I picture chatting with Pat in the smoking shed. 'I think sometimes friends give good advice. And they're cheaper. But I still think therapy can be helpful. When you talk to a friend, you have to think about how they might react to bad things you tell them. You don't need to worry about that with a therapist.'

'I have nothing to be sad about,' Naz says. 'I have work, I have money. The sun is shining. It's all good.'

I wish I could be so happy about such simple things.

Richard answers the door wearing his old-man jeans again and a faded T-shirt with the name of his band across the front. I picture him on the stage at Glastonbury, the screaming fans, wanting him. He shuts the door behind me and heads towards the therapy room.

'Can I see the rest of the house?'

'I'll show you later. I know you like my room; let's get comfortable there first.'

I reach out and pull his arm back to stop him from walking any further. I push him against the wall, press my body against his and pull the back of his head down so I can kiss him.

'Dani, where is your impulse control?' But he's smiling and I know he likes it.

There's an open bottle of red wine and two glasses on his desk. He pours us both a glass.

'I love this room so much. You've got so many books. Have you read all of them?'

'Yes.'

'All of them? Every single one?'

'Well, parts of them.'

'Will you take them all?'

He raises his eyebrows.

'Will you take them?'

'Sorry, Dani. Take them?'

'When you move to the new house.'

'Yes, yes, of course.'

'I made you some brownies.' I take the lid off the Celebrations tub and show him.

'You are sweet. How lovely.'

'They've got hash in.'

'Are you trying to lead me astray, Dani?'

'You were in a band. I thought you'd like to relive your youth a bit.'

He laughs, takes one and eats it.

'Delicious. I can add baking to your talents.' He takes the tub from me and puts it on the desk. We sit down in our usual chairs, but then he gets up for another brownie.

'Don't you want to save some for later?'

'One more, one more. Would you like one?'

'I had one on the way over.'

He smiles and his teeth are stained grey from the wine. He must have been getting stuck in before I arrived.

I stretch my arms and then bring my legs up on the chair so I'm sitting cross-legged.

'You know I said about seeing another therapist? I've booked for next week. David Burgess. Have you heard of him?' I wasn't going to tell Richard, but for some reason, it's just come out.

'What?' Richard stares at me.

'I booked in with a therapist for next week.'

'Why would you do that after you promised me you wouldn't?'

'I don't remember promising. But you don't need to worry. I'm having a phone appointment, so he won't even see me. I'll give a fake name and I'll change your name too.'

'I'm sorry, Dani, but I think you're being immature and ridiculous.'

I shrug a couple of times in the silence that follows.

'I need to speak to someone.'

Richard shakes his head.

'Dani, I cannot stop you from making appointments with other therapists but you cannot, you must not, say anything about us. It would spread in no time. It could get me into a lot of trouble.'

'I wasn't going to. I won't say your real name, anyway. All this has spun me out. I need to speak to someone and get my thoughts in order.'

'You cannot mention my name. Not under any circumstances. Or where I practise from.'

'I thought anything a client tells a therapist is confidential?'

'Therapists speak to each other. It's a small world.'

'That's not fair on the clients they're seeing. Do you speak to your therapist mates about the clients you're seeing?'

'Sometimes, but I never mention them by name.'

I think about the clients he's talked to me about, but he didn't tell me anything that would mean I could identify them. I wonder how they'd feel if they knew he was sharing their problems with me.

'I'll give a fake name anyway – so it doesn't matter.' We've both raised our voices. I show him my palms and then point at the bottle on the table. 'Lovely wine. What kind is it?' I go and pick it up and refill our glasses.

'Stay with what we're discussing, Dani. I think you need to reconsider.'

'Yeah, okay. What's the wine, then?'

I think he's going to carry on having a go at me but he shakes his head and sighs.

'Is it going to mean anything if I tell you?'

'Probably not. Just trying to educate my palate.'

I get up and pick up the bottle of wine, read the label. Pinot Noir.

'From France,' I say, putting it back on the desk. 'You never did tell me if you spoke French.' We stare at each other.

'Dani, it's been a tiring day, and now this. I wasn't prepared for this and I was so looking forward to seeing you.'

'I'm sorry you're disappointed. I was looking forward to it too.'

'I am disappointed. I'm disappointed by what you're saying.' He crosses his arms.

'It all gets too much sometimes. I feel confused and I don't know what to do.'

'I feel confused too, Dani. Do you think I was expecting this to happen between us? I pride myself on being a professional, but you smashed through my defences and now look where we are. It's utterly insane.'

'"Utterly insane"?'

He closes his eyes.

'Yes,' he says.

'You regret it, then?'

I wait for a response but the silence stretches on so long that I wonder if he's fallen asleep.

'It's beginning to look like I might.'

I go and sit on his lap. His breath smells of red wine. The whole point of the brownies was to get him relaxed, not to row.

'I'm not sure I can do this, Dani.'

My stomach drops. I can't lose him.

'I'll cancel the appointment then.'

He kisses me. When we stop, he gestures towards the wine bottle. 'The wine was a gift. I've had a rather important person coming to see me recently. Somebody very much in the public eye. She's very appreciative of the therapy I'm doing with her. She had her secretary send me a case of this excellent wine.'

'Who's that?'

'I can't say. But let's open another bottle.' He takes a bottle from under his desk, opens it and fills our glasses. He takes another brownie and eats it.

'Do you see many famous people?' I say.

'A few,' he says with his mouth full.

285

I want to say, 'Good for you,' but instead, I say, 'Shall we put some music on? Or the radio?' I want to make it relaxed in the room. Get some other sounds in to wash out the tension.

Richard takes his phone and puts on Classic FM. Violins jerk into the room.

'So, have you told *anyone* about me?'

He shakes his head.

'Not even one person? A friend? A sibling?'

'Nobody.'

I want him to have told at least one person about us. It'd make it feel more real. I go back to my chair and drink more wine.

Richard starts telling me about his research into publication number five. I pretend this is my office and he's coming to me for advice on his writing. He talks and talks and leaves no spaces for me to respond or ask a question. I roll a cigarette and hold it up in front of me.

'No, no, you can't smoke in here,' he says.

'Shall I go out front?'

'If you must.'

I leave the front door slightly open and smoke quickly. When I come back, Richard looks at me and makes a gurgling noise at the back of his throat but doesn't seem to be aware he's doing it. The hash from the brownies is kicking in. 'Enough of this nonsense,' he says. 'You look beautiful.' He looks at my legs, my body, my face.

'Thanks.'

The music has changed. Still classical but mostly piano.

'A beautiful young girl.'

'You've got crumbs on your chest.' I make a brushing motion on my own.

He goes to the bottom drawer of his desk and takes out a hand hoover. He hoovers the area around his chair, and his chair, then his chest and looks at me like he's doing something funny. He pretends the hoover is pulling him to the other side of the room, then he sits back down and sighs. 'Come here,' he says, curling his fingers towards his chest.

He unbuckles his belt the moment I stand up. I kneel in front of him.

'Is this what you want?' I free his cock and start stroking it with one finger. I take it in my mouth and he groans.

'Dani, you are so good, so good ...'

Richard leans forward and I stop. He takes his glass and drinks some wine. He looks pale.

'Do you want some water?' I say.

'No, I want you to keep going.' He keeps telling me how good I am.

'How did Becca do this?'

'She doesn't. She doesn't like it. Never has.'

'You told me she did it when you were working late that time.' I remember because of the old-fashioned way he said it – 'pleasuring me with her mouth'. That expression had made me feel squeamish. I preferred 'giving head'.

'I don't remember, Dani. Possibly. If I said it, then it would have been true.'

'Have you told Becca yet?'

'I've alluded to it. She knows it's coming.'

'How did you allude to it?'

'Jesus, Dani. Stop interrogating me. I said to Becca we both know it's over, and now Phoebe has moved out, it will be easier to separate.'

I look for signs he's lying but there are none. I take it in my mouth again. His fingers against my scalp are hard.

'The woman you had a three-year affair with, what was she like?'

'Dani—'

'I want to know.'

'Keep going, and I'll tell you.'

I work it with my hands like I'm slowly grinding pepper. 'Was she attractive?'

'She had beautiful skin, and dark eyes. She was beautiful.'

'Was she as good as me?'

He smiles. 'Almost.'

'Tell me about other women you've been with.'

'Why?'

'It'll turn me on. There must have been other women. You're far too attractive not to have been sleeping with other women, especially if Becca wasn't satisfying you. How many?'

He moans and pulls my hands away from his cock. Pushes the back of my head down into his lap.

'Dani, stop with all the questions.'

It's easier to go down on someone who isn't very big. His breathing quickens and when I know he's about to come, I stop and look at him. He takes hold of his cock and starts pulling on it. His eyes are glazed and his breath ragged. I put my hand on his.

'I want you to come in my mouth. But I want you to speak to me while I'm doing it. Tell me about the other women.' I take it in again, so slowly. He groans.

'You really want to know?'

'Yeah. Who else?'

'Where do I start?'

'Who turned you on the most?'

He laughs.

'There's quite a few of them, Dani.'

I tense my body to stop a shiver.

'So tell me.'

He takes a deep breath and when he exhales, I feel the warmth of it on my forehead.

I sit back. 'Or don't tell me. We can have another glass of wine and chat about your research.'

'Don't you dare stop now.'

'The other women?'

'Okay. You want to know? The women who turn me on are the ones who come on to me . . . the ones who want it. Women like you, Dani, who come in and flirt and want it.'

I sit back and put my hands round it again.

'I thought it was only the one patient, fifteen years ago, or something.' I try to sound casual but my stomach and my chest are filling with ice.

'Slower,' he says and puts his hands over mine, gets them moving with the rhythm and the speed he wants.

I can't act, but Richard is stoned, not attentive to my face, my strained tone of voice. Usually, he'd pick up on it. 'I'm sure most of your clients fancy you.'

He snorts.

'They get off on the attention. It's such a charged environment, especially when relationships and sex are being spoken about. They come on to me. You wouldn't believe the number of female clients who come on to me. And some male ones too.' He reaches for my head, pushes it into his lap. 'Then they're grateful they have a therapist who is so virile.'

I stop and look at him. His eyes are still closed.

'And you have sex with them? In here?'

'I give them what they want, Dani. What they need. One patient suggested I had a harem.' He laughs.

'I was right that time then, when the box of condoms was under the couch?' I want to lean forward and sink my teeth in until they meet.

'I don't know, Dani. What did I say? Possibly.'

'Has anyone ever reported you?'

He takes hold of it himself again, hand moving up and down.

'Why would they? I'm giving them what they want. Most are married or in relationships; they're hardly going to tell anyone. They come in with their tight tops, perfume, wet-look lipstick. They want it so I give them what they want. They speak about their fantasies and they want to act them out. Or they find me so attractive they want some . . . intimacy. So many women are attracted to authority figures. You know that, Dani.'

His head rolls on the back of his chair.

'I'm one in a long line, then?'

'I'm giving you what you wanted.' He looks at me but his gaze is off focus. 'It's what they all want. A good fucking from their handsome therapist. Jung had sex with his patients, so did Perls. It's well documented.'

'So it's all been lies? About the house you've found? Moving in together?' He tries to put my head back in his lap. I shake his hands off and lean back. 'What we were talking about the other day, moving in together?' I stand up and say it louder. He stands up, pulls his jeans up and fumbles over the top button. He tries to take my hand but I don't let him.

'Dani, come on. We were both enjoying the fantasy, but seriously, you really thought . . . ?'

I cover my face with my hands and he takes them away and holds my wrists.

'I'm sorry,' he says.

'Sorry for what? Me? The other clients? Why do you do it? These people are coming to you for help. Do you really think this helps them? Having sex with them?'

He drops my wrists and turns away from me. He shakes his head and makes a noise like he's got something stuck in the back of his throat. He doesn't turn round when he starts to speak and I watch the back of his head.

'Dani, I know it's wrong, but they want it. You wanted it. You wanted it, didn't you? You wanted me.'

'I wanted therapy.'

The only sound in the room is us breathing and the ticking of the clock. I keep trying to yawn so I can get a deep enough breath in.

He doesn't turn round.

'I'll tell you why it happens, Dani. It happens because there are times when the atmosphere in the room is so charged that it's easier to do it than to not. And there is nothing in this world like it. In the space of a few seconds, suddenly, from being therapist and patient, we're fucking on the couch and it is a thrill greater than I have ever known. It is intense beyond words. Raw, animal passion, and that's what makes it addictive and why I don't want to stop. I can't stop. I feel this euphoria.'

I pick up the wine bottle by the neck and raise it. Wine pours down my wrist and arm. I take a step closer to Richard, and raise the bottle higher so it's level with his head. He starts to turn, I need to do it now before he realises. But then I let it drop. The rug is so thick, the bottle doesn't break.

'You piece of shit,' I say.

The skin on his face has paled and looks like cold white wax. He pushes me out of the way and stumbles from the room. I hear the clack of the toilet seat going up and then he's heaving his guts up and groaning in between the retching. I stand outside the door listening, then go back to his room. I want to pull every book from the shelves and rip out the pages. I want to smash his laptop through the closed window. I want to set the couch on fire.

The sick noises stop. I leave the room and go down the passageway. Richard is no longer in the clients' toilet but has left the contents of his undigested brownies and red wine in a lumpy puddle on the floor. I walk into a huge, high-ceilinged kitchen and pause for a moment. Duck-egg blue cabinets and shelves with coloured glasses and books artfully arranged. White walls, wooden floorboards and a light pink rug. It's the most beautiful kitchen I've ever seen. Richard's slumped over the kitchen table, snoring. I can't wake him, even when I pinch his arms and pull at his hair. I take a photo of him, a close-up of his face which shows the dribble of brown sick on his lip and chin. When I think of this educated and sophisticated man, I need a reminder of this night, this sight.

There's sick in the sink coating the plates and glasses, more undigested brownies and spaghetti. I turn on the tap and then think, what the fuck am I doing?

Back in his therapy room, I take the picture of the young girl and her father from the wall and wrap it in the blanket from the end of the couch. I hold it to my chest as I walk home.

Chapter Thirty-Two

I step over takeaway flyers and kick the door shut behind me. I switch lights on as I walk to the kitchen. The sink is full of mugs and glasses poking up through grey water, and the worktops are sticky and unwiped. There's a tea towel on the floor in front of the washing machine, and half of the load has been pulled out of the tumble drier and then left so it looks like the machine is throwing up the clothes. The hard smell of old cigarette smoke lingers, making the air feel it could bite. Jo does nothing domestic, and it's not been on my radar. The last time I cleaned was when Richard came for lunch.

I sit on the balcony, chain-smoking. It's not even ten o'clock. I message Richard to ask if we can talk, then I call his mobile and the landline, but he doesn't answer. I text Jo and she texts she'll be back Tuesday night. Stevie's still at Ronnie's.

I take bottles out from under the kitchen sink: furniture polish, disinfectant sprays, oven cleaner, glass cleaner, bleach. Stevie did so much without me and Jo realising it. I wash up and wipe down all the surfaces. When the hoover gets caught up in the wire and the tube comes out, I kick it and call it a cunt. I fix it and go round hoovering each room a second time to make sure I've not missed anywhere. Every so often, I stop and smoke on the balcony and try Richard. At half two, I go to bed and set my alarm for seven, but I can't sleep and stare at the ceiling even though I can't see it.

I message Babs to say I'm not well. Saturday is the busiest day and I don't like letting them down, but it's the first day off sick I've had. Leanne and Tulsi are constantly off. I get dressed in jogging bottoms and a hoodie and take a rucksack with me. I walk to our nearest supermarket. I fill a trolley with two loaves of cheap white bread, a large block of cheddar, a family trifle, several packets of value biscuits, two two-litre bottles of lemonade, a multipack of crisps, full-fat yoghurts, liquorice all sorts, iced cakes, strawberry ice cream and salted caramel ice cream. I add a frozen chocolate cheesecake, two microwave lasagnes, a pack of six sausage rolls and a large pot of double cream. I buy a box of thirty laxatives from the in-store pharmacy.

I walk home with the rucksack straps digging into my shoulders and two bulging carrier bags. Knowing how much I have to eat and then throw up is exhausting, but I'm going to do it anyway because I do not know what else to do.

One Christmas, the moment Dad and me and Jo sat down to eat our Christmas dinner, I lost it. I knew after eating, I'd be straight in the toilet throwing it all up and it seemed like such a shit thing to do after we'd all put in so much effort, spending the whole morning cooking. It was the first time Dad had spent Christmas with Jo and me for years. He'd made us these wooden sculptures. Mine was of a girl sitting and reading a book, Jo's was of a girl looking in the mirror.

I sat there wearing my green paper crown with my loaded plate of turkey and potatoes and vegetables in front of me and sobbed because I didn't want to eat it all and then be sick, but I didn't know how not to do it. I sobbed and sobbed and Dad and Jo didn't say anything. They were used to me being mental. Then I stopped crying, ate it all, took my crown off and threw it all up.

The lifts aren't working. I stop halfway to put the bags down and have a roll-up. I call Richard while I'm leaning against the wall. If he answers and we sort this out, I'll throw this shopping in the skip at the front of the flats, do something good with my time, study, or go for a walk. He doesn't answer his landline or his mobile, and I don't leave a message.

I unpack the shopping and hide most of the food under my bed in case Jo comes home. I make cheese sandwiches, thick with butter, to eat while the first lasagne is in the microwave. I put some shit on TV so the sound of me chewing and swallowing isn't the only sound in the flat. I lie on my side on my bed, propped up on an elbow, my plate on a magazine in case anything spills. After the lasagne, I eat four packets of crisps, a packet of chocolate digestives dipped in tea, a six-pack of chocolate mini-rolls and half a tub of salted caramel ice cream with double cream poured on top. I take the bottle of lemonade into the toilet and drink some of it, contract my stomach muscles and throw up. I keep going until I've finished the lemonade and I'm bringing up bile. I smoke and do it all again. I shower and wash my hair, take ten laxatives and message Richard. I lie down on my bed and don't expect to fall asleep, but I do. When I wake up, it's five and I'm cuddling one of Ellie's teddies. Richard hasn't called or messaged me back.

I look through the kitchen drawer for the takeaway flyers and order a Chinese, a set meal for six with extra chips. While I'm waiting for it to arrive, I eat dry toast to line my stomach. I take about a third of the takeaway on my plate, chicken chow mein, four chicken balls, beef in black bean sauce, special fried rice and some chips and lie on the sofa watching TV, a documentary about women in prison. The male narrator does this thing where he sounds either incredulous or disbelieving when he's interviewing the women, but I see through it. It's a ruse, so the women open up more. I hope they've seen through him too and they're bullshitting him as much as he's bullshitting them, that it's a double bluff, but I worry they've fallen for it. He's giving them undivided attention and they like feeling important. One of the inmates is running a group for other inmates on anger management. She's got an abrupt, no-nonsense way of speaking but she's also kind. You can see she cares. She reminds me a bit of Pat.

I hear the front door opening. I sit up and put my plate on the table, rub my mouth and tighten the belt of my dressing gown. Jo giggles and there's a deeper voice too. Doug.

'Hey sis!' she says. 'Hey babe, what are you eating?'

'Chinese, they got the order wrong, sent me too much. There's loads in the kitchen if you want.'

I can think of nothing worse than the two of them sitting down and joining me.

'God, no,' Jo says like it's a disgusting idea, but she loves Chinese takeaways.

'You all right, baby?' I can see Doug's muscles through his sleeves. They're steroid big and there's something cartoon-like about the balls of bicep.

'What are you watching?' Jo says.

'A documentary about women in prison.'

'She's obsessed, always has been, since she was a kid, haven't you, Dani?' She rubs her nose.

I nod.

'With prison?' Doug says.

'I find it interesting.' I look at my plate of food on the coffee table. I could talk loads about prison, like how it doesn't work because the reoffending rates are so high, and why can't we be like other countries with a focus on rehabilitation, and how Dad learned to read and write and do yoga while he was there. But

I'd feel disloyal to Stevie if I start chatting away to Doug.

'You like prison or ex-prisoners? Likes a bit of rough like her big sister, hey?' Jo elbows him and tells him to shut up. He grabs hold of her wrists, and in that position, she looks tiny. Her hands disappear in his and she yelps as he laughs. I look at the chips cooling and the beef in black bean congealing and try to ignore the sexual tension as Jo and Doug wrestle and make little excited noises.

'I came back to pick some stuff up. We're going back out. Are you working tomorrow?' Jo says.

'Yeah.'

'I've got a few days off work,' says Jo. 'We might be going away. I'll let you know.'

Her bedroom door shuts, and there's silence. They might be shagging, or taking cocaine, or both. What do I care? I just hope they'll leave soon so I can finish the takeaway because when you take too long over a binge, it's harder to bring everything up. I smoke on the balcony, and message Richard to say we need to talk. On my second roll-up, Jo fakes another laugh and the front door slams. I finish the cold food.

I pause the documentary and take a can of Diet Coke into the bathroom. Afterwards, I splash my face with warm water and look in the mirror. My parotid glands are swollen and make me look like a cross between a pig and a chipmunk. I spray the toilet with bleach spray, wipe it down with loo roll and flush the chain. I smoke a roll-up on the balcony, but when I stand up, I have to sit back down because I start shaking and it's like I have pins and needles creeping over my vision. I take a few deep breaths then I swallow down another ten laxatives with a glass of water and make a cup of tea with a tiny bit of milk. No point going to all that effort to get rid of calories if I'm going to put them straight back in. I watch the rest of the documentary. My mouth is sensitive and the tea makes my teeth hurt, and I have to let it cool before I can drink it.

Pat messages. She hopes I feel better soon and says to ring her if I fancy a chat. I don't respond. I'll see her tomorrow at work. No point staying off work again because I don't have the energy to binge like I did today and I haven't got the money for it either. I lie on my back and call Richard so I can listen to his voice on the voicemail, but he answers. I scrabble around for the remote control and press mute.

'Why haven't you been answering?' I say.

'I don't work at the weekend, but you sounded distressed in your messages. It sounded like you needed to talk.'

His voice, his tone, has gone back to like it was when he was my therapist. It's been one day since I was with him but it feels like months.

'I can't believe what you told me last night.' I say.

'What's that?' His voice is hard and it makes me hesitate a moment.

'About fucking your clients.'

There's a silence and I wonder if he's hung up but then he speaks.

'Do you wish to resume your therapy, Dani?'

'Are you fucking joking? How could I after all this?'

'If you are going to be aggressive, I will end the call.'

I bite my lip and clench the fist not holding the phone. 'How could I start back with my therapy after everything that's happened between us?'

'Dani, I'm not sure I know exactly what you're referring to, but if you'd like to resume your therapy, I can book you in. You sound distressed.'

'I'm distressed because of you, you prick. Don't make out like I'm the mental one, like I'm the one who's been doing bad stuff.

You're the one shagging your clients.'

'I have no idea what you're speaking about, Dani.'

'You're joking, aren't you?'

'I'm going to end the call now; if you would like to make an appointment, you can email, or if you would prefer, I can refer you to another therapist.'

'You are a piece of shit and I'm reporting you.'

There is a silence, and I think he's hung up.

'Reporting me for what?'

'For gross misconduct. For fucking your clients.'

'We spoke about fantasies during your sessions and how fantasies are not reality. I'm going to recommend you make an appointment with your doctor.'

'Don't make out like I'm mental. You are a fucking—'

He's gone.

I headbutt and punch the sofa cushions a couple of times, then I take ten two pound coins from the big glass bottle where Stevie keeps his change. I'll replace them when I'm paid. I pull on tracksuit bottoms and a hoodie and go to the twenty-four-hour garage opposite. I buy two microwave cheeseburgers, a family-size fruitcake, a family-size bar of Dairy Milk with Oreo filling, a large bottle of Diet Coke and two white chocolate Magnums. I eat it all and bring it back up again. I smoke, I take the rest of the laxatives. I watch TV until I fall asleep.

I wake up in the middle of the night because my subconscious was working away and reminded me about the photo of Richard, slumped over his kitchen table with sick on his face. I take my phone and send it to Richard. 'Does this help you remember what happened between us?' I write under the photo. He calls but then it cuts out. I call him back.

'Yeah?' I say.

His voice is low. 'Delete the photo or I will write to Stevie to tell him about Jo. Then I will contact your university to tell them not to let you return because you are unhinged.'

My throat is too dry to speak, but there is no point in speaking because he has hung up.

I delete the photo.

Chapter Thirty-Three

I wake up before my alarm because of the dragging pains in my stomach. My mouth is dark and dry and rotten. After I've been to the toilet, I hold on to the sink while cleaning my teeth because I'm so unsteady. Pins and needles in my vision again. I sit down with my back against the bath. I learned in the CBT course that when you're throwing up a lot and taking laxatives, it messes with the salt and mineral levels in the body, causing you to shake and go dizzy. It can also lead to problems with the heart, but I stopped listening at that point.

I crawl to the kitchen and use the worktop to pull myself up. I sip warm water because cold water would be too much of a shock to the system, and eat a quarter of a banana for the potassium. I roll a cigarette even thinner than usual, but I only take a couple of puffs before I chuck it because the head rush is too much.

Sunday is a shorter workday; I'll be able to get through fine. Despite being the smallest size they make, my work trousers fall down past my hips, so I put on black jeans. I don't know if Babs is in today and even if she is, she may not notice. In the grand scheme of things, it doesn't matter.

I take the lift because I'm shaking too much for the stairs. By the time I get to the ground floor, I've had to sit down even though the floor is filthy, so I know I can't go to work. If standing in the lift is too much effort, I can't work on pot wash all day. I press the number six button, go back up, and go to bed. I don't take my shoes off. I don't get under the duvet. I don't text Babs. Too much effort.

There's banging on the door and I can hear someone shouting my name. It sounds like Pat but it can't be Pat because she doesn't know where I live. I check my phone. It's ten past five and I've got six missed calls from Pat, two from Babs, voicemails, and messages. I take a while to stand up because my head is spinning, and go and answer the door. I lean against the wall on the way for support. Pat's standing there in her uniform with her brown leather bag over one shoulder.

'Hello, love,' she says.

And then she blurs into black and there is a roaring in my ears and then, nothing.

Pat is sitting on Stevie's chair with her crossword book on her lap and a pen in her hand. I'm on the sofa, covered in my duvet.

'Pat,' I say.

'Ah, good. Sleeping beauty is finally awake,' she says.

'What are you doing here?'

'I came to check you were okay.'

I pull the duvet up and use it to dry my face.

'Why?' I say.

'You didn't show up at work, and I couldn't get hold of you. I was worried.'

'What's the time?'

'Just coming up to eight o'clock.'

'In the morning?'

'In the evening. It's Sunday evening.'

I think back to getting in the lift, but I can't remember much after that.

'What happened?'

'You fainted when you answered the door. I would have tried to catch you but I didn't get the chance. You just went.'

'I feel fine.' I go to sit up but get a stab through my right temple that makes me lie straight back down.

'Rest, Dani.'

When I wake up again it's dark outside. Pat has turned on one of the side lamps and is reading one of Jo's magazines.

'Hello again,' she says. 'I'm going to make you something to eat and then I've got to go.'

I can hear her in the kitchen, opening drawers and closing cupboards. It feels good listening. I get up and look for my phone. The battery is dead and I can't think where the charger is. My head hurts too much so I go back to the sofa to lie down.

Pat comes back with two slices of toast on a plate and a mug of tea, and puts them on the coffee table.

'Where's Jo?' she says. 'Out with her new fella?'

'Yeah, probably.'

'Do you want me to try to get hold of her?'

'No,' I say. 'I really don't.'

'I've got to go now, Dani. But I'll be back in the morning. Don't worry about work, I'll call Babs and tell her you're still unwell. I've got time in lieu owing, so I'm going to take that.'

'It's a bit late notice, though, isn't it? For you to take the time off?'

'Don't you worry about that,' she says. She picks her bag up and puts it over her shoulder.

'Pat, how did you know where I live?'

'I made Babs tell me. I know it's breaking data protection and all that, but I was worried. She was worried. You were on the rota and it's not like you not to turn up or call in. And especially because you've not responded to my texts for days. We were calling you all day. I said to Babs I wanted to check you were okay.'

'I'm fine,' I say. 'Thanks for coming here.'

'Don't cry. Eat your toast,' she says.

I don't know if I'm asleep or I'm just speaking to him in my mind.

'What's been going on?' Dad says.

'I'm sorry. I thought I was doing the right thing. I thought therapy would help me.'

'It's obvious that geezer was a fucking idiot.'

'He's a psychotherapist, Dad. He's well trained.'

'Mickey Mouse training. Why do you think he's gone for that kind of work in the first place?'

'I don't know. To help people, probably.'

'Screw your loaf. To get to young girls like you.'

'If you'd been here, it wouldn't have happened. You could have given me advice.'

'You've got to learn to back yourself, Dani.'

'I can't. I need help.'

'A lot of them therapist people are the ones that need help.'

'You're probably part of the reason I was going in the first place.'

'What?'

'I'm not a weirdo piece of shit. You've got to stop calling me that.'

'What are you talking about?'

'All those times you called me a weirdo piece of shit.'

'Dani, I'd never call you that.'

'Dad, please don't deny it – you're making it worse.'

'Look, if I ever said that to you, I am genuinely sorry. You are not a weirdo piece of shit.'

'It's really affected my confidence. I wanted you to be proud of me.'

He holds out his arms wide and I run to him.

'I miss you so much, Dad.'

Pat must have plugged my phone in because I wake up to hear it ringing. Pat tells me she's on the way round. When she arrives, she makes tea while I sit on the sofa.

'How are you feeling?' she says.

'Much better.'

'No offence, love, but you looked pretty bad when you answered the door yesterday.'

'I bet,' I say.

'We were worried about you.'

'Thanks for coming over. And again today. I feel bad you're using your holiday up on this.'

'That's my choice, Dani. I want to.'

'Thanks. I appreciate it. It's nice of you.'

'Do you want to talk about it?'

I speak into my mug of tea.

'It's difficult. I'm not really ill.'

'Come on, Dani,' Pat says. 'People who aren't unwell don't go around fainting like that. Your face was completely white, love.'

'It's self-inflicted.'

'What's self-inflicted?' she says.

Fuck it, I think. She's gone out of her way to help me because she cares. I can trust her. And even if what I'm about to tell her does make her think badly of me, so what? I tell Pat about the bulimia and I wait for her to make some noise of disgust or to have a go at me for it. I cover my mouth with my hand.

305

Pat comes and sits next to me on the sofa and puts her hand on my arm. 'You don't need to be ashamed, love. It's all right. Don't get upset.'

'When I told you I had problems with my eating, I was hoping you'd think it was anorexia, but then I'm too big to be an anorexic anyway. I feel like a complete skank now.'

'You're not, Dani. You're a young girl who's finding her way.'

'That's why I was going for therapy. And because of my dad and all that. And I was getting better. It was good at first. I thought I was getting it under control and working through shit.'

'So what's changed?'

'We've been seeing each other. Outside of the sessions.'

'Who? You and the therapist?' There's such shock on her face I have to turn away.

'We've been sleeping together.'

'You and the therapist?'

'I thought we were in a proper relationship, but he was using me.'

'Jesus, Dani.'

'Remember when you wanted to go and get the earrings for Megan, and I said I couldn't? I was meeting him in Wetherspoon's. We even stayed in a hotel one night – and he's been here, to this flat, when Jo was at work.'

Pat puts her arms around me. She holds me. I don't know for how long. Every time I think she's going to stop, she doesn't, and she keeps her arms around me and she is warm and smells of fabric conditioner and cigarettes.

'Jesus,' she says again. Her mascara is smudged under both eyes.

'I know, I messed up.'

'You messed up? You were paying him for therapy, right? This is a professional with qualifications?'

'Yeah.'

'He's the one who messed up, love. Not you.'

'He kept saying I needed to engage with the therapy and be honest with him. I was trying to do it, but I ended up "seducing" him, he said. I didn't even know I could be seductive.'

'No, he's putting it onto you, and it's on him. How long have you been seeing him for, like that, not as your therapist?'

'A few weeks. He said he was going to leave his partner for me. I thought I was special and this educated, professional man wanted me.' I shake my head and put my hands over my face. 'I've been so stupid.'

'Dani, you're not stupid. He used his position to manipulate you. You're going to report him, aren't you?'

'He said he'll deny it. Who do you think people will believe? Look at me compared with him.'

'You should report him. He shouldn't have been seeing you outside the sessions. There are rules about that kind of thing. There must be. He took advantage of you, Dani.'

'It's not like I'm some victim with no input into what happened. I flirted with him. I was attracted to him. I wanted him to want me.'

'You were paying him to help you. He should have looked into why you were flirting with him and analysed that. He took advantage of you, darling. How old is he?'

'Fifty-one.'

'And you're twenty. For god's sake.'

'I can't put all the blame onto him. I wanted it to happen.'

'You were going to him for help.'

'I was, but I was attracted to him, Pat.' I shake my head. 'I'm so mixed up about it all.'

'Anyone would be. But what he did isn't right.'

I start getting the pain in my temple again.

'I'm so tired,' I say. 'I need to sleep, Pat. I'm sorry.'

'Go and have a lie-down. I'm going shopping to get some lunch for us. You haven't got much in the fridge.'

'You can go, Pat. I don't mind. I'll be fine. I just need to sleep. Thanks for coming over again.'

'Stop worrying,' she says. 'I want to stay.'

I feel better after I've slept some more. After lunch, Pat and I sit on the balcony and she smokes but I still can't face it.

'I did look into making a complaint with the organisation he's registered with.' I bring the website up on my phone to show her. 'The United Kingdom Council for Psychotherapy – UKCP.'

'Are you going to call them?'

'It says before making a complaint, you should try to resolve it with your therapist.'

'I think you've gone beyond that point. Call them up, love, see what they say. He might do it again.'

'He has. He does.'

'He sleeps with other clients?'

'He said they're usually married. That's why he gets away with it. He said they're grateful he's so virile.'

Pat shakes her head. 'Dani, the man is a complete scumbag. You've got to report him. Don't let him do it to anyone else.'

I think of another girl like me. I don't want her to go through what I have. Then I think of what Richard said, about contacting Stevie and my university.

'I can't, Pat,' I say.

She looks at me and doesn't say anything. I can tell she's disappointed from the way she sighs, but she reaches over and squeezes my hand.

We spend the afternoon at the kitchen table, Pat on the laptop Richard gave me, me on my phone, reading about therapists who have been suspended or had their names taken off the register. We realise that most of them are men who have had 'inappropriate' relationships with their clients. The UKCP publish the results of the hearings, and my stomach turns reading about how these psychotherapists abused their positions; how creepy and calculated they were.

'Look at this bit,' Pat says, reading from the screen. 'If it was a psychiatrist or psychologist who had sex with one of their clients, they'd be removed by the General Medical Council. If they carried on trying to work, it'd be a criminal offence because they're regulated professions.'

'I know,' I say. 'I read that before. But it's not the same for psychotherapists.'

'Not a criminal offence for psychotherapists, but it is for psychiatrists or psychologists. That doesn't seem right, does it?' says Pat. 'Where is the logic in that?'

'It's because it's not regulated. Psychotherapists can be struck off the UKCP, but they can carry on practising. Psychotherapy isn't a regulated profession. A psychotherapist can have sex with his clients and even when he's busted, keep on working as a psychotherapist. The title isn't protected.'

'It doesn't make any sense,' she says.

'So there's no point in putting the complaint in because even if Richard is found guilty, he could carry on working as a psychotherapist and carry on doing what he's been doing,' I say.

'But he wouldn't be able to align himself with the UKCP, and if they remove him from their register, they'd publish the details on their website. That'd be worth something,' Pat says.

'Look at this.' I point to the bit I'm reading. The therapist who put videos up online of himself playing love songs on the banjo. What a tosser. That woman was going to him with a history of sexual violence, and he was having sex with her.'

'Can you feel that angry for yourself?' Pat says.

'Right now, I feel stupid more than anything. How could I have been so stupid? I can't believe I didn't see what he was doing. He was using me.'

'You went into it in good faith. Don't beat yourself up. It's him you want to be angry at, not yourself.'

'I shouldn't have been so naive.'

'It wasn't naivety, Dani. It was trust. What a shit world the place would be if we all went around suspicious of everyone. Don't feel bad for what happened. It was not your fault. If you were at fault, I'd tell you. You know that, don't you? That I'd be straight with you?'

I look at the notebook she's got in front of her, where she's been making notes about what we should do next. She's spending her free time helping me. The least I can do is give her the full story.

'Pat, I want to report him but I'm worried he'll tell Stevie about Doug, and contact my university to tell them I'm mental. He said he would.'

Pat laughs. '*Now* you are being naive, Dani. He won't do that.'

'How do you know?'

'It'd be a breach of client confidentiality. Everything you've told me about him shows how he's always covering himself. He won't do that. He's mugging you off again.'

She's right.

We talk a bit more and then Pat gathers her things up and goes. Tells me she'll message me later and to call her if I need anything.

Jo calls me later that evening to let me know that she and Doug are off to Brighton for a couple of nights. She's excited and wants to chat. I put her on loudspeaker and lie on my back. Put the phone next to my ear so I don't have to hold it.

'You know on Saturday, after we came back to the flat?' she says. 'We went to his flat for a smoke, then his mate called and said there was this bare-knuckle fight in east London.'

She's not watching it on Netflix any more. She's living it.

'You were high, weren't you? What were you on?'

'Yeah, all right, Mum.'

'Like Mum would have noticed.' I think about how Doug is the complete opposite of Stevie. Doug's drugs, parties and bare-knuckle fights. Stevie's the sofa, Netflix and takeaway pizza. 'Is that it then, for you and Stevie?' I say.

'Yeah.'

'You're really sure?'

'We've grown apart.'

'You've grown apart from him, Jo. He still wants you.'

'He'll find someone that suits him more. Someone more domesticated.'

I can't picture Stevie with anyone else. I know he worships Jo. Yes, he can be a slob and set in his ways, but his world revolves around making sure Jo's comfortable and has what she needs. Jo doesn't realise it.

'I'll miss him,' I say. 'And Ellie, even though she was a little shit most of the time.'

'You can stay in touch with them.'

'Yeah,' I say. But we both know it never works out that way.

Chapter Thirty-Four

On my morning break, I stand away from the smoking hut so nobody can overhear, and call the UKCP complaints number. It goes to answerphone so I end the call. I could see this as a sign to drop it, but then I think of Diogenes and his view on outspokenness, and that vice and conceit should be exposed. On my lunch break I walk to the park, sit on a bench and call again. This time a woman answers. I stand up so I can take a deeper breath.

'I need to make a complaint against my therapist.'

There's a pause and I imagine she's writing or typing what I say.

'Okay. What kind of complaint?'

'I think it'd come under gross misconduct. We were sleeping together and he said he's had sex with other clients too.'

'Can I take the name of the therapist, please?'

I pause. I think of Diogenes.

'Richard Goode. He works from King's Road.'

'We would need evidence. Do you have emails, text messages, that kind of thing?'

'Not much, but I've got call records of times we spoke late at night.'

'Thank you. That would be helpful. Could you give me your name, please?'

'Dani.'

'Thanks, Dani. And your surname?'

'Do you really need it?'

'If you supply us with enough evidence to approach Mr Goode with the allegations, he will be able to identify you anyway.'

'Day,' I say. 'Dani Day.'

Me and Pat have the same day off, so we meet in the morning to go to the old people's home. I feel what happened at the flat has made us closer and when I see her waiting for me outside the tube station, I want to give her a big hug, but I smile and pat her a few times on the arm instead.

When we arrive at Roden Court, Elaine's walking through reception. She pauses, tilts her head and gives me a slow smile. I turn and walk out before she can say anything. When I get to an empty bus stop, I sit on the red plastic bench and close my eyes. I was so wrapped up in Richard that I hadn't visited Frank for a long time. I'd barely thought of him.

After an hour, I walk back and wait outside for Pat to come out.

'When was it?'

'Last night. Elaine said she went to wake him and she couldn't. She called the ambulance and stayed with him, held his hand. By the time the ambulance arrived, he'd gone. It was peaceful, love, and Elaine was with him, holding his hand. He wasn't alone.'

I remember Frank trying to hold my hand and me shaking it off. Pat takes an envelope from her bag and holds it out to me. It's got my name on it in shaky blue handwriting. 'Elaine gave me this to give to you.' I keep my arms by my sides. 'Do you want me to keep it and give it to you another time?'

'No,' I say and take it from her. I put it in my rucksack. On the way to the train station, I think about Richard telling me about 'dissociation', where the person disconnects. You feel emotionally numb and like you're a different person. I'll have to think about Frank at some point, but not now.

When I get home, I put the envelope from Frank in the drawer of my bedside table, lie on my bed and look at the ceiling. The flat stinks of weed. I try to read some of my poetry books from university but I can't focus. I think about going over to the garage to buy loads of food to binge on, but then Pat calls and when we stop talking, the urge to do it has passed.

On Sunday morning, I wake up holding my breath. For a moment, I can't breathe, don't know how to breathe. My brain has woken me because my body has stopped doing what it should. I look at the glass of water on my bedside table and lean over to pick it up so I can throw it in my face and shock myself into taking a breath, but then my instincts kick in and I'm breathing again.

I sit up in bed and focus on inhaling through my nose, holding it and exhaling as slowly as possible.

Frank has tucked the flap into the envelope rather than stuck it down. I unfold the thin, lined page, which looks like it's been torn from a jotter.

'My Lovely Dani,' he's written at the top of the page. I put the letter down and go and blow my nose. I come back with a fistful of tissue, pick the letter up and carry on reading. He says my visits meant a lot to him and were a high point of his week. I have to put the letter down again. If I'd known they meant so much to him, I would have visited more. But it's easy to have regrets. It's much easier to think 'I should have ...' after the event than do it at the time. At the bottom of the page, Frank's written, 'Be careful with youth, for it flies from us,' and a couple of kisses which look more like crosses because of the angle he's done them at. It wouldn't have killed me to hold his hand once or kiss him on the cheek, but I couldn't. Easier to bang a stranger because it's less intimate. It's good Elaine was holding Frank's hand. It's good some people can do that kind of thing. I hope Elijah managed to say goodbye to him, too.

Jo's with Doug. I can't call Pat because she's spending the day with Megan and the grandchildren. I try Reena and she picks up on the second ring.

'Are you busy?' I say.

'I'm still in bed.' I hear her yawn. 'Big night last night.'

'With the football girls?'

'Yes. We won our match and so we partied even harder. How are you?'

'I'm good,' I say.

'You sound rough.'

'No, I'm fine.'

'Dani?'

'Yeah?'

'Why are you calling me?'

'I don't suppose you could meet for a coffee, could you?'

'Now?'

'Yeah, or later today.'

'No. My hangover is rotten. I can't get out of bed.'

'No problem. I'll see you at work tomorrow,' I say.

'But why don't you come over?' she says.

'I don't want to bother you if you're not feeling great.'

'It's a hangover, Dani. It will pass. Come over.'

'Are you sure?'

'I wouldn't have said it otherwise.'

She texts me her address and I get on the bus. When I get

there, I sit in the living room on a yellow leather sofa while she makes us coffee. I tell her about Frank and she gives me a hug. She's not showered since her night out but I don't care. Then I tell her about what happened with Richard, and that I'm waiting for a date for the hearing.

'You should have listened to me in the café that time,' she says. 'I told you it's not a good idea to date really old men.'

'Yeah, the age difference – it just wasn't right. I don't know what I was thinking. Well, the age difference was the least of it.'

'But still gross,' says Reena. 'Are you worried about the hearing?'

'Yeah. It's going to be his word against mine. But I've got evidence, which is good; call records that show some long conversations late at night.'

'Any other evidence? Photos?'

'No. He was never into selfies. Said he didn't like the culture of it. He was one step ahead, making sure I didn't have any evidence.'

I think about the photo I deleted, how stupid that was and how I should have kept it, but I was scared.

'I wish there was something I could do to help you, Dani.' Reena clenches a fist and hits her knee with it.

'You are helping. It helps talking to you about it.'

'No, something more.' Reena sighs and picks up her coffee from the floor. 'Why don't I book a session with him, get him to make a pass and record it on my phone?'

'I thought about recording him, but I never did because I thought that somehow, he'd know, or I'd be acting all paranoid and give it away. It was hard to hide things from him.'

'I won't find it hard. Let me record him. I want to help you.'

'You'd do that for me?'

'Yes. You're my friend, Dani. I want to help you.'

'I appreciate the offer, Reena, but I don't think it would work so easily.'

'Why not? You haven't seen me act, have you? I'm so good. I could easily fool him into thinking I was some sex addict or something. Then he'd definitely make a pass, wouldn't he?'

'Reena, I know you'd be able to act brilliantly. Your impressions are fantastic.'

'I got a seven for my drama GCSE,' she says.

'Should have been a nine. But I don't know. It doesn't feel right. You'd have to go for weeks and weeks first, probably, before he made a pass. You can't sit through all that. You wouldn't be able to get the evidence in time for the hearing either.'

She jumps up and takes a few steps away, then she turns back to me and starts shimmying her way over. She winks and starts sliding her hands up her body.

'Mr Richard?' she breathes. 'Are you Mr Richard? Can you help me, baby?'

'Reena, stop it. Not appropriate.'

'I hear you've got some exciting and novel ways to help your clients. Want to show me what you can do?'

I'm laughing because I can picture her doing it. Walking into his room, acting, fooling him. Making a fool of him.

'Let me do it, Dani. Obviously I'll be much more subtle than that. Then you'll have the evidence you need. Even if it is too late for the hearing, I could then put in a complaint.'

'You'd really do that for me?'

'Yes, I told you I would. But you'd have to pay for the sessions.'

'Thanks, Reena. I appreciate the offer, but it's not a good idea.'

'So what are you going to do?' she says.

'I'm going to find more evidence.'

'What if you can't find anything?'

'I'll keep going until I do. And then I'm going to make sure he gets what he deserves.'

Reena stares at me.

'Dani, you looked really scary when you said that,' she says, only half smiling.

'I'm going for him. I'm not going to let him get away with it.'

'Good,' she says.

When I get home from Reena's, I put Richard's name into Google and go back further and further, searching for anything at all about him that could help me. I find an old Facebook page advertising his services as a psychotherapist. There are eight reviews, all giving him five out of five stars.

'Richard helped me through a very difficult time. He was professional but warm and I would highly recommend him.'

'Richard provided a space for me to work through the things I was struggling with and I was able to readjust my outlook on life.'

'I've only been seeing Richard for two months but already feel so much better. I know with his skills and expertise I'll be exactly where I need to be in not too much longer.'

The five other people have just given five stars and no comments. I send them all a message saying I had a bad experience with Richard Goode and asking if they always found him to be professional. I say I can see they've given him a great review, but I'm worried about him working as a psychotherapist because I think he's a predator. I include my phone number and say to message me or give me a call. It's a long shot considering they're singing his praises, but perhaps something happened after they wrote the reviews. There's nothing to lose.

Chapter Thirty-Five

I get a letter through the post from the UKCP with a date for the hearing in late September – three weeks before I'm due to start back at university. The thick white paper reflects the gravity of the situation; this is too serious for an email.

I've submitted all my evidence. I was so stupid to delete the photo, but I'm trying to stop beating myself up about that, and trying to stop beating myself up for things in general. I don't have texts or emails, he didn't send anything that would incriminate himself, but I do have records of eight phone calls we had that lasted over an hour and took place after ten at night, and other records of me calling him, too. I'm hoping that at least one person I contacted through Facebook will come back to me, if they had a bad experience with Richard, and tell me about it.

I take the laptop to a shop to see if he's left any evidence on it to show it was his, but there's nothing. I ask the woman to check again, in case she's missed something, but she's adamant it was wiped clean. I'm about to shout that she's obviously not doing her job properly, but realise she's not the one I'm angry at.

I've not said anything to Jo about what happened with Richard, only that I decided to stop the therapy because I was doing so much better. She's either high or on a comedown on the rare occasions I see her at the moment anyway. Also, I don't want to keep going to her and telling her that something else has fucked up.

Stevie comes to pick up his TV when Jo's out with Hayley one evening. He's wearing a khaki vest and when he's taking the TV off the wall, I look at his sunburnt shoulders. 'Sun cream's for pussies,' I remember him saying. I make us a cup of tea and we sit on the sofa so he can show me pictures of Ellie on his phone. I tell him to stop on one of the pictures so I can look at it more closely. Ellie's wearing a dark blue T-shirt with a spaceship on.

'That's a cool T-shirt.'

'Yeah, she's moving away from the pink and sparkly phase.'

I shift slightly so I can look at him.

'Stevie, I'm sorry about what happened with Jo.'

'Shit happens.' He shrugs.

'She's my sister and I'm not going to say anything bad about her—'

'Yeah, I know how you sisters stick together.'

'But I know you cared about her, a lot.'

'Dan, I still do,' he says.

'And thanks for letting me move in.'

'I didn't have a choice.'

'I know, but I appreciate how you tried to help me.'

'Yeah,' he says. 'Help me take the TV down to the car, will you?'

Stevie won't put the TV on the floor of the lift so we hold it. He takes most of the weight.

He closes the boot and we stand there looking at each other.

'Come on then,' he says and holds his arms wide. It's the first time we've hugged. 'Dan,' he says. 'Stop it now; you're getting my vest wet.' He pushes me away and pulls the front of his vest away from his skin. 'Soppy cow,' he says and rubs the back of his hand across his eyes before he gets in the car and drives away.

I could go to the garage now. Buy shitloads of food to binge on. But instead, I go back up to the flat, lock myself in the bathroom and cry.

While I'm on pot wash at work, I spend a lot of time thinking about what draws certain people to become counsellors and therapists. Is it the easy access to vulnerable people, those who are at their lowest ebb? The therapist can sit, godlike, and hear all of the client's shameful secrets and smile gently whilst revealing nothing of their own insecurities and fuck-ups. Does it make them feel superior? Is it much easier to be surrounded by other people's problems than deal with their own?

I try to persuade Pat about my views on therapists, when it's myself I'm trying to convince.

'*Some* people must want to become counsellors and therapists because they have a genuine desire to help people,' I say when we're sitting in the canteen at lunch one day.

'Look at how much they charge, though, Dani. If they cared that much about people, wouldn't they do it a bit cheaper so anyone could afford it?'

'That's why some have the low-cost sessions.'

'Even then, you're still looking at a lot of money,' she says. 'Way out of the range of most people.'

'But don't you think it must be a great feeling to do it well? To help someone and send them back out into the world? Sorted out and able to function better?'

'When you put it like that, yes. But none of the stories I've heard have been good ones. My sister-in-law, you know the one I told you about—'

'Yeah, I know – the counsellor made her all dependent.'

'If you can learn to trust your friends, they're probably a

better option because they're helping you because they care. Not because you're paying them.'

I see the logic in what she's saying. The advice she's given me has been just as good as, if not better than, what I was paying Richard for. And she didn't reject me when she found out what I was *really* like. It made us closer.

'I found an old Facebook page of Richard's. It had reviews from clients. I emailed them all, but I've not heard anything back yet.'

'When was that?' she says.

'Three days ago.'

'Give it time. They may need some time to think before they get back to you.'

'And I was thinking about this woman who used to have the appointment before me. I'm sure he's sleeping with or has slept with her, too. I'm going to try and talk to her.'

'How are you going to do that?' she says.

'I'll just wait for her outside Richard's to catch her before she goes in.'

Pat frowns. 'You might be asking for trouble there, Dani.'

'You don't think I should do it?'

'I'll come with you.'

'It'll be fine,' I say. I want to do it alone.

Sometimes I waver. I think I'll retract my allegation and just get on with my life. I don't need this shit. All my headspace taken up with it when I should be thinking of better things, things that will help me improve my life: friends, university, that kind of thing. But then I close my eyes and imagine I'm invisible. I am in Richard's room, watching him as he prepares for his next client. He stands in front of the mirror, licks his lips and plucks a couple of nasal hairs out with his fingers. 'Gotcha,' he says with each one. He moves the box of condoms from the shelf to under the couch. He goes back to the mirror, tilts his chin and smiles at his reflection. There's a knocking at the door and on his way across the room to answer it, Richard does a little quick step, already getting turned on for the next client he's going to see. She's coming to him because she was sexually abused by her uncle when she was a child. She believes that therapy will help her deal with the negative after-effects that dominate her close relationships.

And after that, I know I have to go through with it. For the women who he might make a pass at in the future. And for me. I want justice.

On Monday, there's still no news from Richard's ex-clients on the Facebook page, so I decide to go to his house to try to speak to the woman. I get to Richard's at ten to five and wait further down the street so there's less chance of him seeing me. At five to five I see her Audi coming slowly down the road as she looks for a parking spot. She knocks at his door. He smiles and gives her a parking permit then goes back inside. When she's putting the permit on her dashboard, I go over.

'Yes?' she says as I stand in front of her. Impatient, posh.

'Are you having therapy with him?' I point to Richard's door.

She lowers her eyebrows. Her forehead doesn't move. Botox. Up close, she looks older than I thought she was.

'That's none of your business.'

She locks the car door and walks towards Richard's. I follow behind her.

'I was having therapy with him, and I found out he sleeps with his clients. Has he ever made a move on you?' She pauses, turns and looks at me with hard eyes. 'It's important, he can't keep getting away with it,' I say.

'Go away,' she says. 'I do not know who you are and I do not want to talk to you.' She waves a hand at me, and I see she's wearing a wedding ring.

I let her walk away. Then I write my name and number on a piece of paper and put it under her windscreen wiper, just in case.

Chapter Thirty-Six

I'm at work when I finally get a message from one of the people who left a Facebook review for Richard. A woman called Anya, who had written that he was 'an excellent, knowledgeable psychotherapist'.

'*Can I ask why you're doing this? You say you had a bad experience with Richard but that could be many things.*' I go to the toilets so I can call her but then think it might be too much. I send a message explaining and Anya texts straight back. She agrees to meet me outside Café 54 in Ealing the next day when I'm on lunch break.

I guess who she is when I'm walking towards the café. She's slim, older than me, with long brown hair and a fringe falling into her eyes.

'Anya?' I hold my hand out.

She shakes my hand.

We queue for a takeaway coffee and I try to think of some small talk.

'You see those women over there?' I nod towards a couple of women in the corner, and Anya looks at them. 'They're drinking herbal tea and they've got cakes. I always thought how good it would be to be able to do that rather than have coffee and a cigarette.'

'What's stopping you?' she says.

'Caffeine and nicotine. But one day I'll do it. I always like to set myself targets.'

Anya and I walk down the street until we find a bench.

'How long ago was it that you were seeing him?' I say.

'Four years ago,' she says.

'Did he make a pass during a session?'

She brushes the fringe out of her eyes and nods.

'He told me I looked beautiful when I was sad.'

A spike of jealousy stabs my chest as I picture Anya sitting on my chair in that room I loved. Richard saying those words to her, calling her beautiful. Then the jealousy is wiped out by anger.

'Did you sleep with him?'

'Did you?' she says.

I nod. 'In his therapy room, at my flat. Once in a hotel.'

'I did, twice. I freaked at him after the second time. He threw one of my shoes at me and said he couldn't see me any more, that I was disturbed and he couldn't help me.'

'He threw a shoe at you?'

'Not in my face or anything. He threw it in my direction but it missed me by quite a way. It was to intimidate me. It worked.'

'Did you report him?'

'I said I would, when I was freaking out at him, but he said he'd deny it.'

'That's what he said to me. It's how he gets away with it.'

She looks around. 'I've got a boyfriend too. He'd leave me if he found out about Richard.'

'Have you been with him long?'

'Five years. That was part of the reason I started seeing Richard. We were having some issues.'

'Maybe he wouldn't leave you. Maybe he'd understand.'

'I doubt it,' she says. 'I wouldn't stay with him if I found out he'd cheated on me.'

'I reported Richard to the UKCP. I've got a hearing coming up. He shouldn't be able to get away with this.'

'Yeah,' she says. And the look that flitters across her face is pained.

There's something soft about Anya. Her hair is soft, her features delicate. I know it sounds bad, but I can see why Richard tried it on with her – she looks like an easy target. Like I was.

'Anya, he can't keep getting away with it,' I say.

'People like him do.'

'Not always.'

'I'm worried nobody will believe me, and it's the shame of having to tell people, and my boyfriend finding out.'

'How will you feel if you just keep it inside?'

'I blank it out. I try not to think about it.'

'But it will still be there, won't it?'

We sit for a while, and then Anya looks at me.

'You're so brave, going to a hearing. Will it be like court?'

'I'm not sure.'

'But what if you go through all that and they don't believe you?'

'I don't know. I just know I'm so angry I have to, or it'll always be there on my conscience – thinking of him doing it to someone else and knowing that I didn't try to do anything to stop it. I can't live like that.'

She fiddles with the lid from her coffee.

'I'm sorry, Dani. I'm not ready.'

'Look, if there are more reports coming in, then it makes my case stronger.'

We sit in silence.

'My boyfriend,' she says.

'Yeah, I know.'

'I don't know what to do,' she says.

'If the complaints keep coming in about him, they'll know it's true.'

I want to beg her, but she's already been manipulated by Richard. I don't want to feel I'm manipulating her too, pushing her into something she's not ready for and making her feel uncomfortable. I don't want to be like him.

'He made me feel dirty,' Anya says.

'You were exploited. You weren't doing anything wrong.' I remember the line Pat said to me. 'You were paying him to help you.'

Anya takes a tissue from her pocket and blows her nose.

'And I feel ashamed for cheating on my boyfriend. He's a nice guy, I don't want this to come out. He'd hate me.'

'You don't need to be ashamed,' I say. 'It won't get you anywhere.'

'He asked me to lie on the couch. He really pushed it, saying it would help. He was asking me all these questions about my sexual history. I felt uncomfortable and sat up and he moved fast. I sensed he'd been touching himself. If ever there'd been a red flag, that was it. But how stupid was I? I kept going back. I was attached to him and I felt he was helping me. He could be so sympathetic. It's bad enough telling *you* this, but the thought of saying it to a room of strangers . . . I'm not sure I could.'

'You could,' I say. 'We can do it together.'

She shakes her head, gets up and walks away.

There's only a week until the hearing. I still sit in the smoking shed even though I've given up. Pat thinks it's funny that I've chosen to give up at such a stressful time in my life, but I say I'm taking control. I'm getting through a lot of Nicorette gum every day, which burns the back of my throat, but it's still better than smoking. And not smoking means I can breathe better, which means I can run for more than five minutes on the treadmill at the gym. The first time I make it to ten minutes I get an endorphin rush which reminds me of taking an E. But running is better because it's not illegal and it's natural. A natural high.

'How are you feeling about it?' Pat doesn't need to say, 'the case'. It's a week away and it's all we talk about.

'I'm shitting it.'

'You're doing the right thing.'

'I know. And think how good it will feel when they find him guilty and he's struck off.'

'Exactly,' says Pat.

'But what if they don't? What if they think I'm making it up?'

'Dani. The fact that the hearing is happening shows that they think you're telling the truth, or you wouldn't be getting the hearing. Remember that.'

'Yeah,' I say. 'It's a good sign.'

'They're taking it seriously,' says Pat. 'And you've got the call records. Those prove he was breaking boundaries. He shouldn't have been calling you like that.'

'Yeah. It's good evidence. They'll have to find him guilty,' I say.

Chapter Thirty-Seven

On the day of the hearing, I wake before five. Six hours to go. I sit on the balcony and smoke. It's already warm and the heat is so close it's making me feel like I'm in a straitjacket.

I wear my smartest pair of black jeans, ones that don't have any rips or holes, and borrow one of Jo's work shirts. Pat wanted to come with me but I said I needed to do it on my own.

I get the tube and a bus to America Square, in the City. My shirt sticks to my back. The building where the hearing is being held is large and imposing with more window than brick. I go through the revolving door. The receptionist is on the phone and ignores me when I walk up to the high counter. When she's finished her call, I tell her why I'm there and she says there's a waiting room on the first floor.

Richard is sitting in the waiting room. He's wearing a beige linen suit and a white shirt. He's looking out of the window and fanning himself with a magazine. I freeze then dig my nails into my palms and back away from the doorway before he can see me. Halfway down the stairs, I trip and have to grab hold of the bannister before I fall. I sit on a stripey green sofa in reception and wait. I text Pat to say that I'm nervous, and I'll let her know as soon as they've made a decision. I add a couple of fingers-crossed emojis and thank her for everything.

'It's what friends do,' she messages back.

The adjudication panel consists of two men and a woman sitting behind a long grey table. Richard and I are seated opposite them, a good two metres apart.

The woman introduces herself and her colleagues. She has little eyes and sweat on her upper lip which she keeps dabbing at with a tissue. The man sitting on her right has a chin that takes up half his face. The man on her left has massive sweat patches under the arms of his blue shirt and is breathing heavily, clearly struggling with the heat. I forget all their names as soon as she says them. Two fans are blowing warm air around the room. The woman makes no reference to the fact the room is stifling.

The woman says why we're here today and reads out my allegations. Richard smiles sadly and shakes his head. She invites him to speak.

'Unfortunately, I had no option but to cease therapy with Dani when she repeatedly arrived at the sessions intoxicated,' he says.

He continues that I got angry when he stopped the therapy, then made the allegations. His voice is soft. He sounds so reasonable and entirely believable.

'I have held a professional practice for over seventeen years, have worked for the NHS as an adviser, taught at the College of North West London and have an unblemished record. There has never been a complaint made against me in all the years I have been a psychotherapist. My wife, my daughter, my family, my friends, my colleagues, and everyone who knows me are appalled at these allegations,' he says.

I want to jump up and scream over his words so they can't be heard.

He reaches for a tissue from the box on the table, dabs his eyes, and apologises.

'The impact this is having on my family is very upsetting,' he says.

He coughs, apologises again.

I tear skin from the side of my thumb then press it against my thigh to stop the blood.

'Dani also made a complaint about the counsellor she was seeing before me, but I understand it went no further, again due to lack of evidence. She has form.'

The panel make notes as he speaks. The man with the big chin asks Richard about his supervisor, and he says he has had the same supervisor for the past fifteen years.

The panel turn their attention to me. The man with the sweat patches asks me about the complaint I made about a counsellor I saw before Richard. I open my mouth but I feel so intimidated I can't speak. I think of Diogenes and his view that deceit must be exposed.

'He's being misleading,' I say, pointing at Richard. 'I didn't put in a complaint about the counsellor, I emailed him directly to tell him I wouldn't be coming back.'

'And why was that?' the woman says.

I clear my throat. It feels like there are razor blades in it and when I talk, my words keep cutting out mid-sentence.

'Because in the first session, he stopped me after I'd been speaking for ages to say he'd better switch his hearing aids on, and in the second session he fell asleep. So Richard is lying,' I say. 'He's using something I told him during my therapy against me, but twisting it. I have never put a complaint in about a therapist or counsellor before.'

The woman asks if I ever arrived at my session with Richard under the influence of alcohol.

'No. I never arrived at the session pissed – drunk, I mean. Once we started having sex, yes, I had a drink once or twice before going over, but not while I was seeing him for therapy.'

The swear word hangs in the air and I feel myself heating up. I reach for the glass of water in front of me and take a sip but my hand is shaking so much that water slops down my chin. I put the glass down and use the back of my hand to wipe my chin but it's still wet.

They ask Richard about the late-night calls. They have my list of the eight dates when I called him late at night. The calls lasted between fifty-three minutes and one hour and two minutes.

Richard nods as they're reeling off the dates and times. He gives an apologetic smile.

'I cannot remember the exact dates, but I took several calls from Dani, late at night, during the time I was seeing her for therapy. She told me she had been unable to get through to the Samaritans one time she tried, and I felt I had an ethical duty as her psychotherapist to speak to her while she was in distress. She was using suicidal ideology; she was alone in her flat and I was genuinely concerned she was a suicide risk. I tried to replicate the therapy hour – as you can see, the calls are roughly the same length of time.'

I point at Richard. 'We were having phone sex for some of those calls. And I've never called the Samaritans. I've never been suicidal. He's lying.'

Big Chin asks me to sit down and suggests we all take a ten-minute comfort break. When we come back, Richard is given more time to defend himself.

'I'm sorry but why's he getting so much more time to talk than me?' I say.

They say he has a right to refute the allegations. They're on his side. I can feel it. Fellow professionals together.

I'm finding it hard to listen now. I clasp my hands together under the table to stop myself from banging my fists on top of it

and screaming at them. I take some deep breaths to calm myself
and catch the end of what Richard is saying.

'Dani and I discussed her promiscuity in the sessions and how
her fantasies about men in positions of authority were intrin-
sically linked with the loss of her father—'

'He gave me his laptop. He put "love" in as the password.'
Richard shakes his head like I'm deluded. 'It was your laptop.
You gave it to me because you bought a new one, when you
came to my flat, for lunch.' I know my voice is getting shriller
and louder, but I can't help it.

'Sometimes, when we dearly wish for something to happen, it
can become confused with our reality,' Richard says.

I look at the panel. 'What I'm saying is true,' I say. 'Please. I
know he comes across as convincing but I'm telling the truth.
I've met another ex-client of his, and he had sex with her. She
told me about it.'

The woman looks up from where she's been writing. The
room becomes still, the only noise coming from the fans stirring
the warm air.

'Can you give me the name of this ex-client, Dani?' the
woman asks.

'I can't say. She told me in confidence.'

'I'm afraid unless you can give us her name, we're not able to
consider this information,' says the woman.

I look at Richard.

'Remember throwing a shoe?' I say. 'To intimidate her? It
worked.'

He swallows and clears his throat.

'More fiction,' he says, shaking his head. 'Fiction upon fiction.
Another invention—'

'I'm not saying who it is because I'm respecting her wishes
because I have integrity, which is something he—'

Big Chin says I must not interrupt while Richard is speaking.

'But it's okay for him to interrupt me?'

Sweat Patches makes a stroking motion with his hand like I need to calm down. He says I'll have another opportunity to speak later. I catch the woman watching as I pick at my cuticles, and stop. I'm sure a sneer passed over her face. I bring my finger to my mouth to get rid of the blood. Richard opens his briefcase and takes something out. I recognise the cover of a card I gave him after I'd been seeing him for a few weeks. It's got a shiny gold star on the front. He asks if he can read it aloud, and they say yes. I cover my face with my hands.

'No, no, no,' I say.

'"Dear Richard,"' he begins to read. '"I just wanted to say I am eternally grateful to you for being such a brilliant therapist. I've felt so much better since I started coming to see you and the bulimia is getting under control. I look forward to the session all week and know that with your help and all the good work we're doing together, I'll be able to sort my shit out and lead a good life. I don't have the words to thank you enough for what you are doing and what you have done, love Dani."'

'I sent that before he made the pass. Please, everything's getting twisted. It's not fair. I know he comes across as much better than me but I'm telling the truth. He's a liar. He has sex with his clients. I had sex with him, loads of times.'

Richard takes out the lighter I gave him and holds it up so they can see his initials.

'Dani gave me this engraved lighter too,' he says. 'Her infatuation at times manifested through the gifting of cards and presents.'

'He's lying,' I say.

The woman holds her hand up and asks me to calm down. I take deep breaths.

'Did you give the card and lighter to Mr Goode?' she says.

'Yes, but—'

'Then he's not lying,' she says.

'He's lying in the stuff around it,' I shout.

The panel say we'll break for lunch now. After that, the panel will discuss what they have heard. We're told to meet back in the room at three o'clock.

I sit on a bench down the street and call Pat.

'The panel believe him, Pat. I can feel it. I might as well go. There's no point waiting. He came across as so convincing, and I lost it and shouted a couple of times. What's the point in waiting?'

'You had the call records, and you were telling the truth. Don't try and second-guess what's going to happen. You don't know what the panel are thinking.'

'Pat, it was obvious in the way they were looking at me when I spoke, compared with the way they were looking at him. And at one point, he made a little therapy joke, mentioned some well-known psychotherapist, and they all shared a moment. I'm not stupid.'

'They believed you enough to get you this far,' says Pat. 'Keep the faith. You've got truth on your side.'

I go back into reception at five to three. At ten past, I'm still waiting and I don't know if the fact they're taking longer to discuss it is a good or bad thing. I'm hoping it's good. It must be. If they were certain I was lying, surely they wouldn't need extra time to discuss everything. Thirty minutes later, I'm called back in before the panel.

The woman gestures to the chair I was sitting in before, but I shake my head. I want to stand.

The woman thanks us for coming. She says the evidence is not strong enough or conclusive enough to prove gross misconduct.

They'll be discussing and advising on the late-night phone calls at a later date, with recommendations for Richard to follow.

Richard smiles and nods. Thanks them.

I look at each one of them in turn and I don't want to shout, but that's how it comes out.

'For an educated group of people, you are *really fucking stupid.*'

I go to McDonald's and order two large Big Mac meals with strawberry milkshakes. While I'm waiting for my food, I get a message from Pat.

'I lost,' I text back.

She calls me straight away.

'Where are you, Dani?'

I tell her and she says she'll be there shortly. I tell her not to come but she insists. I take my food from the counter. I've got time to eat it and throw it up again before Pat gets here. I take one of the burger boxes from the bag and open it. I think of the toilets upstairs and how after eating all this, I'll have to go and buy a large Diet Coke and take it with me to the toilet and be sick as quietly as possible and avoid eye contact with anyone in there when I come out. I close the box and put it back in the paper bag. Then I get up and walk out.

I meet Pat at the train station.

'I lost,' I tell her again.

'Dani, when I texted, I asked how you were, not how it went.'

'They didn't believe me.'

'They didn't believe you, or there wasn't enough evidence?'

'Richard read out this card I'd sent him and showed them this lighter I'd given him. That obviously helped his case.'

'Fucking idiots,' says Pat. 'You can hold your head up, Dani. You did what you could. Next time he gets reported, they'll be all over it. You've done the groundwork for the next person.'

Chapter Thirty-Eight

I make an appointment with a psychotherapist called Sandy.

I've got this internal battle going on; part of me wants to be-lieve all therapists are scum like Richard, but rationally I know it can't be true. I chose Sandy because there's a page on her website about how she and another woman exposed a therapist from the Counselling Service where they'd done their training a few years previously. He made sexual advances towards them, and they reported him. After a fight that lasted a couple of years, where he denied all charges and accused the women of fabri-cating it, he was eventually removed from the UKCP for gross misconduct. I like that Sandy and the other woman didn't give up, even when they were being called liars. The therapist is still practising but at least there's loads of stuff about him online now.

I have to sit on the tube for half an hour to get to Sandy's, but then it's only a short walk from the station. Sandy's room is different from Richard's – for a start, she rents it from a large health centre. The other businesses that operate from there are ones like complementary therapies, reiki and non-invasive plastic surgery. Richard wouldn't work from a place like this. He'd consider himself far too superior to the other businesses. There are no bookshelves in Sandy's room, which is on the ground floor. There is no couch, just a couple of wicker chairs with paisley cushions and a table with a glass jug of water and two glasses on it. And, of course, a box of tissues. There are no pictures on the walls, but three lamps are on even though it's bright and sunny outside.

'Would you mind turning the lamps off?' I say when I walk in the room. 'It's just it seems unnecessary, with there being so much natural light in here.'

'I'm happy to turn them off if it makes you feel more comfortable.' She has a Northern accent. When she's turned off the third lamp and sat down, she smiles at me. I don't like her hair. I don't like the colour combination of blonde streaks in the grey, and it looks coarse as well, but I don't have to like her hair. She goes to speak but I talk over her.

'I know you need to go through all the introductory stuff but I just want to say I was recently seeing a psychotherapist and after a couple of months he made a pass and we got into a relationship then I found out he'd been seeing . . . Well, that he has sex with other clients, and I reported him but they didn't believe me, the UKCP, and I'm coming to you because you've been through something similar so I thought you might be more likely to understand.'

Sandy exhales slowly. 'I hear you, Dani.'

We sit for a moment.

I take a couple of tissues and crunch them up in my fist. I make myself look at her and maintain eye contact, even though it's making my stomach churn, but I have to see how she responds to what I'm going to say. It will help me know if I can trust her.

'Please don't turn out to be weird—' I close my eyes but make myself open them again. 'Because it would be difficult to go through another experience like that again. I'm trying to get back to university and I need to sort my head out.'

339

CARLA JENKINS

'I'm so sorry your therapist did what he did,' she says softly. She doesn't move when she speaks.

'How do you know I'm not lying?' I say.

'I know you're telling the truth.'

'They didn't believe me at the hearing. They were a load of tossers, like him.'

'Dani, I believe you.'

I can't describe how good that felt. Like the little girl could finally put her hand down because she'd been heard.

'What your therapist did was a gross betrayal of trust and ethical boundaries,' Sandy said. I kept repeating her exact words inside my head so I'd be able to remember them perfectly later.

What your therapist did was a gross betrayal of trust and ethical boundaries.

We speak about Sandy's experience of what happened to her – about the similarities in the way the men acted. I tell Sandy it seems like there's a guidebook for predatory men dealing with vulnerable women – they use the same tactics. One of the most common is making you believe that you're leading it.

'I feel bad that I couldn't see what was happening,' I tell her.

'When a person goes for therapy, they're exposed,' Sandy says.

'Perhaps I trusted him too soon.'

'You were doing what you were supposed to, Dani. You had no reason not to trust him. He was advertising as a professional.'

'He said I was seductive and flirtatious.'

'That's what he wanted to see, and then use it to his advantage.'

Sandy's intuitive and insightful. We speak about how my promiscuity is a way of me 'consuming' men, trying to compensate for losing the main one, my dad, and also about my need for affection that I didn't know how to ask for.

In one session, I tell Sandy about how writing stories about

340

Richard where terrible things happen to him makes me feel better.

'I really surprised myself the other day, Sandy,' I say. 'I've never considered myself a violent person – I hate fighting, violence, anything like that, but I gave Richard back a foreskin so it could be slowly pulled clean off while his hands and ankles were handcuffed to metal bars.'

Her eyes briefly widen before she speaks. She clears her throat.

'There have been many studies into the therapeutic benefits of creative writing, Dani.'

'Yeah, I've heard of art therapy and music therapy but never creative writing therapy – it should be more of a thing. I find it very helpful. It's like an outlet, you know? I always feel better afterwards.'

'You need to write,' she says.

'The foreskin one is my sixth story, but I might need to come up with a better title. Do you want to hear about the other five?'

'Why not?' she says.

I lean forward in my chair and tell her.

'You're a real creative,' Sandy says after I do. 'And it sounds like writing is a good place to put this anger.'

'I always feel better afterwards. When I write these stories, I end up feeling sorry for him, and I'd rather feel that than the anger.' I look out of the window at a bird hopping around on the grass. 'I don't want to be one of these people who get consumed by rage, you know? I don't want to let this . . . residue of him influence my life any more than it has to.'

Sandy nods and I know she understands.

I tell Sandy that I've got the bulimia down to once a fortnight and I'm going to work at stopping completely. I think I'll be able to because I'm getting my feelings out on the page, instead of throwing them up.

★

I take the laptop Richard gave me to Cash Converters and make a deal with a stubbly-faced assistant with blue tattoos on the backs of his hands. I consider transferring the money I get for it into Richard's account, but then think about how much I paid him for therapy sessions and use the money to pay Sandy instead.

I write on my phone, or in my leather notebook until my hand cramps and I have to shake it out.

At work, Babs gets Leanne to train me up on the till, which means I can go up to the next pay band. We end up having a good laugh. I've always thought Leanne was a bit of a dick, but I see a new side to her when she's showing me how to work the till. Babs says I can carry on working at Hall & Walker on weekends and holidays when I'm back at uni, because she's never met anyone better on pot wash than me.

In the fourth session, Sandy asks me what I've learned, what good I can take from the time I saw Richard. I laugh at first because it feels like there's nothing positive I can say about it, but Sandy encourages me to come up with one thing, one positive.

I look out of the window at a bird. Sandy has started to identify them for me when I ask. Richard would probably have kept silent. This one's a starling, and I like how its wings look metallic. I like the green and purple flashes shining through the black.

'I liked his room,' I say. 'I loved being in that space. It felt like the kind of room I'd love to have one day. I felt like a better person for being in it. No offence, Sandy; I'm not saying this isn't a nice room. It was just the books he had. Two of the walls had floor-to-ceiling shelves, just books. It was beautiful.'

'I think you can do better than that, Dani,' she says. Her hair looks better when she puts this fifties-style hairband in. It's kind of jaunty. Perhaps I could make a bit more of an effort with my appearance – little touches like that.

'Tell me one positive, Dani,' she says.

'I suppose I've learned that just because you're a professional and well educated, it doesn't make you superior? You can still be a piece of shit?'

She nods. 'You're smart,' she tells me. 'You're getting it.'

And I wave my hand in front of my face and look at a line in the floorboards. I always found taking compliments as hard as giving them, but I'm trying to change.

'Thanks, Sandy,' I say. And I try to hold on to the word 'smart' without blocking it. I smile at her then check the time on my phone and see we're near the end of the session.

'And I've been saving the best news until last,' I say. 'Anya – remember I told you about her? Another of Richard's ex-clients who he had sex with? She called me last night. She said she's finished with her boyfriend and there's something she needs to talk to me about. I think she's going to report Richard.'

Chapter Thirty-Nine

Jo's got the TV on but she's not watching it. She's messaging on her phone, and her eyes are puffy.

'What's up?' I say. She pulls her legs up and I sit at the end of the sofa.

'Doug's ignoring me and I don't know why.'

'Did you have an argument?'

'We've never argued, and he's not been at work the last few days. He's just suddenly stopped responding.'

'The more you message him and the more he doesn't respond, the worse you're going to feel.'

'And this woman keeps liking all his posts.'

'Right,' I say. 'I didn't realise it was so serious between you.'

'What do you mean?'

'Exclusive.'

'It's not.'

She puts her phone face-down on the table. We go and sit on the balcony and Jo smokes. Jo says lots of nice things about Stevie that she would never have said when they were together. I tell her that I prefer Stevie to Doug and the reasons why.

I look at her profile as she blows smoke into the air.

'Jo, with starting back at uni soon, it feels like the right time to be thinking about moving out, but I won't go until you find someone else to split the rent. Or if you want me to stay, for the company, I will.'

She smiles.

'You moved in to sort yourself out, didn't you? And you're sorted now – or doing much better, anyway. Move out.'

'I'll stay until you find someone.'

'I was thinking about moving anyway – getting a studio near work. The drive is doing my head in. I didn't know how to tell you, so it's good you were already thinking of leaving.'

The drive wasn't something she had to worry about when she was with Stevie, as he always drove while she went on her phone.

'Where are you moving to?' she says.

'I'll get a house share with other students. See what's available.'

'That student house you were in before was grim.'

'Yeah, but I don't think they're all like that.'

'It's a good idea, Dan,' she says. 'It feels like the right thing to do. Get more back into that student lifestyle.'

She goes to light a cigarette and I tell her to wait. I go and get Dad's lighter and hold it out to her.

'I'll swap you if you want. You can have the lighter and I'll have the signet ring,' I say.

She looks at it.

'You might start smoking again.'

I shrug. 'Yeah, I might. Or I might not.'

Jo takes the ring off and gives it to me and I put it on. She keeps the lighter in her hand.

'I had this weird dream thing about Dad, the other night,' I say.

'What was it?'

'I'm not sure if it was a dream, actually – you know when you're not sure if you're awake or asleep? Just before you wake up? I was in this trance-like state, anyway. I saw Dad and I

345

hugged him. He told me to back myself.'

She flicks the lighter and and keeps the flame burning for a few seconds.

'Dani, you've always been so strong, you just don't realise it. Dad told me once he admired your determination and the fact you'd never give up. Even when you were a kid.'

'He said that?'

'Yeah.'

I wait a moment to let my throat settle.

'He told me that he thought you'd end up running your own business one day. He always said what a grafter you were,' I say.

Jo nods.

'He had some issues, didn't he?' she says quietly.

'That's why I can forgive him all the bad stuff. He struggled a lot, with his head. And he didn't have any help for it.'

'His anger was off the scale sometimes,' she says.

'He always apologised.'

'That makes it better?'

'He wouldn't have chosen to act that way. It was like he was taken over. Can you blame people for mental illness?'

'He was always there, when you needed him, if you were in the shit,' she says.

'Yeah. Like you were for me when I had the breakdown.'

'Sorry I've not seen you so much lately,' she says.

'You've been busy. Forget about it.'

'I should have more time on my hands now though.'

'Is it going to hurt to be single for a while?'

She nods her head and bites the inside of her cheek.

'I know you see me as your needy little sister, Jo, but you can always talk to me, about whatever, you know; or if you're in the shit, or—'

'Yeah, I know,' she says. 'Thanks, Dan.'

Chapter Forty

My first day back at university goes well. The module I've chosen is 'Shakespeare's Heroes and Villains'. Dad would have loved hearing about that one.

After the class, I go to the uni bar with some of the other students from the module and we speak about the lecture. We exchange numbers while we're in the bar and set up a group chat.

When I leave, I go to call Pat to tell her how my first day back went, but I see it's only half four and she'll still be working. I could meet her from work. Surprise her. Go for a coffee.

Then I realise there's something else I want to do first while I'm still high from my first day back at university.

I walk up the mosaic-tiled path and bang hard on Richard's front door. When he opens it, I slip past him before he can say anything, and run into his therapy room. There's a woman lying on the couch.

'Get up,' I say to her. Her shoes are neatly together beside it, and I pick them up and hand them to her. 'Find another therapist.'

I feel Richard's presence behind me.

'Dani, this is preposterous,' he says. 'Leave at once.'

I turn to face him.

'I had my first day back at university today. I wasn't going to let you ruin that. The whole reason I was coming to see you: to get my shit together so I could get back to university. No, you were not going to spoil that. But I just thought I'd pop in to let you know that Anya has reported you now, too.' I turn to the woman who's putting her shoes on and looking at Richard with a bemused look on her face.

'I had sex with him,' I say to her. 'He has sex with a lot of his clients. If he hasn't made a pass at you yet, he probably will soon – although maybe not after this.'

'What are you talking about?' Richard says. His face is screwed up, and he moves so he's standing between me and the woman. 'Francesca, I'm so sorry. I'll contact you to reschedule this session.' He turns and points in my face. 'Leave, Dani. Before I call the police. How dare you enter my practice like this?'

'How dare *I*? How dare you, Richard Goode. How dare you pretend that you want to help people when your real motivation for doing this job is to exploit people who are struggling. How dare *you*?'

'Get out,' he says.

'How dare you have sex with your clients?'

He picks up the phone from his desk.

'Yeah. Call the police. They'll be hours,' I say.

'Get out, now!' he shouts.

The client shakes her head and walks out just as another woman moves towards the open door to the therapy room, holding a bag full of shopping. She stands in the doorway, staring at us.

'Becca?' I say and she looks towards Richard then back to me, and slowly nods. 'I'm sorry,' I say. 'I was having sex with him. I was his client and he told me he was going to leave you. I'm sorry. He told me having sex with his clients is addictive. He needs to be stopped, and he will be soon. Another ex-client is reporting him.'

'You had sex with Richard? While he was your therapist?' she says.

'Yes,' I say.

Richard moves towards her but she holds out the shopping towards him to stop him coming closer.

'You'll get what you deserve,' I say to Richard. 'It's coming.'

I take one last look around the room. The floor-to-ceiling shelves filled with books, the lamps, the art. All a façade. I step past Becca and out of the door.

'Becca, you need to listen to me,' I hear Richard saying as I walk out, and I can't make out what she's saying back as I walk down the path, but she is shouting and it sounds like he is pleading.

'Goodbye, Mr Goode,' I say. 'And it's time.'

Acknowledgements

Arvon
Mark H
Chloe Fowler
Louise Dean
M J Hyland
Trevor Byrne
Kate Wilson
Emma Hillier
Ros Huxley
Maddy Milburn
Sareeta Domingo

Thank you to you all.

Credits

Trapeze would like to thank everyone at Orion who worked on the publication of *Fifty Minutes*.

Agent
Madeleine Milburn

Editor
Sareeta Domingo

Copy-editor
Amber Burlinson

Proofreader
Kim Bishop

Editorial Management
Sarah Fortune
Carina Bryan
Jane Hughes
Charlie Panayiotou
Lucy Bilton
Claire Boyle

Audio
Paul Stark
Jake Alderson
Georgina Cutler

Contracts
Dan Herron
Ellie Bowker

Design
Nick Shah
Jessica Hart
Joanna Ridley
Helen Ewing

Photo Shoots & Image Research
Natalie Dawkins

Carla Jenkins is a writer and teacher who is passionate about exploring mental health issues in her writing. During the past three years, Carla's writing has been placed in several national and international competitions. She is currently studying for a PhD in Creative Writing at the University of Exeter. Through her business, Raw Writing, Carla runs courses helping those who wish to write a novel themselves.